The Torn Tapestry

THE TORN TAPESTRY

Jane Froud

C

CENTURY

LONDON SYDNEY AUCKLAND JOHANNESBURG

This book is dedicated to
my mother and Pete
in loving memory.
And to Sid, who is one of the
bravest men I know.

Copyright © 1989 Jane Froud

First published in Great Britain in 1989 by
Century Hutchinson Ltd
Brookmount House, 62–65 Chandos Place
London WC2N 4NW

Century Hutchinson South Africa (Pty) Ltd
PO Box 337, Bergvlei, 2012 South Africa

Century Hutchinson Australia Pty Ltd
89–91 Albion Street, Surry Hills, New South Wales 2010
Australia

Century Hutchinson New Zealand Ltd
PO Box 40–086, Glenfield, Auckland 10
New Zealand

British Library Cataloguing in Publication Data
Froud, Jane
The torn tapestry.
I. Title
823'.914 [F]

ISBN–07126–3057–0

Phototypeset by Input Typesetting Ltd, London

Printed in Great Britain by
Mackays of Chatham PLC, Chatham, Kent

ONE

'Tell me, Nina, are you a chi-chi, or just a poor-white?' Moira asked.

Her friends laughed, a chorus line behind her. Against the sunlit sky her hair flamed around her head. She aimed a sharp kick at my outstretched legs on the grass, then turned abruptly and they ran, laughing at her wit, mocking my discomfort. I looked quickly at the other girls under the trees. They studiously avoided my eyes. Her shaft made its mark — my olive skin and dark eyes could well have been those of a girl of mixed African/European blood. I had never thought of that possibility.

My heart pounded hard and the sour taste of vomit filled my mouth.

But it's not true, I thought, so why do I care so much?

Tears filled my eyes and I quickly brushed them away, not wanting anyone to see that I was upset by Moira's taunts.

I should be used to disappointments. My mind went back to the beginning of term, some weeks before, to my feeling of rejection as my parents saw me off on the train at Nairobi station . . .

In the bright African sunshine which somehow had found its way through the grimed glass canopy, dust motes had danced, forming a nimbus around my mother's head.

Her freckled face, framed by a pale straw hat, turned upwards towards the train window and I had seen the

5

beads of perspiration shining on her upper lip. I leaned outwards wondering if, at last, there would be some words of encouragement, of sorrow even, at my leaving.

'Don't stick your head out of the window once the train starts, Nina, you'll get smuts in your eyes' she said, and her head tilted downwards again so that all I could see was the dispirited down-turned mouth. I sighed, feeling that already, before the train had moved, I'd been dismissed — that Mother only stood there because it was expected of her.

Couldn't she even pretend she's going to miss me? My stomach had hollowed with longing. Not even now, when I'm going so far away? The prospect of starting at the convent boarding school terrified me, and I felt vulnerable and alone; perilously close to tears.

Father, smart in his military uniform a few paces behind Mother, took a quick look at his watch.

'Almost time to go!' He put up his hand and I leaned further out of the window, wondering if he expected to be kissed. Instead he shook my hand quickly and stepped back from the train again.

'Don't forget to write to your mother, now, she'll want to know you arrived safely!'

At the next carriage window a woman and her daughter clung to each other precariously, weeping, then laughing at their tears.

My parents looked uncomfortable, standing side by side on the platform of Nairobi station. I glanced at them covertly, willing them to make some small move of affection towards me, then realised that such a move would be an untruth. The emptiness I felt inside was not so much for what I was leaving, because, God knows, I should have been used to that, but fear of the unknown world I was entering.

The whistle blew and they waved politely, small embarrassed gestures. As the train moved I strained further out of the window, still hopeful, keeping them within my view, until I saw that they had immediately started for the exit barrier.

I swallowed hard, suppressing the hurt, knowing that things had never been different.

There was no memory of being held or cuddled even when I was small — not by Mother. My loving comfort had come from Melika. Melika, my beloved ayah. Shutting my eyes, I leaned my head against the window-frame, remembering how Melika had clasped me to her large black bosom that very morning.

'Oh, Nina!' she had cried. 'Is my little girl grown so big now that she can fly?' She had rocked backwards and forwards, almost smothering me. 'What will it be like to wake each day and find you gone? And how will Jamira and Rashidi fill their hours without you?' Melika and her children had been in my life for as long as I could remember.

'I'll be back,' I had mumbled as Melika's arms tightened around me. With eyes closed, I breathed deeply, holding onto the memory of the distinctive smell — a mixture of Melika's dark, musky scent, and the clean crisp starch of her overall.

Melika, Jamira and Rashidi! My constant companions during the past twelve years. Only them — and the voices that came and went, unasked and unanswerable, in my head. Once I had asked Melika if she too heard the silent conversations, and she had 'Tsk'd' at me and said, 'Don't ask too many questions, child, for who can give the answers? Who knows the ways of the Ancestors, or where life leads us?'

'Hello!' A voice broke into my remembering.

I quickly wiped at my eyes with the back of my hand, embarrassed that anyone should see my tears. 'Smuts!' I explained awkwardly.

'Your first term, isn't it?' The girl had bushy red hair and bright golden eyes. 'I'm Moira — and you're —?'

'Nina — Nina Anderson.' I felt her eyeing my over-

7

long gymslip, my cheap socks. She wore a red and white spotted cotton dress and white sandals.

She turned into the compartment.

'You have the top one,' she said, pointing to the fold-away bunk, 'and we'll share the luggage rack for our things.' She stood on the seat to stow away her cases, leaving little room for mine. As she stretched upward I saw her knickers, frilled and lacy. I looked away, reddening, and was glad that the ugly gymslip safely hid my home-made navy blue bloomers.

'We don't have to wear uniform, you know. Not on the train, anyway.' She sat cross-legged on the seat and opened a box of chocolates. 'Like one?'

'Thanks.' My hand hovered over the chocolates, unable to make the choice, unused to such luxuries in the lean post-war days of 1949.

'The letter from school said I had to travel in school clothes. . . .'

'Oh, you don't take any notice of that!' Moira's voice was scornful. 'If we've got a nun escorting us, then sometimes she'll insist, otherwise we wear what we like!'

'How long have you been at the convent?' I asked.

'Two years.'

That'd make her thirteen. I felt much younger, although only a year separated us. Looking quickly at my reflection in the stained mirror above the minute wash-basin, I saw my eyes, huge and dark with apprehension, staring back from my sallow face.

'Little Owl,' Melika had called me. I hated my image — dark brown hair, with fringe cut straight across my forehead. Moira's hair was a riot of wiry curls, totally uncontrollable by the look of it, giving her a transitory appearance, as though she was constantly on the move.

My one battered suitcase was crammed against two kikapu's, the woven palm-frond baskets into which I'd

8

jammed my few possessions. I thought about my cotton dresses, hastily and cheaply run up by the Indian dress-maker, wondering if I should change, then decided I'd be better off staying in the anonymity of the serge gymslip. I pulled off my red tie, undid the top button of my blouse and pushed up my sleeves, uncomfortable in the constrictions.

Moira had eaten her way through half the chocolates. She offered me another.

'Haven't you got any?' Her eyes looked sideways at me.

'No — we forgot them.' The thought would never have occurred to my mother.

'Oh dear! Never mind, perhaps they'll send them on — then we can share them?'

'Of course.' I decided to refuse any more if they were proffered.

'Have you lived in Nairobi long?' she asked.

'Only since the end of the war. We were in Uganda before that. I was born there — Dad's in the Army.'

'We've got a coffee farm — at Muthaiga.' She picked up a book and started to read. I was forgotten, and sat wishing I'd got the corner seat so that I could at least look out of the window.

The train slowly chugged its way down the steep slope that formed the edge of the escarpment. On each side the wide plains spread, brown and vast, with the dark purple shape of Mount Longonot outlined against sun-silvered Lake Naivasha. By sitting forward on the edge of my seat I could see the flamingo-pinked lakes dotted along the floor of the Great Rift Valley — jewels in the dun-coloured landscape — Naivasha, Ele-mentita, Nakuru.

Then we stopped, brakes squealing, and the whole carriage erupted with the noise and laughter of schoolgirls.

'Moira — hi! Good hols? Who're you in with? — Oh!'

The eyes all turning in my direction, appraising, disparaging. I shrunk back into the seat.

'She's Nina. Starting this term.' Moira, surrounded by friends, left the compartment. I could hear their laughter ricocheting back down the rocking corridor as the train drew out of the station again.

'What is it about me?' I asked myself, and studied my face in the mirror once more. 'Am I so ugly? So repulsive?' I half-shut my eyes and through the slits saw reflected a different face — darker-skinned, thick glossy black hair, an embroidered dress of fine spun wool. My hands moved over the rough serge of my school uniform, my own face gazed back at me, pinched and white and unhappy.

It was always so! The thought came. Even then. . . even then!

I shook my head and looked quickly out of the window, chasing the thoughts away, watching the Rift Valley spreading itself around us as the train slowly moved through it, scrubby bush and scattered thorn trees giving way to softer, deeper greens as the engine pulled noisily up the Mau escarpment into the darkening sky. I pulled the mosquito gauze blind down against night insects, and unwrapped my small package of sandwiches, lovingly prepared that morning by Melika, choking on one of them as isolation closed my throat with misery.

Melika, Jamira and Rashidi must have felt this way when we left Uganda, I thought, as though they were leaving all they knew and loved there, and were travelling into hostile territory!

Thinking back over the years I knew I had been alone except for them.

Mother, wrapped in her own imagery, wrote pale poetry and drifted through the days. She worshipped

Father to the exclusion of all others, and I had watched the irritation rising in him at her meekness, an irritation which grew into frequent anger. When he was at home I spent my time fearful of his rages which, like cumulus, rolled up from nowhere and exploded with loud thunder. Storms that shook me with their violence and injustice, and left Mother weeping. I hovered on the edges of the tumult, afraid he'd turn on me, longing to comfort her, knowing I couldn't.

I'd no idea why I was so distanced from my parents, nor did I know what it was that I had done to earn such disapproval. I dared not ask, and whilst not understanding it, I had to accept this somewhat Victorian attitude.

Melika had the knack of appearing at the right moments; when Father was at his most angry she'd take me to the small dark room that served as her home in the servants' quarters behind the house.

'Come, Nina — your father is *kali* — so very angry — today! Stay here with us until he goes to the Club!'

Cross-legged upon woven palm-frond mats, we sat and ate boiled green bananas — the staple diet of Uganda, rolling the pale yellow mashed fruit into small portions with our fingers.

My stomach tightened now, aching as I remembered the illicit meals eaten in Melika's room, meals washed down with hot, sweet tea from white enamelled mugs; the bright voices of Jamira and Rashidi mingling with Melika's gentle wisdom; the soft light of the hurricane lantern throwing our shadows onto the rough concrete walls.

Rashidi, a year older than me, had led the three of us in all we did. As far back as my memory went, he had always been there, the air alive with his laughter. Jamira, two years younger, was the quieter one, following, unquestioningly, her huge dark eyes at times filled

11

with the tears of frustration as her short legs struggled to keep up with us.

We had all been afraid of my father, hiding from his hard eyes. I remembered the day we'd been climbing one of the huge mango trees in the garden when he had appeared below us, berating Kimau the slow-witted gardener. Jamira had shaken so much with her fear that the branch she clutched trembled wildly, the leaves rustling loudly. Rashidi's eyes had met mine, whites showing with his apprehension, and we had at once started to giggle, smothering our mirth until it became so uncontrollable that I fell, literally, at my father's feet.

I had been sent to bed immediately, and through my window watched morosely as the other two played behind the kitchen. Rashidi had climbed dangerously over the garage roof and brought me fruit to eat once darkness fell.

'We couldn't speak for laughing, Nina! Your face was like that of a mouse trapped by a snake when you fell at Bwana Anderson's feet!'

I had not thought it that funny at the time!

Rashidi was dark brown and long-legged and full of mischief; my close companion; my sibling, in a sense. This friendship hadn't been dissipated as it might have been by my starting at primary school in Nairobi, for though I met other children at the school, we lived too far out of town for me to be able to spend time with them, and my parents steadfastly turned down any requests I made to bring anyone home.

No, my friends are Melika's two children, I thought. They are all I need!

And the others, the hidden ones — they were there, too. . . . always there.

'*You've always been on your own.*' They spoke now, their voices confused, almost indistinguishable. The girl,

Noeda, and Bibicol together — then more — a babel. Was I really the only one who could hear them? . . .

* * * *

. . . Goodness knows, the noise was loud enough to wake even the great tyrant Babur in his stronghold far in the mountains of the Hindu Kush; horses moved restlessly, snorting and blowing loudly, their eyes wild, restrained on tight reins by the bold Afghani riders as they waited for the start of the BuzKashi; traders called out the virtues of their wares; and the crowd, made raucous with excitement, shouted encouragement to their favourites and good-humoured abuse to the opposing team.

The tight-packed throng parted at my father's approach, letting us through, and I was conscious of the young men's glances upon me, aware for the first time that my presence made them strut and stare. I turned my eyes downwards, conscious too of my blossoming maidenhood, and dared not look to see where Ibrahim was amongst the jostle of contestants assembling on the plain in readiness for the game.

Though 'game' was perhaps too gentle and frivolous a term for this far from gentle event. This was more a contest of strength and endurance, taking place only on special occasions, such as holy days and the feast day of the Khan, between two teams of the finest, the strongest young men of the tribe, the 'ball' a beheaded, disembowelled goat filled with straw. This goat had to be seized and carried around the goalposts, several miles away, then back to the special pit in the plain from which it was first taken. The victory was twofold, first to the team who won, but mainly the glory was for the man who had actually tossed the goat's tattered corpse into the pit at the close.

To win the BuzKashi was every young Afghani horseman's dream.

As I glanced upwards quickly, I caught Ibrahim's

13

look upon me and felt my face grow hot. Ibrahim, the favourite rider for the team from Kabul!

I slipped quietly into the tent behind my father, drawing my veil tight across my face to hide my heightened colour. I was afraid that now I was sixteen it could be the last time that I would be allowed to attend, since women were by tradition banned from watching so splendid and so gory a display of manhood. But I, Noeda, daughter of Habib Amir, had been privileged from the time I was old enough to ride, tight-clinging, behind my straight-backed, handsome father. Privileged also, to sit beside this man, this God-figure, on soft cushions sheltered beneath the carpet awnings, whilst my mother and the ladies of her entourage stayed cloistered and gossiping in the confines of my father's estate. No one but Habib Amir would have dared to flout the conventions of this all-male company by bringing in a female, no matter how small or quiet she might be. No one dared, either, to question Habib Amir's right so to do.

Thus it was that after the first two appearances I made amongst the select company seated under the awnings, after the sidelong glances and indrawn breaths of approbation, I was forgotten and if not exactly accepted — ignored. Except, that is, by my father, whose hand would reassuringly pat my arm from time to time, and who would pass me sweetmeats and piquant morsels from his own plate . . .

* * * *

. . . A hand on my shoulder was shaking me.

Moira stood over me, her friends grouped behind her, arms linked.

'Are you coming to eat? Oh, I see you've eaten!' She looked at my brown-paper-wrapped sandwiches. 'Pity, it's lovely food!'

They were off again, like a flight of bright birds.

The train buzzed with the sound of their voices late

14

into the night. They came and went, flitting into the compartment; glancing in my direction; ignoring me beyond brief words. I climbed into the top bunk and drew the thin grey blanket up round my ears, trying to block out their gaiety. Feeling lost and desperately homesick, I wept silently; the hot, salty tears running slowly down my cheeks to soak the pillow-case.

The location of the convent, high in the hills above Lumbwa, was a temporary measure taken during the war, when the school buildings in Nairobi had been commandeered for use by the A.T.S. As we bumped round the final corner of the dirt road in a convoy of lorries which had been at the station to meet us, I gasped. The main building was of cedar wood. Large and one-storeyed, built round a central courtyard, set in beautiful landscaped gardens; sweeping lawns, proud-spaced conifers, a copse of blue-leaved eucalyptus and bright flower-beds. It had formerly been the estate of a German Count, still incarcerated for his national-ity — legacy of that war which had raged so far from Africa that it hardly impinged upon our consciousnesses.

Beyond the gracious lines of the main house stood the dormitories and dining-room. Mud and wattle buildings with thatched roofs. There was no electricity, I learned, and the water, what little there was, was pumped up from a dam at the bottom of the hill, spurting brown and uninviting from the few cold taps — precious hot water for twice-a-week baths being heated in huge cast-iron drums over wood-fuelled fires.

We stood, on our arrival, beside our suitcases as one of the nuns went through the roll, assigning us our dormitories, casting the die for my next three years.

'Nina Anderson,' she looked up from her papers, her eyes myopic and cold behind the pebble-glass spec-tacles. I trembled and nodded.

'Yes,' I managed.

15

'Yes, Mother Gertrude,' she corrected me sharply.

'Yes, Mother Gertrude.' My face was burning with embarrassment, and on the periphery of my vision I saw Moira smirk and nudge her neighbour.

Being a non-Catholic in a Catholic school brought its own difficulties. There were a few of us, but we felt like outcasts — or at least I did. Although the nuns were scrupulous in their treatment, their eyes tended to skim over us, tolerating rather than accepting. I longed to be one of them, to be allowed into the chapel — redolent with incense — to join in the chanting, the genuflecting, the Sign of the Cross. Above all, I coveted the bright rosaries and white veils of the Children of Mary. As it was, my non-Catholicism was just one more thing that made of me a second-class person, adding to the guilt which was to taint my life for many years.

In self-defence I had withdrawn further into myself, working hard, catching up with my contemporaries.

Then Moira and her friends had swooped down upon me, like vultures at a kill, as I sat beneath the blue eucalyptus trees during our 'Reading' period one hot afternoon, catching me unawares, making me jump at their sudden appearance.

'Why, if it isn't Nina Anderson!' she had said, looking down at me, her hands on her hips, her gymslip hitched short above her knees. 'You got those chocolates yet? Don't forget, you've got to share them with me!'

My face had blazed bright scarlet. Then she'd let fly with her carefully poisoned dart:

'Tell me, Nina, are you a chi-chi. . .?'

My breath was laboured as I watched her run away, and rage began to build inside me, until I was shaking with it. If she'd been near enough I could well have killed her in that moment. As it was, I forced myself to remain still, sitting on my hands to stop their trembling.

Why? I asked myself, and then, as if in answer to my question: so why let her upset me? She's nothing in my life!

My pulse stopped racing and I leaned back against the peeling bark of the eucalyptus tree, with my reading book slipping from my knees. The valleys below the school grounds were bright green, where the tea fields of Kericho gleamed like sand-shallow sea in sunlight, contrasting with the dark of cedarwood growing in great swathes up the hillsides.

The garden boys had recently cut the grass and the sweet, heady smell vied with the strong resinous scent of eucalyptus, making my heart lift once more.

As the warmth and perfume of the day washed over me, I puzzled at what it was that made people like Moira so antagonistic, so cruel. I longed for home, suddenly, and yet at the same time I dreaded returning to the turmoil there.

Into my lazing mind drifted my exotic friends, blotting out any thoughts of my parents, pushing Moira into the back of my mind. I concentrated hard, trying to catch the images, pull them out so that I could get closer, for comfort, but the effort seemed almost too great in the lassitude of the afternoon.

And yet I couldn't let them go. The dark-skinned girl, Noeda, was laughing, keeping me awake. She was about my age, and full of laughter, with eyes that glowed like dark amethysts below the twin wings of her eyebrows. Around her the others appeared and disappeared as they always did in these dreams — tall men in cloaks and turbans, mounted on wild-looking horses; veiled women, shrouded and secretive; and then — vivid for a moment — Habib Amir, with great jewelled rings upon his fingers.

17

They whirled — the images — misting and then clearing misting again, behind my closed lids . . .

I opened my eyes. The sun still shone, the grass prickled against the backs of my knees. I wondered if other girls also dreamt so vividly, and why I dreamed of places I'd never been to anyway. I frowned, never sure whether I actually dreamed or simply imagined. The dreams had been with me for most of my life, growing more persistent as I grew older. And yet I thought they'd left me, so busy was I with life at school. I had almost unconsciously pushed them away, afraid they might be revealed, shy about their importance in my life. It disturbed me that they had returned so strongly. Usually they were most persistent when trouble stormed at home.

I shook my head impatiently. To hell with them all, I thought, to hell with them! A faint glimmer of guilt that I would be struck down in some way for such blasphemy only marginally tinged my resolution. I'll show them! I said to myself, though what I intended to show them I'd yet to determine.

I jumped to my feet and ran down the gently sloping grass lawns, turning and twisting in the sunlight, feeling dizzy and unaccountably light-headed. I hitched up my tunic, tucking the hem into the elastic of my knicker-legs, and danced to the music in my mind. Then, tired at last, I lay on the grass again, hands under my head, and felt the sun warm upon my face. In the far distance I could hear a dog barking and, in the woodland, cicadas sang, shrill against the coo of ringed doves. An African voice called, starting a long-distance conversation over the tea bushes beyond.

Then the sky was abruptly blocked out, a dark shadow shutting off the warmth, to the accompaniment of clinking beads and crucifix. I opened my eyes and sat up quickly, heart beating wildly once more, shielding my head against the blows I felt sure would be rained upon it.

'What on earth is the meaning of this, Nina Anderson?' The nun's words were admonishing, but I thought I detected the hint of amusement in her blue eyes. She was on reading-duty, must have seen my sudden madness.

I stood up fast, wondering what my punishment would be.

'I'm sorry, Sister, I don't know what possessed me — I just felt I had to move, to run — or I would have screamed!'

She put her hand on my shoulder and smiled. 'The Saints preserve us! Screamed indeed — and in the silence of reading-hour!' She signalled me to pull down my gymslip. 'I thought for a while the heat had got to you, Nina. Now, be a good girl and save the running and dancing for recreation!'

She said no more, and I thanked my stars it was her and not one of the stricter nuns who had seen me. I went, red-faced, towards the classrooms, conscious of Moira's scornful eyes upon me.

Her inference that I looked like a half-caste stayed with me, despite all my bravado, and I worked extra hard because of the feeling of inadequacy it gave me.

How unfair life must be for real half-breeds, I mused, belonging to neither world, rejected by both!

While determined not to let Moira's words reach me, I nonetheless stayed out of the sun, afraid of tanning to an even deeper shade, and I washed my hair frequently, trying to make it lighter, fluffier.

I made tentative friendships with the quieter girls, sharing their studiousness, keeping to the background, in the shadows. But secretly I longed to be like Noeda — flamboyant and bold. Unafraid.

TWO

Jamira and Rashidi were waiting at the gate as we turned onto the dirt track from the main road, at the beginning of the school holidays.

The gloom into which Mother's half-hearted welcome at the station had thrown me lifted at the sight of them, and I leaned so far out of the car window that I almost fell.

'Nina! Control yourself, for heaven's sake,' Mother said sharply.

The driver slowed, and I jumped out several yards from the gate and ran towards them.

'You're back, at last!' Their hands were on my arms and I hugged them both, sensing Mother's disapproval from the darkness of the car as it went past us to the house.

'Yes! Yes! I'm here, I'm home!' I cried excitedly. Melika was coming fast down the drive, her familiar, portly figure constricted by the stiffness of her uniform. She opened her arms wide and I ran to her.

'The days have been so slow! We've counted each one — waiting for this time to come!' Her tears ran with total lack of embarrassment as she held me tightly.

'Oh, how I've missed you, too!' I replied. Inside I was rejoicing that she was still there, for Mother's few letters had hinted that now I was away there was no need for an ayah. 'And I'm so relieved to find you here, where I left you.'

She shook her head. 'For some time I was afraid, Nina. The Bwana wanted us to go since I hadn't got you to look after, and he said we cost too many shillings to keep. But then Njerogi came back from the beer-house too drunk to cook dinner. Bwana got very angry — you know how angry he can be — and Njerogi left. So — where one man's crops cannot thrive, another's flourish. I am now doing the cooking!'

'Dangerous work — in this house!' I whispered.

Meals were indeed the times of especial hazard. Father's temper seemed chafed to raggedness by the very restriction of being trapped with Mother at the dining table. I had seen him more than once hurl a serving dish of potatoes or vegetables at the now-departed Njerogi, with little or no provocation. Never the meat though — meat was too expensive.

My heart sank as I thought of sitting through the interminable meals that stretched ahead. I realised in that moment that this fear of my father was the cause of the ambivalence I had felt as the term drew to a close, the dread counterbalanced by my longing for the warmth and love that came from Melika.

'If you went away from here, I wouldn't want to return,' I said quietly into her ear.

She pushed me away, studied my face sternly. 'Never speak so! Never! You can't choose the people to whom you are born; they are the elders of your own tribe, and as such must be respected!' Her head, with its wiry curls close-cropped, nodded at me to emphasise her words.

Within the shadows of the house Mother sat with a glass of gin and orange in her hand, as though the effort of meeting the train had depleted her.

'Well,' I said conversationally, 'it's nice to be home!'

She glanced up at me. 'Put your things away tidily when you unpack, Nina, the servants have more to do than run around picking up after you.'

I bit my tongue to stop the response. 'Yes, Mother,' I said as I climbed the stairs to my room, cold with renewed disappointment.

After lunch, from which Father was mercifully absent, I went into the garden to find my friends and, watching them at play, wondered what had made my parents employ Melika, widowed and with children, when I was three years old.

Perhaps she was going cheap! At once I felt ashamed at the uncharitable thought.

'Up the hill?' asked Rashidi, catching sight of me. He had grown in the three months I'd been away, and we were awkward, treading warily around each other.

'Yes — up the hill!' I started to run. 'I'll beat you there!'

The long pale grasses caught at my legs as I went, following the almost invisible path towards the hill. Immediately the whole grassland seemed to explode with yellow birds as we disturbed a fever-tree full of golden weavers. At their flight the tree quivered, its branches festooned with their brown-grass nests, like baubles on a Christmas tree. The sight filled me with the exhilaration of familiarity — the weaverbirds had always used that tree, for as long as we'd lived there, and probably before. I laughed out loud with joy, then Rashidi overtook me, his long bare legs impervious to the sticking of blackjacks, the soles of his feet pale against the rich chocolate of his body.

'Wait!' the plaintive wail came from behind. I stopped and looked back at Jamira struggling to keep up with us. Her dress was too large, and the neck had slipped so that a bare shoulder showed.

'Come on — I'll help you!' I put out a hand and pulled her along behind me. Ahead, Rashidi stood near the top, one foot on a tree stump, his eyes shaded by his hand against the sunshine as he looked down at us, his silhouette dark against the skyline. A sense of familiarity filled me, a feeling that I'd seen him standing like this before, but I couldn't remember when, and a sudden rush of affection filled me.

22

'You are slow, like old women,' he taunted. Jamira let go my hand and sat, almost obscured from view by the high grasses. My own breath was rasping in my lungs from the steep climb, and I was glad to wait until we both got our wind back.

Above the brown grass Leonotis plants stood tall, with flower-heads like spiky brown beads at intervals down their stems, each flower-head sprouting slender reddish blossoms. On one of these I could see an iridescent sunbird, probing inside the trumpet-shape for nectar.

'Oh, look, Jamira! Look at that lovely bird!'

She looked, but with the African acceptance of environment, the innate oneness with the land that made them un-astonished by the beauty of their surroundings, she shrugged.

'The honey-bird,' she said matter-of-factly, and we started off, up the slope once more.

'Every time I do this, I swear it'll be the last time!' I complained to Rashidi as we reached the top. 'It's too steep for fun!'

'Your school softens you!' he laughed. 'But for me, Langata School brings strength — both in the head and in the body!' Looking at him I wondered at the direction that strength was taking. There was definitely a difference in him which I couldn't put my finger upon, a separating somehow, which brought a sudden sadness to my exhilaration of a moment before.

'I too will be going to school,' Jamira said proudly. I turned to her and again saw the gulf that schooling was digging between me and her brother. Jamira still held the open trust that had existed between the three of us, and her eyes were steady on mine. Perhaps I had only imagined the diffidence in Rashidi?

I put my hand out to take his and, with only a fractional hesitation, he took it and we walked into the small chapel that was our goal.

23

Immediately my fear left me. The soft pungent smell of the hard-trodden cow-dung floor mingled with the scent of frangipani and oleander flowers packed into jam jars around the stone font. The grass-thatched roof crackled in the slight breeze, sending downwards small fragments of dust and grass to dance in the sunlight that poured in through open windows. There was no glass to keep out the sounds, no doors to be locked against intrusion. The whole structure, mud and wattle, cow-dung and thatch, was in its essentials completely simple, and yet as I entered it was as though every bell, in every church, everywhere, was ringing for me. I couldn't have explained this feeling of complete accord to anyone, but Rashidi felt it too, I was certain, for his normally boisterous nature quietened within the walls, and his fingers, still entwined with mine, tightened slightly.

We had been there many times, but for some reason this time was completely different. Magical, full of unseen presences.

Jamira broke the spell. 'It's so quiet in here today — I can't even hear the goats on the hillsides!'

'Maybe they sleep — the sun's at its highest and only fools like us run instead of resting!' Rashidi replied.

We left the chapel and made for the shade of a large mango tree.

Rashidi climbed onto one of the large smooth branches and took three guavas out of the pockets in his shorts.

'Here! I brought fruit to refresh us!'

I bit deep into the soft pink flesh of the guava, feeling the juices moist in my mouth, the pips scrunchy between my teeth.

'Where did you steal these, Rashidi?'

'From the shamba of Memsahib Potter!' he grinned.

'You'll get caught one of these days!' Jamira frowned at him.

24

'She leaves the fruit to rot upon the ground — surely it's better that we should eat it?' He lay back upon the wide branch, one leg dangling towards the ground.

I found my eyes closing as I lay in the shade on the long, soft grass, and was soon asleep . . .

In my dreaming I was riding a horse, the dust rising to choke me. Far in the distance a fish eagle called, the upward cadence rising in the still air.

'Listen!' I said. 'Is there water near?'

My companion turned to speak. It was not Noeda, as I had expected, but another woman, one I did not know, yet felt I knew well . . .

I awoke with a feeling of bewilderment, and sat up fast to restore myself to my surroundings.

Rashidi's face turned, looking down at me through the branches.

'You snored like an old man, Nina!' He broke off one of the dark-green, glossy leaves and threw it at me. 'Did I tell you I am learning to speak Kikuyu *and* English at Langata School?' His voice was full of pride.

'No, you didn't! You'll soon have four languages then — Buganda, Swahili, English and Kikuyu, while I only speak the first three, and those not very well!'

'Didn't I tell you that the school gives me strength?'

By the time we got home it was late afternoon, and Father was there.

'So you're back then!' he said, looking at me over his precisely clipped moustache. He didn't give me time to answer. 'You've got to stop this gallivanting about the countryside like a native, though. Your mother tells me you've been out already with the Ayah's brats, and I can't say that I approve. You're nearly fifteen, Nina, and should be learning both your position in society — and theirs.'

I was dumbfounded. 'But — they're my friends, Father!' My cheeks flushed with anger.

'Friends, Nina? Friends? They're the children of one of our servants, for heaven's sake! Why haven't you made friends at this la-di-da school you're going to? God knows we pay enough in fees for you to learn at least how to mix with your own kind!'

'I have made friends!' I said, and across my mind flashed the doubt that I'd ever have any really close friends of my own age, my own kind — and I knew I didn't want them anyway.

He picked up his newspaper and swatted at a fly on the arm of his chair. 'Just take notice of what I've said. Friends indeed — where are they then?'

In my room I fumed at his words. How could he so denigrate Rashidi and Jamira and, by association, my beloved Melika? I pictured him, pompous and self-satisfied in his laundered clothes, fat with food and drink, with people waiting upon him hand and foot — and I hated him.

He's not going to make me change, I thought fiercely. Nothing he can do will stop me loving them! I almost wished that my skin was as black as theirs.

My distancing at school had made me more aware of our differences — I had never before thought so deeply on matters like this. Little though I could understand, I understood enough now to see how totally wrong was my parents' conception of African life, and how vast their ignorance. There was nothing in the lives of Rashidi and Jamira that wasn't based on age-old tribal rules; they knew exactly how they were expected to behave towards older people; how to respect the property of others, and their dignity. I had seen how Melika instilled in them the importance of courtesy and of cleanliness. She treated her children, of whom I was one, with utmost consideration. But, above all, she spoke to us, and with us, discussing each

26

question in a manner that did not dismiss that question as unimportant. There was no way I could reach out and meet with my mother and father that way. Mother because she existed in what seemed to be a world apart, and Father because to me he was all-powerful, indomitable and unapproachable. In his presence I felt stupid and inadequate.

I did take his warning to heart, however, being very careful not to let him catch me with Rashidi and Jamira, keeping my hours with them to the times when Mother was busy at her writing or deep in siesta.

Melika was not deceived by my excuses that it was homework which kept me busy — I never could fool her!

'You don't share your time so much with us,' she said one day, 'nor do you come to eat matoke! Has your school made you too important for these things?'

I kept my eyes turned down, ashamed. 'No, I haven't changed, Melika. I feel there's a kind of gulf between Rashidi and me, which I suppose comes from the fact that we're growing in different directions. But it isn't that which stops me from being with you, it's just that Father had ordered me to stay more inside the house with Mother.'

Father, whose presence subjugated us all.

Melika put her finger under my chin, pulling my face upwards so that my eyes had to meet hers. For a long moment she looked at me, then she shook her head. 'Oh, Nina!'

That holiday not only marked the growth of my awareness, but also my ascent to womanhood. My menstrual flow caught me frighteningly and unexpectedly and while I knew, of course, about it from the girls at school, I was totally unprepared for its entrance into my world.

Mother looked at me blankly when I ran to her.

27

'Oh? Yes — well you'll find what you need in the cupboard,' she said.

Melika explained.

'Why can't I speak of these things with Mother?' I asked her as she tucked me up in bed with a hot water bottle to ease my aching stomach.

'Memsahib lives in her head, Nina. She is a writer, and to be thus is to be gifted beyond our understanding. Besides, she knows I am here to look after you, doesn't she?'

I lay thinking about Mother. Photographs of her before she came to Africa showed a totally different person, vivacious and happy. From those faded snaps, her eyes looked out with confidence and the lines now deep etched between her nose and the corners of her mouth were absent. I wondered what she had been like then, what bitterness had soured her so. I wanted her to be different, for our relationship to change, but I didn't know how to approach her.

'It was the same before,' the stranger's voice came again. 'You never were close to your mother.'

'Oh, for goodness' sake!' I said out loud in my bedroom. 'What are you talking about?' There was no answer, and I picked up my book and started to read, closing my ears against the intrusion, not wanting to examine the implications, but wondering at the same time which one of the people in my dreams she was.

Later in the afternoon Jamira and Rashidi came to see how I was.

'Are you ill?' Jamira asked, with eyes wide.

'No, Jamira — I've just got stomach ache.' She shot me a quick look of womanly conspiracy.

'Perhaps you ate too many guavas!' Rashidi teased.

They didn't come right into the room but stood uncomfortably just inside the doorway.

'Come and sit with me!' I begged.

They shook their heads.

28

'No, we cannot, Nina, it is not our place to do so,' Rashidi's face was turned downwards, his bare foot tracing patterns on the floor.

'But I come into your room — we share the mats there!' I protested.

'It's not the same . . .'

At that moment Father walked in, early home from work. He looked at them and his face darkened.

'Get out!' his voice was tight with anger.

They fled, then he turned to me, picking up one of my plimsolls from the floor.

When the beating stopped I sobbed into my pillow, feeling as though I'd been stoned, my flesh raw and stinging. I lay on my stomach fighting the nausea that was a combination of my new adulthood and rage at his cruelty. Then I heard the car start, the sound of him driving away.

Thank God! I found myself hoping he'd never come back.

My head spun. This time I didn't fight the thoughts that swirled into my mind, glad for them to be there, hungry for the company. But there was no solace there either . . .

*　　*　　*　　*

. . . The veiled women smiled slyly behind their headdresses, their fingers painted into strange patterns with orange henna. They pointed in my direction scornfully.

'Why should she be so favoured that she can leave the estate and travel with the Khan like a boy?' one of them asked, her voice sour with envy.

'I'll tell the Khan,' I said.

They laughed and turned away.

'You'll all be punished,' I shouted at their backs. 'Just wait and see! He'll look after me, as he always has done!'

I ran, stumbling over my long garments, through

corridors of marble tile, searching for the Khan, but he was nowhere to be found . . .

* * * *

. . . I awoke crying, to see Mother's face peering round my door, her eyes red-rimmed. She came and sat on the edge of my bed. One hand hovered for a moment above my shoulder then withdrew to join the other, twisting at a handkerchief on her lap.

'Nina,' her eyes came up to meet mine, and I could see they were awash. 'Nina, you must be careful! You know how cross he gets!' She sniffed and averted her head. 'I don't think I can stand much more! These rows upset me so much!'

The bed shook with her weeping. I turned over, wincing at the sharp pain of my bruises, and put my arm up around her back. Her fragility shook me, her backbone sharp against my fingers.

'I'm sorry, Mum! I really didn't do anything wrong, you know. I've always played with Melika's children, and no one's stopped me before now.'

'I know,' her voice came muffled from the handkerchief. 'It's just his *position*, you know. It isn't right for the Major's daughter to be running barefoot with the servants.'

'But they're my friends! Melika was my ayah — she's been with us as long as I can remember!'

'I know — and I don't think I could've coped without her!' She stopped and sat silent for a moment. 'We don't want to lose her, do we? So be good, and do what Father tells you.' She stood up, looking embarrassed, as if she regretted revealing so much of herself to me.

'I do love you, Mum — you know that!' I spoke quickly, longing for her to put her arms out to me. Her mouth tightened, and I sensed her withdrawal, kicking myself for having spoken.

She turned at the door. 'Remember, no more playing about, and they should *never* come into your room.

30

The kitchen and garden are all right, but never your bedroom!'

I lay shivering and bewildered.

In the dark room I saw Father's face. Huge. Enlarged so that I could see every pore of his skin, every nicotine-stained hair of his moustache. His eyes were cold, cruel, as he stared at me.

'Oh, please!' I cried, 'try and understand me, try and love me!'

His face remained stern, unmoved.

'What do I have to do to please you?'

Then the implacable face dissolved, re-formed, taking on sharper features, a dark beard; and I knew it was the man I saw always in my dreams. His clothes were of the finest silk, adorned with gold thread; his breeches made of scraped kidskin; his legs encased in high boots of polished leather. Upon his head he wore a round felt hat with wide upturned brim of soft black Astrakhan fur.

Afghanistan! The name was loud in my mind. He's the Khan! But the Khan is kind, he loves Noeda . . .

* * * *

. . . My father, the Khan, put his hand on my arm reassuringly as, without warning and violently, a thunderstorm base-drummed its accompaniment to heavy downpour at the start of the BuzKashi. Over almost as soon as it started, it left the baked earth aromatic with the indescribable smell of clean water on hot dry dust.

The wisemen later shook their heads and said this should have been heeded as the ill omen it so obviously was.

The shrieks of laughter and shaking out of wet robes by the large crowd were observed disdainfully by the haughty Pathan riders assembling now on the plain, which stretched, steaming, as far as Bactria in the North East and Kabul in the West. Sounds of coughing

31

and the occasional shout of the vendors of the tasty local bread, Nan, took over from the buzz of excited conversation at the sudden rain as the crowds began to settle in their wet clothes. An expectant silence kept the many mouths closed as they sat, breath held, waiting for the BuzKashi. In the quiet a horse blew loudly and pawed the ground. The sea of faces turned towards us, brown skins, white teeth, eyes watching eagerly.

'Let the BuzKashi begin!' my father commanded, his voice harsh in the silence. The message was relayed down to the young man standing in anticipation of this moment outside the tent. He raised a carved cow horn to his mouth and blew a loud and sonorous note, the signal to be ready. The crowd roared as they saw the riders shorten their reins and wheel their fast horses to take up positions for the start, then with hooves flying, a clanging of sticks and stirrups, and a spray of the top wet soil, the BuzKashi was on. The full fat corpse of the goat appeared then disappeared among the jostling horses, fell and was up-tossed again, rapidly becoming more and more tattered as it was pierced by the lances.

This was indeed no gentle sport, not one for the squeamish or fainthearted, but I was used to it and rose, cheering, with the rest when my particular champion, Ibrahim, pierced the goat and held it over his saddle as he galloped full pelt for the outer limits of the course.

Ibrahim — haughty, fearless Ibrahim! I stirred restlessly as I watched his strong body control the fine horse upon which he was now disappearing from my sight. My nipples prickled against the restrictions of my dress as I remembered the quick, illicit handling he had given me the night before, at the feast that preceded the festivities. His fingers, hard and yet gentle, had slipped quickly and unexpectedly into the front of my bodice as I had stood in the shadows watching the dancing and drinking. Wanting to join the menfolk with whom I felt such affinity, hating to be cast aside with the married women and children cooped up in the kitchens, I had crept out, full of envy and excitement, to watch my sisters and their friends make gentle flirtatious play with the riders in the big hall. The fathers kept watch suspiciously, hoping to preserve their daughters as unsullied virgins to be bartered as brides to the best families — the richest families — present.

Hidden behind a column at the very edge of the hall, I watched, wide-eyed, and did not hear Ibrahim as he came up behind me.

'Ah! What is this, little kitten?' he whispered, his arms suddenly tight about me. My heart, already fluttering at the suddenness of his appearance, took off in wild flight as I realised who it was. Ibrahim, half drunk, cared not it seemed that it was the daughter of Habib Amir he was holding. His face and mouth close in against my neck, whispering, nuzzling, his hands moved slowly and expertly to my small bud-breasts, fondling, squeezing, manipulating them until I felt they were swelling to the size of the giant water melons that grew in profusion down by the river.

'So, the little cat is becoming ripe!' he laughed into my hair. His body pressed hard against my back, I could feel his manhood grow, and for a moment fear dried my mouth. Then his hands moved downwards and thrust between my thighs. With such melting moistness of desire, I think I would have surrendered to him on the spot had we not been interrupted by one of his companions loudly calling his name.

'Ibrahim, you ram, where have you got to? Stop chasing the virgins and come over here to listen to this tale of daring we are getting from Mahmoud!' Ibrahim straightened, pulled one of my hands backwards to feel the extent of his desire then, patting me not too gently on the rump, he said, 'Another time, little dove!

Another time, I will pierce the armour of your father's greatness.' I did not understand what it was he meant by this, so dizzy was I with my own desire, but I cared not for his words, only for the fact that he was leaving.

I ran back to the darkness of my room and flung myself, wild-hearted and gasping, onto the piled cushions of my divan. Excitement and fear chased each other through my head. What if I had been seen! What if Ibrahim were to say anything about my presence? I would be severely punished for having had the temerity to leave the kitchens, for having broken the rules so blatantly, for we — the younger daughters of Habib Amir — were closely guarded, nurtured and cultivated as were the exotic plants my father's gardener tended in his hot-houses. And Ibrahim — what would happen to him for his audacity? I lay, eyes closed, afraid and trembling with a mixture of this fear and the new sensation which Ibrahim had produced in me.

I hastily glanced at my father, fearing that he had heard my thoughts as I relived the events of the night before, but he was watching the game, pointing out to his companions that Ibrahim was being overtaken now by the fastest group of horsemen. Too far to be seen clearly, the goat flew upwards out of the cluster of men and horses, then the tight mass of bodies broke up as the chase started once more. Coats flying, lances held high, the hard mountain riders pursued the goat. As they galloped near it could be seen that there was one riderless horse amongst them.

Instinctively, I knew.

'Ibrahim!' I cried, my cry drowned in the same call that sprung up from a thousand throats as the crowd realised that the favourite was not among the riders. Almost immediately one of the grooms had mounted and was on his way towards the body, which I could just see, far out on the plain.

34

'Oh, Ibrahim. No!' I cried within myself, filled once more with longing for the touch of his hands.

The distant body lay still.

The crowd, which had been silenced by the accident, began to make murmurous conversation once more, then, their interest in the game renewed, they shouted encouragement to their favourite teams. Roars of approval, groans of disappointment, blended, swelled and died away.

All this was to me merely a background distraction. My attention was given to the figure of the groom bending over Ibrahim. I longed to run to him and yet was afraid of what I might find. Nausea lead-lined my stomach, and my agitation was such that my father must have sensed it.

'Noeda,' he said, putting his arm around my shoulders, 'you are not eating, my love, and why so pale? Are you not well?'

'Father, I am not ill,' I replied, keeping my eyes downcast lest he should read my secret in them, 'just a little dizzy with the storm.'

He looked at me closely, searching my face anxiously.

'It is unlike you, my daughter, to turn away from food, or to tremble at the fall of a man in the Buz-Kashi. Perhaps you are growing too old to be allowed to come with me any longer.' His eyes speculative, he turned back to answer a question from the man seated on his left.

I strained once more to see what was happening to Ibrahim, but the churning mêlée of horsemen blocked my view as they whirled and twisted, their horses sweat-foamed. Dust billowed chokingly from the earth, now dried hard again by the sun, obscuring my view of the plain. I arose to leave, pausing at my father's shoulder.

'I think I'll go out into the air, Father,' I said. 'This way my head might clear more rapidly.'

'Go with care,' he replied, his hand for a moment over mine on his shoulder, then he turned once more to his companions.

Slipping out of the back of the tent, I pulled my veil over my face and quickly moved to where the grooms and servants of my father's house were gathered. I sought and soon found my special friend, Harun, he who had guarded me so often from early childhood, whenever I accompanied my father on his many and varied journeys. Harun I could trust. If I had not loved Habib Amir as my father so dearly, then Harun was the one I would have chosen to take his place. He was small and bow-legged from many years in the saddle, a man of great gentleness and humour who could make me laugh even when I was filled with the easy tears of girlhood.

'Harun, help me!' I said, as I took his hand.

'Noeda, as always I will do all I can if I consider it the best for you!' he laughed. 'But, dear daughter of Habib Amir, what a time to choose for your poor old Harun! The best part of the BuzKashi is still to come, and I have money on the team from Kabul!'

I felt his reluctance to break away from his friends, but knew that it was not in his nature to cast me aside without even a hearing.

'What is it then that you wish?' he asked, his concentration divided between his loyalty to me and the lure of the game.

'Harun,' I began hesitantly, 'it's Ibrahim – I am anxious!'

Harun looked closer, his eyes twinkling with comprehension.

'So that is the way of it!' he said. Ibrahim and I had romped and wrestled as youngsters in the stables that fell under Harun's care, and many a time he had threat-

36

ened us both with chastisement for the mischief we performed. But that was some few years ago. Now panic mounted in me at his apparent disinterest.

'Harun, please, could you not send more help out to him!' I pleaded.

Harun scratched his thinning grey beard and answered, 'This is against the rules of BuzKashi, since there are so many riders already on the plain, more would add confusion and the helpers might then need help themselves!' His eyes narrowed in thought as he looked towards the spot where Ibrahim had fallen. 'But for you, Noeda, I will break the regulations. At great risk, at very great risk to myself, I am prepared to send one groom on one strong horse to aid the rascal, Ibrahim. Though I am sure there is not much wrong with that young ox.' He shook his turbanned head. 'May it not be that he drank a little too well of your father's wine last night, and now wishes to sleep off his painful head in the sunlight?' He laughed his dry, old man's laugh at me, but I saw that his eyes were not glancing at the food and drink laid out on the mats in front of his friends as they had done when first I asked. He turned and called a young syce standing by the horses.

'Ahmed, mount the grey gelding and ride with discretion round the game to see if more help is needed for Ibrahim.' He patted my hand. 'There, young one, does that please you?'

I drew the veil tighter across my face, fearful that he see too much.

'Go carefully, Noeda!' Harun warned me. 'You are too high-bred to walk among this crowd, you may find the welcome rough and the language not to your liking!'

'Thank you, Harun,' I said. 'But you, of all, should know that I am not afraid. I have always been free to mix with those I call my friends, whether they be groom, gardener or visiting Khan. I fear no man!' This was not entirely true – had I not feared Ibrahim just a little last night? No, it was not him I feared, just his sensuality — and my own, I thought.

I sat on the dust-hard earth, filled with fear and conflict.

'Ibrahim, what have you done to me?' I wondered. 'What new person have I suddenly become, that I fear so for your welfare?' But Ibrahim heard me not, out on the plain.

'Oh, hurry! Please, please hurry!' My impatience got the better of me and I squeezed my way through to the front of the tight-packed crowd, where I could just see through the dust, three horses slowly walking back towards us, one with a bundle across its back. Dark and motionless, limp arms hanging heavy towards the ground.

I tried to swallow, throat constricted, heart hammering. As they drew nearer, I saw that one of Ibrahim's legs hung awkwardly from his body. I ran through the crowd to the perimeter of the game and caught up with the horses, walking with them to the back of the tents. Ibrahim was gently lifted down and placed upon the ground. I bent over his dusty face, and since he made no movement, I put my ear to his mouth, frantic to hear if he was breathing.

'Breathe! Breathe! Please breathe!' I whispered, willing him to live. His head moved slightly and I felt myself go limp with relief.

Harun's hands, with all the experience of his years spent tending Habib Amir's horses, were running over Ibrahim's body, feeling for broken bones, and Ibrahim moaned, a hollow sound from somewhere in the darkness where his soul was travelling. I felt dizzy with joy that he was still alive, and tumbled my hair to his chest, my ears straining for the sound of his heartbeat.

'Noeda!' The voice was harsh, cold. I looked up into the slate greyness of my father's eyes.

'This is no place for you, daughter — return to the

tents this moment! Would you shame me in front of all these people?'

My instinctive protest stuck in my throat. My father was angry, and Habib Amir's wrath was a thing to be feared. His austere face left me in no doubt of his displeasure and, gathering my skirts about me, I ran for the shelter of the tent. . . .

THREE

I never did manage to come to terms with my incarceration at school, feeling myself to be different, an outcast. Moira took a never-ending delight in taunting me, gleefully pointing out my unstylish clothes, my lank brown hair; her eyes forever begging the question, reminding me. While I was there even Noeda seemed to have deserted me. My dreams didn't disappear completely, but they were fragmented, without cohesion or meaning. During the holiday periods they returned more strongly, but they were confused and violent, and I could draw no comfort from them.

In fact my isolation stood me in good stead, forcing me into study. Wrapped in my solitude, chrysalis-like, I pupated from child to young adulthood. I had no idea where my future lay. Father had been evasive whenever the subject was broached, and I felt sure that he expected me to fail the final examinations, thus relieving him of the necessity of even considering the cost of further education.

Therefore, at the end of my final year I waited unenthusiastically for the results and, when the official letter came, I took it to Father with fingers that trembled slightly, afraid of his reaction, whichever way.

'What's this?' he asked, busy with eggs and bacon.

'My School Certificate results, I think.'

He put the envelope down on the table beside his place. 'Hm! Don't expect they'll exactly set the world alight!'

Come on – open it for goodness' sake! Let's get it

40

over with! I begged silently. At nearly sixteen I still hadn't the courage to speak out loud, knowing that to do so would probably make him, out of sheer bloody-mindedness, put the letter in his pocket unopened.

'Sit down, Nina, and have your breakfast.' Mother spoke quietly. Under the table her hand reached out and squeezed my knee. With startled joy, I looked quickly in her direction, but her eyes were turned, as ever, downwards.

When Father eventually, and almost reluctantly, opened the buff envelope, my mouth dried. I tried not to look at him, but couldn't keep my eyes away from the paper in his hand.

'Well, I'll be damned!' he exclaimed, and his dark eyes surveyed me through his glasses, over the top of the letter.

Perspiration prickled my armpits.

'What does it say?' my voice squeaked.

'Seems you've done quite well!' he replied. 'You've passed everything except your maths.'

'Seven subjects?' I couldn't believe it.

'Yes, seven! Well, I'll be damned!' He smiled at me, seeing me, I felt, as a person for the first time.

'Well done!' Mother said. I leaned over the table on an impulse, and kissed her, but this proved too much and her eyes filled. I turned to Father quickly, knowing her weakness would irritate him.

'I never thought I'd get them, even though I worked really hard!'

He picked up his newspaper.

Flushed with excitement, I ran out to Melika's room after breakfast. 'Rashidi! Jamira! I've got my results — I've passed nearly everything!'

They hugged me, and we danced round in a circle with joy.

'That's good, Nina!' Rashidi's voice was genuinely glad. I looked up at him, pleased at his pleasure. He had grown and now stood a good head and shoulders above me.

'Shall we go to the hill?' Jamira asked. 'To celebrate?'

'Of course, the hill!' We hadn't been there for well over a year.

Melika's voice from outside called Jamira.

'Mama, Nina is clever and we celebrate!' Rashidi told her.

'I know — I heard it all at the table. I'm so proud of you, my daughter!' she beamed. 'To be clever, as well as beautiful! We'll be losing you soon to a husband, I think!'

'No, Melika, not me, not yet! We're going up the hill. Could you tell Mother I'm out for a walk — if she asks?'

She nodded. 'But, Jamira, you have to go into Nairobi today, remember?'

'Oh, Mama, can't it wait until tomorrow?'

'You know it can't — the books are needed for school!'

Jamira grumbled but agreed she must go, and Rashidi turned to me. 'Still the hill?'

'Why not?' I started off on the steep climb, feeling the awkwardness between us again, wishing I hadn't agreed.

'How's school?' I asked to break the silence.

'I'm in the top class,' he replied. 'The teachers are pleased with me and there is talk of my going to Makerere College.'

'That would be good — both to be going to college, and for you to be back in Uganda!'

'It is being talked of, that's all.' He closed the conversation.

He should go, I thought. He has far too much intelligence to end up as a houseboy or a clerk in a Government office! I studied his back on the path ahead of me, and prayed that his bright spirit wouldn't be extinguished by colonial bureaucracy.

'I wish we could go to college together, in England!' I blurted, then immediately wished I could swallow the words. There was little enough chance of *my* going – none at all as far as Rashidi was concerned.

He turned and looked at me, and his eyes were empty. 'Nina! Where would the money come from for our journeying?'

'I know! I'm stupid. It was just a thought that flew into my head!'

'Like a hornbill, too heavy in the beak!' he laughed. But we were silent for the rest of the climb, and at the entrance to the small chapel we stood, uncomfortably.

'It's still the same!' My voice was loud in the silence.

We both started to go through the door and, at the slight body contact, parted quickly. Rashidi's hand rested for a moment on my shoulder, pushing me gently inwards, and I could feel the warmth of that pressure still there after he had taken his hand away.

In the quiet of the chapel all sounds were magnified; a goat bleating in the valley below; the drone of a bumblebee on a private quest through the unglassed windows; and in the far distance the rising notes of a fish eagle's call.

'The fish eagle! Listen!' I had spoken out loud, my voice trembling.

Rashidi looked at me, puzzled. 'Yes, Nina, it is a fish eagle! We've heard it many times over the waters of the dam!'

'I know, but this one is special!'

He smiled. 'How — special?'

The sound of the bird was gone, but the notes hung in my head.

'You are strange today!' Rashidi was sitting beside me now, on the hard wooden bench. His hands, pale-palmed, were spread out on the redwood pew in front

43

of us. I wanted to put my own hands over them, to see the white and brown fingers together.

Normally, I mused, I'd do it. Why do I hold back now?

My breath shallowed and my mind slipped backwards . . .

'. . . *The Khan is your father.*' *The voice in my ear spoke clearly. 'For this reason you cannot go against the laws.*'

Don't be silly, the Khan is Noeda's father, not mine! I knew that to be so, had always known it.

'Come on,' Rashidi's voice was loud, an intrusion. 'This place is full of strange sadness today, and we should be happy because of your success.' He held out his hand and I took it, glad that in the gesture he restored what had been.

The shade of the mango was cool as we sat beneath it, looking out over the valley towards the far hills which were purple, miraged in the heat.

'Will you be going to England then?' He looked at me speculatively, chewing on a grass stalk.

'I haven't spoken to Father about it yet. Somehow I'm afraid he'll stop me. Perhaps the money'll be too much.' I'd no idea what the fees would be. At the back of my mind I had the impression that I might be able to get some sort of scholarship. 'I'm so surprised that I did well! I didn't expect to, so I've made no plans. Perhaps there's some way you could come with me, if it's free?'

His face in profile was dark against the bright sky beyond the tree's shade.

'How I wish,' he said, 'that I could.' The awkwardness was there once more.

I spoke quickly to ease the tension. 'Well, we could at least find out. I'm sure quite a few students from Makerere go to England.'

'Yes.' His answer was abstracted; he'd gone away from me.

I looked up into the darkness of the tree.

I've never before, I thought, realised how beautiful the mango tree is; how wide and smooth the branches; how glossy the leaves. The inner bole cut off from the world by the thickness of foliage — secret and secure.

I got up and started to climb, wanting to be there in that womb-like sanctum, safe and enclosed.

Rashidi followed me, his legs and arms more agile, quicker and bolder on the branches until he was high above me. As I looked upwards, watching him climb, I saw his genitals, unfettered by underpants beneath his khaki shorts. I looked away quickly, a sudden rush of desire thudding at the base of my stomach so that I had to sit down, trembling, upon the branch, feeling its smooth hardness between my thighs.

Rashidi climbed down.

'You're still not able to go as high as I do!' he boasted as he sat, straddle-legged, facing me. I dared not look downwards in case I saw again the disturbing evidence of his manhood, and yet I couldn't meet his eyes for fear he'd see too much revealed in mine.

He put his hand on my bare thigh. 'Your legs have no muscles, Nina,' he laughed.

Beneath his hand my flesh burned and I shut my eyes, wanting his hand to travel upwards.

Around the tree, Africa pulsed.

'We'd better go home.' My voice seemed to come from far away.

'Yes.' He too sounded subdued. 'Yes, we'd better go home.' He jumped to the ground and held up his arms to catch me. For a brief moment we stood against each other, then abruptly both turned and started down the hill.

My perception of the physical world was strangely intensified, so that I saw everything with total clarity: the soft grass like water rippled by the wind; the sun — benign — making the trees float, dancing, in the heat-

45

haze; Rashidi's back, straight and strong in front of me. There was a stillness, an expectancy, as though the birds all held their song — waiting.

An echo of the pressure of Rashidi's hand upon my thigh burned as though it was imprinted there.

Oh, God! I thought. Not this — not this! I knew the consequences for both of us.

In an unprecedented fit of pride and generosity, Father suggested taking us out to dinner at an hotel in Nairobi that night, to celebrate my results. Unfairly, perhaps, I wondered if he was celebrating my success or his own by association.

The house was brittle with gaiety. I'd never seen Mother so dressed up, so animated.

'Is my hair all right, Nina? Should I comb it a different way!' She looked at me anxiously. 'I'm going to wear my turquoise-coloured silk dress, and pearls. Yes, definitely my pearls.' She chattered uncharacteristically and I braced myself to be enthusiastic, to hold for her the short-lived bubble of pleasure, when all I wanted was to lie upon my bed and capture the essence of that afternoon, distil it somehow.

'The turquoise will be lovely, Mum, and perhaps you'll let me do your hair. We can put it up — look — with my combs, and that'll show off your neck with the pearls around it!'

'If you don't think it'll make me look silly?' Indecision clouded her face.

I rummaged through my own sparse wardrobe, finding in it a dress that I'd been given to dance in on Mother Superior's feast day at school. It fitted now — pale oyster taffeta with heart-shaped neckline and a full skirt that swirled around my suntanned legs. I caught sight of myself accidentally, a reflection of a reflection in the three-way mirror, so that I was not

46

looking directly at myself, but had a sideways view, as if of a stranger.

I wasn't unhappy at the sight, surprised to see how slender the dress made me, how my new-formed breasts stood proud, my neck long under the heavy brown hair which Melika had tied up for me into a pony-tail. In the mirror my eyes were huge in my face. A face not pretty exactly, more madonna-like, oval and smooth.

I could do with a little colour, I thought. But not too much or father would explode. Whatever else, I wanted that night to go well, for Mother's sake more than for my own.

I went through to her room. 'Will I do?' I asked.

She looked up at me and I saw reflected in her face the pleasure I had felt at my own unexpected image.

'Oh yes, Nina! You look lovely! What have you done? There's a look about you I've not noticed before!'

Have you noticed anything about me — ever? I asked silently.

'Can I have some make-up?' I realised there certainly was a singing inside me which was showing in my face. It's the relief of having done well at school, of pleasing Father, I told myself. But I knew this was not the truth.

He was expansive. Proud Papa, escorting us to the dining-room of the Avenue Hotel; ostentatiously ordering wine, making requests to the orchestra, with Mother blushing and nervous as he led her to the dance floor. I tried to swallow the embarrassment that rose, threatening to choke me, as he queried the bill at the end of the evening, paying it with poor grace.

He was quiet on the way home, and I could see Mother's mounting fear. Sitting behind them in the car I saw that her carefully up-piled hair was starting to come loose, straggling tails across her shoulders, emphasising her vulnerability.

Oh, please God, don't let him be violent tonight! I

47

prayed, trying mentally to count how many drinks he'd had. Sometimes the good Lord hears one's impassioned pleas, and this night, for once, he did. Lying in my room, tense, I strained for sounds of combat, but there was nothing but silence.

'Thank you!' I said to the Unknown, and bit hard upon my knuckles to try and stop the tears that would not be stopped.

At least Noeda doesn't have to drown out the sound of her parents arguing, I thought, though I doubt if her mother would have the temerity to answer back to Habib Amir either! How similar, yet dissimilar our lives! I wished that it was me, pampered and loved by my father, the Khan. My whole being seemed absorbed in that exotic world; a world so much more alive and exciting than my own.

But Noeda seemed to take it all for granted.

I allowed my senses to be submersed in hers . . .

* * * *

. . . The kitchens in the courtyard of the mosaic-patterned mansion were redolent with strong spices, and clamorous with the chatter of the cooks and serving girls. Normally I loved being there amidst the hub-bub and clatter of cooking pots, but today I sat, bridling my impatience, in wait for my father's call.

We had ridden home at the close of the BuzKashi in silence. Tense silence, not the companionable gaiety we usually shared, my father and I. Perched behind him on the large black stallion, I stared miserably at his uncompromising back, begging him silently to forgive me.

I had waited anxiously for his call, but heard nothing from him that evening, nor yet the next morning when I wandered forlornly into the kitchens in search of my friend, Bibicol, who had served there since we were both small children.

Bibicol, with the laughing face and round, firm little

body – recipient of all my secrets. She looked up eagerly from her work as I entered, thirsty for tales of Buz-Kashi. Then, seeming to sense my mood, she said, 'Noeda, your face wears the look of a young calf that has been taken from its mother. Yet you went only yesterday to the BuzKashi.' She grinned ruefully, for my privilege in this respect was the cause of much envy. 'It is your usual custom to bore us all to the verge of sleep with your lengthy tales of the game. What happened to furrow your brow in this way?'

I sat down beside her on the bench where she worked, straddle-legged, kneading dough into large lumps for baking. Bibicol at that moment was the only person in the world I could possibly confide all my doubts and fears to. I knew so little of love and its physical counterpart, which little knowledge had been garnered from talk amongst the kitchen girls, from their jokes and the whispered confessions. True, I had witnessed the crude joining of the farmyard animals, but found it difficult to relate the untidy, flapping awkwardness of the ducks mating to what I understood of 'love'.

Ibrahim had quickened my interest and awareness and, with this quickening, my girlhood seemed to be slipping away from me.

The sensations I had experienced at his exploratory touch were such as I had never felt before. Had my proud sisters experienced the melting desire that he had induced in me? I wondered. I thought not, cloistered away as they were in their purdah, and in the narrowness of fear and protocol. I knew, with sadness, that as soon as I became too obviously ripe, my bloom would be hidden away from the eyes of men, too, my long dark hair hidden beneath an enshrouding veil, my face covered, my body encased from head to foot in the folds of the long dress, the chadri, which all women wore. I felt suddenly the weight of sorrow that was woman's lot, and longed to be free, to be a boy as I had always longed. Free to ride with my father forever, free to take part in the BuzKashi myself. I sighed, long and loud, and Bibicol nudged me hard.

'Noeda come back — your mind is travelling far today! What has happened? Please tell me, dear one!'

Stumbling with words, and suddenly a little embarrassed, I started to tell the events of the last twenty-four hours.

'Noeda!' Her voice was a startled squeak as I reported Ibrahim's boldness at the feast. 'He could be hanged for that, and you — '

'I know, Bibi, I know! And that is why I fear my father now, though how he could know anything —?'

'I'm sure he cannot possibly know. It is your own guilt that makes you so fearful!' Her ever-ready laughter was infectious, and we were soon convulsed with mirth, the near-hysteria of adolescence.

'Why, you sly cat — to have a young man touch you so, and within sight of all!'

'But, Bibicol, it was unexpected. He was so suddenly there!' I replied. 'And I felt . . .' I paused, lost for the right words to describe the warmth in my loins, the nerve-end expectancy. '. . . I felt that the cat might start to purr!' I finished lamely.

I realised then, with shame, that I had forgotten about Ibrahim's accident.

'How can I find out how he is, Bibi?' I asked.

'I haven't been out of the house all day to listen to the talk of the stables,' she said, 'but I'm certain that if he were dead, the news would have reached the kitchens by now.' She frowned in concentration. 'I will find Ahmed when I go to collect chicken eggs, and see if he can give us any enlightenment.'

Good Bibicol! I gave her waist a quick squeeze of thanks and went back to my room.

'Noeda!' It was my sister's voice beside me. I had slept for a while, exhausted with apprehension. 'Noeda!

Father is calling for you.' Salima was older than me by three years, and her round face glistened with the sheen of overindulgence, for she loved to eat. Her eyes were small and malevolent as she looked down at me.

'Come — he wants you in his rooms immediately. What have you done, favoured one? He didn't speak with the usual softness of tone that he uses when he speaks of you. Don't tell me that you have incurred his displeasure? You — who he indulges more than any of us!' Her tone was bitter.

My heart sank. My dear, loved father! I wondered briefly if Ibrahim were worth the risk of losing Habib Amir's affection, and hastily flung my veil around my head and ran.

He was sitting silently when I entered, and he contemplated me gravely for a moment before smiling and holding out his hand.

'Daughter, come here!' he said, and drew me down to the cushions beside him. 'We have to talk about the future, you and I. It was mentioned to me several times at the BuzKashi yesterday that you are developing into a young woman, and the elders feel that the time has come for you to be so treated. In the absence of any sons, Noeda, perhaps you have become as a son to me, and I have grown so accustomed to your companionship that I had not noticed how beautiful you are growing!' He pinched my cheek affectionately. 'But we cannot have the people say that Habib Amir does not honour the conventions.' He laughed a little ruefully. 'I sorrow greatly, Noeda, for you and I have become as one during the past years. It is not lightly that I will give up the joy of having you constantly by my side.'

Stone-heavy with dread, I looked at him. Had my half-formed fears of yesterday so quickly been brought to reality?

'Father, you can't just leave me here, shut up on the

51

estate — I am surely to be allowed the freedom I have always had?'

'No, this cannot be, my love,' he said quietly. 'Your mother and sisters also have been complaining about the favours that you enjoy by my side. I fear for you, Noeda, for women can be vicious if envy takes possession of their hearts!'

'But, Father, I will die in the confines of the house. Please try to think of some way we can overcome this.'

'Daughter, even if I could, I would not, for the people here look to me to set the morals. If I were seen to break the rules regarding women, then my authority would be in jeopardy.'

'Father . . . !' I began again.

'No more, Noeda!'

In vain I wept and begged him to allow our carefree companionship to continue. In my grief and horror at the thought of being shut in purdah with the other women, all thoughts of Ibrahim had vanished. I did not even feel relief in the fact that it was not because of him that I had been summoned. So far was he from my thoughts that I started when my father said:

'Oh, I am sure you will be glad to know that Ibrahim is not as badly hurt as was first suspected.'

'I am glad,' I managed. 'What happened to him?'

'His leg was crushed and it seems the bones may not mend well, but it is his pride that has suffered the greatest wound.' He gave a short laugh. 'For the favourite BuzKashi rider to fall so soon in the game is an indignity not to be borne, but time will heal both wounds, I am sure!'

Habib Amir rose and, taking me by the hand, pulled me up to stand in front of him.

'Yes, you are grown,' he said, moving his hands to my shoulders. 'Oh, little bird, I hate to clip your wings, but it has to be.'

'Father . . . please!'

He turned abruptly and left the room, but not before I had seen what looked suspiciously like the glisten of a tear in his dark eyes.

I fled down the corridors to the quiet of my rooms, where I wept bitterly at the simultaneous loss of childhood and freedom . . .

*　*　*　*

. . . I woke next morning with a searing headache, which I preferred to blame on the excitement of the previous evening rather than my dreams.

It was as though the day before had never existed — Mother was pale and weepy, and Father was truculent over his breakfast. It was not, I decided, the right moment to bring up the question of University and England.

Melika was shelling peas out on the back lawn. She smiled at me as I sat down beside her.

'Did you enjoy yourself last night, Little Owl?' she asked.

'If you call sitting on top of a volcano that might erupt enjoyable, then yes, I suppose so. But for Mother I was pleased. I've never seen her look so good!'

Melika sighed. 'I remember when I first came to Memsahib,' she said. 'She was happy then. And pretty, too. You were so small — a little, round, brown-eyed girl, and not a naughty child. Oh yes, she was happy then, Nina, singing at her work and with many friends. And Bwana too was not disturbed by anger as he is now.'

'What changed?'

'Well,' she looked at me sideways, 'I don't really understand. All I know is that they went to England on leave. He came back some three months earlier than her. Things were never the same after that. But I can't tell you why, because I don't know . . .'

I was silent, wondering what cataclysmic event had so altered my parents' lives, puzzled by the veil which

53

shrouded them, at the strange shadows that life threw, so that there were many undercurrents, unrevealed.

I'd lived with these two people always, but it was as though I had seen only one dimension — and that, it appeared, wasn't the truth at all. Not even, perhaps, half the truth! I wondered if I'd ever really get to know them — ever break through the barrier. I know nothing, I thought, about how they've spent their lives. They've existed in my mind simply as my parents, and now I find that isn't the case at all. On the contrary, I am only a very small part of those lives. Lives which are darkened and shuttered against my intrusion — and against each other!

How little I understood, too, about the other life I myself led inside my head. A separate existence to which I turned ever more frequently, longing for the comfort of familiarity which Noeda gave me.

FOUR

Some days later I stood in front of Father, hands gripped tight behind my back.

'Is there any chance of my going to University? I could do, you know, with the grades I got!'

His head came up from behind the East African Standard. Through his glasses his cold eyes surveyed me for a long moment, then he spoke:

'University? Are you mad, Nina? Or so stupid that you can't take in what's happening in this country? Here!' he pushed the newspaper at me. 'Read about it — read about how this Mau Mau thing is getting out of control! Cattle and sheep mutilated, farms set alight! The Kukes are determined to get us out at any cost. And that means we *all* might have to go to England, girl, not just you!' His hand holding the paper shook, so that the sheets fell to the floor. He swore as he bent to pick them up. 'Bloody hell! Can't you see we'll need every penny?'

'Yes, I see.' My heart sank, but there was justification for his fears. Rashidi had told me, months before, of the gangs that hid, filthy and lice-ridden, up in the forests. How they waited, with pangas, knives and stolen guns, for the time to come for them to strike and regain what they regarded as their land, stolen by the white man — the Mzungu. He had spoken almost wistfully, as though he wished he could join them, even when I'd cried: 'But, Rashidi, violence isn't the answer! Killing and brutality won't gain them one acre of that land, and it isn't your battle anyway — you are a Bugandan, not a Kikuyu!'

'It's not that simple — not just a matter of Kikuyu

55

and Mzungu. The white man has robbed all Africa of its lands — taken our birthright from us, from Cairo to Capetown.'

I had not thought of it like that, secure in my dual relationship.

'It's true, I suppose. But not this way, Rashidi — not by massacre and mutilation! It should be done through the Government, through legislative discussion, surely?'

'No amount of talking and promises will bring justice. We have all had to carry our kipandes too long.' He had thrust his hand deep into his pocket and brought out the small cardboard identity pass, the humiliating document which all black people had, by law, to carry. 'This kipande which marks our movements — like the brand-mark on the white farmer's cattle! No, you are wrong, Nina, this is not a battle that can be won with words, with promises — there are too many now in the forests, armed and ready. Too many who have eaten the Mau Mau oath.'

'But there are a lot, too, like us, who are friends, surely? Many of the farms who take care of the workers — who really care?'

'Really care? I wonder. The next few months will show who really owns this land, the Africans or the Mzungu who came, like vultures, to eat our heritage!'

'Is danger that close?' I shivered at his words, sharing his dichotomy.

And so rode Alexander the Great; Genghis Khan, too — across the whole of Persia and into Afghanistan, with devastation in their wake, I thought. They too mutilated and murdered in the same way the Mau Mau are doing.

I looked now at my father and saw how the hair above his ears was growing grey.

'What shall I do then?' I asked.

'What will we all do?' he spoke brusquely. 'They're

56

going to recruit more troops for the Kenya Regiment and the King's African Rifles. Meanwhile, we'll have to get hand guns, and you both will have to learn how to use them.' He waved his hand at Mother and me. 'Thank God we've only got one Kikuyu working for us — Kimau — and he's so stupid that I doubt if he's been indoctrinated.'

At the edge of the Langata Forest, later that week, he put up a tin can as a target.

'Now, use the gun as though you were pointing your finger. Think of it as an extension of your hand,' he said. I shut one eye, squinting along the barrel.

'No, no, *no*! Do that and you'll get a hell of a kick-back. Your arm's too rigid, Nina,' I relaxed my arm slightly and pulled the trigger, shaken by the jolt.

'That's better — just keep trying!'

But I don't want to shoot anyone! I thought.

Mother was white-faced. 'I can't do it!' she said, 'I simply can't do it.' The revolver looked huge in her hand; too heavy for her thin wrist.

'Oh, for goodness' sake, what's all the fuss about? Don't you want to be able to defend yourself?' Father shouted at her.

She raised the gun again and held it at arm's length as if it were attacking her.

'Squeeze the trigger! For goodness' sake — squeeze the bloody thing!'

I saw tears start down her face. Father threw the target down upon the ground.

'Leave it! Forget it! If you can't even try, then be it on your own head if they kill you!' He stormed off to the car and started it up, revving the engine impatiently as we ran to climb in.

He wouldn't let the subject be, but raged on about her weakness all the way home. Then, unexpectedly, he turned on me.

'You'd better watch out, too. That wretched boy, Rashidi, he's at Langata School, isn't he?'

'Yes.'

'A breeding ground for terrorists, I hear. Perhaps he'd better go back to Uganda, and quickly. Who knows, we've probably got an oath-taker in our house already, with him there!'

I was immediately indignant. 'Rashidi's not a Kikuyu! He's loyal, I'm sure of that. No one could be more trustworthy than Melika — or her children!'

'Huh! That's what we all say about our servants, and how many have already been proved wrong, eh?'

'No — not Rashidi. I would swear to that!'

'I hope you're right, Nina, but I still think he should go. Certainly, you must have nothing more to do with him.' He looked at me over his shoulder. 'You're not too old to have a damn good thrashing, you know!'

I glared at the back of his neck, at the roll of thick, coarse flesh pushed upwards by his collar, and wished with all my heart that he was not my father. Wished that I were that other girl — the one in Afghanistan, whose father loved her.

Later, Mother, emboldened by her fourth brandy, said, 'I think Nina's right, you know. Melika and her children are our friends, they'd defend us if there was trouble, I'm certain.'

I could see the anger in his eyes. He poured himself another drink. 'I don't trust him — any of them. Nor should you. You — of all people!'

She shrank back slightly in her chair. 'They're not all bad, William . . .' The drink in her hand tipped, spilling a few drops. She scrubbed at the damp patches on her dress with a handkerchief. 'Melika's part of the family. Think how she's stood by us all through the years!'

Purple rage suffused his face.

Please! Please God! My silent prayer was frantic. Please make her shut up — please!

'In fact, I'm surprised she's stayed so long — considering,' Mother continued, the danger signals unseen. 'I think she'd give her own life to defend us — or Nina, anyway!'

I could sense the tension growing; knew she'd gone too far.

Father sprang up and was across the room fast, standing over her.

'What the hell do you know, you drunken old sot, mm? You — who couldn't even mother a son for me!' With a violent movement he tossed his whisky into her face.

Rage burst inside my head.

'Leave her alone, for goodness sake!' I shouted. 'You talk about her and the Africans as though they're not human! They're not animals, you know!'

'That's where you're wrong — the Mau Mau *are* animals, and all the blacks could go the same way — riddled with superstition and oath-taking!' Spittle flew from his mouth as he spoke. 'And you, Nina, you're just a stupid child — blind to the reality!'

I wanted to kick at him, to shout and swear and smash my fists into his face. Instead I jumped up from my chair and ran out into the night.

Behind me the mosquito-gauzed door banged shut.

There was no moon, and the path was invisible. My anger propelled me upwards, instinct finding the right footfall, the climb dissipating my rage until by the time I reached the top of the hill, it had dissolved, leaving instead an anguish of spirit that was far more painful.

Entering the chapel I breathed deeply, taking comfort in the familiar pungent smell, and felt my way to one of the pews. Praying had never come easily to me, but this night I made the Catholic sign of the cross with hand to head, to heart, from one side to the other,

and prayed with everything I'd got: 'Mother of God —
help me! Help us all!'

The night quivered around me, its noises strange
and out of context. I began to imagine dangers that
weren't there in the crack of a twig, the sudden upward
flight of a nightjar. My breath quickened and the hairs
on my arms stood erect.

There's someone there! I cursed myself for my stu-
pidity in coming so far from the house, sure that I was
surrounded, seeing menace in every dark shadow. Then
I slipped slowly and quietly to the floor between the
pews, lying there upon my stomach with mouth dry.

There! I thought, I can definitely hear someone! And
again! Holy Mother of God, protect us and preserve
us. Hail Mary, Mother of God! I wished I'd learned
the words.

A silhouette in the doorway, dark against the mini-
mal lightness outside. I stopped breathing altogether,
but felt my heart thudding loud.

'Nina?'

'Rashidi! Oh God, how you frightened me!' I got up.
'I thought you were the Mau Mau!'

'You are stupid to come here alone,' he said. 'We
heard the shouting in the house, and when Mama went
to see if you were safe, she found your bed empty . . .'

'Does Father know?'

'No, he drinks much, and knows nothing. We
thought it unwise to tell Memsahib, until I tried to find
you.' He passed his arm around my shoulders. 'I knew
you'd be here!'

'Can we stay for a while? At least until my heart
stops pounding so hard!'

'Of course. I told Mama that it would only be if I
did *not* find you that my feet would rush me back down
the hill again.' He looked out into the night. 'There's
no danger here, of that I'm sure. Nothing to interest
the gangs up here on this lonely, empty hill!'

We sat, as ever, underneath the mango tree. The moon rose, large and orange, over the far hills. Below us, the lights of the town sparkled in the blackness like a candle-lit procession, and the night was calm once more.

'I feel stupid — running like that! But there was so much talk of trouble and guns and murder — I couldn't stomach it, or my father's temper any longer. Mainly, I think, because I'm frightened; afraid for Africa, for you and me — for all of us!'

'There is much sadness and anger here now,' Rashidi was lying on his back, hands under his head. 'This has to happen, Nina, we have to regain our heritage, our independence.'

'At such cost? So many lives? Can anything worthwhile be gained that way?' I asked.

'Yes! Oh, yes!' He was silent a moment. 'The teachers tell us much in school. They talk of Algeria, of Ghana, of Angola and Mozambique. It seems that independence from another nation's rule rides often on the back of revolution.'

'And you, Rashidi, what will your role be?'

'I am not committed yet. Like you, I've a leg on either side of the doorstep. What I fear is the pain that comes when the door is closed, from one side or the other.'

'I'm so frightened that you'll go — that I'll never see you again!' I struggled with the words, feeling them jagged in my mouth.

'I'm afraid, too. Perhaps that's why I stay?' His arm was around my back, undemanding. I lay down beside him, my face against his neck, and the rich musky scent made my senses reel, the earth turn and swing beneath me. I moved my mouth towards him, wanting my lips against the dark satin of his skin.

'Nina — no!' He sat up quickly.

His face was as black as the night, and the pale

61

moon reflected in his eyes as he turned to where I lay. Then his hands, in trembling inexperience, fumbled at the buttons of my shirt, moving inside to feel my hardening nipples.

'And here — down here!' My hand guided him and, frantic now, we tore at each other's clothes, unable to stop. In the moonlight his naked dark skin shone as though it had been brushed with a thin film of oil, my own brown limbs made pale by contrast. His hands were hesitant, stroking the soft hair of my mound, and against my thigh I could feel the hardness that proclaimed his own desire. My body arched towards him, open and demanding.

'I thought it would be painful,' I said into the quietness afterwards.

'It should be painful,' he agreed, 'for the pain would heighten the joy even further!'

'Oh, Rashidi, what have we started?'

'It started a long time ago — you know that, surely?'

'Yes,' I said. And so I did. Longer than we realised!

'If anyone knew, there'd be trouble,' I said.

'We tell no one,' Rashidi promised.

'No one?'

'No one!' We clasped hands to seal the agreement.

And once again, around us, Africa pulsed.

My face next day wore a look upon it that shouldn't have been there. I tried hard to rearrange my features into their usual mask, and thanked goodness for the fact that my parents were once more engulfed in their own secret griefs, so that I passed unnoticed through their lives.

Melika, however, was by far too astute. 'By the look of you, Nina, you have found a boy!' she teased. 'Are you struck by the spirit of love? Is it that which makes your eyes shine like the moon reflected in a pool; your cheeks glow like a sun-ripened guava?'

'What nonsense!' I replied. 'I'm just enjoying being home!'

How is it possible, I wondered as I spoke, to feel such intensity of joy and guilt simultaneously? I couldn't tell her who caused my high spirits; what it was that drugged my senses!

I had started a course at secretarial college which filled my days, but I lived for night-time; waiting impatiently for my parents to go to bed so that I could climb out of my window, down over the garage and go, on feet speeded by desire, up the hill to lie with Rashidi under the tree.

The winds of destruction that blew across Kenya seemed to skirt the small chapel built of mud, cow-dung and thatch upon the hill; somehow, too, they did not cause the dark purple-green leaves of the mango tree to flutter and rustle. Up there, in the dark, all was quiet and light, and full of new-found pleasures.

For four weeks we met like this, wrapped and absorbed in each other, oblivious to the inner voices that just as surely spoke within us both, warning us. No hint of impending doom was allowed to impinge upon our passion. Not once, with my hands on Rash-idi's tight-curled hair, did I stop and wonder at the consequences. I shut my eyes and let him work his magic upon my willing limbs. Rashidi, with his laugh-ter flashing brightly in the dark brown of his face! And I, escaping from reality, searching desperately for affection.

Drunk with sensuality, we crept home in the early hours, when the sky was just beginning to take on the opalescence of dawn, to part in silence and return to our respective sleeping places.

It was on one of these mornings, when I had carefully

climbed through my window, that the light snapped on, and Father stood with his hand at the switch.

In that appalling, stomach-shrinking moment, I froze. In the second before he spoke, I was acutely aware of every item in that room, of every sound within the house — sharp and unnaturally loud.

'Well?' His voice was calm, more threatening than if he had stormed. 'Well?' he repeated, louder this time.

Mother stood just outside the doorway, looking in, anxiety greying her skin. Behind his back she shook her head at me.

The room began to spin. I thought I was going to fall, and put out a hand to touch the plunging, swinging wall, to stop the movement, feeling as though I would suffocate within the circle of accusing eyes.

'I — I just went outside. I couldn't sleep.' Even in my ears the excuse was feeble.

'Outside, Nina? With Mau Mau everywhere?' He folded his arms, containing his anger against his chest. 'Why didn't you answer, then, when I called? When we all called?'

Mother spoke, 'We were about to send for the police. We didn't know what had happened!'

Beyond her, Melika and Jamira, anxious-eyed. Rashidi stood in the background and, for an instant, it was as though he was a stranger — he evoked no feeling in me. Nothing except sickness lying in my stomach like a large heavy rock, and the desire to push through them all, out into the fresh morning air.

'Where were you?' My father's relentless questioning continued. 'Outside, yes — but where? And was the ayah's boy with you? Were you with him, eh? Like a bitch on heat in the long grasses!' His eyes were apoplectic, and small specks of saliva flew with his furious words.

I looked at Melika, and she — my beloved Melika — caught the look and, interpreting it, knew.

'Rashidi slept beside me and Jamira in our room,' she said.

Father turned to her. 'You'd swear to that, woman?' he demanded.

'Of course, Bwana,' she answered.

Rashidi's eyes looked everywhere except at me, his expression blank — rejecting. I almost hated him then.

'I climbed a tree at the bottom of the garden,' I said, my voice less shaky now. 'And lay on one of the branches. I must have gone to sleep there!'

'Don't you ever *dare* do that again! Things are difficult enough without you causing all this worry!' His hand whipped across my cheek, knocking me backwards against the wall.

I stared at his retreating back.

Melika put her finger to her lips before she too turned, shepherding the huge-eyed Jamira and an evasive looking Rashidi away.

Mother came quickly to me. 'For God's sake — Nina! For God's sake!' Her hand came up and almost touched me.

I longed to have her hold me, to comfort me, but knew there was no possibility of that happening and, following that knowledge, I wished I could run away. That there was somewhere I could run to. Somewhere real, not just that place in my head where I usually went.

It was several hours before I slipped away, and there was no joy in it when I did . . .

* * * *

. . . The folds of the chadri were heavy and smelt musty as the sewing woman slipped it over my head.

I struggled, suddenly frantic.

'Take it off,' I shouted. 'I will suffocate! Take it off!' I fought with the enveloping material, trying to free myself.

65

'Come, Noeda, you make more noise than a tethered goat,' cackled the old woman.

I hated her. I hated the chadri, and I hated my father for enforcing what seemed to me a quite unnecessary rule in my case.

'Leave go of me, woman!' I pulled away from her and threw the loathed dress upon the floor.

'Eh!' she clucked, gathering it up once more. 'You ungrateful creature. I have spent many hours in the making of this finest chadri, and you behave like a tiresome child!' She sidled closer, her black eyes running over my nakedness as I stood fighting my tears at the window. I felt her rough hand on my buttocks, and my muscles tightened.

'You are no longer a child, though, one can see that in the roundness of your hips and in the softness of these little beauties here.' Her hands moved to my breasts.

Sickened, I slapped her away and grabbed the chadri from her.

'Get out, you filthy old witch!' I hissed through teeth clenched in anger and fear. 'How dare you touch me thus. I will inform my father of your insolence!'

She stood looking at me with hatred. 'Huh!' she replied, 'and since when can it be said that you are above being handled? Your father no doubt would like to hear what I observed at the feast. You did not slap Ibrahim for his boldness then!'

She came closer and defiantly placed her hands over my small breasts before turning with a harsh laugh and leaving the room. Burning embarrassment and rage reddened my cheeks.

'Daughter of a pig!' My hands shook as I held the repulsive chadri against my nakedness. Desolation and loneliness weighed heavy on my shoulders and I sank into a corner of the room, my hot skin pressed against the cool of the walls. There as I sat, crumpled, the tears came fast.

I do not know how many hours I stayed crouched like a trapped animal. It was Bibicol who found me and helped me to my feet.

'What is this?' she asked. 'I come with news for my friend, Noeda, and find a spiritless female sitting on the floor in her place.' She took the chadri from me and examined it.

'Ho! I see!' She looked at me, feigning sternness. 'Noeda is too important, I take it, to be treated as a woman. She would prefer to keep to her room, wearing nought but her skin, while us lesser beings can at least venture outside, safe from the lecherous glances of villainous menfolk!' She held the garment up against herself. 'See how soft it falls around my body!' She turned and twisted, holding the material out to its full width. Fluttering her long eyelashes, she drew a fold of material across her face so that only those eyes showed, twinkling. 'Keep away, you defilers of women!' she simpered. 'Touch me not, for I am shrouded in purity! Keep away, bold BuzKashi riders, keep your wicked hands to yourselves!'

I could not but be infected by her gaiety. 'You are a foolish creature, Bibi, and I love you dearly. Here, help me try the hideous thing on. At least you will not be mauling at me like that frustrated old woman who sewed it!'

Bibi handed me the chadri. 'Ah, I see the old witch has made herself known to you! Even the female goats run at her approach!'

Vividly, I could picture the female goats scampering, udders full and flying, to escape the ministrations of the old woman. I began to laugh, and weakened by my long spasm of crying, found the tears begin again.

'Oh, Bibi! What am I to do? I can't spend the rest of my days tied up like some old chicken in this thing,

67

unable to run free in the grass on the hillsides with you. And my father, too, will no longer allow me to ride with him. Can it be he doesn't love me any more?'

Bibicol put a comforting arm around me. 'It will not be long before I also have to cover myself,' she said. 'There is no way we can avoid it. You know how the law is, Noeda, and your father, being Khan, can hardly be seen to flout the conventions.'

We sat, silent and sad, bonded by our mutual horror at the thought of years of purdah. And yet this was the fate of all women. I wondered if everyone felt as I did when the time came, and realised how lucky I had been with the freedom that had been mine.

'Eh! I forgot the news which brought me running to you in the first place. I saw Ibrahim! It was but a glimpse, I'm afraid. He is alive but does not speak, and Harun has made a bed for him in one of the empty stables, where he is being cared for.'

My heart lightened somewhat at this news.

'How can I get out to see him?' I asked.

Bibicol looked at me, puzzled. 'Noeda, after all that has happened today, do you still not realise that your life is to change? You are no longer able to run free as a child, you can't go to the stables, let alone see Ibrahim!'

My despair returned. 'Think of something, Bibi,' I entreated. 'There must be some way around it?'

Bibicol shook her head. 'I doubt it, but of course I'll try and think of something. I must, however, now return to the kitchen or I will not be here to think of anything at all!'

She left me, and I stood listening to her light footsteps running down the corridor. At that moment I would have given anything to exchange my life for hers. I knew that in spite of the fact that she would have to wear the chadri and keep the rules of purdah, she would not be as restricted as I was. She would only have to be veiled when on the streets, because she worked in my father's house. Bibicol was of peasant stock and came from one of the wandering Persian tribes, whose women went free and unveiled. Lucky Bibicol! I thought. She can, if she wishes, return to the border and rejoin her family, to ride with them, following the flocks up the mountains and down again to pasture. Return to the carefree life, constantly moving, pausing only to sit and weave beautiful traditional carpets, like those that adorn every room in this house.

I sighed and my skin prickled at the feel of the material from which the chadri was made. It smelt unfamiliar and my stomach heaved at the memory of the old hag who had made it. If she had seen me with Ibrahim, who else may have witnessed our embrace? I wondered. Would she dare tell my father, in view of her own transgressions? I had heard vague talk of the woman in the kitchens, but had not understood the innuendoes until now.

'Allah,' I prayed. 'Be merciful! I surely meant no harm.' I shrank within the chadri, seeking to hide myself from the probing eyes of all misdeeds, feeling small and lost in its hugeness.

Bibicol, change places with me — please! Then — change places . . . My thoughts raced along this new path. I turned to look at myself in the anonymity of the chadri. Yes! With the bukra pulled over my face I could be any woman.

I must speak with Bibi.

Hoping to avoid the questions of my mother and the sneers of my sisters, I went out into the inner courtyard, towards the kitchens. The tiled floors felt cool to my bare feet and the courtyard was unusually empty and quiet. I loved this part of the house, though it was rare to find myself alone, for it was here that the young children of the household played, and their laughter and chatter normally filled the place. The house was built around this court in which my father's gardeners had planted varieties of palm, so that it was a place of shade and safety. Here, the women gathered to gossip in the evenings, their children sleepily playing on the bright tiles around them.

I stood and ran my hands over the rough trunk of a date palm that I had watched grow taller year by year at the same time that I was growing.

'Ho, tree!' I said, 'you are trapped as I am in this courtyard. Yet, would I could change places with you!'

The tree, naturally, did not reply, so I patted it and, pulling my chadri up into a bundle around my waist, I hopped from one red tile to another, as all the children did, in the knowledge that should the other coloured tiles be trodden, the great Babur himself would descend from the far Hindu Kush and take the miscreant off to his hide-out forever. Thus I hopped, half-child, half-woman, alone in that beautiful courtyard with the palms for witness.

The chadri hampered my progress, and I slowed, trying to copy the odd undulations that seemed to be the normal method of movement adopted by all other chadri-covered women. I tripped and sat giggling foolishly for a moment.

A gardener came into the court, and looked at me with some surprise from the sides of his eyes. I coughed delicately and trying to muster some dignity, gathered myself off the floor and walked towards the kitchens.

'Bibi!' I cried as I saw her. 'Come, I have things of importance to discuss with you!'

'Noeda — I see you are dressed now as befits the daughter of Habib Amir.' Her eyes twinkled with suppressed mirth as she dropped me a mock curtsy. 'What does her highness require of me?'

I drew her into a quiet corner and excitedly put forward my half-formed plans.

*
70

The moon hung low in the east late that night as I crept, cat-footed, through the door of the kitchens. I cursed the light it cast upon the white walls against which I was silhouetted.

Bibicol, from the shelter of the doorway, waved me impatiently on, and stood watching as I ran for the shadows by the outbuildings in the yard. The clothes I wore were hers, all spice and wholesome kitchen smells, and I walked head down with her veil closely drawn around my face.

A dog barked loudly and suddenly in the darkness, and I stood for a second, heart beating frantically. I had forgotten how far the stables stood away from the main house, distance magnified by my apprehension. I moved faster and the buildings, surrounded by tall trees, loomed nearer. A man's voice, sleep-laden, spoke and was answered by a laugh from his companion. I must go with caution; I now knew that there were at least two people awake. I shut my eyes and tried to visualise the stables, wondering which one Harun would have put Ibrahim in. Most of the large stables were occupied by my father's Arab horses, mainly stallions, but with two of the best brood mares in for safety against theft. The other mares and foals would be out somewhere on the vast estate.

There were two small stalls at the far end of the square of buildings, for use if a horse needed extra attention, or was unfit. I presumed it must be in one of these that Ibrahim was lying.

Breath held, I moved into the yard, keeping well into the shadows. A chicken woke with a startled flutter as my foot touched it, and ran squawking — surely loud enough to wake even my father's household. I froze, waiting for movement, and as none came, ran quickly toward, and then into, the stall where I guessed Ibrahim to be.

71

In the darkness I went down onto my knees, feeling out with my hands to find where he lay.

'Ibrahim!' I whispered as I touched the sleeping body on the piled straw. He stirred and muttered, still not awake. I leaned over him and, my lips against his ear, spoke yet again. 'Ibrahim, wake — for I have come to speak with you and can't stay long, lest I be missed.'

Ibrahim raised his head, his eyes glinting in a shaft of moonlight beamed in through the open doorway.

'Noeda! What are you doing here at this hour?' His voice was gruff with sleep, and I drew back, feeling chastised. Where now the bold lover? I sat back on my heels, silent. Ibrahim put out his hand and, cupping it around the back of my neck, drew my head downwards until I lay with it against his shoulder.

'How often I have dreamed that you would creep, to lie beside me in the velvet night, and now I wonder, am I still dreaming? And here I lie — broken!'

I shifted my body into a more comfortable position, while keeping my head where he had laid it, so full of fear I was that if I moved away he would not pull me back.

'You knew, I'm sure, that I couldn't keep away!' I said, throat dry with shyness. 'The charcoal ember to light the fire has already passed between us two, Ibrahim!'

'More than one ember is carried in my burner, Noeda,' he replied, and I smiled at the sudden picture this remark brought to me — carrying the burner with the lighted charcoal, constantly swinging it to keep the coals alight, was a job that the youngest boys did, not a BuzKashi rider of Ibrahim's status.

'Come, lie beside me for a short while,' he said, drawing back the furs with which he was covered. His voice was gentle now, as were his hands, running over my alert breasts and smoothly over my flat belly.

'Oh, that my leg did not hinder me so!' he whispered.

72

He took my hand down to feel his hardness and, knowing so little of what to do, I left it there, feeling the movement and an answering response in my own loins, so much so that I moaned softly with longing for him. He kissed me, long and slowly, tongue searching as I lay trembling.

Then suddenly he pushed me roughly from him.

'Go, child, for the love of Allah, go!' His voice was harsh. 'Why play games of which you have no knowledge?'

I sat up, startled and shamed. 'I only follow the rules you set,' I began.

'Go away, leave me alone. Wounded as I am, I cannot take advantage of your foolishness, for which, daughter of Habib Amir, you should be most glad!'

'But Ibrahim, my heart is . . .'

'No more nonsense,' he interrupted. 'Talk not of love to me, Noeda, for there can be no such thing between you and me.' He turned his head away and said no more. I sat stunned at his sudden change of mood, and then, feeling foolish, I stood up and walked towards the moonlit doorway.

Did I hear his voice say quietly: 'Go with care, little dove!' or was it just the singing in my ears that my flush of embarrassment brought?

It was not till I stood, panting with fear, in the cool courtyard of the house that I realised I had not told Ibrahim that my freedom was gone, that no longer would I be able to ride barelegged, perched behind him on his horse with my hair flying as we galloped across the plains. No longer would he be able to speak with me — or even see me properly, shrouded as I would be in my chadri. I leant against the coldness of the tiled walls and wept as the shadows moved with the moon across the house.

There Bibicol, anxious-eyed, found me cold and sad in the early hours.

'What happened?' she begged, her hand pulling at my arm. 'Didn't you find Ibrahim? Were you seen? Oh come, tell me what it is that has upset you so!'

'Bibi, he doesn't want me,' I sobbed into her shoulder, 'and I forgot to tell him that I will not be free to see him again. Can I have imagined the love I thought he had for me, Bibi? Or does he play so with all the girls who are willing?'

'I have heard he likes to tease the daughters of the stable hands,' said Bibi, her warm arms around me. 'But so far I have heard no great mischief of him. Perhaps it was his wounded leg that made him treat you thus. Come, let me take you to your bed, for even if you don't have to rise with the cockerels, I do!'

She took me down the silent corridors to my room, and helped me onto my couch. . . .

* * * *

. . . Someone was shaking me — a voice calling my name . . .

'Bibicol?' I asked. My eyelids were heavy, and I was reluctant to open them.

'Nina! Nina! Rashidi's gone. I thought he went to market with Jamira, but she came back alone and hasn't seen him.'

My head ached, and I was confused. 'He fell . . . I saw that myself, at the BuzKashi. He's hurt,' I told her. Melika's face above mine creased into a puzzled frown.

'What rubbish are you talking, Nina? It's five o'clock and you've slept all day after the trouble in the night!' Her voice was thin with anxiety. 'Rashidi's too large for me to punish now, but we neither of us slept — talking until it was time for me to cook your father's breakfast.' In her lined face, her eyes were bleak. 'What have you two been about? I can't believe that you could be so foolish!' She sat on the bed beside me. 'Is he the one who brought the sparkle to your eyes?'

I nodded, wordless, still not wholly back from the other world.

'And to think I didn't read the signs! You both know it is forbidden! That's why he's run, for sure!' She rocked on the bed, weeping.

'Perhaps he's only gone to work out what to do, to put his thoughts in order,' I suggested, but I didn't believe this myself. 'I just hope he isn't doing anything stupid.'

She turned and looked at me, accusingly. ' "Stupid", you say, Nina, but *you* should have known better! You with your good education, your knowledge of the Mzungu laws!' She clicked her tongue against her teeth in exasperation. 'What can I do? Tell me, what should I do? Shall I stay here, or go to look for him? My son — my stupid, stupid son!'

Yes, indeed, I should have known better. Should know too of the wrath Ibrahim's actions would invoke in Habib Amir if he was found out.

I put my arms around Melika. 'I don't know what to say — I'm so sorry!'

'Sorry, Nina? What good is that now?' She pushed me away impatiently. 'Sorry won't undo your actions.' She left me then, alone with my confused thoughts, and I found I couldn't separate dreaming from reality, didn't want to. It was easier, by far, to dream . . .

* * * *

. . . When I awoke next day I was almost grateful to the hated chadri for the privacy it would give me. I could not bear the thought of my sisters questioning my pallor, so I pulled the folds over my head and let the heavy material fall loosely around my body. I felt soiled and heavy, the young bud of my love for Ibrahim bruised by the rebuff I had suffered. I pushed the chadri away from my face and looked in the polished silver disc that served as mirror, half expecting to see the image of some stranger there, so different did I feel.

75

But no, my face was the same, graver than normal perhaps, but my dark eyes, olive skin, straight nose and soft full mouth — all were the same as they had been every other day of my life.

I pulled a face at myself, and laughed. 'Noeda, where is your free spirit? The wearing of this dress can't suppress the character within, surely — even if it makes me look like a sackful of young chickens on the way to market!'

Arms akimbo, I flapped round my room, making clucking noises and, catching a glimpse of myself in the mirror, laughed so much at the absurdity of the sight that I fell onto the cushions of my couch, weak and gasping. 'Ha! They will not succeed in framing me into the pattern of their mindlessness,' I vowed and, gathering myself into order, I went out into the house.

My mother and sisters were sitting on piled carpets, fat as sleek cats, gossiping and picking at the platefuls of sweetmeats that were scattered amongst them.

'See! The boy has become a girl!' One sister sniggered, looking at me out of the sides of her eyes.

'Are we to be honoured with your company, Noeda?' She lazily turned her plump hand and looked at the henna-stained nails, 'or are we not of sufficient interest to merit such favours?' Her voice, sour with malice, was sugared but lightly to hide her jealousy. I made no reply.

'Lost her voice as well as her privilege to travel with the Khan,' said another of my sisters — this one I liked least of all. She flicked her long ugly fingers at me. 'Sit down, youngest sister,' she ordered. I sat, loath to draw too much attention to myself.

'Huh!' she said at my lack of reaction. 'Don't tell us that the donning of woman's clothing has turned you into a woman at last!'

I could resist no longer. 'If you are comparing me

with yourself, older sister, then I am not a woman, nor want to be.'

She arose, eyes blazing and walked across to me.

'So, cat, you are still without respect for your elders,' she hissed, and, with a swift movement, slapped me hard across the face. I started to get up to retaliate but, suddenly calm, sat down again, turning away from her and biting hard upon my tongue to stop the angry words from overspilling, somehow managing to remain quiet, sitting stiffly upright and ignoring the spiteful cross-talk that went on around me.

The days passed slowly as I schemed and dreamed of ways to escape from the boredom that their company meant; weeks of enduring the endless gossip, learning with little enthusiasm how to braid my hair, to henna my nails, to embroider elaborate chadris — and the most important lesson of all, how to curb my tongue.

Bibicol was my only refuge in those gloomy days, and even her I saw less frequently since it was pointed out that I should not visit the kitchens too often. She came to my room at night and we would sit crosslegged, whispering together, well into the early hours. Many impossible, improbable schemes did we devise for my freedom, but none seemed to be in any way practicable.

So it was, one clear night just three weeks after I had ventured to the stables, that Bibicol came breathlessly into my room.

'Why, Bibi,' I said, 'I had thought you were not coming tonight, you are so late!'

'Shh — I have news for you,' she gasped. 'Ibrahim has left — Ahmed came to the kitchens tonight to tell us. He is going to Bactria, to his uncle's home, to rest there until his leg is completely healed.' She wiped her damp face with her veil and sat beside me. 'Ahmed could tell me no more, try though I did to question him. Everyone begins to think that it is I who is interested in Ibrahim.'

'That may be no bad thing, at this stage,' I said. 'But how is Ibrahim to travel?' I laughed a little ruefully. 'I have grieved so much over his ill-treatment of me, that I have not thought to question his health. Though his reactions would indicate that he was only wounded in the leg and not elsewhere!'

'Noeda, you are as wanton as a cat in season!' she reproved. 'Ibrahim is still unable to walk on his hurt leg but manages quite well to move around with the help of a stick. Ahmed says he is able to sit a horse so, as you say, it is only his leg that is damaged.'

'Certainly it is not his heart!' I sighed. 'My damage would seem to be of a more permanent nature!'

'Nonsense! You are but a child, you will fall many times in love before you become a mother — and after, I'll warrant!' She paused. 'Though not, I suspect, with the man who it is rumoured has been picked for your husband.'

'What, Bibi? What did you say?' My breath halted with apprehension.

'Talk — only talk, Noeda!' she replied in confusion, and started to straighten the carpets and cushions busily.

'What talk, Bibi?' I demanded, shaking her shoulder. 'Come on, what is this? What man, and who has been saying this?' My voice rose in frustration and horror.

'There has been general gossip in the kitchens, as ever,' she sighed. 'I don't know how much truth there is in it, Noeda, and this is why I have said nothing until now. The name of Shamlu Gadir, the son of the Khan of Begram, is the one that is whispered.'

'Oh, no!' I gasped, 'not that fat pig!' I had seen Shamlu at many of the BuzKashis. 'He is old. Old and ugly!' Desperately I clutched at her hand, hoping that she would deny the words she had just spoken.

'He is, indeed, not a young man,' said Bibicol, 'but

he is rich, and his father, who is very old and ailing, is even richer!'

'Riches, Bibi! You talk to me of riches?' I snapped. 'All the gold in Hindustan would not induce me to marry that — that creature!'

'What has been arranged has to be so,' Bibicol reminded me. 'If your father and Khan Gadir have made a pact, no matter what your feelings are, it must be kept!'

'Never!' I stood up, furious and frightened. 'I go now, to see my father!'

'He is not here,' said Bibicol, hastily rising, too, and holding me by the arms. 'Did you not know that he left this evening to go to Ghanzi?'

So my incarceration in the women's quarters meant that where normally I would have known my father's movements, and indeed been a part of them, now I didn't even know that he had gone.

'When will he be back?' I cried.

'I don't know. But calm yourself, for the love of Allah! You are not getting married tomorrow, or even next week. Wait for confirmation before you go to your father. I told you — this is but kitchen talk!'

'Yes, I know. But kitchen gossip usually has the truth buried somewhere in the coals!' I sat down and looked up at her. 'Bibicol — what am I to do?'

'Wait quietly, sweet one, let me try to find out how much truth there is in this talk first. But you too must listen carefully, you may learn something from the gossiping of your sisters.'

She leaned down, kissed my cheek and left me.

FIVE

The following month my blood didn't flow and nausea made me dizzy in the mornings. Mounting panic sent me to the brink of hysteria.

It can't be! Surely it can't be? I cried silently. Please God — don't let this happen to me! What can I do?

I waited another twenty-eight days, hoping that it was the worry over Rashidi, coupled with the rift between myself and Melika that had stopped my menstruation. When nothing happened the second month, I knew there was no doubt.

I carried the anxiety with me constantly, heavy with despair.

There was no one in whom I could confide, no one who could advise me. Telling Mother and Father was out of the question — they of all people mustn't find out. Melika was cold and distant, still blaming me for our transgression; and Rashidi — heaven alone knew where he'd got to, what he was doing.

In the hot nights I lay restless and afraid, longing for sleep because I knew that sleep would bring dreaming. I needed those dreams, needed the loss of my own identity as Nina. I cried into the darkness when they eluded me, terrified for Rashidi, fearing for his safety; sure — somehow — that he'd gone to the forests.

He can't have joined the Mau Mau, I tried to convince myself, he's far too intelligent to be swayed by oath-taking, to be afraid of spells and curses — the Kikuyu Thahu! News had filtered back about the bestiality of the oaths — rituals involving the utmost degradation. Inside me, somewhere in my intuitive core, I knew how the demeaning of African pride, combined with frustration, had sent many like Rashidi upon the quest for national freedom.

Worry and unhappiness took away my appetite, and the nausea brought on by pregnancy and lack of sleep was exacerbated by my fear of Father's anger should he find out what ailed me. Finally I became so weak that I couldn't go to college.

'I'd better call the doctor.' Mother looked at me, indecision making her voice sharp. 'You've been unwell for over a week now — it can't just be a bilious attack.'

I stood up quickly. 'No, Mum, please don't. I'm sure I'll be all right, honestly! I feel a bit better today.' I pulled a dressing-gown on over my pyjamas. 'I probably ate too many mangoes! That'll teach me!'

She didn't seem entirely convinced, but her relief at being spared making the decision was palpable.

'If you're sure . . . ?'

'Perfectly!' Seeing a doctor was the last thing I wanted.

I dressed and went out into the garden.

The world swung and spun around my head and I put my hand against a tree, waiting for the motion to stop. Then sickness overtook me and I retched until my eyes streamed and my empty stomach ached.

When at last I finished, I found Melika beside me, her eyes anxiously studying my sweating face.

'What have you two started, Nina? Is it what I think, that makes you vomit?'

I couldn't answer, but sat down heavily, glad to be in the shade of the tree.

'Memsahib doesn't suspect?' Her voice was low.

I shook my head. 'No, she wanted me to go to Doctor Gordon, but I managed to convince her otherwise.'

Melika lowered herself onto the ground beside me.

'Nina! What are we to do? What *can* we do? There will be great trouble for you — and for me — if they find out. And now your trouble is mine, because Rashidi is my son, and the child has my blood, too!' She plucked a stem of grass and chewed on it reflectively.

I leaned over and buried my head against her shoulder, hollow with loneliness. 'I'm so frightened. Please don't turn your back on me! For a while I thought you had — I was so alone then. Jamira has kept away too, so I felt no one cared?'

'You are my daughter,' Melika's voice was solemn, 'ever since you were three years old. I may be angry with you, as I am angry with my son, but I would not desert you — either of you!'

I sighed with relief. Melika would do it. Melika had always been there to wash and clean my wounds, to soothe my hurts. She'd find a way.

'First we'll have to get medicine,' she said. 'I'll go to the medicine woman and get what is necessary.'

'Will you need money?'

'Oh yes! Nothing is free, girl!'

I thought about my small horde of notes, salted away from birthday and Christmas gifts, hoping I'd got enough, glad to shrug off the responsibility onto her strong shoulders.

Father demanded my presence at dinner. We sat, the three of us, uncomfortable with our revolvers strapped to our waists.

'Your mother tells me you haven't been to college for a week.' His voice broke into the silence, making me jump. 'Are you ill or just sulking?'

I put down my knife and fork, pleased to have an excuse to stop the pretence of eating. 'Of course I'm not sulking! Why should I be?'

'Well, knowing how much you thought of that wretched boy . . .'

'Rashidi? Oh, I expect he's gone back to Melika's family in Uganda. He always said he wanted to go back there.' I kept my voice casual, though my mouth had dried, hoping that would be the end of it.

He looked at me disbelievingly. 'What is it then? You're not going to waste all the money I've paid out for your secretarial course, are you?'

'No, of course not!'

I didn't know how long I'd be able to continue. Melika hadn't contacted the medicine woman — the Mzee Muganga — yet. I wondered briefly if the woman had means of finding missing persons, if she could locate Rashidi for us.

Melika discreetly removed my uneaten meal before Father noticed it.

'I've just got some sort of bug — that's all. I'll be okay in a day or so.'

'She won't see the doctor.' Mother's forehead was puckered.

'Well, if she's not that bad, there's no point paying out medical fees.' He closed the subject, duty obviously done.

She sighed. 'I still think it's something more than that, Nina. You're sick all the time and not eating. It could be amoebic dysentery, you know.'

Shut up! I implored silently. Shut up or he'll surely guess!

'For goodness' sake, leave her alone! If she gets worse then call the quack!' He turned to Melika. 'And you, Ayah, have you heard from that boy, eh? He's not planning to murder us all in our beds, is he?'

Melika's eyes blazed, then she looked away. 'No, Bwana, I'm sure he's not. How could he repay all the kindness that way? He'll write soon from Uganda, I'm certain.' She paused. 'I'm sending Jamira there soon, to stay with my brothers, and to be out of danger from Mau Mau. She'll find him and tell us.'

I could see that she too was unsure, afraid.

A few nights later she brought me a bitter, pungent drink.

'What on earth's this? It smells and tastes foul!'

83

'Drink it! Just swallow it quickly. The Mzee mixed it from the plants that bring away an unwanted child. I only hope we're not too late to move it.' She stood over me as I gulped back the revolting mixture, fighting the reaction of my stomach to bring it straight back.

'Lie down and shut your eyes to stop the sickness.' She placed a damp, cold flannel over my forehead and eyes, and gently stroked my hair until the threatened vomit subsided.

I pushed the flannel away from my eyes. 'How can we find Rashidi, Melika? Do you really believe he's in Uganda?'

'No. Like you, my heart is filled with dread, and at night — when darkness brings terrors — I'm more and more sure that the freedom fighters who recruit boys from Langata School have led him into their ways.'

'But Rashidi's not stupid! The threat of Thahu surely won't frighten him into joining the gangs?' I didn't want to believe this to be the case, couldn't believe it of him.

'My son has been brought up to know what is wrong, Nina, and what he has done to you — what you have done together — makes him full of shame. He could well feel that there is no other course open to him. He couldn't stay here because of your father's anger — for fear, too, of his own love for you. If the whole truth were known then he would be taken by the police to prison. Perhaps, too, he thinks that if he isn't here, then you will be safer, too.' She turned and looked at me. 'Does he know about the child?'

'No, I only knew myself after he had gone.'

She shook her close-shaven head. 'Aiee, Nina, let's pray to Mungu that Mzee's medicine works!'

How would Habib Amir have reacted if Noeda and Ibrahim had found themselves trapped like this by a child of their passion? I wondered, and then knew that his anger would have been equalled by sorrow at their

84

betrayal. Sudden excruciating pain, a mixture of grief and undefined terror, gripped me, crippling in its intensity so that I cried out with it: 'Oh no! Dear God, no!'

In the night the mixture worked, but not in the way we had hoped. I spent long hours helpless, vomiting into the toilet. In my bed, later, weak and aching, I wanted nothing more than death. Sick at heart, both at what I knew was happening within me, and what I thought must be happening to Rashidi, I stared into the blackness. Too wretched and stricken even for tears, I closed my eyes against that darkness, and hoped with all my heart that it would never be necessary for me to open them again, or that I could run away, far away, where no one would find me. Despairing, I cried: 'Come on, Noeda! Where are you? . . .'

* * * *

. . . I lay awake, fretful and afraid, thoughts of Shamlu Gadir churning my stomach. The idea of leaving the house to look for my father and to stop, if I could, the arranged marriage, began to form in my mind.

I knew only too well what the consequences of breaking the tradition would be, but my fear of punishment was not as great as my desire to escape from the dreadful prospect of being married to a man whom I did not know, but about whom I heard disturbing tales of excesses and depravities beyond my imaginings. Unversed as I was in the mysteries of the fleshly union of man and woman, I did know how my nerve-ends had leapt into awareness at Ibrahim's touch. The thought of anyone as gross as Shamlu Gadir touching my tenderness filled me with nausea and despair.

Late one evening, a week after my father had left, Bibicol crept into my room, anxious to see if I was asleep. I sat up, resolution suddenly strong in my heart.

'Bibicol!' I said, holding hard to her soft arm, 'I have thought of a way in which I can escape from this trap,

85

to seek my father and to leave forever the cat-talk of the harem?'

'Oh, Noeda!' sighed Bibi, eyes rolling heavenward in horror at my words, 'don't jest thus with me. Isn't life hard enough for us women without being thrown into disgrace with your wildcat ideas?'

'No, Bibi, listen. I think we could get away with this quite easily . . .'

'We? Who said *I* was to be a conspirator with you? Love you dearly as I do, Noeda, there are limits to which that love will take me?'

I pulled her down onto my cushions. 'Shh, Bibi, let me think this out more carefully. Your family — this is the time of the year that they start their journey downwards from the mountain peaks for the winter, is it not?' Bibicol nodded. 'If we were to join them, who would think to look for the daughter of the Khan amongst the wandering Qashgai?'

Bibicol looked at me, puzzled. 'But Kabul is many, many days' travel from where the members of my tribe pass closest to Afghanistan,' she said. 'How then can we make the distance between disappear?' She stood up and solicitously tucked in my coverlet. 'Sleep now, friend!' she said. 'You are obviously tired and distraught. I am sure that the cockerel's crow will bring new dawning to your mind as well as to the mountains of the Hindu Kush.' She turned to leave.

'No, Bibi, I am quite serious,' I said jumping up, and starting to walk the bedchamber as I thought out my plan. 'Don't mock me, or feel that my mind is asleep. I am sure that it can be done, and that it must be done now if we are to get away before our lives are tied completely to the paths my mother and sisters have set.'

Bibicol sat cross-legged in the corner of the room, doubt fighting with excitement in her eyes. 'Tell!'

I stopped pacing and stood looking out of my window

to where the tall mountains stood dark and threatening in the clear night air.

'Tomorrow, it must be tomorrow night, when as now the shadows creep round the outside of the compound, and the dogs — like the guards — are full of food and sleep. That is when we will go!' Sure now in my own heart of what I was to do, I no longer felt afraid of the consequences, only that my plan would not come to fulfilment.

'You, Bibi, must bring me, at sundown tomorrow, clothing that matches yours, so that we go as sisters, but not too light that the moonlight catch us in full glare. Make also some provision for food and water, dear one, for it may be many a day before we can openly eat.'

Bibicol shook her head. 'What then, do we walk from Kabul to the far hills of Persia?'

'No! Oh no!' Impatient, I waved a deprecating hand at her. 'Do you take me for a fool?' She shrugged, a gesture of familiarity which I chose to ignore. 'No, we take first a small walk to the stables, and from there two horses will be our wings!'

'But,' she insisted, 'the syces — what of them? They will, for sure, hear us stealing the horses.'

'Whose horses are they? Can one steal one's own horses?'

'Your father's horses!'

'My father's horses are my horses!' I retorted, flash-angry at her obstruction of my plans. I was determined to have no logic stand in my way. 'You will take some wine to the syces when the evening dew falls upon the grass, and tell them that it is a gift from the Khan in gratitude for the way in which Ibrahim was looked after. Oh, Bibi, surely you can trick them with your honeyed tongue — I have heard you do so, many times before!'

She laughed, but unsurely still. 'Yes, I suppose it can be done, but . . .'

'But, but, but! Come on, has the fire, the daring, gone out of your soul with the development of your woman's breasts?'

'Not so, but . . .' She suddenly jumped to her feet and came to me. 'Noeda, I have an even better idea! Two women riding unescorted will raise questions everywhere. Why not dress as men? That way we will raise little attention!'

'Friend! You are brilliant as the evening star! But where, oh where, can we get clothes that are neither too grand nor too lowly to call for comment?' I thought for a moment. 'Wait! Didn't Ibrahim keep a chest in the stables? There may be at least enough clothes in that for us to disguise ourselves!' Overwhelmed with excitement, I did not want to wait another day. 'Can't we go now to see what there is?'

'Hold fast, sister,' she replied. 'To be caught before we even start would be as a feast quickly stolen away from the eyes of a starving man!' She stood, brow puckered in thought. 'No, I'll go early tomorrow to gather eggs from the stable hens. It will not be difficult to go quickly into the stall Ibrahim used and to snatch what I can!'

I laughed. 'You'll come back waddling like a fat duck, with clothing tucked up your petticoats!'

'Shh! Let's not raise any questions with your sisters as to why your usual sad face suddenly laughs,' said Bibi, and with a final hug of farewell, she disappeared silently down the corridors.

I lay staring at the moon-cast shadows on the walls, my mind jumping from plan to plan, from hope to hope, from fear to elation.

I awoke in the pale sea-green dawn, and my excitement catapulted me out of bed. The household was still. In the silence of their silk-draped bedchambers, my sisters slept. I imagined them there, soft, perfumed and pampered, and I sang softly to myself at the prospect of escape. When sounds of life filtered up the corridors from the kitchens, I quietly opened my door and, my bare feet making no noise upon the tiles, made my way there, unable to wait for Bibicol any longer.

'Bibi! Bibi! Where are you?' I muttered as I looked first in one room and then in the other. Two sleepy-eyed women yawned a half-hearted greeting in my direction as they scooped out the ashes from the fires of the previous day. So used were they to my presence in the kitchens that it hardly impinged upon their consciousness.

'Have you seen Bibicol?'

'She went for eggs, or milk, or — I don't know — something!' one of them said in reply. 'She was up even earlier than the chickens today, so she will not be long, I think, Noeda.' She rubbed her eyes and stretched, her huge bosom making the material of her top tauten until near bursting point.

'I couldn't sleep, and when I heard you here, I came for company.'

I stood by the door and watched for Bibi, until at last I saw her walking quickly but clumsily from the stables.

I turned to the women. 'Can I have tea, or is the water not yet ready?' And they resumed, as I had hoped, the task of getting the fires going, blowing on the embers to set the red flames flashing. Whilst they were occupied, I beckoned Bibicol to hurry, and she waddled into the kitchen for all the world like a donkey about to foal.

My laughter threatened, and I let out a snort I couldn't control but, turning it to my advantage, made it into a fit of coughing and, with Bibicol at my side, all solicitude, rushed out of the kitchen towards my

89

room. There we collapsed onto the cushions in uncontrollable laughter.

'Oh, Bibi! What a sight you are! I take it from your size that my surmise about Ibrahim's clothes was correct?'

She wiped the laughter tears from her eyes. 'What am I to do with you? If anyone had touched me or startled me, I would have dropped the strangest things from under my skirts!'

She stood up, and lifting her clothes revealed assorted garments tied roughly round her legs and hips. From the front of her bodice she fished two Pathan hats, soft suede with astrakhan brims; in the basket of eggs still hanging from her arm, hidden under a top layer of straw, riding boots and a thick leather belt with a knife and scabbard attached to it. I couldn't believe the amount she had managed to secrete as the pile on the floor grew. When she had finished, she threw her petticoats up over her head and, revealing her naked, plump little mound with its soft pelt of dark hair, she pirouetted round and waggled her full bottom at me – round, white and dimpled!

'Oh, Bibi, you fool!' I gasped and, as she let her skirts fall into place again, we joined hands and danced round our pile of plunder.

'Come on, let's try them on!' I exclaimed, knowing my sisters and mother would be deep in sleep and that Father was not there. We dressed in the odd mixture of Ibrahim's clothes, strutting and posing in breeches and shirts, leather waistcoat and a jacket, pulling up our hair under the hats. His boots were not too large for Bibicol's wide peasant feet, but my smaller ones felt lost inside the heavy leather.

'Hm!' said Bibicol, her hand caressing her chin in a gesture my father always made when weighing up a problem. 'Hm, now let me see, boy, where can we find boots that will make you walk less like a hobbled water buffalo and more like a mountain goat?' Her imitation of my father convulsed us once more.

'Come on, we'd better undress and hide these things again — I'll just have to stuff the boots with fur or something.'

'I have it!' she exclaimed. 'How stupid we are — your own father's boots will be better. His feet are unusually neat for so masculine a man, and even though still large, they will not be as bad as these.' She stuffed the second pair of boots back into the basket to be returned to the stables, and I told her I would go to my father's quarters, if I could get past his personal servants, and steal a pair of boots. We hid the clothes under the furs and cushions of my divan, and I pulled the chadri over my head again.

My father's rooms were across the courtyard to the north-east. There was no sign of activity and, blessing the fates for my luck, I crept into the ante-room and then through to where my father's robes were kept. Trying to make as little noise as possible, I chose what looked to be the least heavy but strongest, high, polished boots, and since I was already guilty of theft, went through his clothes and selected any items I could remember that Bibicol had not managed to get, including two heavy woollen cloaks. I tidied up the slight disorder I had made and spread out the clothes left there, to hide the fact that some were now missing. Copying Bibicol, I lifted up my chadri and wrapped the clothing around my middle and, in the enveloping folds of the grown, put a boot under each of my armpits. I opened the door very slowly until I could just see through the crack that there was still no one around to catch me there, then squeezed my bulk through and walked as slowly and with as much dignity as I could muster, back to my room.

The day dragged, hours turning to days, and my impatience made it nigh impossible for me to sit quietly, listening to the prattle of the women at their sewing. My restlessness took me round and round the room, until my mother said: 'For the love of Allah, Noeda, what ails you today? You are driving us all crazy with your pacing. If you can't be calm, do please go away to the courtyard and play with the children there for a while.' My sisters laughed but I — relieved — went, glad to be out in the yard with the voices of the children in my ears and no watching eyes to criticise my mounting excitement as the day wearily turned on past the sun's zenith and into the pastel pink and turquoise of sundown.

It was deep into the night hours, long after the last voice in the house was stilled, that Bibicol and I, whispering and moving as silently as two snakes, slowly and carefully eased the door of the kitchen open, freezing in our actions as a baby somewhere in the house started to cry sleepily for a few moments.

Then we were out, two shadows across the moon as we ran to the stables to the sudden soft whinny of one of the horses.

'Shush! Shh!' I reached up and put my arm around the horse's neck, stroking his nose to calm him.

'Did you give the syce wine?' I whispered, low.

'A lot, and gave him much of my kissing, until he was drugged with both!' answered Bibicol. 'Though I don't know which was the most potent, my kisses or the wine!'

'We need not ask! Poor Ahmed, he must have thought paradise was near!'

While we talked, soft and low, we were saddling the horses, wrapping cloth round the jangle of the stirrups and mouthpieces to silence them, our own hearts beating wildly with fear and excitement as we did so. We took two fine stallions. Bibicol was a shade alarmed at their size and spirit, but I knew that we needed good, fast animals, and I had ridden both before, across the plains with Ibrahim and Harun.

As we led them out their hooves made what seemed an overloudness in the jet-black silence of the night. We walked them slowly and steadily, our rolled-up blankets, food and goatskins of water tied across the backs of the saddles. We wore my father's cloaks, which had the double advantage of being both warm and dark-hued, to blend with the night.

My breath was sharp in my throat, my chest tight with apprehension, and it was not until well clear of the compound and stables that we mounted and set the horses away at a gallop.

The moon acted beacon to our flight, silvering the track so that it shone, like an arrow fired straight from Kabul towards the dark mountains.

'Wait! Noeda — don't go so fast that you leave me . . . !' Bibicol's despairing shout followed me. I slowed my animal until she drew up at my side. Her eyes were huge, wide with fear, her hands clutching tightly at the horse's mane as she crouched low over its neck.

'I'm afraid I'll fall, Noeda. You forget I am not used to riding, as you are!' Her voice was hoarse with her fright.

'I'm sorry, Bibi, I spared no thought for that. We'll go slower until you become accustomed to the feel of the animal beneath you. Sit upright, thus, and push your feet hard into the stirrups for, should you lose them, then you would indeed fall!'

Bibi's reply came on a choked sob. 'I can't do it, Noeda — I'll hold your progress back!'

'Of course you can, Bibi!' I replied, determined now that nothing should stop our escape. Had we not managed to leave the confines of the estate without detection? I took the rein from her hand, steadied the horse

93

until he stopped blowing and rolling his eyes, and smiled at her, masking my own nervousness.

Glancing over my shoulder I could detect no sign of pursuit, so I allowed the animals to take their own pace, reassuring Bibicol with a confidence that I was far from feeling myself. Gradually her hysteria diminished and I increased our pace slightly until we were travelling at a jogging trot.

'See!' I called, 'it's not so difficult!' I loosed the rein so that she travelled on her own, but my hand was ready to reach out for it once again if necessary.

'Whee! Noeda, I can do it! But where to now?' Her shouted question came as she pulled on the rein and we both slowed to a walking pace.

'Straight across, using the track to Herat. I went most of this way with my father some year or two ago and, if I recall aright, it is fairly straightforward. Best that we ride tonight and then go off the track to sleep, away from searching eyes during the day, don't you think, Bibi?'

'Aren't you afraid at all of what we have done?' Her face was solemn as she looked at me in the moonlight. 'The Khan will be very angry when he returns to find us gone!'

'I am not allowing myself to think about his fury, for Habib Amir's rage can be formidable, as we both know too well from the past.'

'Indeed, he is a just man, but if pushed too far his temper knows no limit! I have trembled at times, even when it was not I who caused his displeasure.' Bibicol gave a half-laugh.

'I do not fear his anger so much as his worry at my disappearance.' I suddenly realised this was the truth, but could do nothing to alter things now. 'I hope only that he, being so close in feelings to me, will understand why I have to go, even if as Khan he cannot approve. But with luck on our side, we may reach him before he returns home, and I will be able to plead with him to stop this marriage to Shamlu Gadir.' I did not want to think too deeply about how he would react to my disappearance. Perhaps it would be better to keep believing that he would be more angry than anxious.

'Come on, Bibi, let's ride fast to try and cover as much ground as possible before the day breaks.'

The moon was lying low now, and once it had dropped below the hills we would have to slow our pace for fear of the horses stumbling in the darkness. We had only a few hours until sunrise, and I knew that Bibicol would be missed before I was. I hoped that the surmise would be that she was warming the bed of one of the grooms. With fortune, no one would look for me until midday, and we would therefore have twelve hours' advantage. Because of this leeway, we decided to ride on after an hour or so's rest, whilst the pitch darkness of night gave way to translucent day. We pressed the horses hard over the rugged uphill climb, and though the air froze our breath as it left our mouths, the animals' flanks were foamed with sweat, this in turn growing crisp with the icy wind.

'Brrr! I wish I were sleeping, warm and comfortable in my bed in Kabul!' wailed Bibicol, rubbing her fingers to get the circulation going. 'We must be crazy! I don't think I have ever been so cold and stiff!' She wrapped her rein round the high pommel of her saddle, then folded her arms, putting her hands into her armpits to try to warm them. 'Thank goodness we are wearing your father's cloaks, Noeda! Can you imagine how we would have frozen without them?'

'I, too, am beginning to wish we had not started this adventure, but it is done, and we cannot return now. Be patient, it will get warmer later in the day!' I wondered how she was going to last, and whether I had been mistaken in bringing her away with me. The first real cold awareness of what we had done made me hold my breath. I quickly switched my mind away.

'We'll stop as soon as we find a suitable place, as far off the track as possible, and then we'll light a fire and get warm,' I said, with a voice that trembled slightly now.

She smiled a little ruefully. 'I'm sorry, I don't mean to whimper! I would have been both hurt and angry had you decided to leave me behind. I'll be better after rest and food — and when my legs and arms grow less sore and stiff from the length of time riding.'

We left the track soon after and, threading our tired horses through the rocks and scrub, made our way deep into a wooded gulley where we were well out of sight of any travellers. Bibicol slid down wearily from her horse and stood awkwardly in the knee-high riding boots. Her hair was escaping from under the Pathan hat, and long dark strands hung untidily across her face. She moved slowly, like a wooden toy on the end of a stick.

'Ooee! Noeda! I'm crippled! My legs won't work and my back, I'm sure, is broken!'

I laughed at my poor friend's plight. 'You should have come riding more often with Harun and me,' I said. 'Come, give me your horse, I'll take the saddles off and rub both of them down. When you have loosened up your legs a little, try and find wood for a fire, and we'll eat.'

As I slid the saddles off the horses I heard the cry of a fish eagle far in the distance, and suddenly I felt cold with fear, and it was as if someone spoke in my ear: 'The fish eagle – listen!'

I looked around, wondering where the voice came from, and saw only Bibicol rubbing her arms and legs.

'Did you say something, Bibi?' I asked.

'No, I merely moan with my aches!' she replied. I shrugged my shoulders and dismissed the sound as imagination. But as I gathered great handfuls of dried grass and rubbed the horses clean of their sweat, I felt uneasy. The stallions snorted and blew their appreciation as they ate the grass I put before them. I threw thick goat-hair rugs over their backs against the chill, and tethered them carefully to the bushes with strong cords.

By the time I rejoined Bibicol she had a good fire burning with a pot of water heating over it, suspended on a pole held in its place by two sturdy branches cut from a tree with Ibrahim's sharp knife.

'There!' I exclaimed. 'You are better already, and looking more like a boy again now that you've pushed back your hair under that handsome hat! In fact, if it were not for a suspicious softness about your chest, and a slight broadness of hip, I would say you make a very passable young man!'

Bibicol made her voice deep. 'Comrade! Rest your fine, manly legs here beside me and take drink!' She handed me a cup of steaming hot tea and I clinked it against hers in a toast to our conspiracy.

We camped all the rest of that day beneath cliffs honeycombed with the nests of birds, and took it in turns to keep watch to the busy sound of their domesticity. I took the first turn, to let poor Bibicol sleep for she was exhausted from the ride, and found it hard indeed to keep my own eyes from closing. In fact I fell asleep more than once, sitting with my back resting against a tree trunk, and jolted awake each time my head fell forward.

Evening found us stiff and not much rested, but we made hot tea again which improved our spirits, until we saddled up to start our ride into the darkening hills. . . .

* * * *

. . . It was dark when I woke, and I turned on the light to look at my watch. Four o'clock in the morning! And yet I felt I had been asleep for weeks! I turned off the light again and lay staring into the unlit room, thinking about Noeda, Bibicol and Habib Amir, now so much part of my life that my waking hours were beginning to be as inescapably interwoven with them as my sleeping ones had been. Noeda and Bibicol, their journey, the escape from the estate in Kabul, had become vivid, so exciting and real that it was only with difficulty that I could divorce myself from it all.

'Who are you?' I threw the question into the night.

There was no answer. My thoughts turned then to Rashidi, and I was filled with an almost unbearable aching of desire for him. I lay on the bed, shaking, and my hand pressed downwards between my thighs, simulating the feel of his body there, within my own.

SIX

'I've been trying to wake you for many minutes,' Melika's voice was hoarse with anxiety. 'What is happening? I thought for a while I was losing you!'

'The medicine hasn't worked — all it did was make me ill and then give me dreams in which I travelled to another time, in another place!'

She stroked my head gently, silent, as if she could find no words, no answers to our shared distress. Then she spoke:

'Don't let your heart be so troubled, Little Owl! I'll find a way.' Her eyes were distant, and I knew then that her grief went deeper than my own, because it was her trust that had been destroyed. Trust in her beloved son, Rashidi, whom she had reared in all the ancient traditions of her tribe to respect the laws, and above all to be honest within his heart. Her own trust, too, in the validity of those laws, was now called into question.

She took me, later that day in the heat of the afternoon while Mother slept, down winding, red-murram paths deep into the Langata Forest, to a small cluster of huts hidden within the thickness of bush. The track was rough and I stumbled frequently, feeling perspiration running down my back.

'It is here that the Mzee lives,' she whispered, and gestured me to stay still. 'Mama Muganga!' she called, and a figure appeared at the doorway to one of the huts. 'May we come to visit you?'

The woman nodded, and we went towards her. I don't know what I had expected. In my imagination any sort of witch doctor or medicine woman would be dressed in fantastic clothes with necklace of leopard's teeth, festooned with furs of colobus monkey, and with headdress of porcupine quills. But the Kikuyu woman in front of us was clothed in traditional brown dress, a white cloth wound round her head, and bedecked with earrings and bracelets of many-coloured beads.

Her eyes widened as she looked at me. 'Is this the one for whom you sought the special medicine?' she asked Melika.

'It is.'

'Then why did you leave it so late?'

How does she know? I wondered. Her eyes were hard upon me.

'We weren't sure — we didn't know ourselves what the trouble was — she is young, and her flow is not always regular,' Melika explained.

'You bring her *here*, in the forest — to me? Don't you realise how dangerous your action?'

I looked at Melika, wondering in which way she meant. My silent question was answered.

'The gangs hide here, they come to me for care in the sickness that they get from the forest. If the Askari, the Police, saw you or followed you . . .'

'No one saw us come,' Melika interrupted. 'We came the longest way.'

'But the danger is twofold — first you bring a Mzungu through the Mau Mau lands, and then you risk the discovery of my work by the Askari. Where, in the first place, did you find my name, the directions to my home?'

Melika looked uncomfortable. 'Before I came to you, I had heard talk upon the wind, in the way that such news is gathered and blown, like seed. But this was the wind of Africa, not of the Mzungu.'

I could see the Mzee was still angry. I felt the chill of her resentment emanating towards me.

'We aren't welcome here, Melika, let's go!' I whispered.

The woman turned her eyes upon me once more.

'Yes, indeed, you are not welcome, white girl. And the child that you bear, even though it carries within it the blood of Africa, cannot be taken from you by me. I will not help you — Mzungu,' she spat the word. 'Go to your own white doctor — let him use his knife to free you from your guilt!'

Her words struck me, harder than any physical assault, and in that moment, I realised that up to then I had not thought of what was growing inside me as a child. It had not formulated as a living being within my consciousness, and now I knew that I wanted the baby more than anything on earth. Wanted that small tangible proof of the love that Rashidi and I had shared. And, sharp again, I felt the tug of grief at my heart, and knew somehow it was for the unborn infant, though I couldn't understand why.

Walking in front of me, Melika seemed somehow smaller, as though our encounter with the Mzee Muganga had caused her to shrink. Back down the path came the sound of her tongue clicking against her teeth in indignation, punctuating snatches of talk in her native Buganda.

'Melika!'

She looked at me over her shoulder.

'It's not your fault that the woman wouldn't help me!'

'Tcck! I know that — it is just a sign of the times we are living in. But move quickly, Nina, for now I'm afraid to be here.'

I, too, was deadly afraid.

We went fast and silently for the rest of the way. Out of the forest she relaxed slightly. 'There is one more chance,' she said. 'I've heard talk of an Indian doctor who will take away an unwanted child.'

My heart dropped. 'Melika — I think I want this baby!'

101

She looked at me incredulously. 'Are you mad, Nina? With an understanding father it would be bad enough — but with Bwana as he is! And now, with his hatred inflamed by Mau Mau! How could there be a worse time for you to tell him that you carry a black child?'

'I see that, but it's Rashidi's child! Rashidi — whom I love. Black, white, what does it matter — it is *our* child!' Briefly, Moira's taunt flashed in my mind. I pushed it away quickly.

'Hush now, girl. You know it cannot be!'

'What's so wrong, Melika? We're two people — no matter what colour our skins. We love each other — that must be enough?'

She 'tcck'd' again. 'Nina, you know that is not so. What would your father have to say?'

'Father would never forgive me!' That was an understatement! 'But I don't think I care. I'd leave home and go to Rashidi, wherever he is. I only know I must hold the child, mustn't lose it!'

Melika frowned at me. 'And Memsahib? Have you thought how she would suffer? No — we will try to get this Indian doctor, for all our sakes.'

'But . . .'

'Speak no more about it, Nina, it has to be done.'

And I followed her, inexplicably lead-weighted with sorrow and loss.

The doctor was dressed in a grey pin-striped suit, his shirt collar undone, and he wore no tie. The small, dingy surgery was deep in the heart of the shanty-town area of Nairobi. Portraits of King George and Nheru hung, crooked, above a vase of dusty artificial flowers. The room smelt of ghee and garlic; his hair was shiny with Brylcreem.

I sat on the edge of a chair, facing him across the wooden desk. He took a carefully folded, but slightly grubby, handkerchief out of his pocket and delicately patted his mouth with it.

'Well, Miss, er . . .' he consulted the pad in front of him, 'Anderson, is it?'

I nodded.

'Well, and what is it I can be doing for you?' The sing-song Asian accent, the spicy smell, the heat of the small room, all combined to make me so dizzy that I felt I was going to throw up. I gripped my hands together.

'I was told you might help,' I blurted.

'Help you — how?'

You bastard, I thought! You know precisely what I mean! Stop playing games with me!

'Why, may I ask, have you come to me, instead of to your own doctor?'

'It's just that I was told . . .'

'Told? Told? Who is it who is telling you? And what?'

'Oh, hell! I'm pregnant!' Tears of frustration and confusion spilt down my face. I brushed them hastily away, furious at my weakness.

'So, you are pregnant, but still you don't answer. Nor do you ask the question — you want an abortion, is that it?'

'Yes, of course it is!' Anger was beginning to take over. 'Why else do you think I'm here.' But inside I cried. No! No!

'Oh yes, of course, you wouldn't come to an Indian doctor if an English one would help. That's the truth of it!' His tone was nasty. 'Well, I'm afraid, white girl, that you'll have to have your baby.'

'So you won't help me?'

'No, why should I? If you are so stupid, so indiscreet, then you must bear the consequences. Go back to your own doctor, Miss Anderson. This operation is illegal, you know, and I don't want to lose my practice here!'

No, I thought, I'll bet you don't.

103

He got up and opened the door, shaking his head.

Humiliated and angry, I walked out into the noisy streets, but inwardly and against all common sense, I rejoiced.

This time the child *must* be born! This time?

Later, Melika looked bleakly at me in the flickering light of a hurricane lantern in her room.

'You'll have to tell Memsahib,' she said, 'there's no other course.'

'I can't — I just can't do it! I'll have to go away somewhere — somehow — until the baby is born.' There was no way I could find the courage to tell my parents.

Fear for the child made my breathing shallow. I knew in that moment that there was no turning back now. I'd have to go on, without their help or approval.

Melika's face creased with concentration, then she said, 'We could go to my sister, Leah, in Mombasa!'

A strange mixture of exhilaration and excitement suddenly flooded me.

'Leah! . . . Leah! . . . Leah!' The name reverberated in my head. A shiver tingled my spine.

Then my breathing deepened again. 'To Leah? How? How could you go?'

'Jamira has gone to Uganda, Rashidi is — only God knows where — you are my only child here now.'

'Yes, but how can we explain if we both go?' I couldn't see Mother and Father accepting the fact of us leaving together.

'I'll ask, saying I need to go to Jamira, in Uganda, to look after her. But really I'll go to Mombasa.' She smiled at me. 'Then you can follow after a few weeks!'

In the darkest hours of the night, the questions circled round and round in my mind. Melika's idea didn't seem a very satisfactory one, but it would have to do. Yes, I'd have to go, I was sure of that — knew it had to be. I had to go to Leah, whoever she was. There

104

was no way I could stay and face Father's anger, or
Mother's distress. I'd go — as Noeda had gone with
Bibicol — we'd face the hazards of the journey . . .

* * * *

. . . Hazards indeed!

The sky was scudded with fast-moving clouds,
through which the moon played hide-and-seek. A cold
wind needled its sharp fingers through our clothes and
we rode, silent in our discomfort, unable to move fast
with the horses over the rutted track.

'Can you see the way, Noeda, it's darker tonight
than the inside of a charcoal burner!'

'Not really, but each time the clouds clear the face
of the moon, I try to see ahead! No matter, for I am
sure we are still going in the right direction — away
from Kabul. But the slowness of our pace worries me,
for my father's men know this track well, and will be
able to ride fast and sure.'

I was justified in my anxiety for in the early morning,
soon after we had gone off the track a short way, to
make camp for the day, I heard the sound of horses'
hooves beating hard over the track.

Bibicol was singing gently, her relief at being on the
ground again after the rough ride obvious.

'Shh, Bibi!' I said urgently, putting my hand out to
touch her arm, 'Listen! Can you hear the horses?' She
was silent and, copying my gesture, put her arm around
her horse's muzzle to still it. The horses fidgeted nervously, and I prayed they would remain silent. The
riders were but three hundred yards away from where
we stood sheltered in a thick clump of trees. I thanked
the stars that we had decided to stop before the sun
showed its head, for the semi-darkness of the hour and
the drifting mist meant that our tracks off the main
route would not be spotted, or I hoped not. I tried to
pinpoint the nearness of the group of riders, but could
not see them.

We stood, frozen with anticipation. I could feel the pulse in my neck beating hard against the skin, and my mouth was dry with fear.

A loud command broke the silence, unnervingly near, and both we and the horses jumped, startled.

'Shh! Whoa, my love!' I said, low and gentle, afraid the sound would not come from my throat. Bibicol was holding her horse steady with difficulty, her head close in to its neck, stroking and caressing it for calmness. For what seemed a long time the riders thundered past. I tried to estimate how many there were, perhaps twenty or twenty-five, but it may have been less, the sounds distorted amongst the rocks and by the muffling of the mist. Then in a moment they were gone, the sound of their passing disappearing into the distance like a roll of thunder blown away with the wind.

My shoulders fell with the easing of tension, and I realised how stiff and tight I had been holding my head and neck. I patted my horse, and moved my arms around to loosen the constricted muscles.

Bibicol still stood with her head pressed hard against the horse.

'Come on, they've gone.' I went across and turned her from the animal. Her face was drawn and white, and her eyes filled with the tears of relief.

'I thought we were discovered,' she let the words out on an expiration of air, as though they had been breath-held for a lifetime. 'Do you think they were after us, or just travellers on the same route?'

'I can tell no more than you. But whichever, we did not wish to meet with them. Neither of us are yet quite comfortable in our new roles as brave Pathan riders, I think!'

'No,' said Bibicol, 'and in my terror I think I have almost wet my breeches. Had they stopped to talk, how could I explain my inability to make water standing up?'

'I had not given thought to that!' I exclaimed. 'We will have to be very careful not to get caught squatting like the women that we really are!'

Our tensions released themselves into laughter at the thought of the predicaments our lack of male equipment could bring.

'Should I light a fire?'

'I think so, Bibi, the rate they were riding they would hardly be looking over their shoulders for telltale wisps of smoke.' I paused, wondering. 'But I don't know, if they have been following our tracks, then when the light is stronger, they will see we are no longer ahead of them, and may turn back. Oh! I am not sure Bibi, but — yes — make a small fire with the driest wood you can find.'

'We would be better moving further away from the track,' she said, 'for here, we are right in line with the direction they have taken, and if one or two are sent back, the smoke would act as a signal to lead them straight to us.'

I conceded she was right, and we wearily pulled ourselves back onto the horses and made our way through the thick scrub to a safe and hidden spot well away from the track. We slept fitfully through the day, half listening for the sound of riders, and in the evening we waited until well after the light was gone before we kicked sand over our small fire and saddled up the horses once again.

'I wonder, should we continue down the track, or cut across rough ground to rejoin it further on?'

'That way is hard, even in daylight — wouldn't it be foolish to risk it on so dark a night?'

'Bibi, it may be the wisest in the long run, for if they are tracking us, then they will not find our marks.'

'There are so many now along the track that they themselves have made, they would surely be hard put

107

to pick ours out? Whereas out in the scrub two lone horses walking would cause suspicion.'

I could see the sense in what she said. 'Perhaps you are right! We will try it, at least until the moon gives us its light, for when that happens, not only will we be able to see our path more clearly, but we too will be more visible for searching eyes to find.'

Slowly we took our horses onto the track and walked them, our senses alert for any sign of movement, and our ears keen for the slightest sound. So on edge were we that a nightjar, rising suddenly with a screech, made us both jump and set our pulses racing so fast that we could hear the loud pounding of our hearts.

'Noeda, I don't like this,' Bibicol's whispered comment was hoarse with apprehension. 'Can't we turn around and go home?'

'How, now, having been away for two nights, can we go back dressed like bandits? The punishment would be instant purdah and confinement for me — and you, Bibi, would be banished from the estate and either sent to the slave markets or returned with ignominy to your family, so what can we do?'

I felt guilt rise in me that I should have brought her to this situation through my impetuosity. I hadn't, I realised, thought out our escape properly. Had not weighed the consequences if we were caught, not yet planned what we would do if we were not. The answers hung upon whether we found my father before he returned to Kabul. If I could but speak to him, explain, surely he would think of some excuse to get us back to the estate with no scandal. But did I want that? To return to the chadri, and the prospect of marriage to Shamlu Gadir? My every fibre rebelled at the thought, and yet as I looked across at Bibicol, I wondered again what I was leading this dear, faithful friend into. She spoke just as I was about to say we would turn back and face the consequences.

'Of course we must go on, Noeda, there is no choice now, for either of us. We will survive the journey, I'm sure — how can we fail, two such brave and valiant souls? All we have to do is to get to the border beyond Herat. Now, what could be easier than that?'

'Dear Bibi, what would I do without you!' We rode, happier now, but still careful and on our guard.

The moon came up, full of joviality, wanting to play games. We cursed its brightness for making us so vulnerable, but then blessed it again when we needed its help to pick our way up the side of the valley. The ground was rock-strewn as we came out of the thick undergrowth in the valley, and our horses found the going hard. We dismounted finally and climbed with them to the top of the ridge.

'Let's rest here for a while,' Bibicol's voice was rough from the climb.

'It is a good spot to stop anyway. From here I can see right down the valley in both directions.' Indeed, in the clear light of the near-full moon, the track silver-snaked its way, weaving through the rocks and trees at the valley bottom, to disappear into the foothills to the east and west of us.

'That way lies Koshuck and then, onwards, Herat. Once we get there it is not so far to the border, Bibi, to Meshed or Merve, and we will pick up the trail that leads us to your tribe from there.' I had travelled as far as Herat with my father, and had not any real knowledge of the distance to Merve from there.

Bibicol sat on a rock and took off her hat to shake her hair free.

'This hat caused my head to itch. I hope it is just heat and not fleas!' She hung her head between her knees and rubbed her scalp hard.

'Hold on, I do not want your fleas! We may have to cut off our hair, Bibi, if we cannot find either my father or your family. But I feel sure we will find the Khan in Herat, for I can see no reason for him going to Balkh or Ghanzi at this season of the year, and in Herat he has much business.'

'Oh no, Noeda, I cannot cut off my hair — not my beautiful thick hair!'

I looked at her. Indeed her hair was beautiful and it would be sad to chop it off.

'It may not be necessary, Bibi, and we will only do it as a last resort, if detection is threatening!'

'Whee! I was afraid that the boys would be deprived of the pleasure of running their fingers through it, Noeda!'

'If it is full of fleas, I shouldn't think they would want to anyway!'

She threw the hat at me.

A cold blast of rain caught me nodding with sleep, and I stood up quickly. Bibicol still slept, her head against the rocks. I looked to see if I could find a lightening in the sky where the moon rode behind the clouds, and cursed when I realised we had wasted a good two hours there in sleep. The rain was squally, but it was enough to chill us through, and the wind that blew the rain away stayed with us, making us feel wetter than we were. As we prepared to mount our animals once more, I looked down the valley and, in a brief moment of moonlight, saw riders coming, almost beyond sight, moving slowly, two of them casting from side to side in search.

'For the love of Allah! We must move fast, Bibi!' I cried, prodding her into action. 'They are coming to look for us!'

Bibicol gave a cry of distress and jumped quickly onto her horse. Unmindful now of boulders and other pitfalls, we set the animals at a fast pace.

'Which way?' she asked.

'To the north for now, to put as much distance as

we can between us and the track,' I said, my mind all at once very clear. 'Then we make a big half-circle back round to the west again and rejoin the track further on.'

'Surely they will send men onward to keep a lookout for us?'

'That is possible, and we will have to deal with each obstacle as we come to it. For now, keep silence and ride as fast as your horse will go!'

We rode hard, along the crest of the ridge, and then down the other side, our mounts slipping and sliding on the downward slope. There was a narrow valley at the bottom and, though it was not as far north as I had hoped to go, we turned into it and followed its twisting way westward.

The river that ran through the valley here was shallow, and we were able to take the horses at a canter through it, with the sides growing steeper and the valley narrower until we came to a defile sided with sheer rock, and the water came faster over a series of small falls.

'Can we get up those, do you think?' Bibicol's face was white with the strain of the ride already.

'Yes, they're not high. It'll not be easy, but so much the better, for no one would think to seek us through there.'

So narrow was the pass that two horses could not travel abreast. I threw a rope to Bibicol.

'Fasten this around your waist, Bibi, and I will secure my end in the same manner. That way, if one of us falls into the water, the other can pull her out!'

I dug my heels into the flanks of my now reluctant horse, and made him turn towards the rush of water of the first fall. He reared in refusal, but at the third attempt, made a good jump up and over the rocks into the comparative stillness of the water beyond. Bibicol's stallion balked too, ears flattened and nostrils flaring

111

with fear. I held tight to the rope and wound it around the pommel on my saddle.

'Come on, boy,' I encouraged, and the horse, in a sudden rush, gathered itself together and made the leap, landing badly, but unhurt beside me, in a spray of ice-cold water that drenched me to the skin. I cursed, but realised it could not be helped, and we continued upstream, over more falls and through deeper pools until the valley flattened out, and we were at last able to wade ashore.

'I'm frozen!' Bibicol, with teeth chattering, beat her hands against her arms. 'Stop for a short while and let me get off to stamp my feet, for I have no feeling left in them and cannot control the horse.'

She slipped down and fell as her cold-deadened legs gave way under her.

I dismounted quickly and pulled her off the ground, holding on while she gingerly moved her legs to get the blood flowing free once more.

'Ow! Ow! It feels as though I am walking on upturned thorns!' Her fingernails dug into my arms as she pounded each foot in turn hard onto the ground. Then she let go of me and ran up and down the small spit of land beside the river.

'Very elegant! Very fierce and warlike, my fine friend!' I laughed, but I was worried by the delay, and hesitated before I joined her in running to warm my cold, wet limbs, until we were loosened up enough to remount and resume our ride.

'We'd better stay with this river as far as we can,' I said, seeing that it wandered now through flat ground. 'I'm sure that if we were followed, our trackers would have caught up with us by this time.'

We travelled for hours without seeing a living thing, neither bird nor animal nor man, and for this we were thankful, though the haunting silence invested the night with an eeriness that left us edgy. For all that, we made good time for a while, because of the openness of the terrain but, towards dawn, the river once more grew narrow as it ran through the foothills of another ridge, and the riding got more difficult as the sides of the valley grew steeper. The sky was taking on the paleness of approaching sunrise, so we decided that it would be wise to stop where we were, and tackle the rougher journey when we were rested.

We found a sheltered hollow by the riverside, soft-grassed and shielded from the worst of the wind by thick tufts of strong murram grass and stunted thorn bushes. There we made camp, glad to get a fire going for warmth and to try to dry out our wet clothes.

I was awakened around midday by the sound of voices, and stood up fast to look down the river, where I could see a band of men and horses slowly making their way from the flat plainsland into the narrow defile.

'Quick, Bibi, quick! Wake up! We are discovered once more!'

Bibicol jumped up, eyes confused, not really aware of where she was or why she was there, and jammed the Pathan hat over her hair. We rode hard over the rocks, sure by now that the pursuers must have seen us, and lengthened the distance between us a little. But as we went, we saw the rains coming, saw the sky turn purple and heavy with clouds. Then the thunder roared down the narrow canyon that confined us. The skies tipped out their entire contents into that narrow river bed, or so it seemed, and the river, with a speed that was unbelievable, rose higher and flowed faster.

'There must have been a cloudburst further on!' I shouted pointing to the side of the valley. We heard the rumble of the water and, turning our horses, we raced to reach a patch of open ground. Already the river was a coffee-coloured torrent, and we could feel the pull on our horses as they struggled to reach the bank. I grabbed hold of Bibicol's reins and kept the horses close as the current tried to drag them away. Then we were scrambling for safety, the animals' eyes white-rimmed with their terror, and Bibicol sobbing with a harsh rasping sound. Our small supply of food fell, and was carried off downstream as we slipped and slithered over the rocks. We stood at last cramped together on an uncomfortably narrow ledge, and my breath, too, was rasping in my over-worked lungs.

I looked back downriver. The sudden swell had obviously caught our pursuers unawares, and I could see that horses and men were in the water, some managing to cling to rocks, others swept fast downstream. I prayed that none would die, for if they were men from my father's estate, then the chances were that I knew their wives and children well.

The rain fell more heavily then, and obscured my view. Bibicol held tight to my arm in fear at the crashing of the thunder. I shut my eyes, worried lest we lose the horses, afraid too that by running away I might have caused loss of life to my father's men — if that was who they were.

The horses fidgeted nervously, precarious on the narrow ledge and, in my ears, unexpectedly, I heard the words:

'There is no escape, you see, girl, no matter how far you travel!' A stranger's voice, a woman. But I didn't know her or why I should hear her voice.

An accountable anguish squeezed my heart and stomach, and the sting of tears made me blink my eyelids open. I shook my head to rid myself of these strange emotions. I'm tired, wet and hungry. I told myself. And that would account for it. For never have I been caught thus by such a storm, not even when out riding with Habib Amir.

I sat, bewildered, holding Bibicol close in mutual comfort until, at last, the storm clouds moved away and left us in sudden still calm. Calm, that is, except for the river which poured its mud-brown liquid fast over the rocks, hurtling branches and clumps of vegetation downstream with its force. I eased myself upright and tried to see a way for us to climb with the horses from our ledge to safety. I was afraid that one of the animals would step back and fall into the water to be swept away.

'Hold my hand, Bibi, and we'll edge along this rock. See — if we can get the horses over this bit, then there's a fairly wide bank which the water hasn't covered. Let's try to get to that first, and then assess our position to see what we can do!'

Bibicol nodded dumbly, as if all speech had been drained from her. She shivered uncontrollably with fear and cold. I gave her a hug of reassurance. 'We can, dearest, always go back the way we came when the river goes down, and give ourselves up. My father's humanity, surely, would ensure us a fair trial and his compassion?'

She managed a small smile, and nodded her agreement.

Carefully, we led the horses and with some difficulty made the safety of the bank which I had remarked upon. There were large rocks to one side of it and, as we went towards the shelter that these offered, to my joy I saw a narrow rift, just large enough, I hoped, for a horse to go through. Steep and jagged, this narrow defile led upwards, and in the clear air left after the storm, I could see the skyline, high above our heads, at the end of it.

'Look, Bibi! A way out!'

Her face lit up at last. 'Can we get up there? Remember, I am not as slim as you! And to tell the truth I am exhausted with what we have already been through.' Indeed, the pallor of her face, and the blueness of her lips confirmed this statement.

'Of course we can make it, Bibi! You are young and strong — stronger than I am, in fact, and though it's steep, it's not very far!'

We tied the ropes from one horse to the other and then between the two of us for safety. The climb was bad, and several times the horses slipped and we all moved backwards, but after about one hour I reached the end and put out my hand to haul Bibicol up the last few steps. We both then pulled upon the rope tied to the animals until we all stood, triumphant, at the top, in a clear warm day so far removed from the nightmare of the storm that we might have been in another world.

Wearily, we unsaddled the horses in a small clump of trees and left them to crop the grass while we stretched our tired bodies out on the ground and fell asleep, with the afternoon sun drawing the moisture from our wet clothes. When we awakened the night was into its second hour of darkness, and a bitter wind tore at us.

'Have we tea, Bibi?' I asked. 'I know most of the food is lost, but can we not at least build a fire and make a hot drink to carry us through the rest of the dark hours?'

'We are lucky — yes, we have tea and some honey to sweeten it with. There may also be a little bread in this one bag I have left. The rest is gone and we will have to find a village or market place tomorrow to replace it, for we cannot continue at this pace on empty bellies.' She drew in her breath and searched her pockets. 'I just pray I have not lost our tinder-flint, for if that be the case then we *are* lost for we can't light a fire!'

'I have mine, Bibi! Thanks be!'

We gathered what fuel we could, and made a hot drink in the flames of the spluttering fire that eventually we managed to coax out of the damp wood.

'Must we ride tonight, Noeda?'

116

'No, we could both benefit from a rest, and so could the horses I think. It seems our followers have been put about by the flood, and won't in any event find our narrow path out of the ravine in the dark.'

We rolled up in our blankets and made ready for sleep. My overtired mind played tricks, however, and though exhausted I found myself suddenly awake in the middle of the night and had difficulty in stilling my thoughts.

The birds sang an exultant chorus to the rising of the sun as it slowly revealed itself next morning, throwing off veil after veil of gossamer cloud, pink and gold and soft magnolia. I turned over to see Bibicol busy with the fire. Dishevelled, and with her hair about her face, she looked enchanting. She was so feminine that I wondered if we would ever get away with our disguise should we be caught.

'Bibi, I see you make tea! How welcome that will be!'

'It is the last of our supplies, I fear, so we will have to make the most of it, and, here — this is the last piece of bread. Rather hard to the teeth, but it will fill a small hollow inside us.' She looked at me and laughed. 'Oiee! Noeda, what a sight you are! Your hair looks like blown grass and your clothes are all apart!'

So, I looked like her!

We drank tea and tidied each other up so that when we had finished we looked more like boys than girls in boys' clothing.

There was no choice but to ride that day since we had lost both our bearings for Herat and our food. We decided to strike out to the south, hoping to hit the track again, and then travel westwards. We were rested, and relieved at having thrown off the pursuit, and the need for food had not yet become urgent, so we sang as we rode in the warm light. Songs of love

117

and songs of war — of Ghengis Khan and his raiding hordes who rode roughshod across Afghanistan, of how they swept through Herat, Bactria and Baniyan, leaving destruction in their path; and we sang, too, of Timur who brought us back to Islam, and of the good Shah Rukh, who brought peace for a while and dotted the countryside with mosques of great delicacy and beauty.

Bibicol taught me songs of robust and earthy flavour from the kitchens and stables, and these we sang with great liveliness, deepening our voices and slapping our thighs. Then she lifted up her sweet voice in a nostalgic song from times gone, a song that was part of the heritage of her tribe:

'The tribe has left, the dust remains;
The sun has gone, the yellow remains.
I never kissed those dark eyes, the sorrow remains.'
So soft and haunting was the sound, so evocative the words, with the eternal spirit of longing and losing, that a sadness came down upon my sunny mood. For the first time since we left Kabul, I longed for my father, and for the warm security of the years of my childhood, sheltered by his affectionate and caring companionship.

The song died, and we rode in silence then for a while, with nothing but the wind to keep us company. It was not until the evening that at last we saw the track ahead of us; a camel train travelling along it, throwing plumes of dust into the hot air.

'If we hurry now, we should meet those travellers before they go too far towards Kabul,' said Bibicol, digging her heels hard into her horse to get it moving, as she set off towards the dust. I followed fast, and it was not long before we reached the track to await the slower-moving camels. We inspected each other to ensure our disguise, and, satisfied that no long hair showed, no glimpse of soft breast would give us away,

118

we sat, straight-backed on our horses, ready for quick flight should the need arise.

The camels came swaying towards us, heavy-laden with merchandise, the dust kicked up by their large circular feet giving them a floating, ghostlike appearance, riding above the ground. Their double humps rolled from one side to the other, so that they looked like old men who had taken too kindly to the wine bottle. We put up our hands in greeting as they drew close, and the man mounted on the lead animal shouted his order to stop, the order coming back, echo-like, to us as it was relayed down the line.

'Greetings, young men,' he saluted us. 'What news of the road ahead? Have you had sight of bandits or such along the route?'

We assured him we had not, as he eyed us suspiciously.

'Well, from the cut of your cloaks you are not thieves yourselves unless, of course, you came by those clothes through thievery. If you are what you appear, then where do you journey to?'

'Herat is our goal, but we had misfortune on our way,' I said, telling but briefly of the cloudburst, and asked if he and his fellow travellers could spare a little food. By now, having reassured himself that our motives were not nefarious, the man had dismounted and, calling to his woman, bade her give us food and drink.

'In fact,' he said, 'we could well make camp now, for the night, and if you two youngsters would care to join us, you will be welcome.'

Bibicol and I looked at each other, a little afraid and unsure in our disguise, but I nodded, and we accepted with gratitude, the thought of hot food and company overcoming our caution.

The dusk fell fast, as it always did at that time of the year, and in the darkness around the fires, with the flames playing their flickering shadows across our faces, we felt safe, at least for the time.

'You are young to be travelling without retinue or guards,' said our host. 'And from your talk you come from good families. How then are you alone?'

I cleared my throat and thought hastily.

'We travel to my uncle at Herat, from Kabul,' I explained. 'We wanted to do this alone, for we are becoming men, and do not need Ayahs to play nursemaid any longer. Our father was in agreement to our going as a test of our endurance and resourcefulness, for soon we all travel north to meet Babur's force.' As an improvisation I felt this to be brilliant, and I saw the light of amused admiration glint in Bibicol's eyes.

Later that night she whispered low, as we lay for sleep, 'Babur, huh! I can imagine what we two would do if we came face to face with him or his army!'

We suppressed our laughter and vowed to be awake before daylight in order to escape the risk of detection. We were ready to mount before break of day, and bade farewell to our host.

'Koshuk is but a short ride from here,' he told us. 'You will be able to replace your lost provisions there, I'm sure, but you are welcome meanwhile to whatever we have to spare.'

We thanked him, but took only enough to see us through that day, and rode away, much pleased with ourselves over the success of our first encounter.

It took us three days to get to Koshuk, and we were near starving by the time we reached that small and unimposing town. It had, to our relief, a busy market place, serving several outlying villages and lying, too, upon the trade route from Farah and Herat to Kabul. I left the bartering for provisions to Bibicol, for I had no idea of what we needed, or indeed of how to set about the business, sheltered as I had been in the household where the daughters of the Khan were not permitted to take part in anything considered so vulgar as bargaining in the market place.

I watched hungrily as she went first to one trader and then another, matching prices and, ever mindful of the slenderness of our purse, choosing the best and least expensive items. She strode through the crowd in her riding boots, hat firmly pulled down over her abundant hair, keeping her speech quiet, fearful to argue too much lest her voice grow high and sharp in tone, and give her away. I was proud of her performance and silently applauded her. Stout-hearted Bibicol!

She came back laden with purchases.

'Here!' She tossed the loaves of nan bread to me in what would have been deemed a deeply disrespectful manner back in Kabul, but she softened the gesture with the laughter of our shared conspiracy that lit up her large black eyes. 'Come, good brother, let us leave this scurvy place and away on our business!' she said, deep and authoritative, and climbed with as much dignity as she could in her tight-seated trousers, onto the horse. Once out of earshot we let go the laughter of relief; we had succeeded in our deception!

On the outskirts of Koshuk we found a teahouse, a lowly place built of mud and roofed with straw and branches, the roof extending outwards from the walls to form a shelter under which travellers could sit to drink hot sweet tea either on its own or mixed with goat's milk. A delicious smell of spiced meat met our hungry senses and, in unspoken agreement, we dismounted.

The owner of the teahouse, seeing our fine, if travel-stained, clothing, came out hastily, eager and obsequious, flicking the dust from a wooden bench and table for us to sit at. We ate well, and, keeping our voices low, fell into talk with a trio of riders who came in after us. From them we heard of the hunt that was taking place for two men who had seized and murdered the son of the Khan of Chesht, a small town near Herat. The men who spoke to us were one of many small groups which had been formed to track the two murderers down.

Bibicol and I exchanged quick looks. Perhaps, then, our pursuers at the river had not been from Kabul, not my father's men after all. My spirits rose a little.

'Well, we are not your murderers,' I said firmly. 'We go to Herat to visit an uncle there, and we have seen no fugitives on our way. In fact, it seems we were mistaken for those villains earlier, and made fast our escape, believing ourselves chased by bandits!' That, I hoped, would explain our flight up the river, should it be reported.

'There's a handsome reward for the capture of these miscreants,' one of the men told us. 'So, young masters, should you come across them, either capture or kill them, and fast too, before they do the same to you!' We laughed our bravado, and left them before too many questions came our way.

'We must be even more careful, Bibi, for capture by either the pursuers or the pursued would inevitably lead to the discovery of our masquerade. We mustn't allow ourselves to be over-confident on the strength of our successes so far!'

'Can you imagine the faces of those pursuers if they caught us and stripped us for beating!'

I was more aware of the fury that my father would show if we were caught and sent back to Kabul!

The track grew rougher and more difficult leaving Koshuk, winding through valleys and over the foothills of the jagged, red Paropamisus mountains. Both the terrain and renewed caution made our progress slow, for we did not wish to drive our horses to exhaustion, wanting to keep some of their power and speed in reserve in case we needed it. We rode in isolation for three days, coming to Chesht as the evening sky began to darken. There was a strange and feverish air of tension as we came even to the outskirts of this small mountain town. Groups of people stood talking in lowered tones, or moved through the rough mud streets at a faster pace than was normal.

I turned in my saddle to speak to Bibicol. 'I don't like the feel of this place. Perhaps we should ride straight through and make camp further on?'

'That may lead to questions, Noeda, for surely the natural thing would be for us to rest here now that the night creeps up behind us?'

'We could perhaps find a meal and then move on.' I was nervous and felt the sweat prickle my armpits, though the evening was cool. We dismounted, clumsy in our apprehension, and felt the eyes of many upon us. Bibicol coughed and near choked as she tried to suppress it. I thanked Allah for the fading light which gave us a little protection, and we looked around for a teahouse. We led our horses across to a tree in the middle of the main square, and tied them there.

'Shall we unsaddle?' asked Bibicol, quietly.

'I think not, it would be well to eat quickly and make our departure as soon as possible.' The hairs on my neck and those fine ones on my arms stood erect and tingling. 'I don't care for this at all — we are in danger here, Bibi!'

Bibicol looked at me. 'I think you imagine things, Noeda. All seems quiet and calm to me!' She tied the reins of our horses with a quick, firm motion and, hands in her belt, led off to the teahouse. I followed with foreboding.

The owner came forward reluctantly to serve us. 'I am about to stamp out the embers of my cooking fires,' he grumbled, 'so make your order quick and simple.'

We asked for tea, bread and cheese, hesitant to

123

request hot food, and the man banged our order down in front of us, spilling half the lukewarm tea in so doing.

Bibicol's eyes blazed. 'What is this, you dog?' she shouted at the man. 'Is this how you serve the sons of the Khan of Koshuk?'

Koshuk! I thought. Why Koshuk? Then I realised she had nearly slipped up and said 'Kabul' and it was commonly known throughout Afghanistan that Habib Amir had only daughters and no son to carry his line.

The man bowed his head low and went quickly through to his cooking fire where we could hear him blowing up the flames to build up the heat once more.

'That was foolish, Bibi, was it not?' I asked. 'We don't want to draw any more attention than necessary to ourselves.'

'Neither do we wish to waste what little money we have got on food or drink that is valueless,' she retorted, all eyes. The owner of the teahouse returned with fresh tea and placed it before us.

'I apologise, sirs, I meant no discourtesy. This town is saddened by the murder of our Khan's son, and at present we are wary of strangers. Please tell me if there is more you require. I will be honoured to serve you.'

Bibicol winked at me. 'No, my good fellow, this will suit our needs. I take it then that the murderers are still not caught?'

'No, there are many searching for the men, but chances are they will escape justice if they have gone north over the mountains towards Maimana or Bactria.'

'What reasons for this murder?' I asked.

'If it was done by those we suspect, then it was revenge, for there has long been a feud between our Khan, Abdul Pashtoon, and the Khan of Farah, Ghulum Zubair. A bitter and bloody feud that has caused much unhappiness and death. It is one that started many hundreds of years ago in the time that

Ghengis Khan turned family against family in his destruction of our land.' He shook his head reflectively. 'Maybe further back, to Alexander even.' He scratched his beard and spat into the dust of the floor.

'What do you know of Alexander?' I asked, curious to learn more of the legendary figure who had shaped the destiny of our country. The old man's eyes reflected the red embers of the fire, and we felt we were listening to a storyteller of long ago as he began:

'I do not know too much, but one story I will tell you for it is worth the sharing. You know Alexander had two horns — like a ram's horns — growing from the sides of his head?' Bibicol and I shook our heads for we had not heard this. 'Well, he didn't want anyone to know about these horns so he covered them with long hair. Only the manservant who tended him knew, and he was sworn to secrecy. But the manservant just had to speak, so he whispered the secret into a well. Soon reeds grew from the well, but whenever anyone made a flute from them no music came out, only the words: "Alexander has two horns!".'

This was not what we had expected, but we joined his laughter at the tale.

'What about the wall — is there such a thing?' Bibicol prompted.

'Well, Alexander had two sons. He divided his kingdom between them. But they were always arguing about the boundary, so Alexander built the wall to separate them. And this argument may have been the start of the feud that still divides tribe from tribe, brother from brother, and has brought about this latest murder. I do not know, for I am old and tired and my eyes have seen too much to be able to judge true from false any more!'

Perhaps we were lucky that it was so!

We sat talking until well into the night to this old man, whom we had disliked so mistakenly when we first arrived. He offered us the use of one of his rooms for the night, and stabling for the horses which we accepted gladly for it was late and we were very tired.

But for all my tiredness, I was restless and found difficulty in getting to sleep. In my dreams when I eventually slept, I was in a different place, a strange place . . .

* * * *

. . . In the morning I was tired and stiff, almost as though I too had ridden the rough track with Noeda and Bibicol.

I got up as quickly as my aching legs would allow, and ran for the bathroom, racked with morning-sickness.

How could those two have managed it? I wondered, as I washed my face afterwards. They're both so young to undertake a journey of that magnitude!

I looked at my white face in the mirror above the basin. But then they're the same age as me! And I'm about to run away, too, to avoid Father's anger in the way that Noeda is escaping the wrath of Habib Amir!

Filled with giddiness and a reoccurrence of nausea, I envied Noeda her freedom and her ability to ride away with Bibicol, knowing that someday, somehow, I'd have to come back to Nairobi and face Mother and Father.

I shut my eyes and breathed deeply, longing to be there — on the dry, rocky route between Kabul and Herat.

Melika's voice broke into my wishful thinking.

'Come on, Nina! You'll be late for college!'

I knew I'd soon have to start making my preparations to leave for Mombasa.

SEVEN

In the fourth month of my pregnancy Melika left. Mother's distress at her departure was matched by her annoyance at having to find a replacement cook.

Father was away, to my relief, on a special course to recruit and train the Kikuyu Home Guard, a body of men supposedly 'loyal' to the White Government, but whose chances of survival were, even to my untutored mind, pretty slim. In Father's absence I seized the opportunity to break the news to Mother that I, too, would be leaving.

'Nina! But you can't go! William . . . !' Her eyes were wide with apprehension.

'I've applied for a job in Mombasa,' I lied. 'I'll be all right! Several girls I knew at the convent live there, and I'm sure I can stay with one of them until I can find a place of my own.'

She stared at me without speaking, her face expressionless, so that I couldn't tell whether she mourned my going. Perhaps, I thought, it'll be a relief not to have me around. I felt I was a constant irritant, a sort of burr, in her marriage.

Her words surprised me: 'I'll miss you, Nina. I'm so alone, you know!'

Oh, hell! I thought. Her eyes filled, and I put my hand on hers. For the first time in my memory she didn't resist, didn't push me away.

'It's better for me to go,' I said. 'Perhaps without me here you two can grow closer?'

'The time for that,' she sighed, 'is long past.' Then she turned away.

My heart ached for her, but I knew that there was no way I could stay.

'Anyway,' she looked at me, and now anger had replaced the anxiety, 'you'll have to wait until he gets back. There'd be the devil to pay if you went without permission.' She paused. 'You're only sixteen, for heaven's sake!'

I was all too aware of that. But I also knew that he'd stop me, for whatever reason, and it wouldn't be long before my pregnancy became obvious. Then, without doubt, all hell would break loose. I *had* to go, and towards this end I schemed, secretly packing my clothes, counting out my remaining savings. When I found I hadn't enough for the train fare, I resorted to taking money from Mother's handbag — feeling guilty and ashamed at the theft. I reassured myself that it was for the best, it was, after all, what Noeda and Bibicol had done.

Then, one hot afternoon, while she slept, I left the house quietly and caught the bus into Nairobi and to the railway station.

As the train slowly pulled away in a swirl of smoke and steam, headed for Mombasa, I knew I was leaving my childhood behind, and I shut my mind to the anger that I knew Father would inflict upon my mother at my leaving . . .

* * * *

. . . The Khan's wrath would know no bounds, but there was nothing else I could do now.

I opened my eyes wide with fear as rough hands grabbed at me in the pale pre-dawn light. I saw Bibicol snatch up her hat and pull it quickly over her hair as the two men who stood over us turned from me to her.

I, too, picked up my headgear and with one free hand pushed it onto my head. My other hand was tightly held in the grasp of one of the men. They pulled

128

us upright and pushed us without pause towards the doorway.

'What are you doing?' I cried. 'What right have you to disturb the sons of a Khan in this brutal and discourteous manner?'

'Keep silence!' The tone was brusque, as we were propelled forward. I was greatly afeared that we were attacked by robbers or by murderers.

'We have very little money on us,' I said. 'But if that is what you want, then please take it.' I struggled to release the thongs that tied my money pouch to my belt, but my fingers shook and the knots would not come free to my one hand.

'We want no money, we are not thieves, though you may well be so!'

I wondered if the teahouse owner had revised his opinion of us and had called for help, but then I saw him, blear-eyed with disturbed sleep, held by yet another man.

'What misfortune have you brought to my house, young rascals?' he began, anger and fear making him splutter.

'We have done nothing,' I began, but the man who held me pulled me roughly over to where their horses were tethered.

'Get up behind me,' he ordered and, not wishing to appear guilty in any way by refusing, I complied, though my throat was tight with fear and my breath shallow.

Thank goodness we slept in our clothes, I thought, and as my mind caught itself in this small, stupid reassurance, I began to panic about the reason for this abduction, and what it could mean. I did not have time for much speculation, for we rode at full gallop then, out of Chesht, northwards towards the grim, dawn-lit mountains. It was all I could do to keep my seat and hold onto my hat, and often I felt myself slip backwards. Praying we would reach our destination before I fell off, I held tight to the edge of the saddle in front of me. Though perhaps, I thought, it would be better to die now, quickly, through a fatal fall, than endure torture, or discovery and probable rape. But then — what of Bibicol? I strained round to catch sight of her but, in danger of falling yet again, straightened up without glimpsing her.

After what seemed hours of riding, but was more likely to have been less than one, we slowed down and I saw ahead the outbuildings, stables and gateway of a big compound.

Khan Abdul Pashtoon! The size of the estate gave me the answer to our destination. It was large, so he was obviously a man of some importance. But surely they did not think we were the murderers? I swallowed hard, dry-mouthed. How could we prove our innocence without disclosing our own secret? I looked again over my shoulder and found Bibicol, eye-whites showing with fear, and her face ashen grey in the cold light. Oh, Bibi! Keep your head! I implored silently. And don't weep! For the love of Allah, don't weep! I was near to tears myself.

We rode through the gateway and into a large court-yard within.

'Dismount!' The order came, curt and cold. I did what I was told and was taken across to where Bibicol and the keeper of the teahouse stood, bewildered and frightened.

'We have done nothing wrong!' I tried to keep my voice steady. 'Once we have spoken to the headman, he will see we are of good family and release us. And you, good friend, I will speak for you and assure them that you did nothing but serve two passing travellers.' The old man stared at me with large mournful eyes, red-rimmed with his terror.

'You do not know these people,' he muttered, low.

130

'Stop that talking, or I'll have you beaten!' shouted one of our captors, hitting out at me and catching my shoulder so hard that I staggered. I was about to remonstrate but caught Bibicol's frightened look and curbed my tongue.

We stood in the courtyard while the sun slowly rose over the rooftops and, at last, a group of men emerged from the house. Was this Khan Abdul Pashtoon? I wondered, but decided that he was not one of the five or six who came towards us. These were obviously guards, or fighting men of some sort with knives at their belts and clad in high, polished riding boots. We were roughly pushed to stand before them, and I looked up at the man who spoke, taking in only that he was tall and bearded. I clasped my hands behind my back tightly to hide their shaking.

'Well?' he asked sternly. 'Who are you and what are you doing riding thus through difficult country with no bodyguard If your clothes speak for you, then you come from good families — or are the clothes not yours? In truth they do not fit you well, and from the state you are in, you have no others. Give a reasonable explanation or I will be forced to believe that you are not what you claim.'

'Sir,' I answered, eyes downcast, my voice struggling through a throat constricted with fear. 'We are indeed of noble family, riding on a trial of endurance to fit us for encounter with the tyrant, Babur. Our clothes, like our provisions, got swept away in a cloudburst, and we are left with what we stand in!'

He stood, legs wide and a hand on his chin. His eyes narrowed as he studied us. 'I don't know whether I believe you, but certainly you don't look or speak like murderers. In fact, my feeling is that you are too young and weak to be capable of that deed, almost tied still to your nurse's skirts, too young to be men, yet too old to be boys.' He stood for a moment longer in thought

131

then walked over to the owner of the teahouse and put his hand on the old man's thin shoulder.

'Old man, you should not be here. I will see you return unharmed and with some compensation. But, remember, it is the rule in Chesht now that all strangers must be reported, and you did not do so, did you?'

The man bent double in his bowing. 'No, my lord, I did not, and for this I beg forgiveness. The young men came late, and by the time I had given them food it was even later, and we fell to talking then. I did intend, truly, to report them early this morning, but your men came before I could do so, sir. But I am sure the young men are who they claim, for I found them unworldly and courteous. Their hands are soft, like those of women, not hard and rough, as would be those of men used to violence and life in the saddle!'

The headman signalled to one of our captors. 'Escort this good man back to the town, or he will lose business.' He drew some coins out of his money pouch and gave them to the owner of the teahouse. 'This, my friend, will repay you for any loss of trade this morning.'

The old man bowed and salaamed his way backwards to the horses, and we watched as he went.

'Now,' said the headman, turning back to us, 'what are we to make of you? Have you any way of proving who you are?' He paused. 'Perhaps I should have you beaten. That way the truth may be revealed!'

I looked directly at him for the first time and, as my eyes and his interlocked, I felt a jolt, akin to recognition, travel through me. I felt I knew this man intimately, and saw the shock reflected, too, in his eyes. And yet I knew that we had never met. His forehead furrowed in a frown of bewilderment.

'Who are you?' he asked, and his voice no longer held the tone of authority.

'We are the sons of the Khan of Koshuk,' I stated

in a voice that shook despite my efforts to control it, hoping against the fates that he didn't know the Khan of Koshuk.

'No — I meant you — who are *you?*' he asked musingly, then realising how strange a question this was, he shook his head. 'The sunlight is in my eyes, and for one moment I thought I knew you well?' he said, then turned to Bibicol. 'And you? How are you finding this "test of endurance"?' His voice still held more than a hint of disbelief.

'Almost beyond my endurance, sir,' she replied, and I saw her face flush. I held my breath, knowing how close she was to breaking point.

'You are both very young,' he said, and turned away to pace the yard where we stood. We waited and in the silence I could hear the pounding of my heart, so loud that I was sure everyone there could hear it, too. Bibicol sniffed and as I glanced at her I saw her quickly rub at her eyes. Be brave, dear Bibi, my silent plea went out to her. She looked my way and, seeing my eyes upon her, gave me a watery smile.

The bearded man returned to stand in front of us. 'I am fairly sure you are what you say. Fairly sure, but not certain,' he said. 'There is something which gives me pause — but I cannot put a name to it!'

Dear Allah! I thought. This man is too perceptive for my liking! I moved closer to Bibicol and gently nudged her with my elbow.

'We are young, sir, and had much trouble persuading our father to let us travel thus. We don't want him to know we have failed in any way, so we beg you to tell no one, lest the news travel back to him.'

The tall man suddenly laughed, his brown eyes reflecting specks of golden sunshine, his mood changing abruptly. 'So that is the way of it! This is to prove your manhood, is it? Come on, come inside to my rooms and have some food.' He looked us over, critically. 'A

133

good wash and some clean clothes would make you more wholesome, too. Did you say you had lost everything in the waters of the river?'

My breath came fast — an exhalation of pure relief.

Bibicol spoke up quickly. 'Yes, everything! Our clothes, food, and worst of all, our money for the journey, leaving us with what little we had in our small pouches.'

Take care. Bibi! Take care! Don't push our fortune too far. What money did we lose — and what other clothes? I kept these thoughts to myself.

'Come,' he said. 'We'll soon re-equip you. We can't let the sons of a Khan ride thus, looking and acting like beggars! I am Rsul Rahman, Headman for Khan Abdul Pashtoon, and I must explain why you were subjected to this questioning.'

'No need,' I told him. 'The man from the teahouse explained the trouble here.'

Rsul patted my shoulder. 'Good, then all I can do is apologise for the treatment and hope you will understand.'

'A wash and a change of apparel would be most welcome, Rsul Rahman,' I said. 'And so, too, would a meal before we go.'

'Must you leave so fast?'

'Yes, need we go yet?' echoed Bibicol, obviously enjoying herself now.

I frowned at her. 'We have far to travel, Behar.' The name was a flash of inspiration. 'And our time is somewhat curtailed for we have lost much due to the flood.' I was still full of apprehension, and wanted to get as far away as possible from this man whose eyes seemed to read my very soul.

Bibicol's lower lip pouted. 'A day wouldn't make much difference, and I am bone tired with riding,' she complained.

'Come on, boy,' encouraged our host, 'your brother

134

is right, you could do with a day of rest — and to visit the barber!'

My hand flew instinctively to my hair, and I felt the wisps escaping from under my hat. 'Indeed we could!' I tried to sound nonchalant, though my hand shook. 'Let me ponder on it while I wash, and we will see how we feel after eating. In any event our horses are back in Chesht!'

'My man will bring them back with him after delivering your teahouse friend, so there is no problem in that direction. Think hard, young friends, for I feel badly that you were so roughly handled. Your horses, too, could probably do with a rest before you continue.'

He clapped his hands for a manservant, who led us away to the washrooms. When we emerged, wrapped in soft warm towelling, our travel-worn garments were gone, and clean clothes lay in their place.

'Bibi, I am afraid to stay too long. This Rsul is too clever a man to be deceived for any length of time. Already he looks too close — and you, Bibi, forget you are "Behar" and flirt with him like a woman!'

She let out one of her deep chuckles, and truly it was a joy to hear, for I don't believe we had laughed in our old carefree manner for many days.

'Behar, indeed! And what name have you chosen for yourself, I humbly ask, oh brother?'

'I haven't thought — what of "Nadir"? That is close enough to allow of a slip of the tongue should you call me Noeda accidentally!'

'Oiee! Noeda, you are clever, clever, clever!' She clapped her hands and strutted in the clean clothes. Certainly they were a better fit than the motley assortment that we had been wearing, and I saw, too, that soft suede shoes had been left for us to wear inside the building.

'Ah well, perhaps we can stay until tomorrow!' Cushioned in the luxury of cleanliness once more, my caution left me. 'But we will go to the barber, Bibi, though it sadden you to lose your hair, for it is dangerous to wear it loose. He could cut it a little and then plait it so that we can wear it in a knot on top of our heads, like the Sikhs and Pathans do, beneath their turbans.'

She sighed, but agreed that it had to be.

'I nearly fell, holding hard my hat on the back of that horse!'

We finished dressing and, calling the manservant, bade him take us first to the barber, and then to Rsul Rahman. As we followed behind him, I felt lighthearted, a sense of great excitement and inexplicable wellbeing flooding through me, for which I could find no reason . . .

* * * *

. . . Melika met me at Mombasa Station next morning, and we travelled by taxi over Nyali pontoon bridge and along the rutted, dusty road that led eventually to the Arab town of Malindi, passing through Leah's village of Mikendeni on the way.

At our arrival a handful of grubby children gathered around the taxi, welcoming its unusual presence in the sleepy village. With bare legs and toes greyed with dust, they stood silently watching the driver as he cradled a mug of hot sweet tea which Leah gave him. He leaned against his vehicle, a city-slicker in his black trousers, white shirt and sunglasses.

Leah's hut was in a cluster of buildings which sat squat like mushrooms, among tall coconut palms whose grey trunks carved parabolas downwards to the sandy soil.

The interior was dark and cool after the blinding sun outside.

'She's come, my daughter!' Melika led me in and motioned me to sit down. I lowered myself onto the mat, awkward with my enlarging belly. Well into my fifth month of pregnancy, I had found it increasingly difficult to conceal from Mother the fact that my clothes were getting too tight, and I had taken to wearing large floppy jumpers even on the hottest days, much to the puzzlement of my friends at the secretarial college.

'Welcome, daughter of Melika!' Leah's smile was bright against her dark brown skin, seeming to light up the dark interior of the hut. A shiver tingled up my spine as she spoke and as I looked at her, I felt I had known her forever.

'Don't be afraid, we will look after you here until the child comes.'

Oh yes, I thought, I know you will! Though I had no idea of why I felt so certain.

'I'm glad to be here!' I answered her, so glad indeed. 'And I thank you for your hospitality!'

'We've made ready a hut for you!' Melika's excitement matched my own. 'And the carpenter in Mombasa made a bed!'

I knew I was indeed honoured. Most Africans slept on straw mattresses, or simply curled up upon palm-frond mats on the floor.

'I don't know how I'll repay your kindness,' I said to Leah. I wondered if she, too, felt the spark of recognition that had flown between us.

She 'tcck'd' with her tongue against her teeth, dismissing the necessity for any thanks. 'You are Melika's daughter, and the child is of our blood. Therefore you are our family, as we are yours.'

Somehow I knew that Leah was indeed a part of my life — and, inexplicably, part of Noeda's, too.

'Is there any news of Rashidi?' I asked Melika later.

'We have heard nothing.' Her smile had gone now. 'And truly our hearts are heavy with grieving.'

'And Jamira?'

'She writes from Uganda to tell me she is at school and well, but has no news of her brother either. I fear

137

there's no doubt now that he has joined the fight for freedom, with the Kikuyus.' Through the sadness of her words, I felt I could hear a hint of pride — of envy even.

It must be so dreadfully hard for people like Melika who have lived so long with the Europeans — with their loyalties so divided! I thought, looking at her loved and familiar face.

'He must follow his heart, Melika, do what he believes to be right. Let's just pray that he hasn't been forced into murder and bestiality by Thahu!'

But my heart felt heavy in my chest when I thought of Rashidi, and I was racked with guilt and remorse both for him and for myself.

EIGHT

My stomach swelled gently, and my skin browned in the reflected sunshine as I walked the soft silver-white sands and swam in the warm sea of the lagoon, safe from sharks behind the barrier of the coral reef. I learned to eat posho, the crushed maize porridge which was the staple diet of the villagers, and to make myself loose-flowing dresses from bright-coloured cloths — kangas — which were sold in the market. I was content, for once, wishing that there was no need for me ever to leave the simplicity of the life. And I shut my ears and eyes to the stories that filtered through. Blood-chilling accounts of udders being slashed from cattle, of decapitated corpses, whose heads were never found; of heightened fear and tension. The time of 'The Night of the Long Knives', the day when the Bushbuck Horn would sound and all the Mau Mau initiates would attack as one man, ridding Kenya of the white settlers who had stolen their lands, was close. Too close. It had become a reality, no longer some vaguely feared and nebulous threat. The whispers grew. I didn't want to think, or hear, or see any of the signs, torn as I was between the two — the black and the white.

I wrote to my parents using a Post Office box number, and this raised no special comment in their infrequent, impersonal replies. It was easy to close my mind to them — to their problems, to my own problems that were entwined with theirs. My small mud-and-wattle hut with its thatch of palm was a sanctuary. The wood-framed bed, webbed with strips of rubber cut from old inner-tubing, was my inner sanctum within the sanctuary. When I was in there, with the

139

door tight-closed, no one disturbed my solitude, not even Melika.

And all the time Leah was there, her presence tangible, our as yet unspoken-about bond a comfort and a reassurance which I didn't really understand.

The heat and stormy rains of December gave way to cooler January, and the coral-creeper vine slung its pink cascades of tiny flowers from branch to branch in the scrub around the compound. Bougainvillaea flamed bright against the whitewashed walls of the huts, and the sea lay smooth as jade beyond the brightness of the sand.

On a still, calm morning, as dawn broke in a blaze of gold over that sea, Kerri was born.

The contractions announcing her arrival had started just before midnight, and I had called, frightened, for Melika.

'We must send for the midwife in the next village,' she said at once when she saw what was happening.

'Can't we wake the shopkeeper and get him to telephone for an ambulance?' Totally unprepared, I was convinced that I was about to die.

'Which hospital, Nina?' She shook her head. 'You can't go to the African hospital since you have no passbook, no kipande, and the European hospital would ask too many questions — why you didn't go for examinations and so on.' She felt my contracting muscles, counting the minutes between the spasms. 'The midwife is trained in the hospital, Nina, she knows how to bring a child into the world!'

My screams echoed through the palm grove, and in the light cast by the lamp outwards through the open doorway, I had seen the whites of many eyes as the village women looked on anxiously.

The pains came fast. I felt the moisture run down my legs, and I was mortally afraid.

'Don't let me lose this child!' I cried, 'not this child,

140

too!' But I'd never lost a child! In lucid moments I wondered if Noeda had. Noeda whom I knew so well!

Noeda — who was me!

When eventually the midwife arrived, breathless and dishevelled on her bicycle, the child's head had crowned, and she barely had time to wash her hands in the bowl which Melika held ready.

'Dear God! I can't go on!' I cried, 'Oh, Holy Mother of God — let me die! Oh, Melika! Help me!' How Melika survived the tightness of my gripping hands I'll never know. Then with a rush the baby came, as if she could not wait a moment longer to be free.

'Aaaah!' The sound came simultaneously from Melika, Leah, the midwife and the assembled villagers outside, followed by shrill ululations of joy that filled the morning air and greeted my small, coffee-brown daughter and the dawn-red sun at one and the same time.

As the first thin wail came to me from where the midwife was cleaning the child, my stomach contracted and I put out my arms.

'Let me see! Let me see! Is it a girl or boy, Melika?'

'She is a girl, Nina, a daughter for us all! Oh, how small and skinny, like a little frog — a kikerri!' And thus, in the pink light filtering through the door, she was named 'Kerri'.

The small dark head wobbled as Melika passed her to me, and as I saw the soft indent at the top of the baby's head, I was filled with an internal dissolution, a melting, similar — inexplicably — to sexual desire. I held her against me, longing to squeeze her even tighter, almost wanting to devour her, to savour her taste, her smell, the feel of her tight-curled black hair.

'Oh, Melika! Melika!' The tears rolled down my face. She put her arm around my shoulders, her cheek against mine and we laughed and cried together.

'Oh, she's safe — she's safe, after all!'

And she was mine.

The midwife's voice cut into our rejoicing: 'The girl will have to go to hospital, she needs stitching. The child was so eager to enter the world that she has torn her mother.'

I looked at her, frightened now.

'No, don't worry,' she reassured me, 'it isn't bad, but still will need a few stitches, which I cannot do! I'll go now and wake the store-owner and ring for an ambulance to take you.'

'Which hospital?' I asked, not wanting to leave the warm familiarity of my hut.

'It'll have to be the European one,' she replied, and went out into the morning sun.

'Don't be anxious, Nina,' Leah patted my hand. 'Just say you were visiting the village.'

'But what about curfew — the fact that you are supposed to report all visitors to the local police?'

The man at the teahouse in Chesht had failed to do so . . .

'We aren't in the Mau Mau lands here, the rules are not so strict since this is the Giriama tribe.' Leah smiled at me.

Would the guards once again take me to Abdul Pashtoon's estate?

The nursing sister's eyes went from Kerri to me, but though her lips tightened, she said nothing. Doctor Phillips was not so reticent.

'Why on earth haven't you booked in, gone to have blood tests and so on? Not very sensible, was it?'

'I went to a clinic in Nairobi,' I lied. My heart constricted for no reason with a terrible fear and within my head I cried: 'My child, oh God, my child!'

Doctor Phillips called my bluff. 'Well then, I'd better ring the clinic for your records,' he said.

My eyes filled and I turned my head towards the wall.

His voice softened. 'Your parents don't know, is that what it's all about?'

Yes, I thought, that — and something else . . . something terrible, that I don't understand . . .

He picked Kerri up and undid the cloth in which she'd been wrapped. 'Oh! My poor, dear girl — I see!' He handed Kerri to the nurse. 'Take her through and clean her up.' His hand took mine, gently now. 'First we'll stitch that tear for you. It won't take long.'

Throughout the indignity of the stitching he talked to me, keeping up a constant flow of friendly chatter, never once questioning, and afterwards, when Kerri lay in my arms, clean and fresh in a hospital nightdress, I put out my hand and took his.

'Thank you!' I said, then reddened as a smile creased lines round his eyes.

The inevitable questions came, but I would not be drawn on either Rashidi or my address. Eventually, and angrily, the hospital administration gave up, and after a week in hospital I ordered a taxi to take me back to the village.

Before I left, Doctor Phillips came to give me a final checkup.

'You'll do,' he said. 'Come back in a week and we'll take out the remaining stitches.' He produced a large parcel. 'I've taken the liberty of gathering a few bits and pieces for Kerri. I hope you won't be offended. It's only nappies, a few nightdresses, vests and so on. My sister had a baby a year ago, and these were hers. You're not too proud to take second-hand things, are you?'

Rsul gave us clothes that fitted us at Abdul Pashtoon's estate — we'd not been too proud to take his help then . . .

'Of course not! And thank you, that's really kind of you. I didn't know quite how I was going to cope, I must admit!'

'Well, you can't go to work. Not right now, can you?'

He looked at me thoughtfully. 'Have you considered having the baby adopted, Nina?'

'No!' I was adamant.

'I do understand how you feel, but,' he paused, 'she isn't white — and how are you going to explain that away to your parents?'

'I can't, I don't think. Father's really bigoted. He'd throw me out, I'm sure.'

'And your mother?'

Poor Mother!

'I really don't know. She's got enough to contend with . . .'

'How old are you, anyway?'

'Sixteen — nearly seventeen.'

He sighed. 'Lord, you're so young to be saddled with a child — let alone a . . .'

'Go on, say it — "half-caste" — that's what you were going to say, wasn't it?' My anger flared. What right had this fresh-from-England doctor to make judgments?

'It's bound to lead to difficulties in this racist society. Be fair, Nina, I was brought up here, just as you were. Kenya is as much in my blood as it is in yours! The Kikuyu are my blood brothers, my friends from childhood!'

I felt chastened, ashamed of my quick judgment. 'You surely don't condone Mau Mau?'

'I don't condone their methods, no of course I don't. But I can appreciate the frustrations that have led to the unrest.' He shook his head. 'Come on, this is too serious! All I wanted to say was that if you ever need help — someone to turn to — I'm here!' He took a pen out of his pocket and wrote on the paper covering the parcel. 'My name and telephone number — and you can leave a message if you can't get through to me.' He turned at the door. 'Think carefully about the possibility of adoption. I know how difficult it is for you to

144

contemplate parting with the child but give it consideration, for your own sake. If you want help, contact me, okay?'

On the way home my fingers traced his name on the parcel: Doctor Paul Phillips, number 32 Nyali Estate, Mombasa. Telephone number 805. And I wondered.

I saw the totos running towards the huts as we approached Mikendeni village, and then Melika came out to meet me.

'How we have looked forward to this moment!' She took Kerri from me, and pushed the shawl away from her small face. 'She is beautiful, this granddaughter! See, Leah, how soft her hair, how smooth her skin!'

The two women led the way into my hut.

'Look!' they chorused in unison.

In the middle of the small room stood a woven basket crib, soft-blanketed and festooned around the edges with garlands of strung frangipani flowers.

Emotion made it impossible for me to speak. I realised again how honoured I was, since African babies slept beside their mothers, or travelled slung against back or side in knotted cloths.

This crib was special. With Doctor Phillips' parcel of clothes, I was well and truly supplied.

'You are my loved family,' I said when I could speak. 'How happy I am to be here!' And indeed I was.

And yet in the night hours, I still searched backwards, hoping that in my past I'd find the answers . . .

* * * *

. . . Rsul was outside with his falcons, we were told. And, after exchanging our soft slippers for boots, we joined him there. He sat high on a white horse with a bird upon his wrist and, yet again, as I looked at him, I felt the sudden tension in my stomach. Bibicol, at my side, whispered:

'How alike, he and the bird! The same alertness of

145

eye and quickness of movement!' She spoke my thoughts.

'Shh, Bibi, don't let him see that glint of admiration in your eyes, or he will wonder somewhat at our morals!'

'Ah, yes, I am too old to be a boy lover for this handsome man — and I forget we are not women now!' She suppressed a giggle and we strolled towards Rsul.

'Ha! There you are, young men,' he greeted us. 'And by far more suitably attired now. I sport for a short while with my birds, if you care to watch, and then we'll eat together.'

I was glad to hear this for my stomach grumbled loud with hunger, Bibicol's rumbling in chorus. She nudged me, and I could see she was having difficulty in suppressing her laughter.

'Indeed, Rsul Rahman, that sounds very agreeable to me,' I said.

We watched as the beautiful, fast-flying birds made patterns of movement across the white-blue sky; marvelled at the acuteness of their hearing and eyesight as they dropped straight out of the sky at the sound of Rsul's whistle, and caught the bait of meat from his hands without faltering in their flight.

He sat, engrossed with his birds, so much a part of the performance that at any moment I felt he would spread wings and soar skywards to join them. In my imagination, suddenly, I felt as though I, too, would fly, turning and twisting in the sunlight with him, in matched harmony and co-ordination.

'. . . do you not agree, Nadir?' Bibicol spoke. 'Nadir, I asked you a question! Where have you gone?'

'Sorry, Behar.' At least my wits were sharp enough to pick up the use of our new names. 'I was dreaming and did not hear you.'

'It matters not,' she sighed. 'I only asked whether you thought, as I do, that the birds must love the man to come back at his call and not take their chance at freedom.'

'Who would want to be free, with such a master?' I winked at her.

'Not me, Nadir, not me! I would be quite happy tied to his wrist forever!'

'Behar!' I tried to sound stern. 'Your eyes should be turning to the young maidens of the household now. You must soon learn to demonstrate your manhood!'

Her laughter exploded through her attempts to remain straight-faced, and I, too, could not control myself, tears of mirth seaming their way down my cheeks. I put my arm about her shoulder and we walked a little distance away to try and regain our composure before the falcons were once more fettered.

Rsul rode over to us and jumped off his horse.

'Come, we shall eat. You must be hungry now since you have had nothing since last evening.'

'We are, indeed, famished!' Bibicol's cry was heartfelt.

He took us then to his own rooms, which were comfortable but furnished in spartan manner, and there we sat down to a large and satisfying meal. It was whilst we were relaxed and full that a man came fast into the room and threw himself down on the cushions. Dusty and tired-looking, he took a long drink and then said:

'Rsul Rahman, forgive my appearance in this manner at your meal, but I have ridden hard from Kabul with news.'

My heart missed a beat.

'Of what, friend? Have our two villains been caught?'

'No, not that, but Habib Amir, the Khan of Kabul, has lost one of his daughters. She and one of the women servants are missing from his estate, as are two of his best horses.'

147

Rsul's eyes flickered briefly towards me. I froze, not daring to look at Bibicol.

'The Khan has asked for all to be on the lookout for these two girls. He does not know if they have gone of their own wish, or whether they have been taken as hostage, for his daughter's clothes have not gone.'

There was a moment's silence, and I could sense Rsul's look upon me once more. I cleared my throat and, keeping my voice as low as I could manage, I said, 'I hear the Khan of Kabul has many daughters and no sons. Surely the loss of one of these girls is of little matter?'

'I am told it is the youngest girl,' he replied, 'the one most dear to his heart. It is said she even accompanies him to the BuzKashi, and I seem to remember a small girl child always beside him when I have gone to the game.'

Allah save us! I prayed. What if he recognises me now! I pulled my hat down over my forehead.

'If she was so favoured,' put in Bibicol, 'one would have thought her to be better protected. No doubt some childish prank these two little girls are playing!'

'The daughter is some sixteen years or so, I understand, and already there was comment upon the suitability of her appearing unveiled in public with Habib Amir!'

Allah! Oh, Allah! I pulled my eyebrows together in a frown and, with my elbow resting upon my knee, sat with a hand across my mouth as if in thought.

'I am sure they cannot have gone far, clad in women's clothing, without someone having spotted them. They will, no doubt be playing games in the hills around Kabul — or after the local BuzKashi players, perhaps?' Bibicol said, straightfaced, but kept her eyes from meeting mine. I prayed silently that she'd speak no more, afraid her voice would give us away.

'The Khan of Kabul is a fair and just man and will

148

reward anyone generously for news of his child. So keep your eyes and ears alert on your travels, Nadir and Behar. And woe to the man who harms a hair of her head!' Rsul smiled at us, his dark eyes creasing to reinforce the laughter lines that already gave such warmth of character to his face. But again those eyes returned to look at me, speculatively. His hands, I saw were unusually slender and long-fingered for a man, and across my mind flashed a picture of him seated to play the saz, which was a sweet-sounding two-stringed lyre. Fast following that picture, in the busy market-place of my mind, came another — of those same slender hands reaching up to lift me down from my horse.

I blinked hard to bring myself back to the moment, in time to hear Rsul bid farewell to the messenger from Kabul and to suggest that we rest awhile and, when the sun had lost a little of its heat, join him to ride around the estate.

'I think we should leave now,' I said to Bibicol later, in the privacy of our room. 'I'm sure Rsul suspects something!'

She shook her head. 'No, Noeda, you are too apprehensive. If he thought anything amiss, I'm sure he'd say so. He is not, I believe, a man who would avoid the truth.'

I nodded, but I was uneasy still.

In the cool of the early evening we rode, the three of us, contentedly. I felt more at ease with Rsul now, and as the time passed it was as if we had been friends for many years. The Khan of Chesht's estate was vast, not perhaps quite as big as my father's, but of goodly proportion, and we rode well over it onto the plains where the sun slanted across the valley, highlighting the ruins of an ancient village, long abandoned. Brown mud ruins in a dusty brown sea, they lay deserted now, but dry husks though they were, the houses sang loud

149

to me of the men and women who had lived and loved and coupled there, as if their lives and thoughts had imprinted themselves upon the walls like frescoes.

'This village is one reputed to have been wrecked by Ghengis Khan,' Rsul told us, 'though I cannot see the reason for its despoliation, since it was not fortified, nor does it stand in any strong strategic place. Who knows, the people here may have incurred his anger by refusing food — or their womenfolk.'

'Can we stop here for a short time?' I asked.

'Why, of course!' He laughed. 'I, too, could well stretch my legs and relieve myself!'

Take care, I thought, take care!

'Do you need to make water, Behar?' I asked.

'No, I hold mine like a camel, brother, as you well know.'

I could hear the slight snarl in her voice as she answered my teasing.

'But you go ahead, Nadir! I will dismount and take a short walk among the ruins.' Her triumphant look put me in my place.

We strolled slowly among the quiet ruins until we were shielded by them from Rsul, then each in turn kept guard.

As I leaned against the walls in the fading sunlight, they seemed to vibrate, transporting me back, until I felt almost as if I were there that day when Ghengis Khan and his men rode in. I saw the guards with swords upraised to kill, but they were not of the Mongol race — they seemed more as I imagined Alexander's men — with helmets and short leather tunics. My flesh chilled.

When we got back to Rsul I asked, 'Are you sure it was Ghengis Khan and not Alexander from Greece who devastated this place?'

'I have always been told it was Ghengis, Nadir, but legends get changed in the telling, so who knows —

perhaps it was from earlier days.' He looked at me wonderingly. 'Why do you ask this question? Have you a knowledge of history or are you just letting the feelings of this place rule your mind? There is a story, too, that the spirits are loath to leave these ruins. Many a man has returned white-faced from riding at night through here!'

'I have no special interest, Rsul, but the buildings do appear to hold a feeling of a strange sort. And somehow I feel Afghanistan is doomed to devastation, always!' I said nothing of the guards I'd seen, the dark and dangerous shadows.

'I felt nothing. What are you talking about? Old tumbled ruins — what rubbish!' Bibicol broke in quite fiercely because she had no share in this conversation.

I asked suddenly, I knew not why, 'Do you know Ibrahim, the BuzKashi rider who fell this year?'

'But yes, of course I know him! Who in Afghanistan has not at least heard of Ibrahim? I knew him first when we were both boys and he visited his uncle in Bactria, for that is where my family live also. Is it not true that he went back there to rest his broken leg?'

'I believe so, but we do not know him well. We have heard, of course, of his courage and daring in the game, and for this reason would like to know him better.'

I wondered now if I would ever see him again, and fear for the future flooded me. I missed Habib Amir, Ibrahim, and my dear friend Harun intensely in that moment, and sharp tears stung my eyes until I deliberately shut my feelings away by concentrating on Rsul and Bibicol.

'This was not always an arid place,' Rsul told us as we rode on. 'When Alexander came through, it was a green and fertile land with water canals everywhere. Then, after Alexander came Ghengis Khan, who with his Mongols ravaged the area, filled in the canals, massacred the people — then the sand and wind took

151

over. That is why you will see so many ruined cities on your travels.' He seemed so knowledgeable a man that I wished we could ride with him as guide, but I knew that apart from the fact that he could not leave the estate, our own position made such an idea an impossibility.

Late that night, as we relaxed in the privacy of our sleeping quarters, Bibicol whispered, 'I am so tired. It is hard work being a man all the time!'

'Indeed, that is so, but how less boring than tending the cooking pots, Bibi, or sewing and gossiping with my sisters!'

'I feel that I could willingly deal with such boredom to be back safe in the peace and security of your father's estate!'

'I, too, wish we had given more thought to the consequences of our flight. But now, having come this far, I can't see what else we can do but continue. Our hopes of finding my father before he went back to Kabul and pleading with him are now dashed since he is obviously there already. I cannot explain to him why I felt I had to leave, and I am truly terrified of his wrath and displeasure!'

'Surely he would forgive, even if he dealt firmly with you to begin with?'

'I don't know, I would hope so, but I'm sure that he would insist on this marriage to Shamlu Gadir, and of course on my going into purdah. And I hate to think what reprisals you, dear friend, would have to bear. No, Bibi, I cannot tolerate the thought. We'll have to go on now and hope that the search will not catch up with us. Perhaps, after a little time, his wrath will mellow and we can dare to return and plead for forgiveness.'

I could not sleep that night, my mind circling with possibilities and probabilities, and I wept hot tears of desperation through the long dark hours.

With new clothes, food and money given to us at Rsul's insistence, we made ready to leave Khan Abdul Pashtoon's estate next day.

'Who knows, I may yet see you in Herat,' Rsul said, 'for I travel there quite often — and, too, you might be glad of a resting place here before you undertake the long journey back to Koshuk. For in some strange way, I feel we are at the beginning of a long friendship, and I hope this feeling to be the truth!'

I felt it was not a beginning, somehow, but more a continuation, though I could not understand why.

Rsul put his arms around our shoulders as we walked across the courtyard to where the horses stood, blowing and champing on their mouthpieces. His hand on my arm felt warm, and I was aware of the slight weight of it, all my senses concentrated on that small area of my upper arm. Then we reached the horses and Rsul stood back. For a moment I was unable to move, the feelings in my limbs returning slowly, as though the circulation had been for a short time cut off.

Bibicol nudged me. 'Come on, Nadir! You are half asleep this morning, we will not make much progress if you continue in this manner!'

'Too much food last night, I fear, but the morning air will soon sweep away the sleep!'

I did not want to leave, and my legs weighed heavily their reluctance as I mounted. Rsul stood watching us, his arms folded across his chest, and for a moment I saw bewilderment once more cloud his eyes as he looked at me. Then he came across to stand beside my horse, and held his hand up to mine.

'Nadir, young friend, go with care. I feel concern for your safety and I am reluctant to let you continue your journey without an escort. Will you let one of my men ride with you?'

'That is kind, Rsul, but we travel alone. It is part of

the test we have been set, and by Allah, we have come this far with no harm to life or limb!'

He didn't look convinced, and though I saw the comfort of having an armed guard with us, I could also see the complications.

'Don't worry!' Bibicol spoke bravely, 'I will keep watch over Nadir, and Nadir will be my bodyguard — this way we'll both be safe!'

'Go with Allah then!' he said, and his eyes held the question once again.

NINE

'Are you managing?' Paul spoke across the basket.
Kerri gripped mindlessly at one of his long fingers as
he touched her hand.

'Yes.' I pushed any difficulties to the back of my
mind. 'We're fine! I've got my ayah there to help.'

'Good!' He motioned me to the examination couch.
'We'll soon have you cleared up here.'

His face, sharp in profile against the window, was
timeless, as though he had walked out of some ancient
tapestry.

'Do you ride?' I asked, into the silence.

'I used to! Don't get time now, I'm afraid. Why?'

'It's just that I could picture you on horseback,
somehow.'

'Like a cowboy?' he laughed.

'No — more from Persia or Afghanistan — with a
falcon on your wrist!'

'As long as you don't visualise me as a knight in
white armour.' His eyes were studying my face. 'I don't
think I'd be much good at this job clanking around in
chain mail!'

He was talking down to me as if to a child. I bit my
lip and blinked, furious to feel the start of tears.

'There we are!' Paul pulled off his surgical gloves.
'You can get up now. It might feel a bit uncomfortable
for a while, but that'll soon go.'

I swung my feet to the floor and pulled on my clothes.

As he reached the door he stopped. 'It's lunchtime!
I think we should go out and have a meal somewhere,
don't you?'

I thought quickly about the small amount of money in my purse.

'I can't, I'm afraid,' I said, embarrassed.

'Come on — my treat for not making a fuss about your stitches!'

His hand under my elbow guided me through to the outer office. Kerri slept, her mouth making involuntary sucking movements.

Paul took up the handles of her basket. 'It'll be nice to have company. I usually grab a quick snack in the canteen.'

He stopped the car outside the Manor Hotel.

'Oh, no!' I thought. 'I can't go in there.' I looked down at my faded dress.

'You look fine!' He read my dismay.

I'd forgotten what such food tasted like, and ate like a glutton; forgotten, too, what it was like to be waited on. The wine made my cheeks burn, my tongue loose.

Paul looked at me steadily with his dark and disturbing eyes, and once again the strange jolt of recognition travelled through me. My breathing shallowed; then the moment passed and I was sitting, shaky and trembling, as he talked, the conversation fitful, changing from one subject to another, inconsequentially.

Kerri, oblivious to us, slept on.

'I'm half-drunk with food and wine!' I said as we left the hotel.

'I'll run you home.'

I hadn't told him that I lived in Mikendeni village. 'You'll be late back to the hospital. I'll be fine, honestly!'

He smiled. 'That's true, I suppose.'

Kerri woke with a hungry wail. My milk began to flow in response to her cry, making my breasts tingle.

'Could I feed her before I go?' I asked.

'Of course!' Paul opened the car door for me and put Kerri's basket on the back seat.

I cradled her dark head against the blue-veined whiteness of my breast and she drank with loud gulping sounds, interspersed with small sighs of contentment.

'Beautiful!' Paul's voice was quiet. 'I've never seen anything so beautiful!' His eyes were incandescent and, briefly, a small frown of puzzlement creased his forehead.

I, too, was content, at one with Kerri and Paul, enclosed within the womb of his car. As he put his hand over Kerri's curls, one finger accidentally touched my breast. The hot winds of desire blew through me. They came from deep within my body, crescendoed and left me shaking. I shut my eyes and concentrated on Kerri's pulling mouth.

When I got out of the car, Paul leaned through the window. 'Is there anything I can do, Nina?' he asked.

Oh yes! Yes! So much you can do, Rsul!

'No, I don't think so,' I replied. Just take me, right now; throw me onto the ground, here, and make love to me! The thoughts brought blood suffusing to my cheeks.

'If there is, let me know. Promise?' he said, starting the car.

I nodded, my voice lost, my breath short and fast.

Bouncing back to Mikendeni in the noisy bus, through the euphoria of the afternoon, guilt overcame me as I realised that since Kerri's birth I had spared little thought for Rashidi. Now a surge of longing filled me, and I found that I was weeping silently, the large drops plopping onto Kerri's sleeping face.

He may never see her! I thought bleakly. Pain, like a knife-thrust between my ribs, made me gasp . . . *nor may I ever see Kabul again, or hear Habib Amir's voice raised in merriment . . .*

I opened my eyes. The palm groves stood calm in the still air, and beside the road goats browsed, watched over by naked children who waved as the bus

157

threw up its enveloping dust. I blinked at the brightness, trying to shake off the headache which had tightened its band around my forehead.

I was puzzled that it should be now that Rashidi intruded into my consciousness. I had deliberately shut my mind to him, immersing myself first in my life at Mikendeni, and then in the joy that was Kerri. Now, inexplicably, I was dead-weighted with fear for him.

And what is the link-up I asked silently, between Rashidi and Ibrahim? Why do I keep hearing, seeing, dreaming about the people in Afghanistan? I wondered if they were part of my past, ancestral echoes from somewhere deep in my psyche. Wondered, too, if there was such a thing as reincarnation and, if so, whether groups of people could reappear together in a future life. If that was possible, it would perhaps account for the sense of recognition which I felt. Was I Noeda, I wondered, and, if so, why was I so immersed *now* in that long-gone life?

The motion of the bus was soporific, the day hot and hazed as I puzzled. Perhaps they were only dreams, after all . . .

*   *   *   *

. . . Bibicol and I rode in silence for a while and, when I turned to look at her, I could see tears running silently down her soft cheeks.

'Oh, Bibi, why do you cry? It is not far to Herat and thence to your tribesfolk. I am full of confidence now, for if we managed to deceive so hawk-eyed a man as Rsul, we should have no fear of detection from others!'

'That is why I weep, Noeda! For how long do we have to keep up the deception? Rsul was not entirely sure — that much was obvious, and you, Noeda, how long could you have kept up that manly camaraderie? I saw the light beginning to glow in your dark eyes — I think it would not have taken much to start a blazing

158

fire there, had you been able to admit your maidenhood!'

I had to agree that Rsul was more than a little attractive to me, but then he was an extraordinarily good-looking man and, like as not, Bibicol's own pulses had been set racing.

'A handsome man, I agree! But Bibi, I am searching for Ibrahim, remember?'

'Ah, Ibrahim, bold dashing Ibrahim! How could I have forgotten?' She sniffed, and wiped away the tears with the back of her hand. 'But never in a thousand years would Khan Habib Amir allow you to wed Ibrahim, for his family has not the same standing as yours, or that of Shamlu Gadir.'

'Never, never will I be tied to Gadir!' I shouted, for I knew that would be a living death to me. 'No, Bibi, I would rather die, or ride, a virgin always, than submit to that obese pig!'

Bibicol looked at me, large eyes alight. 'I see you now, dear friend, wrinkled and crabbed with age, forever astride a horse, riding the mountains and through the Dash-i-Margo, that dread Desert of Death!'

'I would do that in preference to losing my maidenhood to him. The very thought of that large body heavy upon mine makes my stomach turn!'

'But Ibrahim is another matter?' she teased. 'Or even Rsul, perhaps?'

'Ibrahim's body is firm and young, and Rsul sends my senses reeling! But let's stop talking of them, or I'll be overcome with desire, and swoon, falling from my saddle. Then you will be left to travel alone!'

We laughed and spurred our horses into a gallop for the very exhilaration of the wind in our faces.

Seven days it took to get to Herat, and we were weary to the bone when at last we saw its walls, pink-tinged with the setting sunlight. We camped outside that night, deciding that we were too tired to face the challenge of keeping up our disguise. Next morning, early, we rode into the busy town, which served as a trade centre for merchants from as far afield as China, India, Arabia and Africa. We went slowly, letting the variety of noise and scene wash over us: camels grumbled their heavily loaded way; in small, dim little stalls the silk merchants wound their skeins, the fine thread shining like silver even in the darkened shelters; traders of all nationalities cried loud the virtues of their wares, their voices raucous, while heavily veiled women pinched at tomatoes, red peppers and oranges, to feel the quality. All around, voices haggled and bargained over purchases.

A fine yellow dust coated people, produce and buildings alike, and spread a film over the bright carpets laid out on the ground for inspection.

We stayed only long enough to buy food, and then rode on, anxious to put as much distance as we could between ourselves and any pursuit.

From Herat we decided to ride to Meshed, for Bibicol thought that we were more likely to link up with her kinsfolk there than further north. The going was rough and the track dangerous. The second day out from Herat my horse stepped into a deep rut and stumbled. I slid head first down its neck, landing hard and painfully on the rocky track. I put out my right arm to push myself up, and the sharp pain in my wrist caused me to cry out.

Bibicol dismounted and came quickly to me.

'Oh, Noeda! What have you done — where does it pain you?' She lifted my arm, and I bit hard upon my lip to stop myself from calling out.

'Can you move the fingers?' I tried, and nodded.

'I think it is not broken, by the grace of Allah, but I will strap it anyway, just in case.' She started over towards her horse.

160

'How is my animal?' I asked, concerned more now, that it be sound.

'It seems unhurt, Noeda, certainly all the legs are whole.'

'Thank goodness for that, at least!'

She tore a strip of material from one of our rugs, and cast around for a straight piece of wood, until she found a dry branch by the track. She split this lengthwise and placed the flat side against my arm, strapping it firmly in place so that my hand could not be bent at the wrist. The pain of this action made my eyes stream, and I cursed myself and the horse for our clumsiness.

'How can I ride with my arm thus?' I asked irritably.

'Come! Be thankful it isn't your leg or your neck. Put your sound arm through the sleeve of your jacket, and I will button the garment up with the bad arm inside. That way it will be protected and kept still. You have but twisted it, I'm sure, and with a little care it will mend fast!'

Each pace of the horse jarred through my body straight to my wrist, which throbbed and burned as though I held my hand in the embers of a cooking fire. I moaned to myself, full of self-pity, until Bibicol, hearing, turned her horse and faced me.

'You sound like a woman in labour! Is the pain so unbearable?'

'Yes, it hurts greatly, and I would give much to be safely at home, at rest upon the cushions of my bedchamber, rather than jolting sharply on this uncomfortable beast!'

'Shall we stop as soon as possible, then? It might be wiser in the long run, since rest may make you stronger for the ride ahead.'

'Oh, Bibi, I do not at this moment care whether we are caught or not!' I was near tears with pain and an emptiness of heart.

'Just keep going slowly. I will ride ahead and find a

161

good place to make camp.' She rode fast down the track.

As I watched her ride away from me a flow of love for my stalwart companion flooded through me, and I realised how much I abused her good-heartedness. I set my jaw firm and made a silent vow to try not to put too much of a burden upon her young back.

The horse idled along, and I allowed him to pick his own way through the ruts and boulders of the track, knowing that in this manner he would take the smoothest route. Bibicol was fast disappearing, her horse's hooves sending up a spume of dust to mark her passage. The sun warmed me and the gentle motion of the horse lulled me into a half-sleep . . .

'Noeda! I've found a good place. Come, we'll make our way there and rest. Your wrist may be better tomorrow, if not — then we'll rest yet another day. We have provisions enough, and the place I have selected is near a fresh spring of water.'

I followed her, languid in the saddle.

The camp site was indeed ideal. A way off the main track and sheltered from it by rocks, it was a grassy enclosure, shaded by olive trees, and gay with the sound of water from a small but lively spring. I slipped gratefully from the horse and, cupping my good hand under the spring, splashed the cold water over my hot face.

'Do you have waking dreams, Bibi?' I asked as we lay, cooled and quiet, later that day. She turned onto her stomach, a grass stalk between her teeth.

'I don't understand you. What do you mean, "waking dreams"?'

'At times, when I am wide awake, it is as though my mind closes to the things around me, and I find myself looking at a different place, with people I do

162

not know — in the same manner as dreams come unbidden when we sleep.'

'The fall from your horse has jarred your mind! Rest, Noeda, and you will return to normality!'

'No, Bibi, I am serious now. It is not just today that this has happened to me, but recently these "dreams" come often, and I am much puzzled by them.'

'Poor girl! I always knew you were a misfit in your father's household. No wonder your sisters were uneasy in your presence!'

I sighed, sad that she could not comprehend, and let myself drift into half-sleep once more, wondering at all that had taken place in the short time since the BuzKashi. So short a time, and yet it seemed many moons had risen, full and pregnant in the night sky, and fallen again, thin shadows of that fecundity, each month.

And where was Ibrahim? Where Habib Amir? We rode in the wrong direction for encounter with either of them. And if Ibrahim had travelled northwards to Bactria, I could see no way in which we could cross back over the Paropamisus mountains and reach that far place, for the cold weather was fast overtaking the heat of mid-year, and soon the passes would be clothed in snow. I concentrated on Ibrahim, trying to bring him into my mind, but his face eluded my memory. I could not understand why this should be, for I knew him well.

The sunlight flickered and filtered through the leaves of the olive trees, making patterns of light and shade dance upon the rumps of our horses as they stood grazing. My wrist stopped aching and I turned to tell Bibicol so, but found her asleep, a gentle snore rippling her upper lip.

I lay back and tried once more to catch Ibrahim behind my closed eyelids, and of a sudden he was there. I imagined him seated beside me and, the warmth and comfort of that place caressing me, I felt a flood of such

163

longing come over me that I cried out with the strength
of it.

TEN

Melika's face, when I arrived at Mikendeni, was bleak.

'I've had a letter from Jamira,' she explained. 'She speaks of Rashidi, but it is not good news. She's heard that he is definitely in the forests of the Abadare mountains, and that he only just missed capture by the Askaris the other day.'

'Where did she hear that?' My pulse quickened. It made no difference really where she'd heard it. It would be no better for him if he tried to hide in Nairobi, I thought. If the Askari stop him and look at his kipande, his fingerprints on that will give his identity, no matter how well he changes his appearance. I knew that if Rashidi was really involved with the gangs now, his only chance would be to stay hidden in the forests, or to go to the Kikuyu reserve and hope some of the squatters around Nyeri would hide him on their shambas there.

My chest tightened with pity as I imagined him in the forest, wet and frightened, sitting through the cold nights unable to move for fear of treading on snakes or bumping into buffalo; unable to come home, to be warmed round the fires or fed and cared for by Melika.

Oh, Rashidi! Why? Why? I shivered, sharing his fear in my imagination.

Melika put her hand on my arm. 'Nina, what are we to do? I am so afraid for Rashidi!'

I put Kerri's basket down on the ground and held her to me.

'What could you do if you went to Jamira, Melika? How would that help Rashidi? There is little you can do but stay here and pray, going from here to look for him won't save him from the bullets!'

'No, I understand that, but I think I should go to Uganda, to Jamira. That way at least he'll have somewhere to go if he can escape from the forests.'

'God grant that he has the sense to do that,' I said. 'The King's African Rifles and the Kenya Regiment, too, have bombs and mortars and modern guns, to fight against pangas and knives. There's talk that there will be soldiers coming here from England, too. What hope have the Mau Mau to succeed against such odds?'

Leah spoke then, her eyes far away. 'They can't hope to win the battle against such forces. But in the end justice must be done!'

I sighed, feeling my unwilling involvement in the conflict between black and white, seeing injustices on both sides that could never be resolved.

On the grapevine we'd heard that the oaths, the secret oaths of the Mau Mau, were changing now, becoming more widespread, more horrific. Special group-oaths were being enforced upon the young men, virtually tying them to a long commitment, like conscription to the army. Rashidi had explained the forest oaths to me, many months earlier, the ones which guaranteed protection to secret hideaways; caches of arms; meeting places. But these oaths had been mild in comparison with those that were now being administered. He'd told me about the arch through which initiates had to crawl, made of crudely cured animal skin with sheep's eyeballs transfixed to it by seven Kieapple thorns; the banana trough of blood from which they had to drink whilst swearing the seven oaths of allegiance. It appeared that now the rituals were even more grotesque, full of sacrifices too bloody and horrific to be retailed.

My flesh crawled at the thoughts, and I turned to

Melika in the brightness of Mombasa, far from the horrors of Mau Mau.

'Shall I come with you to Uganda?' I asked her.

'No, stay here with Leah for now. Kerri is so small, and she needs you — and your milk.' She pointed at the milk-stains on my bodice.

And I, traitor that I was, felt a *frisson* of desire at the thought of Paul, whose tapering fingers had accidentally caressed me there.

A few days later Melika waited in the early morning for the bus, her belongings tied in a huge bundle by her side. Leah and I stood together, a little apart from her, as if already she had left us.

'Please get Jamira to write to me with news of your arrival,' I pleaded. 'We'll be anxious to know that you're safely there.'

'And you, Nina, will you write letters? I'll miss you and Kerri so very much!'

I nodded and we clung together with our tears mixing.

Then the bus came fast along the road and I kissed her wet cheek and helped her on board. Leah and I stood watching the dust cloud disappearing towards Mombasa.

'Tcck!' Leah clicked her sadness. 'Will we see our sister again? These days are so terrible, and I'm afraid!'

'Oh, damn it!' I looked down the road as if my eyes could will the bus backwards. 'I forgot to tell Melika not to let Rashidi know about Kerri, if she sees him!'

'Why this?' Leah's voice rose questioningly.

'Because I think he's got enough worry upon his shoulders. Already his life has been made complicated and dangerous by me.'

'This is true — would he have gone away otherwise?' She sat down and pulled me onto the grass beside her. 'But you cannot take the blame for what happened

167

between you. Your paths were linked,' she looked at me quickly, 'in times past. The ancestors decreed it so.'

'I don't understand.' She surely couldn't know about those others!

'It is difficult for me to explain it to you, Nina, for in our language it is not easy to unfold the layers that lie behind our minds, our souls.'

I sat bolt upright, bells ringing in my head. 'What . . . what's that you say?' Perhaps Noeda wasn't just my imagination or the wild contortions of my dreaming mind!

Leah smiled. 'It is as I thought,' she said. 'The ancestors have placed their mark upon you! We both have the sign of the spirits on us, and we have the sight!'

I smiled and shook my head wonderingly.

'I am serious, Nina, you have the gift,' Leah rebuked me. 'It is merely that you don't know how to use it.'

I looked at her sideways. 'If that's true, Leah, then why didn't it stop me from causing Melika and Rashidi such pain?'

'The reasons will be told.' She nodded her head to emphasise her words. 'You'll see, Nina!'

And you, Leah — who are you? I queried inwardly. All the while I'd been in Mikendeni her presence had enveloped me, but I couldn't see why this was so. I had almost avoided her, rather than question the effect she had upon me — a familiarity that was almost awesome. And yet she herself was anything but awe-inspiring. She was small and plump, younger than Melika by some five years, unremarkable. But now her eyes had taken on a luminosity that made them huge in her face. A cold shiver made my flesh goose-pimple — there was definitely something . . . Then Kerri woke with a wail and I went to her, and the tension in the atmosphere subsided.

The weekly post brought a letter from Jamira with news of Melika's arrival, but nothing about Rashidi. It also brought a letter from Mother, on a rising crescendo of hysteria.

'When will you come back, Nina?' she implored. 'The situation here is terrible! Your father is still away with the army, and I'm alone and very frightened!'

I sat in the shade of the casuarina at the beach edge and looked out to the horizon, Mother's letter sliding off my lap. The blue sea rolled away before me, exposing razor-sharp coral and seaweed, and the sky arched, clear and cloudless. I wondered at the desperation that had driven her to write so revealing a letter. The months since I'd left Nairobi stretched into years in my mind, and I had to concentrate for a moment to bring her face into clarity. My memory was more for emotions than faces, and emotions seemed almost to be all that was left of the past, evoked now by her letter, demanding to be remembered. The hurt, the lovelessness, the loneliness. Not just this recent past, I thought, but that other one which somehow has become more real to me.

Now I was torn again between Mother's need for me and Kerri's. Kerri, two months old. I sighed. There was really only one answer, since there was no way I could take the baby to Nairobi.

I picked up the letter again, flipping through the paragraphs, letting her pain wash over the top of my head — afraid to open my heart for fear of pain's echo there. Then, on the last page, a paragraph stood out as if written in red:

'Late the other evening, Rashidi came. At the knock on the door my heart came into my mouth, as you can imagine, for fear of it being Mau Mau, but he called through the door and I let him in. It's as well your father wasn't here — you know how he feels about Rashidi! He looked thin and wild, somehow, and didn't stay long. He wanted to know where Melika and Jamira were so I gave him their address. He asked after you, too, believing for some reason that you were in England at university! Then, as suddenly as he came, he went again. Very strange!'

Rashidi! His behaviour as inexplicable as Ibrahim's in my dreaming. So at least he was alive — free! Then why this sudden contraction of my heart, the sharp pain, tissue-tearing in my chest, so intense that I couldn't breathe? He might be free, but I had lost him. Oh, Rashidi!

And Ibrahim, too, was lost to me . . .

I wrote a long letter to Mother, giving her what comfort I could, and promised to visit her within the next few months.

By then, maybe, I can put Kerri onto the bottle and leave her here with Leah, I thought, travelling on the bus into Mombasa, having decided to post my letter there. I wanted to see Paul, too, needed his common sense and advice.

Catching sight of myself in the glass door of the hospital, I nearly turned away. I looked bedraggled, and my dress was creased and old. My hair was caught up in an elastic band at the back of my head, and Kerri was slung, native-fashion, in a kanga tied across my chest.

The receptionist looked at me from her desk, her eyebrows raised in question. 'Yes?'

'Could I see Doctor Phillips, please? Doctor Paul Phillips.'

She studied me for a moment. 'I'm sorry, I'm afraid you can't. He went from here last week — gone to Nairobi on transfer, I believe.'

I went back out through the door, feeling alone, betrayed. The noon sunlight was as dark as if it were midnight.

*

At the time of the next full moon, Leah's daughter, Mirriamu, gave birth to a boy. No hospital for her, no cradle made. The midwife came and delivered the child, and Mirriamu waited then for a name to be chosen by her husband and the elders.

Leah took the extra duties and after the first day looked exhausted. She yawned and stretched her arms, sitting near the cooking fire.

'It is bad to be a woman,' she said. 'There is no time when one of us is away. Still the shamba has to be hoed, the plants sown or watered. Then there's wood and water to be collected.'

I looked at the men sitting, shaded by the pandanus trees.

'The men should help more, Leah. They only fish for a short while each day when the tides are right, the rest of the time they sit and gossip or spend the money they earn from fishing in beer-houses.'

'It has always been so. We have no time, and the maize dies in the heat of the sun. Sometimes a man will help in the sowing or harvesting, but this is rare. It is not their place.'

'Surely they could fetch water or collect some firewood, especially now that there's a curfew because of Mau Mau.'

I had seen how the women rushed to do all the work in time to get back to the compounds.

Leah 'tcck'd.' 'Never! The custom has come from way past, and will not change!'

'Why don't you get together, speak to the elders, the District Commissioner? This is no way for a woman to live, rearing the children, working in the shambas, never stopping, and getting nothing for themselves out of it.'

'The men want us to be ready for their pleasure at night, too, Nina! For sure, it's better to be a man!'

It was so, too, in Afghanistan, amongst the nomads anyway.

171

Not in the cities, though — there the women were shrouded, protected by the chadri. The work was done by servants, eunochs and headmen. Better perhaps to be free, even though the work was unfairly loaded!

Next morning I went with the women to the fields, slinging Kerri into a carrying cloth on my back, so that her head bobbed against my shoulders as I walked.

'There's no need for you to go!' Leah protested. 'You are not born to this!'

'It doesn't matter, Leah. I'm ashamed that I've been so wrapped up in myself and Kerri that I didn't think to offer help before now!'

The heat beat down, hard and ruthless, making the perspiration run down my face and between my breasts. Kerri stirred, restless on my back, so I wrapped her in the cloth and put her in the shade.

Leah had shown me how to wield the hoe — the jembe — beating it down into the hard earth between the newly sprouted maize. One step forward and a downward thrust with the hoe; step, hoe, step, remorselessly in the hot, hot sun.

Across the large cleared shamba the women worked, their soft voices filling the day, endlessly cheerful.

How can they do it, I wondered, day after day, year after year? My back ached and my mouth was gritty with dust kicked up at each blow of the jembe.

Leah began to sing, the other women providing a rhythmic chorus:

>'Oh great clouds,
>Clouds that carry the water,'
>   'Hey — aaah! Hey — aaah!'
>'Climb, climb over the hilltops,
>Fly, fly over the waters,'
>   'Hey — aaah! Hey — aaah!'
>'But do not fly to Kilimanjaro,
>Kilimanjaro is the thief of our water,'

172

'Hey — aaah! Hey — aaah!'
'Fall, water — on the coastlands,
Here on the dry earth by the sea,'
    'Hey — aaah! Hey — aaah!'
'That the maize grow tall and healthy,
That the cobs grow fat and sweet!'
    'Hey — aaah! Hey — aaah!'

So the singing continued, Leah improvising the words as she went, the chorus giving a time — a beat — to the lift and fall of the hoes.

I could hardly breathe, and my feet were blistering in my sandals. It was almost impossible to keep up with the others.

Leah stopped in mid-song and looked at me. 'Are you all right? Don't overtax your strength the first day out! Remember, we are used to this work. Even when small, we work with our mothers in the fields. The boys are always fortunate, watching over the herds and playing!' She shook her head. 'But when the rains fail, it's us women who get the blame!'

The shade felt like heaven as I slowly lowered my aching body down beside Kerri. Between my shoulder-blades pain stabbed, as my muscles rebelled. I lay on the spiky brown grass, let the tension drain out of my body, and fell instantly asleep . . .

* * * *

. . . The loom click-clacked in the background as the Qashgai women worked unendingly through the hot daylight hours.

The black goat-hair tents of the Qashgai stood harsh against the light sandy soil, and the rhythmic click-clack, click-clack of a carpet loom made a background of sound against which the moving fresco of goats, gaily dressed girls, turbaned men, and half-naked infants, seemed to dance in the opaque heat waves.

Bibicol's voice rang clear and young, but the words

173

were strange to me, for we were now near Meshed and the travelling people of that region spoke a dialect all their own, similar to ours in some words and phrases, but differing enough to make it hard for me to follow.

The pageant of movement stopped, halted by her call. All faces turned in our direction, eye-whites bright against the brown faces; the children with their grubby fingers pushed into their mouths for reassurance.

Without speaking we dismounted and walked the few separating yards, so that it could be seen we came in friendship and unarmed. I put my good hand over my heart in greeting.

'Salaam,' I said, and Bibicol, following my example, went forward and in their tongue spoke to the elderly men who sat on their haunches looking at us with suspicious curiosity. There was a deal of arm waving and fast talking then, of which I could understand only a word here and there, but it seemed the conversation was not proceeding in too happy a manner. I could tell from Bibicol's rising tone that she was becoming exasperated, and I touched her gently on the arm.

'What is passing between you?'

'Because I am not as myself, they are treating my questions warily, and so far I have been unable to find the whereabouts of my family.'

'Leave it for now. Let's just ask for time to rest ourselves and our horses, and perhaps for a little water, if they have any to spare. We will approach the subject of your tribe again when their suspicions have calmed.'

'I had not thought how our disguise could work against us here. If we had but stopped to consider, we would have foreseen this difficulty!'

'Yes, but Bibi, remember that the danger of pursuit is not gone — and how could we have travelled with women's clothes in our bedrolls? That would have raised many a question if we had been searched. The chances are that Rsul's men went through our scant

174

belongings anyway, when we were taken from the teahouse.'

She agreed, and put forward our request for hospitality. Immediately the hostility of our reception vanished to be replaced by the normal friendliness that was typical of the nomads of the Persian-Afghanistan border, these laughing, gentle people who spent their lives in constant movement, up to the high pastures in the summer months, and down to the lowlands when winter covered the rich grazing of the foothills with a thick coat of snow. They travelled thus, whole households together for company and protection, goat-hair tents folded and tied to the overloaded backs of patient donkeys and mules or, if the tribe were rich, on camels. Along the route they would stop and, depending on the quality of the pasture, stay for a day, a week or a month, setting up the tents so quickly that it seemed they had always been there. And at every stop the weaving loom took pride of place, the clacking of the wooden bobbins providing a constant reminder of their industry as the women threaded the rich colours through and back, knotting and twisting the threads into vibrant life, with fifty knots to each square inch of carpet.

As we sat, shaded by a canopy made of woven camel hair, cups of hot tea sweetened with honey were brought from the cooking area. We squatted on our haunches with the menfolk in a silence broken only by the loud sipping of liquid from the small teabowls, and we eyed each other over the brims.

I looked to Bibicol for a lead, since I was not familiar with the customs and manners of the Qashgai, and it was not until all the bowls had been set upon the ground that she spoke.

'For that excellent tea, we thank you. Your camp is good and your cooking embers well cared for.'

I gathered this to be the traditional way.

'You are welcome to our humble camp, and to what poor provisions we have,' came the answer.

These formalities done with, Bibicol talked quietly and without undue emphasis on our search for her family. I hoped, indeed, she would leave the subject, since we needed to establish our credibility with these people before exploring further.

'They ask how you came to be wounded,' she turned to say, 'and if there is anything they can do to ease your wrist.'

'I thank them, Behar, but the pain is lessening, and I'm sure all will be well by tomorrow.'

The old men nodded their heads. I wondered if they understood what we said, and made note to be careful.

'I have told them that we come with messages for Bibicol's family, and that we have travelled far to get here.'

'Tread carefully, the news from whence we came could just conceivably have travelled this far. We have, after all, dallied on the way at Chesht, and this makes our position more dangerous.'

'I think not, though I am not pressing it. We are but distantly related to this girl and her tribe, and being young men of breeding, are in no hurry to follow in the dust-wake of the sheep and goats.'

'True, Behar, my brother. You have taken well my lead regarding care, I see. Do you think we will be given the usual hospitality for which the Qashgai are famed?'

The elders looked at each other and smiled in pride, confirming my thought that they understood more than they had admitted.

'Our accommodation, poor though it be, sirs, is yours to share with us, and you are welcome to stay for as long as it pleases you, for we do not often have strangers to bring us news from far Afghan.'

We salaamed our gratitude and, the hour being right,

we took off our boots and joined in the chanting of the Quran, bowing low to the west, towards the heart of Islam, the birthplace of Mohammed. Strange how, in that desolate place, with no muezzin to call out the time for prayer five times a day, all work stopped simultaneously as those of the Muslim faith kneeled low to touch the ground with their foreheads, and affirm their loyalty to Allah and to his son, Mohammed.

Closeted as we had been in Kabul, Bibicol and I knew little of the male rituals, and had only heard the readings from the Quran at Ramadan or other religious festivals. We watched the men of the tribe, and followed closely their actions. We would have to learn quickly, for no man of high breeding would be so unversed in the rituals of Islam. All boys were tutored long and intensively from early childhood, and the chanting of the Quran was second nature to them. Bibicol and I didn't know the words or the verses, and could only make inarticulate sounds, to appear to be reciting freely.

The evening slid into the silence of dusk, and we sat talking whilst the star of evening, the 'heart star' as we called it, sent showers of shimmering sparks towards us from the safety of the sickle-moon's embracing arms. We told a slightly altered version of our adventures from Kabul, and had the elders clicking their tongues in sympathy at our losses in the river, at our mistaken identity as murderers in Chesht, and at my fall from the horse but a day or so ago.

Then we slept rolled in our blankets, under the eyes of the stars once more, and to the accompaniment of the high-pitched singing of the sand as it was blown into soft shapes by the ever-present wind.

We stayed with this tribe for several weeks, while my wrist mended, and gradually we built up their trust in us. Walking one evening, we heard in the quiet of the lavender dusk, the most beautiful rhythmic singing.

177

We turned and moved quickly in the direction of the sound, drawn onwards by the sheer enchantment of it.

As we rounded a rocky hillock we saw them, silhouetted against the pale mauve sky that bore witness to the sun's departure; four men of the tribe who sat cross-legged on a prayer mat, their beads moving in time to the chant, through their long brown fingers. Each turbaned head dipped in its turn towards the centre of the circle, so that there was a continuous snake-like flow of movement, round and round. With words that came straight from the Quran, each man's voice came and went separately, but in such harmonic accord that there was no break, and the music made magic which hung in the air and hypnotised us into motionless wonder.

'In the name of Allah, the Merciful, The
    Compassionate,
Praise belongs to Allah, the Lord of all Being,
The all-merciful, the all-compassionate,
The Master of the Day of Doom.
Thee only do we serve; to thee alone we pray for
    succour,
Guide us in the straight path,
The path of those whom Thou hast blessed,
Not of those against whom Thou art wrathful,
Not of those who are astray.'

I looked at Bibicol as the outline of the four singers grew blurred in the fading light, and saw that tears ran unchecked down her face, as they did down mine.

We crept silently away, leaving the singers to their exhaltation, and did not speak for we could not, so deeply were we moved.

The women of the Qashgai were not forced to wear the chadri, they dressed in brightly dyed cloths, strong serviceable skirts made gay with many petticoats, so

178

that when they walked their skirts swung in perpetually dancing movement. Their hair was braided with bright threads and cowrie shells, and their big dark eyes were emphasised with rims of black kohl. They were so full of laughter and song that to be with them was a joy.

One girl in particular took it upon herself to be our constant companion. Fatimettou was thirteen years old, and a lithe, lively girl, small-boned and as quick as the cicadas whom she rivalled in the amount of noise she made. I had never heard anyone sing as often as she did, not even Bibicol. Her voice was sometimes soft and honeyed in ancient love song or lullaby, other times loud and strident as she sang the songs of the desert wanderers. Bibicol and I warmed to her open-hearted-ness and wandered far with her as guide. She showed us many things, including the dexterity of the weavers' art of selecting the colour for each knot of the carpets they wove. She took us far out into the hills to seek dyes for the threads and to find the bush from which the leaves were plucked and dried to make henna. This was the small insignificant plant, she told us, that Mohammed was supposed to have named 'the chief of plants' and with whose dye he coloured his beard.

As I listened to her, I had the sense of having heard these things already, but couldn't remember where. I spoke to Bibicol about it later and she answered:

'Sometimes the knowledge of herbs and plants comes to one from many, many years past. Instinctively, a person can have the understanding of what is good, and for which sickness a certain plant must be used. It is in the blood, inherited somehow in the same way that the similarity of a physical feature is passed from generation to generation.'

'A sort of echo from past memory of the tribe, perhaps?'

'Perhaps! Who knows these things? But look only at the birds — who tells them to fly all at once to the north or to the south? And how can they find their way back unerringly, year after year? They, too, must pass the map within themselves from parent bird to fledgling.'

It took but a few days for me to gain an understanding of most of the talk that flowed and bubbled around us, and I, too, could make myself understood without much difficulty. Once it was accepted that we came with no intent to harm, the tribe took us into their hearts and it was as though we had always been with them.

I could see now why Bibicol was the dear, sweet soul who had been my closest companion since we were both but eight years of age. I sat one day upon a rock watching her and Fatimettou chasing each other through the boulders. My beloved Bibicol, of all people the closest to me — closer, I realised with a start, than even Habib Amir, and certainly more so than my mother or sisters. I chewed upon a stalk of grass, pensive, and realised with sadness that I did not even know how she had come to be working for my father in Kabul. I had never thought to question her presence there, so used was I to it.

How had she come to be in service to my family? Had she been sold as a slave in the markets, or taken in payment for some favour granted by Habib Amir? I watched the two girls, one in bright skirts and decoration, the other incongruously clad in man's breeches, but alike in their joy for living, their eyes bright with laughter and their voices ringing out with enjoyment at their game.

Bibi, you should be here, with your lovely warm people. Not cooped up in the confines of a kitchen in Kabul, at the call of the cooks, and as the butt of my mother's scolding tongue should anything not be to her liking. I had been bred to be waited upon and nurtured, and it had simply never occurred to me until now that this was injustice. No one, I thought, had the right to feel superior to another, or to subject that other to a life of slavery. My instincts and the conditioning of my childhood warred within me. Bibicol was just as much in bondage to me now as she had been to my father, for I was too afraid to think of leaving her and continuing on my own. The realisation came that if we were to return to Kabul I, being Habib Amir's daughter, would be punished — and severely — but for Bibicol's part in our escapade, she could quite certainly be executed.

There was no going back now.

'Look, Nadir, I have captured this gazelle!' she called across to me, her arms pinioning Fatimettou from behind so that the girl could not move, squeal and wriggle though she might.

'It is a fine doe, Behar, the skin will make a good mat for your feet to rest upon in your tent!'

Fatimettou broke free, and their chase resumed.

'Oh, Bibi, what have I done to you?' Tears of self-recrimination stung my eyes as I sat there on the sun-baked rock with the sound of their happy voices shimmering through the heat. I knew then I would have to leave her when we found her tribe and, having made this silent resolution, I felt a mixture of grief and relief.

'Whooee! I am melting like a lump of candle tallow in this heat!' Bibicol threw herself down onto the ground beside me. 'Fetch me water, girl!' she commanded, mock-stern, to Fatimettou, who ran — did she ever walk? — to the water bottles.

The days passed happily until the time came for the tribe to move onwards towards the south. This came as a welcome respite in some respects because, during the latter part of our stay, I became worried by the obvious attraction that Fatimettou felt for Bibicol. Her childish affection began to take on a flirtatious quality and I could see, standing back a little as I was, that

181

her eyes turned often to Bibicol, and the expression
held in them was the beginning of infatuation. Short of
disillusioning her, and thereby the rest of the tribe, by
disclosing our true identity, it was the best course that
we should depart, and soon. I was even more concerned
when I caught the girl's father and mother in earnest
conversation with many a glance thrown in Bibicol's
direction.

Allah preserve us if they should offer Fatimettou to
Bibicol in marriage, and Allah stand by our sides even
closer if we should have to explain our reasons for
refusing!

I approached the head of the tribe shortly before the
day of their move.

'We will have to leave you, though it fills our hearts
with great and bitter sadness, for we have grown to
think of you as our family. We must fulfil our mission
and return thereafter to Kabul where our duties are
waiting.'

'We had hoped to travel longer with you,' he replied,
'but my admiration for your steadfastness grows daily,
and I understand your need to continue northwards to
Merve. Insh Allah, by the will of God, we will find our
travel routes crossing again, and soon!'

Fatimettou's smooth oval face crumpled as we said
our goodbyes, and it was all Bibicol and I could do to
remain dry-eyed and firm in our resolve. The girl ran
into the women's tent and emerged again with a small
furry bundle in her hands.

'For you! So that each time you look at him, you
look at me; every time you smooth the hair on his back,
your hand reaches out to mine.' So saying, she thrust
into Bibicol's arms a small golden-brown puppy. The
generosity of her gift reflected the depth of her feelings,
for the honey-coloured hunting dogs of the Qashgai
were very precious possessions, and famous for their

182

intelligence and fearlessness in defence of the herds that they guarded.

'But I cannot take him . . .' began Bibicol.

I jumped in quickly, we did not want to hurt the feelings of these kind people. 'The gift is certainly unde-served, Behar,' I said, 'but we will be truly honoured to accept this small animal, and I am sure he will lead us back to you far sooner than we could have found the way on our own!'

'He will be named Alexi, after Alexander the Great, for he will travel far and no doubt establish a name for himself wherever he goes!' Bibicol pronounced, lifting the wriggling little body to her face. 'Ho, there! I greet you, Alexi!'

Alexi's liquid brown eyes swam in gratitude for being thus named after so famous a man, and his small tail waved his pleasure. Bibicol passed him to me, and with such an excess of movement that I near dropped him, he wriggled close to my face and put out his ridiculously pink tongue to splash me with quick licking.

'Enough, brave warrior! I have this day already cle-ansed my skin! He will remind us both of you always, Fatimettou, and of the kindness you have all shown us here.'

Bibicol took the pup back from me and stowed him carefully inside her jacket, and we went fast then, afraid to stay longer lest our emotions betray our femininity.

We rode silently for a while, and then Bibicol started to sing in a soft and gentle manner, as if she were lulling a child to sleep.

'Ho, Bibi! Do not sound so melancholy! We should soon find your people, and that will be joy indeed.'

She smiled her acknowledgement. 'Come, then, Noeda, let us sing as we used to, and thus raise our spirits so they fly once more to the tree tops.'

We sang loud and cheerfully, reminding each other, as each song ended, of yet another still unsung, until

183

our voices grew quite hoarse, and even the sun took refuge from the noise behind the far hills at our backs . . .

* * * *

. . . The women stopped for a midday break.

'Here, Nina, eat this.' Leah handed me a large chunk of coarse bread. 'I cooked extra sweet potatoes with the evening meal yesterday, so we have those as well.'

I bit into the red skin of the sweet potato, suddenly ravenous. 'This is good!'

The talk flowed around me.

'Why is it that we are women?' one of the younger women, Mwange, asked, 'to work all hours for our men?' She moved her head from side to side. 'Just to enable them to buy more cattle, and then to watch them use those very cattle to pay the dowry on younger wives!'

'Is Juma looking then?' Leah asked her.

'His eyes search out for the young girls. Those whose breasts have firmness, before they are pulled by the feeding of babies. Ah, I fear for myself now — he will no longer seek my sleeping mat except when the girl bleeds!'

'It will be one more person to till the fields — see it that way,' Leah comforted her.

'Is that to be my life, then? For the rest of my days? To toil in the shamba, to gather wood, to fetch the water, to cook the meals?'

'It is our lot!' They nodded their heads in sympathy with each other.

'You are lucky, Nina,' Mwange said. 'The white women are Memsahibs, with servants to do their work. They do not toil in the fields!'

'Sometimes,' said Leah, 'misfortune brings in its wake fortune. It was so for Melika when she lost her man to the blackwater fever, and went to work as ayah to your mother, Nina.'

184

'Ah,' the others agreed, 'to work in the house of a Mzungu can be a good job for a woman.'

'But when a man goes to work as cook or houseboy or gardener, then his wife still tills the land, still works to feed his children, seeing her husband but seldom. It is not often that a man sends money to his family when he works for the Mzungu. He spends it instead upon clothes for himself and for paying prostitutes.'

We sat in the shade and shook our heads in sympathy with each other.

My skin burned darker in the sun and my feet grew hardened to the stones of the shamba. At night, after my muscles had become accustomed to the work, I slept deeply, waking only to feed Kerri when she howled her hunger.

She was growing fast, round, fat and beautiful, with enormous dark eyes and soft black hair. If only Rashidi could see her, I thought, but still there was no news of him.

ELEVEN

'Jomo Kenyatta will come before the courts soon,' the shopkeeper told us, 'but he has a white man to defend him! Heh! What chance has he of justice that way?'

We sat upon his dusty steps and listened to the radio. The newsreader's voice on the crackling radio was scathing:

'There are rumours of a rescue attempt, but Kapenguria, where Jomo Kenyatta is confined, is heavily guarded by tanks and troops.'

The shopkeeper spat contemptuously into the dust. 'It is not Jomo Kenyatta who leads the revolution. No, not him, for hasn't he had the English schooling anyway? The dangerous ones are those who hide, like the leopards, high in the forests, striking at night, lying low by day.'

He switched off the radio and shuffled back into the darkness of the duka, through the large tins of kerosine and sacks of maize meal; past the shelves where a conglomerate of items, from Brylcreem to bars of yellow Sunlight washing soap rubbed dust-coated shoulders; to where a smoke-grimed hurricane lantern awaited his match.

In the twilight outside we sat in silence, deep in our own thoughts, facing our own fears and speculating about the increasing violence. We still couldn't believe that the bestialities could be turned against the Kikuyus' own kith and kin — let alone the Europeans.

There was an edginess everywhere, even amongst the placid Giriama tribe; a waiting, and in the fading light outside the duka at Mikendeni we looked at each

186

other, men, women and me — the Mzungu girl — and our eyes were full of anxiety.

'Now the simis will be sharpened, the guns loaded. Now the killing will begin in earnest,' said one of the elders, 'and we are the ones who will suffer, not knowing which way to turn!'

The next day a letter came from Mother, a cry too desperate to be ignored:

'William has been wounded, Nina, in a fight with terrorists. He's in the military hospital and I've only been allowed to see him for a short time. The doctors, as usual, have told me very little. I'm really worried, and think it imperative that you come back to Nairobi immediately.'

Immediately! I looked at Kerri crawling in the sunshine, and my heart sank. Father, wounded?

The Khan? Could that indomitable man be hurt?

The questions tore through me. I couldn't imagine my father brought down, reduced.

At the thought of Habib Amir, I felt myself dissolve with fear, my mouth drying in anticipation of seeing his cold look upon my face. He'll never forgive me for running away! How will he punish me, I wonder? I found my hands were shaking uncontrollably.

Leah stood, pounding maize in a large wooden quern, and at that instant her head turned in my direction and her eyes asked the question. She handed the heavy pounding stick to Mirriamu and came to me.

'What makes you look so anxious?' Her hand, for a moment, rested on my shoulder, and the touch sent a tingle down my spine.

'It's Father. He's in hospital, and Mother calls me to go back to Nairobi!'

'You're worried about Kerri, is that it? There's no problem. She eats posho and fruit now, and Mirriamu has milk enough for two! Kerri'll be safe with us — you know that!'

187

'Yes, of course!' It was obviously the only way. It was out of the question for me to take her to Nairobi. Mother had trouble enough without the additional shock.

'I don't know how long I'll be away — it could be days! Until I get to Nairobi there's absolutely no way of knowing just how badly he's hurt.'

Guiltily, I realised I felt no compassion for him, just an overriding dread.

'Nina! Just go! Have you enough money for the train fare?'

'Mother sent me some.' That in itself seemed ominous and uncharacteristic. 'I'll leave then, on the first bus that comes along tomorrow.'

Leah smiled her encouragement at me. 'It'll be good for you to go to Nairobi, Nina, you've been away now for over a year.'

I was filled, suddenly and inexplicably, with anxiety and homesickness, and Mother's face came to me with a clarity of detail that I'd been unable to evoke before. She needs me, I thought. This time she really needs me!

Kerri gurgled and cooed as I packed my few possessions, and with tears threatening, I watched her crawling in the fading light. Her face was up-turned towards me, and Rashidi laughed through her eyes.

'Thank God I've got you, sweet Kerri!' I said, picking her up and swinging her high towards the thatch, so that above my face she crowed with laughter and dribble splashed my cheek. I was so thankful that my child had been born after all, with her bright spirit and beautiful, coffee-brown body. 'Problems or no problems — you give me so much joy.' And yet the joy was almost a pain within my heart as I spoke. I knew that soon I'd have to think about our future, but there was no time right then. Or maybe it was just that, frightened, my mind made excuses not to think too

188

deeply; time warped and altered so much for me now, waking or sleeping.

The wood-fuelled engine belched dark smoke which enveloped Mombasa station in a gritty cloud. I pushed through the crowd and struggled along the narrow corridor until I found an empty compartment. Then I waited impatiently for the whistle that announced our jerky departure, as the train filled.

Unable to afford a sleeping berth, I sat cramped beside a large sweating woman with two fretful children. Blessedly I'd managed to get the window seat, and at last the children slept, legs and arms sprawled on the prickly fabric.

The long hot night stretched unendingly. I rolled my head, trying to ease the ache in my neck.

'Hot, isn't it?' The woman next to me wiped her forehead with a far from clean handkerchief. Our conversation had been desultory, her energies directed at trying to control the children.

I wondered how she'd cope, this large lady from suburban Manchester. She shut her eyes and soon her mouth slackened into sleep.

I stared out into the unbroken darkness, my body loose and rocking with the 'chugga-da-chugg, chugga-da-chugg' of the steam train along the dirt-dry track. As the engine followed the curving rails ahead, I could see the sparks fly upward, the lit carriage windows stringing out like bright beads against the blackness.

I must have dozed, for the next thing I knew was the squealing of brakes and a juddering as we slowed to stop at Voi station.

I peered through the mosquito netting at the noise and unexpected activity, strange in the middle of the night, in the middle of nowhere. My companions slept on.

A generator throbbed, bringing electricity to the

189

station buildings, light flooding forward to reveal the bustle of the crowded platform. African women, huge bundles on their heads, babies hip-slung, ran to join the jostle to climb into already-crowded third-class carriages; Asian women drifted by in swirls of saris, followed by thin-legged children; vendors walked the length of the train, offering up oranges, bananas, hot sweet cakes to the passengers. I pushed up the gauze and leaned out to buy some oranges.

As I handed over the money, I looked upwards and saw Rashidi. I felt the sudden pounding of my heart, the constriction in my breathing. It seemed an eternity before my voice could make its way through the tightness of my throat, into a shout:

'Rashidi! Rashidi?'

He turned, eyes searching for the source of the call. It was him, though at first I thought I'd been mistaken, he was so different — filthy and long-haired.

'Wait, Rashidi, wait!' I scrambled over the sprawled legs, tore at the door and ran down the corridor to jump down onto the platform.

He came towards me, eyes puzzled, frowning. 'What are you doing here, Nina?'

I laughed nervously. 'I could ask you the same thing!'

His eyes were wild and evasive, the pupils large.

'You shouldn't be seen speaking with me, it might make questions in people's minds,' he said.

'Were you going to catch the train?' I asked, and hated myself for recoiling from his rancid smell.

'No,' he shook his head, the tatters of his hair swinging against the grimed coat. 'No, I was expecting someone. One of our men.' He looked at me closely. 'Have you money, Nina? Give me some if you have.'

I put my hand in my pocket, thinking of the meagre coins in my purse. 'I can let you have a little, but I haven't much.'

190

'All Mzungu have money!' His voice was bitter. He hawked and spat upon the ground and, in that moment he seemed to have diminished, to have shrunk somehow.

I pulled out my purse and counted out ten shillings. 'No — give me all of it.' He snatched the purse from me. 'You can get more from the Major!'

He turned away, then stopped and looked at me with eyes that portrayed the desolation of his soul. For a moment I glimpsed the old Rashidi, then his hand came up and touched my cheek, briefly, gently, and he pushed his way into the crowd, thin legs shrouded by the over-long army greatcoat. As I watched I felt emptied, drained of the love I'd held on to for so long — cheated somehow — as though the boy I'd known had been replaced by a total stranger.

I shivered, suddenly cold in the humidity, shocked into immobility.

'No! Oh, no, no!' My voice sounded loud in my ears, but went unheard, drowned by the crowd that closed around his disappearing figure.

Stunned by disbelief, I wondered numbly if betrayal was always to be my lot. My movements towards the train were leaden, unreal, like a slowed-down film track. I pulled my heaviness upwards, back to the compartment as the whistle blew, steam escaping with a loud hiss to mock my misery.

Throughout the night my dichotomy tore at me, causing physical anguish so intense that at one stage I cried out with it. Love for Melika, for Leah, for Kerri, warred with my disillusion, a disillusion fired by my father's inbuilt belief that all Africans were savages, incapable of rising above that savagery. I wondered if he was right. Was the divergence between black and white too deep for bridging, too steeped in ancestral differences, not only of colour but of belief, of culture?

Weary beyond sleep, I stared out into the tropical

191

night, saw the flat plains silvered now by a half-waned moon, the kopjes assuming strange prehistoric shapes; thorn trees, flat-topped and shadowed, sheltering who knew what predatory enemy. My grief, too, was beyond weeping, the void within leaving a leaden ache, numbing coherent thought. I felt bleak and dangerously ephemeral, the future uncertain, too short for reparation, the past intruding, repeating inexorably; images of Bibicol, Habib Amir, Ibrahim and Rsul chasing each other through my mind, blocking my thoughts of Rashidi, and Mau Mau.

Rashidi, who had become a wild fanatic fugitive, no longer the clean, bright youth who'd entered me, sown the seed of our child. Disappointment left a bitter taste on my tongue and I felt dirtied, wondering if this cynical, wild animal had always lurked behind his smiling mask; whether it was the projected image thrust upon him by my love that had made him what I wanted him to be. And whether, in the same manner, my own desperate need may have projected images upon my unconscious, filling my inner world with scenes from some distant, unreal past.

'No!' I told myself firmly. 'No — they are real! I was there, I know — I just *know*, they're real.'

I moved out of the compartment again and stood in the darkened corridor, my forehead pressed against the glass of the window, jerking and swaying with the train. I pushed down the window and leaned out into the wind, wanting to scream my anguish into the uncaring African night.

A herd of wildebeest fled, disturbed by our passage, their multitude of thrashing hooves churning up a cloud of dust which, in the star-shimmer, became an opaque and milky sea. Ahead, the train curved, bejewelling the darkness. A smut flew into my eye.

'Oh, damn you! Damn and blast you all to hell!' I shouted, the shout whipped out of my mouth by the wind, my tears stinging my cheeks and washing out the smut. I put my head down on my arms and wept. Cried for Rashidi and the part I'd played in his dissolution; went on crying for my mother; for my father whom I'd never known, might now never know; cried for Kerri and the father she'd never have either; for all the loneliness; the misunderstandings; for the past and for the future, the whole of Africa; for humanity, feeling myself dissolving, melting into the whole morass; losing my form so that I became one with the grief everywhere.

When I stopped, my body ached, my eyes were swollen and stinging, and I shook violently.

And why? Why the familiarity, the inevitability?

Pale streaks of dawn lit the walls of the escarpment on the last climb upwards and, with the lessening of darkness, so, too, my heavy heart lightened, purged by the weeping. I knew that although my feelings for Rashidi had transmuted from love almost to revulsion at our meeting, I would carry the memory of that love always, encapsulated in Kerri. Hold it within my centre, precious.

Clearly and distinctly the thought came to me: the ties had to be severed, cut cleanly. And I realised Rashidi would have joined the gangs anyway, that our entanglement and its consequences were merely the catalyst, the touch-paper.

Across the lightening sky a shooting star flared, travelled westwards and then disappeared.

I went back into the darkened compartment and curled up on the seat, exhausted, my mind slowly calming. I still have Kerri and Melika, I reassured myself. Leah, too . . . Leah, who in some way was special.

And Bibicol . . . Bibicol is special, too . . .

* * * *

. . . The small dog, Alexi, proved a mixed blessing on the dusty track towards Merve. On the one hand he delighted us with his enthusiastic desire to please, and the glee with which he gave us his undivided love and loyalty; on the other, as he grew rapidly larger, he was more difficult to carry.

He learned quite soon to sit in front of either Bibicol or me on the horses, shifting to keep his balance. He was still too young to run any distance beside us, and valiant though his attempts were, his small legs would give out after a while and he would sit, tongue lolling and eyes apologetic, waiting for one of us to dismount and lift him up. At night he lay between us, limbs jerking in dreams of great chase, but senses always alert for any discordant note in the symphony of night noises. If any such change came, he sat up quickly, ears up and small black nose wrinkling to catch any drifting smell of danger.

It was this alertness of his that had us upright with all nerves stretched one moonless night, several days after we had left Meshed.

'What is it?' breathed Bibicol.

'I don't know yet, but obviously he heard something.' Indeed, Alexi stood, one paw lifted from the ground, and a low growl vibrating his throat.

'Shh, Alexi!' I ran my hand along his back to quieten him, and felt the ridge of hairs that fringed his backbone, erect and rough to my touch. He would not be calmed so, moving as silently as I could, I picked up Ibrahim's sharp knife and stood looking into the blackness. The night was so dark that I could see nothing at first, though my eyes ached with the search. After a few moments, I heard them — horses being led, two as far as I could tell, slowly and almost silently in our direction.

I put my hand out to touch Bibicol, and pressed hard upon her shoulder to warn her to keep down and quiet, then I moved carefully towards the smouldering embers of our fire and, with one sharp movement, kicked a half-burnt log that lay on top, sending up a shower of bright sparks which lit the blackness. In this transient light I saw two men, almost upon us now, but halted in their progress by my sudden movement.

'Stop! We are armed and ready to take you!' I shouted, a slight tremble in the first word almost giving away my nervousness.

'Nadir — is that you?'

'Rsul?'

'Indeed it is! And I thank Allah to have found you! We thought for an instant we might have stumbled upon bandits!'

'What are you about — so far from Chesht?' I asked.

'And who do you bring with you?' chorused Bibicol.

'Aha! A surprise for you two young braves. You spoke of your admiration for the finest BuzKashi rider in Afghanistan and, see, Rsul brings him to you!'

Ibrahim! My mouth dried completely, and I swallowed hard and looked at Bibicol in horror. Her eyes were huge in the fire glow, and she lifted her eyebrows in hopeless question.

Ibrahim stepped forward and I went towards him slowly, with the light of the fire behind me, throwing my face into shadow. Keeping my voice no louder than a whisper I greeted him: 'Welcome, Ibrahim! My brother and I have long admired you!'

He came out of the shadows, his walk uneven, favouring one leg.

'We heard of your fall at the BuzKashi. Your leg is nearly mended, I see.'

'It is almost as before, but causes me pain after much riding — and I have done little else these last weeks.'

'You have come far?'

'From Kabul!' He frowned as he looked at me, and his answer came hesitantly.

And we had thought him safely in Bactria!

'What news of Kabul?' I was afraid to hear his

195

answer, but spoke to fill the silence which was full of questions.

'It is not a good place to be these days – the Khan's daughter is missing . . .' Again he faltered, his head on one side and his eyes narrow as he looked at me, '. . . and the Khan is torn between grief and anger. I myself am engaged on the search for the girl, both because I have known her from childhood, and also since I enjoy the patronage of Khan Habib Amir in the BuzKashi.' His look flew from me to Bibicol and back again.

This was worse than we had ever anticipated. I was sure he recognised us, for if any man could penetrate our disguise, Ibrahim was the best qualified. We stood silent, our thoughts no doubt running in the same direction. If he had but come alone, we could have explained, for we sought him anyway — but what of Rsul?

'May we sleep by your fire, friends?' asked Rsul who had stood, watching and listening to the exchange.

'Forgive my ill manners,' I said quickly. 'Behar, stir the flames beneath the waterpot and make a drink for our fellow travellers.'

Bibicol pulled at her hat until it sat forward on her head, shading her face, and occupied herself with the fire. As Rsul and Ibrahim turned to their horses to lift the saddles and give the animals food, Bibicol's urgent whisper came: 'What shall we do?'

'I don't know, Bibi! Let's pray, Insh Allah, that these two will leave before daylight reveals our features in all detail!'

'If not?'

'Then we must leave early, instead. We will have to plead we are short of time to meet with the Qashgai, near Merve.'

'What reason can we give for our need to meet this tribe so urgently?'

196

'The reason will come to me if necessary — hurry now, for they approach!'

As the men returned I sat, back to the fire, with Alexi's wet nose thrusting into my hand for reassurance.

'Where do you go from here, Rsul?' I asked.

'For the moment I go with Ibrahim. The Khan of Chesht has given me leave to travel awhile in acknowledgement of the success my men had in capturing the murderers of his son.'

'Ah, so they are brought to justice? We need no longer look over our shoulders for fear of meeting these thugs?'

'That is correct — they were found soon after your visit, and have been executed. We just trust there will be no more reprisals to follow.'

We sat drinking sweet tea with Rsul and Ibrahim, talking quietly and, on our part, very carefully. Even so I could see the puzzled frown cross Ibrahim's brow from time to time.

'Come, friend!' At last Rsul stood up. 'We should sleep, for the hour is late, and we travel on towards Merve at first light tomorrow.'

To Merve!

'Why are you going to Merve? It is but a small village, I believe.'

'Nadir, we go there to seek the Khan of Kabul's daughter,' said Ibrahim. 'Her servant girl is of the nomad tribes, and it is a remote chance that they could be there. In any event, I am bound to check for I promised Habib Amir so to do.'

That meant we would have to change our plans.

'What shall we do, Noeda?' whispered Bibicol after we had wrapped ourselves up in our blankets to sleep.

'Shh, Bibi, I don't know yet. Leave it until tomorrow and we will see what happens. It may be that we can take another route.'

'But then we will miss my family.'

'I know, that is the difficulty. I don't see the answer yet. Sleep on the problem and see what dawn brings.'

I slept not at all, for this confrontation with Ibrahim was the hardest test we had had to stand so far, and I could not believe that he would not feel the same tug of recognition that had jolted my inside when he had walked out of the darkness by the fire. I wondered if men perhaps did not suffer from the tearing ache at the back of their throats and down to the stomach that I felt, knowing that he was lying there, the other side of the low-burning logs.

Daybreak found me saddling our horses, and in the silent greyness that preceded the first burst of birdsong, Ibrahim of a sudden was beside me.

'So early, friend?' he asked, stretching and yawning. 'Could you not sleep either?'

'I was restless,' I replied.

'I, too, could not subdue my thoughts,' he laughed. 'It was as though I badly needed a woman to comfort me, for I ached in every part. A soft body beneath mine would have eased the discomfort.'

I turned the other way, hot with embarrassment.

'Ah well, maybe in Merve the peasant girls will be obliging.'

Was this how all men spoke to each other?

'Did you find relief with the girls at Meshed, or are you and your brother interested in other directions?' he pursued the questioning.

'Sir, we are but boys,' I stammered, not prepared for this line.

'Boys! And yet old enough to travel alone across Afghanistan. Don't tell me that you have not experimented with the serving girls at your father's estate?'

'Maybe!' I left my answer short, and turned to see if Bibicol was stirring.

The day was beginning to lighten and I wanted to

get away. Ibrahim put his hands upon my shoulders and turned me towards him, scrutinising my face in the pale dawn.

'Are you sure we have not met, Nadir? You seem more than a little familiar to me.' He put his hand up and took off my hat. 'Yes!' The word came as a hiss. 'I thought there was that about your voice and the shape of your shoulders which called out to me. Noeda — what is this?'

'Oh, Ibrahim, I beg of you, keep silence!' He took my hand and drew me away from our sleeping companions, behind an outcrop of rocks.

'How can I now keep silence?' he asked. 'I am here to search for you and to return you to Kabul.'

'Ibrahim, we left Kabul in part to search for you, and I cannot return, not now — I am promised to Shamlu Gadir, and I would rather the vultures picked my bones clean here in this far place, than share my life and my body with that man!'

'I did not know of this betrothal! I can see now the reasons for your flight, but you cannot run forever, girl. Your father is heartbroken, and one day you will be caught — and then what?'

I could not reply, for this question was the one that grew and grew in my mind, try though I did to push it away. I stood, mute with misery; Ibrahim by my side was silent, too.

The birds, all at once, started to announce the day, loud in the half-light, and with the rising crescendo of song Ibrahim and I turned simultaneously to each other and I was close held against him.

His hands, insistent at my breast, were hard, and hurt me, and I feared that he would tear my shirt. I pushed away from him.

'No, Ibrahim, not this way!'

'You hunger for me too, Noeda.'

'That may be, but I am still the daughter of Habib Amir!'

'It is you who needs to be reminded of that fact, and if it be so, then return with me to Kabul that I might claim two rewards — the money that your father offers for your return and, in addition, yourself as my bride.' He pulled me back, his hands upon my buttocks, pressing my body against himself. 'Don't be so virtuous, Noeda, you forget who it was who crept into the stables at Kabul! Was it not you who lay beside me, hot for my lovemaking? It was only my broken leg that stopped me pleasuring you then. Why now play the innocent with me?'

I struggled free and moved away from him.

'Come on! Come on! You desire me, as I desire you — why not admit it? We are both "men" after all!' he laughed and made a coarse gesture with his arm.

'Oh, Ibrahim, don't talk so!' I was saddened at his lack of delicacy. 'That time was then. Now I have difficulties enough without seeking more!'

'Oh, keep your precious virtue! The reward Habib Amir is offering is by far more attractive than you or your skinny body!' He pushed me roughly to one side. 'I only make play for you to further my chances with your father, anyway!' He turned away and with a sharp movement plucked a stalk of grass to chew upon. 'Think on it, Noeda. It may be the only course open to you, and if you persist in this masquerade, then the cost of my silence would rob you of your bride price as a virgin.'

'Do you threaten me, Ibrahim?' I asked, but there was no time for a reply as Rsul's voice came from the camping place to ask where we were.

Ibrahim led the way back, for all as though nothing had transpired between us. Bibicol, busy with the fire, looked quickly at me and, catching my bleak look, her eyes turned then fast to Ibrahim.

'Rsul — Nadir and I have been discussing our plans, and it would seem to be the sensible thing for us to ride together to Merve,' Ibrahim announced.

Rsul's dark eyes studied my face. 'Are you sure this is what you want, Nadir?'

'Ibrahim tells me that you are going that way, so we may well travel at least part of the route with you.' What else could I say, with Ibrahim's threat above my head?

Both Bibicol and Rsul looked puzzled. I could understand the former's bewilderment, but in no way found explanation for Rsul. I went quickly to Bibicol.

'Come, Behar, help me load the horses while your pot of water heats,' I said urgently.

Under cover of the girthing and loading of our animals, I endeavoured to let her know a little of what had transpired.

'What will we do?' she whispered.

'We go along for the time being,' I replied. 'This is not the Ibrahim we knew! Something has changed him — we will no doubt fathom it out later.'

Rsul came over to help with the horses. As he stood close behind me to reach over and hold my bedroll steady, I had to bite my lip to stop myself from turning to lay my head upon his chest for comfort.

But I hardly knew this man.

I picked up Alexi and buried my face for a moment in the soft loose skin around his neck.

Throughout that long day's ride I battled with my hurt bewilderment at Ibrahim's manner. I spoke but little, for I could find no words. Bibicol, seeing my distress, kept a flow of talk in an endeavour to divert attention away from me. Alexi, sitting my horse between my thighs, turned from time to time, eyes full of apology in case he was the cause of my grief. I let my horse fall back behind the others, needing to be alone with my thoughts, and my body became one with the smooth motion of the animal, lulling me into half-sleep. A sleep in which strange dreams haunted me. Figures, dark and half-known; sometimes seeming to be Ibrahim or Rsul, then changing, merging — the same, but somehow different.

Ahead, Rsul was waiting, with his horse turned back.

'Nadir, Nadir! What ails you? In vain I have spoken your name for the past few moments. Are you unwell, friend, for you are singularly silent this day?'

I found difficulty bringing myself to the moment, and my throat ached with unshed tears.

'Rsul! Thank you for your concern. No, I am not ill, I think just overtired for I couldn't sleep last night, and now my waking hours are filled with images and strange imaginings.'

'Ride on, Ibrahim, and you too, Behar!' he called, and put his hand out to catch the bridle round my horse's head. 'We will follow, and catch up with you later.'

Both looked back — Bibicol with concern, and Ibrahim's glance held warning. Then they turned away.

With Rsul leading my horse, we slowly went along the track until we found a small grove of trees, shaped and gnarled with the winds that blew over the plains. Here Rsul dismounted and, putting up his hands, caught me as I, too, slid down.

'Come, you need to rest awhile, for your face is white and your eyes dark-rimmed with fatigue. Lie here in the quiet and find your spirit.' He led me to the shade and, when I sat, he pulled off my boots and laid them upon the ground beside me.

'You are much younger than I thought.' His hands were gentle, expert, as he rubbed my aching feet and legs. 'Perhaps your father was wrong to let you come on so arduous a journey!'

202

'We wanted to,' I replied hastily. 'We need to become men.' How near the truth was that statement!

I lay back and shut my eyes, falling immediately into deep and troubled sleep, again filled with strange images and unknown people.

Rsul's hand upon my shoulder shook me awake and Alexi, pushing against my body, sighed deeply.

'Ho! Nadir! You dream. Such sad dreams they must be to make you weep so! Come, wake and take a drink of water to replace the moisture that flows from your eyes!'

I sat up quickly. 'I was far away from here,' I said, 'and yet the two places were entwined, as though somehow I am two people!'

He smiled, eyes thoughtful. 'I know that feeling well! A half-sleeping, half-waking realisation of the oneness of all time, as if our ancestors from times past come crowding in to stand and say: "But we are *now*, not *then*!". Perhaps that is why I feel I know you so well, Nadir?'

I was on the very edge of telling him the whole of my story, for I could no longer bear the dishonesty with him. But he stood up then, and walked away to sit upon the rocks.

'Try once more to sleep, boy,' he said, his voice a little abrupt. 'Without the dreams this time!' As I looked at him he turned his face away, but not before I saw once more the question written there.

'Oh, Alexi, my emotions nearly betrayed us then,' I whispered as the puppy flopped down upon the ground beside me. His soft, as yet unpricked, ears felt like velvet in my fingers, and he gave a short contented grunt before falling asleep. I followed his example without realising it, and woke an hour later to see Rsul preparing the horses once more.

'You wake at the right moment,' he called over to

203

me. 'I was just about to rouse you, for we must ride now if we want to catch the others before night.'

I stretched, a great stretch that pulled each muscle, each tendon in my body into wakefulness. 'Yes, I am rested! Come, Alexi, give me your example of new vigour!'

Alexi, full of life, ran circles in the sand, chasing birds, leaves, his own tail, and barking at his shadow.

'You foolish animal!' I watched and laughed with Rsul at Alexi's antics, content in that moment's shared pleasure.

'There is a small pool of water in the hollow of those rocks if you wish to cool your face, but I should not risk the drinking of it.' Rsul pointed. I was grateful to be able to get out of sight for a few moments to relieve myself and splash the lukewarm water over my hands and face.

'Ready?'

'Yes, and thank you, Rsul, for that short break. I feel restored again.'

'Don't push yourself too far, Nadir, your health is more important than any other consideration.' He paused. 'Already I feel you have taken yourself far beyond your strength. Even in the few weeks since I saw you at Chesht, your face has grown thinner, and your eyes more strained.'

'A sign of maturity, perhaps, Rsul?' I said.

'No, you are mature in an unusual way, Nadir, a way which puzzles me greatly, for you are unlike any other young man I know. You seem more sensitive, more seeing somehow, even — if I may say it without offence — like a woman in your intuition and grace!'

'My upbringing has been gentle, Rsul, and that is one reason that we have undertaken this journey,' I replied. I would have to take more care. I tried to ignore the buzz of warning in my mind. The air between us shimmered with unsaid words, and even the grasses for an instant were motionless, as if waiting.

I called to Alexi, to break the mood, and as he skittered to me, I shut my eyes and breathed deeply to control the flutter of my pulse against my skin.

'Let's go!' I cried when I could find my voice, and we turned our horses out from the trees, leaving their paper-dry leaves to blow once more alone in the desert wind.

Later, when we had joined Ibrahim and Bibicol, and sat in the coolness of the evening, Ibrahim's voice made me jump.

'I'm sorry, Nadir, if my rudeness upset you. My leg hurt after the riding and the pain at times makes me forget my manners.'

I looked at him across the fire. Now what?

'If we are to ride together, we cannot fall out,' he smiled. 'Forgive my roughness, boy?'

I looked at Bibicol and she shrugged her shoulders at me. 'I don't know,' she said.

'Of course, Ibrahim, we have to remain friends, and there is no cause for us to be otherwise. I sorrow to hear that your leg pains you so. Behar, where are the leaves that Fatimettou gave us to make poultices for my arm when it ached?'

Bibicol produced the leaves from her saddle bags, and with hot water we mixed a poultice of such pungency that our eyes streamed.

Rsul stood up. 'I'm tired, friends, and your brewing is making me cough!'

He moved away, to curl up in his cloak for sleep beyond the ring of light cast by the fire.

'Shall I do it?' asked Bibicol.

'No, Nadir is to apply it!' said Ibrahim quietly, but in such firm manner that I could not gainsay him.

He stood up and let drop his breeches, so that I had to avert my eyes from the sight of his manhood.

'Come!' His laugh was bitter. 'We are all men together. Surely you are not so modest that the sight of another man sends your stomach queasy?'

'Of course not,' I managed, 'but would you sit, please, so that I can apply the poultice.' Ibrahim sat, and with all my attention on his leg, I layered on the pungent leaves, wrapping them firmly with cloth.

He caught my hand and pulled it upwards. 'There!' he whispered, looking to see that Rsul slept. 'Feel how my passion grows, Noeda, even though you hide your body in man's clothing.'

I tried to pull my hand away, but he held it there, palm downwards over the bareness of his genitals, and I felt the blood pulse there, engorging him.

'Stop it, Ibrahim, stop it!' I was shaking with rage. 'Rsul will see, and Bibicol!'

'Bibicol may have her turn if she so wishes,' he whispered back.

Humiliated, I snatched my hand away, face burning. 'Why are you acting thus? It is not in your character to be so. In all the years I have known you, you have never shown this cruelty. What ails you, Ibrahim?'

He slumped back then, his eyes black with despair. 'I don't know why I behave thus with you, Noeda. You are my dear, dear companion of childhood. And not only that, the daughter of my good friend and protector, Habib Amir, so my treatment of you is doubly inexplicable. It is almost as if I am not myself these days, somehow I want to hurt you, for reasons that I cannot understand. I love you well, Noeda, and my desire for you is very strong, as you have found. And yet I am compelled to treat you like a harlot, as though I hated you!' He paused in thought. 'No, I do not hate you, girl, but I know that to love you is fraught with danger.'

'What danger? Habib Amir?'

'Partly, for he would not give his approval, fond though he is of me. But it is something more than that.

There is something about you that causes me to fear, and thus I punish myself, by punishing you. Forgive me, it may be that my fall at Kabul fractured my mind as well as my leg!' He stood up abruptly and pulled on his trousers, over the bandages.

'Don't blame yourself too harshly, Ibrahim.' My mind suddenly clear, I knew he could not help himself, that some dark part of his nature tore at him, making him behave this way.

Ibrahim looked at me, puzzled. 'I do not follow you, Noeda.'

'And I do not follow myself, Ibrahim — but let us take hands in a promise to try not to destroy each other any more.'

'I will need your help, for my moods are black and overpower me at times!'

We embraced and, with slight embarrassment, each looked around for diversion.

I had forgotten Bibicol was there, and went quickly to her. As we lay close, with Alexi snoring gently between us, she whispered, 'What was all that about, Noeda? Today so much has happened that my head is spinning, and I have had no chance to speak to you!'

I put my arm out and hugged her to me. Alexi protested sleepily, and then resettled.

'Oh, Bibi! I, too, am confused beyond belief. This last week has been most strange, and I feel I am no longer myself. Almost, I seem to be standing to one side and watching the extraordinary events. Even my dreams are confused and unlike any I have had before.'

'Maybe we are over-fatigued?'

'That is possible, but we will rest when we find your family. It is Ibrahim who worries me most, for he knows the truth, and I fear that with the rapid changing of his moods he may betray us.'

'But you longed to see him so much! Now that he has found us, you wish him to go?'

'I do love him, Bibi, but the quality of that love has changed somehow. I don't understand why, but I do realise that though he sought me, it was not for *my* sake that he did so. I love him now for our long comradeship through the years, but no longer as a lover. Which in itself is a contradiction, for even this evening, while repulsed by his desire, at the same time my own body responded! But I know physical love between us is against my destiny. Don't ask me why or how I know, Bibi — I just *know*.'

'Oh, friend, you are a puzzle to me. I find it difficult to understand your thoughts these days. It seems that our journey has changed you from my simple, happy friend of Kabul, perhaps rushed you into womanhood, although at times you seem still but a child!' She sighed. 'But I love you still, Noeda, and together I'm sure we will overcome all the troubles that seem thrown in our way like large rocks on our track!'

She kissed me warmly, then snuggled her head into my shoulder and slept.

I lay, listening to the night chorus of frogs in some distant river, and in my imagination it was the stars that called and answered each other, not the frogs. But they answered my silent questions not at all.

Ibrahim's behaviour was exemplary for the next two days. He was courteous, gentle and thoughtful, but still there was something missing. The essential gaiety of his personality that had characterised him all the years I had known him, was gone. The silent young man who rode with us now was nothing akin to the bold-hearted and somewhat wild BuzKashi rider known to all of Afghanistan. It was as though Ibrahim had ridden away, leaving his shadow seated upon a horse with us.

We each of us engaged him in conversation, but were defeated by his morose, though polite, response. Rsul wore a perpetual look of worry, and I felt for him, especially as he was the only one of the four who had not even a hint of what could be causing the constraint in our attitudes.

On the evening of the second day he took me to one side.

'Nadir, I am very concerned over Ibrahim, for he is not himself at all. I am afraid he made this long journey too soon after his accident.'

'He is certainly different, even from the first evening,' I replied.

'I am going to try to persuade him to return to Chesht with me, and give up for now the search for this girl.'

'It may be difficult to make him see the wisdom of that, Rsul, but try — do try!'

When we returned to the fire Bibicol and Ibrahim were talking together and there seemed a glimpse of the old teasing manner between them. A quick surge of jealousy swept through me — Ibrahim is mine, Bibicol. Then I checked myself and the feeling disappeared, for I knew he was not — could never be.

Alexi, throughout this journey, had been torn between Bibicol and me, loving us both, and terrified that either should feel he favour the other. He ran backwards and forwards between us constantly. This evening, in the fire-glow, Rsul bent down and stroked him, and Alexi, instead of running away as he normally did from anyone other than Bibicol or me, almost turned himself inside out jumping to lick Rsul's face.

'Here, little eel, calm down or you will exhaust yourself,' he said, and his long fingers on the puppy's sides blended into the soft honey-brown of its fur. Alexi sat quivering in anticipation as we cooked our evening meal, holding himself back with difficulty from coming too close to the cooking pot.

The two men rode together ahead of us the next day, leaving Bibicol and me some little way behind, and at the setting of the sun they told us they would be leaving the following morning.

'For I don't feel Habib Amir's daughter would have come this far! More likely she has gone northwards towards Bactria,' Rsul said.

'It has been many weeks now since she and the servant girl went. I feel they would have been found by now, if they are still alive.' Ibrahim kept his eyes straight ahead, looking at neither Bibicol nor me and, as we two exchanged quick glances, I put my hand up to my mouth to hide a smile there, and found Rsul's look upon me.

'We shall miss your company, of course,' I said, 'but you must not waste your time any further. Ride back to Kabul to see what news there is in that far city!'

'I doubt we will be travelling that way ourselves, but I do hope our paths will meet, and soon,' added Bibicol.

'It may be sooner than you think,' replied Ibrahim, 'for I may not return to Kabul to admit to the Khan that I have failed to find his daughter. I will rest with Rsul for a while yet, and perhaps we will be able to travel together on your return to — where was it?'

'Koshuk, Ibrahim, Koshuk!'

'Ah, yes, Koshuk! I know the Khan there well, it surprises me I have not met his sons before now.'

Rsul must have picked up the undercurrent in this conversation, though the words were normal enough.

'Is there some mystery that you are keeping hidden from me?' he asked.

'No! No, not at all, Rsul,' laughed Ibrahim, with another quick flash of his old self. 'It is just that — um — well, just that Kabul and Koshuk are great rivals in the trials leading up to the great BuzKashi!'

What fabrication, Ibrahim! I thought. Ah well, it would suffice.

I caught a look in Ibrahim's eyes, a reminder of the

210

warmth and mischief that had caused me to love him as a youngster. I smiled a secret smile back at him.

Oh, Ibrahim, why can't we live without complication? At that moment I felt almost that I would be happy to ride away with him.

'But you remember, Nadir, what I said to you!' His voice was once more cold and a little harsh. The sudden swing again from light to dark brought me back to reason.

TWELVE

'Can you take a taxi, Nina?' Mother's voice on the phone was blurred.

'No, my purse was — it was snatched at the station.' There was no time for explanations.

'Oh!' She sounded confused. 'Oh — I see. All right, I'll get the driver to come and fetch you then.'

I sat in the hot sunlight, a stranger in the city where I'd grown up. Already I missed the suck and hiss of the sea, the pounding of the huge translucent breakers on white sand. Nairobi was all noise and bustle — too many people in too much of a hurry.

Kerri would be awake now, down in Mikendeni, with her plump legs in the air, playing with her toes in the shade beside the field while Leah worked. I longed for the feel of her firm, round flesh, the smell of milk and talcum powder, and I was unbearably lonely for her, in the busy station forecourt. My breasts stung, tingling and exuding small droplets of milk at the thought of her.

Paul came then, unexpectedly and strongly into my mind, making my nipples ache with a different yearning, prickling against the material of my dress. I shut my eyes and saw his face in my mind, the strong jawline which contrasted with the softness of his strange, amber-brown eyes; the straight, slightly too large nose; his mouth upturned at the corners. The thoughts evoked in me a wanting, an intake of breath that left me dizzy and vulnerable.

I wondered why he had gone from Mombasa so suddenly, feeling the rejection of his departure, the withholding of himself. And yet I was sure he had felt something — such an emotional tug surely couldn't be a one-way thing? It was impossible that he had not sensed the impulse that charged the air between us. Perhaps he had, I thought and, seeing the danger, held back. Perhaps fearing that he might burn if he let me come too near; anxious not to lose his self-control.

I recalled his fingers against my naked breast, and my mouth dried. Was he aware that I was there at all, that I wasn't simply a patient? Did he see *me* — small and dark-haired with eyes that must surely have given me away? Then a sudden thought made me flush with embarrassment and shame. Could it be because of Kerri? Because I'd had an illegitimate baby — and she was black? A chi-chi.

I stirred uncomfortably, seeing in my mind his thick shock of hair, wanting to touch it, to push my fingers through its density. I'd seen how it was echoed by the short hairs on his arms, the dark triangle at the neck of his shirt.

Perhaps Paul couldn't forgive my transgression — Kerri's conception? Couldn't he accept the mixture of colours? Was he too hidebound by the unwritten code that made of such mixing 'half-castes'? Was that the reason he'd not contacted me again?

'*Habib Amir can no longer claim the bride price!*' *It was Ibrahim's voice in my ear* . . .

The thought chased my desire.

I don't even know Paul — don't know whether he's married, has children! I shook my head, facing the reality of the busy traffic in front of me. I realised then, even more clearly, that I had finally shrugged off my guilt over Rashidi. He had no claim over me. He had chosen his path.

No, I thought, what occurred between Rashidi and me should not have happened, perhaps, but it did, and I've got Kerri as a result. But there was no way it could have been long-term. Rashidi was there when I needed that love. I wasn't prepared to hold on to the wanting — he'd gone and with him went that particular illusion. I wouldn't forget, but on the other hand neither would I carry the ember around with me like a coal in a charcoal burner, fanning it to keep it alive.

Rashidi — and Ibrahim — their parts were played now.

In the sunshine my mind wandered, blotting out the anxiety about Mother, my worry over leaving Kerri, the confusion I felt over Paul — leaving my guilts and uncertainties . . .

*   *   *   *

. . . Then Bibicol was with me, her presence comforting and familiar, her earthy common sense reassuring. We'd find her family, I was certain of that, and perhaps make our home with them.

But in my heart I knew this couldn't be. I'd have to return to Kabul and make my peace with Habib Amir.

Next day when Rsul and Ibrahim had gone, we found a pool amongst some bushes where we stripped and bathed and were thus more wholesome when we saw the nomads' goat-skin tents in the distance. Sheep and goats grazed on the stubbled grass and, from time to time, through the perpetual blanket of dust, we glimpsed a ghostly rider, clad in flapping sheepskin, or a barelegged herdboy seeming to float on the miraged air.

'Is it your tribe, Bibi?' I asked as she stood in her stirrups, eyes shaded to see.

'Difficult to tell from here,' she replied. 'So, now what do we do? Let down our hair to be girls again, or wait as men?'

'We'd better make sure before we let go our disguise,' I said. 'After all, it didn't take Ibrahim long to recognise us, so your family will soon know you.'

'That I doubt,' she answered, 'for I have not seen

214

them since I was but eight years old, and I think I have changed a little from the small girl I was then.'

I had not thought of that.

We rode towards the group of people who had gathered, standing together, to greet the strangers riding into their camp.

'I'm nervous now,' said Bibicol, her knuckles white on her reins. 'Not as much as when we were being chased up the river, perhaps, but in a different way!'

We got closer.

'Yes — they are there!' she exclaimed. 'See the man leaning on the stick? And the woman in a red shawl, that is my mother, and he my father!'

'Take it quietly, Bibi. Let us feel our way before revealing ourselves.'

She cleared her throat nervously before calling out a greeting in the Qashgai dialect. Smiling faces turned upwards to us on our horses, and hands were held out to help us dismount.

'Welcome! Welcome travellers!' said the man, Bibicol's father.

'We are here to camp at least for a few days, so please give us the pleasure of staying with us awhile.'

'The pleasure of sharing time with you will be for us!' I stumbled with the dialect, thanking our stay with Fatimettou's family for the fact that I could speak it at all.

Bibicol said nothing, emotion robbing her of her voice, and I saw her hands tremble as she took the tea bowl offered by her mother.

We learnt that they had travelled for many days, down from the highlands before the onset of winter, and that they had seen no one since leaving the village of Merve, some three days earlier. Nothing about the missing girls from Kabul.

'We come from Kabul!' I said, suddenly. Biblicol, her father and mother all looked at me, waiting. 'How long is it since you saw your daughter, Bibicol, who went there to the Khan's estate?'

'It must be some seven or eight years, I think. How long, Mojgan?' her father asked his wife.

'At least that long. She was eight years old when the Khan took her. A small, sickly child, whose health made journeying with us a dangerous thing for her. He promised she would return when she was old enough and had proved her strength was back completely. It seems so long ago.' She sighed, and the man put out his hand to touch her arm.

'The time will come, and at least she is living well, without the difficulties and hazards of our travelling life!'

Bibicol could contain herself no longer and, pulling off her hat, she undid her plaited hair and let it fall around her face in a crinkled cloud.

'You have to wait no longer — I am here!' she laughed and stood up, Alexi rolling off her lap onto the sand.

The man and his wife clapped hands over mouths opened in astonishment, and for a moment no one could move.

I felt a strange detachment, sitting there, part of the scene but apart from it. Then the jubilation burst out, with all members of the family called, and the news relayed again and again.

'It's Bibicol! She's back!'

So, my father was going to return her to her people anyway! Perhaps this would make things easier for me when I returned to Kabul.

It wasn't until the excitement had abated a little that Bibicol's father came to where I was sitting with Alexi.

'I am Abdul,' he said. 'And I thank you, young sir, for bringing back our daughter! But how is it that she travels thus alone with you, and dressed in man's clothing with no other women or guards?'

Here comes the difficult part, I thought.

'I, too, am not what I seem!' I replied, about to tell him all, but somehow holding back at the last moment. 'But, rest assured, Bibicol is safe and well, and this you can see by just looking at her!'

'The looking pleasures my eyes, for I thought to die before she ever returned!' he said. 'Daughter, come and properly introduce your companion.'

Bibicol came towards us, her eyes full of questions for me. Imperceptibly, I shook my head to let her know I wanted to remain 'Nadir' for the time being.

'Nadir is a good friend, and has guarded me well on our long journey,' she told her father. 'Now, could we perhaps rest for a short while, as we, too, have ridden without stopping for many weeks.'

I felt that Abdul was not entirely happy at being given a somewhat non-committal answer in this way, but he called for his wife and she and two other girls led the way to different tents. I had forgotten that Bibicol and I would be separated because of our sexes. I saw her look over her shoulder at me and shrug.

I called out to her:

'I'll be unloading the horses, Bibi, in but a few moments, if you wish to collect your bedroll.'

'Oh, yes, I will come now to get it!' We made our escape quickly to where the horses stood patiently, still saddled.

'I didn't know whether to reveal myself or not,' I said. 'What do you think, Bibi?'

'Perhaps it is best to stay as you are, for anyone searching will be looking for two girls, not a man and a girl.'

'True — but in honesty I grow tired of playing the part, and long to be as we were before the BuzKashi, young and innocent and untroubled!'

'Days that are gone are like blown seed, Noeda, we

217

cannot put them back into the seed-pods, they each have to mature in their own way or perish!'

'And we've come nigh to the latter a few times!'

So it was decided that I would remain as Nadir, at least for the present. We were joined then by a group of youngsters clamorous to carry our bedding and cooking pots into the camp. Bibicol went with them while I tethered and watered the horses.

That evening Bibicol emerged amongst a flutter of girls, dressed in her sister's clothing. The journey had thinned her formerly plump body down to pleasant proportions, and indeed she seemed to have grown a few inches taller. Her hair glistened from fresh washing, and in it were woven ribbons and beads that danced around her head as she moved.

Abdul drew in his breath in appreciation as she approached.

'Daughter — that is more fitting! You have grown very beautiful, but who could expect less with a mother such as yours!'

Mojgan and the girls all laughed, the sound silver in the dusk.

'Yes, Bibi, you have grown from a handsome boy into a beautiful woman in a few short hours!' I teased. Looking at her, thus attired, and surrounded by her laughing family, the tears came to my eyes, and I knew myself to be alone.

In celebration, Abdul had ordered a sheep killed, and the smell of roasting meat made our mouths water. Alexi was beside himself with excitement, and could not sit still, running from one person to another, but always back to me, as if to make sure that I was still there and had not abandoned him to this noisy tribe. At times the smell of the food became too much for him to bear, and he would let out a yelp of hunger.

Later he curled up beside me in the tent, and seemed to know that a great sadness filled me, for he lay near

218

to my face, one leg across my neck and his nose so close to my cheek that I could feel his warm breath upon it. I wondered if Ibrahim, lying somewhere out under the same skies, grieved as I did for the passing of our shared youth and the end of expectation . . .

*   *   *   *

. . . The loud and sudden sound of a car hooter shook me out of my reverie, and I smiled as the driver put my small suitcase into my father's Citroën.

'You made me jump, Samwelli! I must have fallen asleep,' I said.

His eyes in the mirror were speculative.

'Will you be staying to help Memsahib?'

'I can't!' I wondered how much pressure was going to be put upon me not to return to Mombasa. 'How is my father, Samwelli? And what happened?'

'Bwana is near to death, Nina.' He paused. 'And Memsahib . . . the Memsahib, too, is unwell.'

'In what way — unwell?'

He shrugged. 'You'll see. She is worried about Bwana Anderson — we all are. He was caught by Mau Mau in an ambush.'

'Shot?'

'No, not shot. Hit with knives, pangas. His neck, chest. Truly, I don't know how his spirit has remained here until now.'

It was worse than I'd feared.

'Where did this happen? Did the gang come to the house?'

'No, we are loyal. Even Kimau, the garden boy, has not taken the oath – or so I believe to be true. Your father was leading a search party in the bamboo forests of the Abadares. Most of the company were killed, the others ran for their lives. All but one sergeant, and he carried Bwana dowr the mountains to the camp at GilGil!'

'Have you seen him?' I was burdened with anxiety and guilt.

'Servants aren't allowed in the military hospital — only Memsahib.'

Poor Mother. I felt a sharp stab of resentment that Father should be so ill, and she so incapable; then hated myself for my callousness.

Mother was hardly recognisable. She'd grown thin in the year I'd been away, her face gaunt, the skin a transparent membrane stretched over the bones so that I could see the dark hollows of her skull. Her blue eyes burned within their sockets, and her need was there, plain to see. My stomach tightened with sudden grief and compassion for her.

'Oh, Nina!' Her eyes were awash now and her hand shook as she wiped the tears away.

I put my arm around her shoulders and felt their fleshlessness — an indictment against me. For a moment she leaned her head against my chest, then she pulled away.

'I feel so useless — William lying there. I can't do anything to help him.' As her head turned upwards I caught the brandy fumes, wondered that she should be drinking this early in the day.

'When can I see him?'

'Later . . . this afternoon. They're a bit strict about visiting at the hospital.' She paused, fumbled for her handkerchief. 'He's in intensive care, you know.'

'Samwelli told me.' He had also told me she wasn't well. Was this what he meant, that she was drinking? Perhaps it was her way of combating the worry.

'Could I have coffee?' I asked, to ease the awkward silence. 'Something to eat? I'm famished.' I'd had nothing since I left Mombasa the night before.

'Oh — of course! Sorry.' She called for the houseboy, gave the order.

'Aren't you going to have anything?'

'I can't, Nina, I just can't eat at the moment. Somehow food seems to choke me.'

'Mum — you're losing so much weight!'

She gestured impatiently. 'I'm all right, don't fuss me!'

The hospital was bare and smelt of disinfectant. It had a parade-ground feel about it, and I almost expected to hear the clump of booted feet, instead of the silent footfall of soft-soled shoes; to hear orders shouted, not given quietly.

I looked through the window of the intensive care unit to where Father lay, isolated; a pale grey form, with tubes attached to him.

We donned gowns, masks and caps, and I felt perspiration prickle my forehead, finding the gauze over my face suffocating, claustrophobic. When we got to the bedside, I didn't know him. Relief made my voice loud:

'It's not him, Mum! It's okay, it's not him!'

Not the Khan!

'Don't be so stupid, of course it's William!' Mother's eyes blazed.

I looked closer, saw that indeed it was my father.

'They've shaved off his moustache!' I was shaken by my inability to recognise him, and by the realisation that I knew so little of him that without the thin line of hair upon his face he was someone I had never seen, never known.

Mother held one of his hands, tears running unchecked down her face, and irritation filled me once more that he should cause her so much unhappiness.

This is my father, I was self-admonishing, ashamed at my lack of filial grief. No matter what he's done, after all, he's my father. I forced one of my hands forward over the crisp white sheet and touched his fingers. They felt cold, clammy, as if he were already dead. I pulled back quickly. He opened his eyes,

221

blinked slowly into focus and then saw me. The eyelids stayed wide, and he tried to speak, running the tip of his tongue over his dry lips.

'Nina?' The sound was little more than a croak.

'Yes, Father, it's Nina.' I leaned over him, revulsion gone, eager to hear his words.

'You're back then?'

'Yes, I'm back.'

Back from Merve now.

He swallowed painfully, eyes losing focus again briefly.

'Shouldn't have left her — your mother. She needs your help, never could cope.' Even now there was an edge of cruelty in his voice.

I bit back an angry rejoinder.

'I'm here to do what I can,' I said.

There was a long silence. I thought he'd gone back to sleep, and jumped when he spoke again.

'It wasn't her fault, you know.' I strained nearer to hear him. 'I'm to blame for it.'

I wanted to batter him with a thousand questions, but I couldn't. An aura of potency still emanated from him, dominating me, making me inadequate.

Mother sat in the chair by his bed and laid her head on his arm, her shoulders shaking.

I started to speak, to make light of the comment he'd made.

'No — wait!' he interrupted me. He lifted his hand and awkwardly I took it. 'Try to forgive us — me — Nina. Try to forgive!'

A wave of pity, almost of love, engulfed me. Then his hand slipped from mine and he was asleep.

'Do you want to go, Mum?' I asked her.

'In a moment. Just give me a few minutes.' Her voice came muffled.

I walked round to the bottom of his bed, picked up

the clipboard of clinical notes which hung there, trying to make sense of the medical jargon:

'Severe lacerations to head and L. H. side of thorax. Operation successful. Recovery impeded by syphilitic debility.'

I hung the clipboard back onto the iron bed rail, not understanding what it meant, but somehow uneasy.

'Come on,' I was impatient to be out of there, my voice harsh.

'All right, dear, all right!' Mother looked bewildered, a little frightened. 'Although there's still ten minutes of visiting time.'

'There's no point in staying, he's asleep.' I stood by the door waiting, with my heart inexplicably pounding fast, painful within my ribcage, and the sour taste of vomit in my mouth.

I drove fast up the road towards home, wondering at my anger, at the panic that threatened to choke me. Mother sat quietly, blank-eyed, beside me. Looking at her, my anger softened.

'Try not to worry, medical science works miracles these days!' I tried to keep a note of optimism in my voice though, in fact, I felt little hope. Father was already wearing the mantle of death. Briefly, I wondered if by some ironic quirk of fate, Rashidi had been involved in the ambush, then pushed the thought away.

'Bloody Mau Mau!' Mother's voice in the silent car made me start. It was the first time I'd heard her swear.

I pictured the ambush, the troops fighting their way through the razor-sharp bamboo, making too much noise to be wary. The sudden swish of the slicing pangas, knifing through the darkness; the rancid smell of the terrorists mingling with the sweet odour of blood.

Afghanistan, too, had run red with blood spilled by the Mongol hordes led by Ghengis Khan . . .

Oh, dear God! I thought, the full horror of it coming

223

into my awareness, hurting me. And Father, down in the mud, amid the bamboo spikes, bleeding to death. Thank God someone had stayed, brought him back.

The medical notes burned into my memory: 'Severe lacerations to head . . . thorax . . .' But what the hell did the rest mean, 'recovery impeded by syphilitic debility'? Had father, that upright pillar of morality, contracted syphilis? If so, there were questions to be asked, spectres to be exorcised. I smiled grimly. Somehow, incongruously, the thought that Father had slipped from his rigid code made him more human. Then my hands on the steering wheel tightened. What about Kerri? Could I have inherited the disease and passed it on, unknowingly, to her? Oh God! God help us!

Mother spoke. 'You'll stay here, won't you, Nina? You can easily get a job in Nairobi.'

There was no way I could break the news now, or explain who Kerri was, what she was. The problems seemed insurmountable, unbearable, and I felt helpless and frightened. When we got home, I lay down on my bed and shut my eyes. I could cope better with Noeda's troubles . . .

* * * *

. . . It was while watching Bibicol at the carpet loom, her bright happy voice mingling in chatter and song with the other weavers, that I knew I must leave her, and soon. For in the weaving of threads, the blending and twisting of different colours to form the all-over intricate pattern it was as though I saw in parallel a kind of plan. How each life, a strand in the whole, be it silk or wool or coarse camel hair, was dependent upon the interaction of the other strands, and yet at the same time independent of them. The threads came together at the appropriate time and place to form the pattern, and then dispersed, each in its own direction, knotted off, alone.

224

Thus the loving, beautiful pattern that Bibicol and I had made through these years of our youth, had come to the time of knotting off. The warm, homespun fabric of her nature, no doubt would be woven into many different designs throughout her travels to high pasture and down again.

My own, silken perhaps, through the accident of birth, was more likely to tangle and snarl, by nature of its fabric. I was terrified by the thought of continuing without Bibicol, for I loved her dearly, and had come to rely upon her practicality in organising the more mundane needs of our journey, which included the purchasing and cooking of our food. This quite apart from the fact that she was the recipient of all my secrets, and the one person whom I could trust utterly. But in the same way that the voices in my waking dreams had instructed me to let go of Ibrahim, I knew that I had to relinquish my hold on Bibicol so that she could grow in her own way.

This decision having been made in my mind, I set about secretly preparing for my departure. This new secret person I had become, unable to share my intent with the one person who knew all my thoughts, grew more adept in the selection of items of food and equipment that would be needed when I left. It took some time to make these preparations since, in a way, I had to steal each article from my kind hosts, and I took, too, small amounts of money daily from the money belt which Bibicol had worn, to carry our small resources. I hated this theft, and only took what I felt were basic necessities to take me through — to, I knew not where.

Bibicol and Alexi followed me as I walked in the hot afternoon a few days before the tribe planned to continue its journey south. It was the dead hour of the day, when all the animals and birds in the bush that surrounded the camp seemed to keep silent conspiracy with their human counterparts at rest in the shade of

225

the tents. I could not lie still, for I knew that when Bibicol's family moved, then I, too, must travel, but in a different direction.

'Ho, Noeda! You walk too fast in this heat,' she panted, catching up after Alexi, leaping at me, had told of their arrival. 'Dear one, I have seen a quietness in you this past week that I cannot account for. Are you not happy here with my people?'

'I would be happier if I were free to be myself with them, Bibi. But how can I do that now? I am certain they would be hurt and angry at our deception, and from their talk I know they esteem Habib Amir greatly. It would put them in too much duplicity if they knew they were sheltering his daughter.'

'I wish now we had been open from the start!' Her eyes overbrimmed. 'I miss being close to you, Noeda! And while I love my sisters and the whole of my family, it will take time for me to build the relationship whereas, with you, well, we are as left hand and right hand, are we not?'

'The closeness will grow with them, I'm sure, and think how free you are here! Not forced into work, but willingly giving of your time and labour!'

She sighed and took my hand. 'How long, do you think, before we can tell them who you are?'

'That I don't know, but the time will come when they can be told. First I want to be sure that you will not be punished for your part in my escape!'

When the morning came for camp to be struck, I made my getaway in the pre-dawn bustle and confusion, and rode a short way off the track behind them to watch, through my heartache, as the gay caravan moved off towards Meshed. The sound of their voices eddied back to me on gusts of wind, interspersed with the occasional snarl of an ill-humoured camel, angry at being aroused so early in the day.

'Go with Allah, sweet Bibicol!' I whispered to the

226

wind, and knew that she, too, would ache with the pain of separation when she realised I was not with them. I had longed to hold her close the previous night and to explain to her why I must go, but I had known that she would insist on coming with me.

It wasn't until the last goat had disappeared from view that I looked around and found that Alexi lay half-concealed in the grasses behind me. I was sure he knew he was not supposed to be there for, instead of his usual exuberant greeting, he lay, flat on his stomach, as if wishing to sink into the hard earth, motionless except for his eyes which, whites showing, gazed at me apologetically.

'Alexi!' I said, despair, anger and love warring within me. 'What are you doing here? I put you safely in the basket strung from Bibicol's pack mule!' Alexi wriggled an inch or two forward, hopefully, and his tail, not totally in control, gave a small jerk.

I got down from my horse and knelt down in the dust beside him.

'Oh, Alexi! Did you know?'

He leapt up then and gave me such a greeting as though I had been away for months. I sighed. There was no course now but to take him with me. I dared not rejoin the caravan, for to see Bibicol again would completely dissolve my resolution. Picking him up, I mounted with him, and set off at as fast a pace as the horse would go, towards Merve. From there I knew not where to go, perhaps to Bactria, and then home to Kabul, if I dared.

Weary in the afternoon, I found a shaded place to stop, and we slid down. I pulled the reins forward over the horse's head and left them hanging loose to the ground, for all Habib Amir's animals had been trained to stand as if tethered when this was done.

I looked around for some wood to make a fire on which I could heat some water, but saw none near. I was too tired to search further, so I sat with my back resting against a rock, and drank some lukewarm water from my water-skin. It had a brackish taste and I took but one mouthful, then proffered some to Alexi and the horse.

I should eat, I thought, for it was many hours since my last meal, but the effort of getting up and fetching food from my saddlebag seemed too great. Instead, I lay down with my hat over my eyes and fell into jerking, uncomfortable sleep.

When I woke it was already dark, and a cold wind screeched across the plains. I wished I had taken the time to search for firewood earlier. When my eyes became more used to the blackness, I managed to find some scrubwood and dry grass which I piled up to light. Bibicol had always attended to our fires, and my hands were clumsy as I tried again and again to strike a spark from my flint. I succeeded at last in making a small flame, but this was soon extinguished by the wind.

'Oh, Alexi! I can't get it going!' I cried, after renewed attempts. Alexi sat, doleful and shivering. I stood up and walked away from the small pile of wood, knowing that if I stayed, my impatience would grow and I might kick the kindling to the far Hindu Kush.

I stood in the cold air and looked up at the sky.

'Oh, Bibicol! Dearest Bibi!'

The stars looked down at me, impassive. I went back and tried once more. This time, by standing between wind and fire, I managed to shield it enough for the bright orange flames to take hold. Alexi barked his approval.

'Come!' I told him. 'We must search for more fuel, or we spend a cold, cold night!'

He reluctantly followed me away from the warmth, and we gathered what small quantity we could, with our fire acting beacon for us in the darkness.

I heated water for a drink, and cut strips of dried meat for Alexi and myself to eat, but had not the energy or spirit to cook anything. In honesty, I had not even watched what Bibicol did, taking it for granted that hot food was there.

Alexi came and leaned his small body against me, feeling my need and, at this small gesture of love, I could no longer hold back my tears.

'Oh, Bibi, I miss you far more than I thought possible. I miss your warmth and companionship and your ableness!'

Alexi, overcome with anxiety, sent up a small howl, and tried to lick my face dry of tears. I hugged him to my chest.

'What answers can you give me? Can you advise which way we take, and the course we should set for the future?'

The night noises seemed loud and menacing. I laid Ibrahim's knife close by me and built up the fire as much as was possible to ward off any danger until morning rescued us.

We rode more slowly, Alexi and I, the following day, so as not to weary the horse. We stopped for a while in the afternoon, but I did not sleep, and after an hour or so rode on, as the sky was restless with small clouds. I wanted to reach the first foothills of the uplands that evening if I could, for I felt snow in the air, even though the sky was bright yet, with only small clouds acting as messengers of the coming bad weather beyond the horizon. At the top of a hill I stopped in the red-gold of the setting sun, and looked down across the plains. Far to the north the mountains stood in pale layers of blue against blue, and already the night mist was draping veils of opal grey round the foothills. Somewhere, quite close, a wild cat coughed its warning, and the birdsong grew intense as though each bird had a last, urgent message to impart before sleep.

I felt my solitariness acutely, seated there upon my fidgeting horse. I could see no way ahead, no clear path to tread. My hopes that Ibrahim would be the one to share my future were now dashed, for he and I were destined not to be woven together. Looking out into the disappearing glow of the sunset, I felt again the tug of my unconscious and knew that somehow, Ibrahim's thread and mine had tangled and caused a defect in the tapestry of our lives, a defect which might take many ages to unpick and weave again. Of no point now to try and retrieve the lost pattern by spinning a cocoon of silk around the memory.

It came to me then that my father, through the very conditioning of our system, had bound us all to his estate thus, from my mother down to the humblest stable boy. And we had seen no wrong in this. Indeed, I wondered, was it so wrong? Each person there played his or her role, and was provided for, in the majority of cases, happy to be part of the whole that was the estate. Was it not rather a question of free will that concerned me? How many there, given the choice to go or to stay, would have chosen to remain?

The case for women was not one for consideration in that context, either. Purdah kept women from any social activity. It was a requisite of the religious law everywhere, and was not questioned. I had, by my actions, flouted this law, and I knew with certainty that if I returned home, Habib Amir, for all his love of me, would be bound by this to punish me severely, and I would never be free again, even if my marriage to Shamlu Gabir were cancelled because of my conduct.

So I sat, isolated in the darkening day, with the despair of all women, everywhere, rising from somewhere deep in the darkness within me at the unfairness of our lot, and I cried aloud to the sky: 'Oh please tell me — why?'

And through the tears that now released themselves, I knew that no one could answer that question for me.

The days continued lonely, and the night times desolate. Without Alexi's small, warm body to keep me company, it would have taken very little to make me turn back, but I continued at good speed, keeping off the track wherever possible and, skirting to the east of Merve, I joined the trade route which went through to Bactria and from there on to Samarkand and Kunduz. I was faced with a long ride across part of the vast Turkoman Steppe which stretched, so I had been told, far to the sea called Caspian in the path of the setting sun, and to the north of the Elburz Mountains. I was doubly glad that I had thought to include heavy sheepskin leggings and a cloak amongst the items I had taken from Bibicol's family for, shortly after passing by Merva, Alexi and I, emerging before dawn from our camping place, found ourselves in a cold, blue, wind-whipped world. The snow had fallen overnight, early this year, and it already mantled the mountains ahead of us. These mountains appeared to me higher than any I had ever seen, and the prospect of the months ahead filled me with apprehension. I spurred my horse on, hoping to make as much progress towards Bactria as I could before the passes became blocked.

By noon that same day the trail became icy and treacherous, and Alexi shivered in my arms. In the half-hour before darkness came upon us, we found a stone hut half hidden in rocks, its flat mud-covered roof already taking the sheen of frost in the fast cooling air. I approached diffidently, not sure of a welcome in this bleak place, but no answer came to my knock and the door opened at my push. Inside it was empty, save for piled straw in one corner and a crude cooking hearth of heavy stones. It mattered not. I led my horse in through the low doorway, his shoulders missing the lintel by a mere hand's-width, and unsaddled him in the somewhat cramped space.

'There, my good companion!' I said, after I had rubbed him dry of sweat with straw, and thrown the blanket across him. 'You may share our quarters with us, for I fear the night will turn bitter, and you have served me too well to risk losing you through greed for space!'

By this time I had learned the necessity of gathering firewood before doing anything else, so Alexi and I set off on our nightly quest, and found to our joy that stacked behind the hut was a large pile of cut wood. I wondered who had lived in this wild and lonely place. Obviously someone who intended to return, for a long time had been spent in the gathering and chopping of fuel. Jubilant, I carried a goodly amount into the hut and got a fire going quickly. I felt myself in great luxury, having a roof and walls around me after so long spent sleeping in the open.

When I opened the door next morning, the snow fell inwards. I could not believe that such an enormous blanket of whiteness had fallen thus, without my hearing it. Alexi could not comprehend the strange new substance, and sniffed at it suspiciously.

There was no way in which we could get through the high drifts that blocked the track as far as I could see. I struggled, waist-deep, to the higher bank at the back of the hut, to find that I could not see even the way we came, so I slithered down the steep bank again, back into the hut, and warmed myself at the fire. It looked impossible for us to move either backwards to Merve, or forward to Bactria. The snow was early and unexpected, and I thought back with amazement to the short distance past when I had been watching Bibicol play with Fatimettou in the blazing heat of the dust-laden plains. And, thinking of Bibicol, my heart was heavy with loneliness for her sweet companionship, for our shared laughter and for the tribulations we had faced together.

The days stretched into a week, and I was kept captive by more falls of snow. Unable even to leave the hut without scraping a narrow passage around the outer walls to get to the woodpile, I spent most of my days in digging this pathway and bringing the fuel in for our precious fire. The hut became acrid with the smell of urine and droppings, for Alexi and the horse could, of course, not go outside. This smell, together with the smoke from the wet wood, caused my eyes to stream constantly.

My water supply soon ran out, so I melted snow in my cooking pot over the flames for drinking, and as the days passed with no break in the weather, began to cut our food to the barest minimum.

Towards the end of the second week, I was down to the last strips of dried meat — all else was gone. I became weak, and slept most of the time. Collecting the wood was a nightmare, and had more snow fallen to block my path, I would not have had the strength to move it.

Alexi's ribs showed, sharp, and the horse, too, became hollow and gaunt. As I became weaker, I lost the will to care what happened to us. My stomach cramped with hunger, and my head ached unendingly.

'Alexi!' I moved my hand, which felt too heavy to lift, to touch his quivering body. 'If we must die thus, let it be quick.' Alexi could not move, but valiantly tried to wag his tail. My hand dropped down, and so near to death were we, that I remember no more.

THIRTEEN

'Michael's coming over this evening.' Mother turned from the telephone, some time later.

'Who's Michael, for goodness' sake?' I didn't want to see anyone, or have to make conversation.

'William's aide, Captain Michael Blake.' She poured herself a brandy, added a small splash of water. 'He's been marvellous! So helpful over the past week.'

I looked at her and swallowed my protest. She was so frail, lost somehow, and I didn't know her at all.

'Help yourself to a drink, Nina. I suppose you're old enough now?' She frowned. 'What are you? Eighteen? Or is it nineteen?'

'Nearly eighteen.' It was eleven months until my birthday, but what did it matter? I poured a glass of orange juice.

'Cheers!' We contemplated each other over our glasses.

'I hope you'll stay . . .'

'What's he like, this Captain Blake?'

We spoke together, awkward in the confinement of the room, like strangers.

'Sorry, Mum, what did you say?'

Her empty glass rattled as she put it down. She sighed. 'It's just . . . oh, I don't know. William could die; you're away; even old Melika has deserted me . . .' The brandy bottle clinked again against her glass.

I knew the feeling of aloneness only too well.

'Come on, don't be so pessimistic! I'm here; Father's in good hands! As for Melika — well, I miss her as much as you do! I tell you what — tomorrow I'll write to her in Uganda, ask her what's happening, when she's coming back.'

She managed a small smile.

By the time Captain Blake was due she'd downed six brandies. I had watched anxiously, trying to coax her to eat more than a mouthful of dinner. She'd become quite coquettish, changing into fresh clothes, putting on make-up and making an attempt to pin up her hair. My eyes prickled as she stood leaning against the sitting-room door, obviously posing, so thin that the dress engulfed her, with lipstick slightly smeared over her lip-line.

'You look great, Mum!' I took her hand, made her turn around. 'That's the spirit!' I looked down at my own soiled clothes, still smelling of wood-smoke from the train.

'I'd better change, too.'

I wondered what I could put on, aware of my lack of choice, then rummaged in my suitcase and brought out a faded dress, and while the houseboy ironed it, washed and tried to tidy myself up.

My reflection in the bathroom mirror stopped me short. I hadn't really looked at myself for a year, and I was startled by the stranger staring back at me, arms raised to her hair.

I was tanned a deep golden brown from working in the shamba, my dark hair bleached into auburn and dark russet. My eyes seemed huge, shadowed slightly with tiredness, and my breasts were full and firm, pulled upwards by my raised arms.

Good grief! I'm a woman — not a girl any longer! I stared into my brown eyes, and saw that they were the colour of sweet sherry, flecked with small specks of gold.

Are you really me? I wondered. Do I really look so like Noeda? I had become accustomed to the old image of Nina Anderson, small and skinny with sallow skin and lank hair. This new vibrant reflection needed time for assimilation, solitude for familiarisation. I smiled at myself and my heart lurched as I saw Kerri reflected there and realised that she, too, was in my image. I pressed my cheek against the coolness of the mirror. Kerri! Kerri! Oh, how I love you!

Then my mood suddenly darkened as the word 'syphilis' wrote itself against my closed eyelids. I picked up the East African Standard, focusing my thoughts on the words, trying to stop the panic that rose, threatening to engulf me altogether.

'The Mau Mau situation worsens,' the printed words took shape. 'Armed Askari are patrolling some of the farms, but this is an almost impossible task due to the vastness of the area. However, the compulsory call-up of all European men over sixteen for service in the Police Reserve or Kenya Regiment, should help matters. Great things, too, are expected from the African "Specials" and the Home Guard and these brave men should set an example to those loyal Kikuyus. Already many Meru and Wakamba tribesmen are serving.' I put the paper down, puzzled by its blandness.

The tension everywhere was growing, and the murders which had always happened to 'other people', never oneself, were no longer a remote possibility. Pistols and revolvers of all sorts were worn strapped to waistbands, by men and women alike. I found the gun which father had taught me to shoot, and carried it, albeit reluctantly, everywhere I went. Vainly I tried to get Mother to try again, but she couldn't or wouldn't, and I had to be content with insisting that she at least had a small pistol strapped to her belt.

'The Lancashire Fusiliers will be arriving shortly,' the newspaper article continued. 'They will be followed by the Inniskillings, The Devons and The Black Watch. It is understood that the RAF will bring bombers, with which to blast the terrorists out of the Abadare forests.'

My flesh chilled — what if Rashidi were there, cowering and cold in the target area? How could they hope to win, those dark and desperate men? The pressures were beginning to tell on them, even now. More and more tired and hungry terrorists surrendered daily, and were immediately sent to 'interrogation' centres. I didn't want to imagine the methods used by the interrogators.

Later that evening Michael Blake arrived. He was fair-haired, fresh-skinned, very British, smart to perfection in his khaki uniform, and meticulously correct in his manners. Embarrassed, I watched Mother, clumsy in her efforts to flirt with him, grotesque in her make-up with her little-girl voice.

Oh, stop it, please stop, I entreated silently. She turned to me, glass in hand, spilling its contents.

'Isn't Captain Blake a handsome young man, Nina?' Her voice was unnaturally high.

'It's the uniform, Mother. It makes them all look handsome.' I took her glass away, put it on the sideboard. She frowned at me, then laughed.

'Oh dear, does my daughter disapprove of me drinking?'

'No, of course not! I just don't like getting splashed!'

Keep it light, I thought. She's just about at the end of her tether.

Michael caught my eye, and smiled. 'Doesn't Mrs Anderson look good tonight? She's stood up to the worry so well, you know.'

Realising he was trying to tell me he understood, I found myself flushing, caught out. I was acutely aware of my worn dress, the scuffed shoes, and I resented him for making me feel ashamed of myself, of Mother.

'How about some music?' I said. The battered old radiogram still stood in the corner of the room. I picked through the records — *Oklahoma, Annie Get Your Gun, Kismet;* Bing Crosby, Dinah Shore. The music was

237

scratchy, the sound tinny, but it filled the awkward corners, the silences.

Mother stood up. 'A dance, Michael?'

He rose, gallant, and took her in his arms in the cramped sitting-room. I pulled the coffee table out of the way.

The telephone jangled, breaking into the music. I knew what it would be before I picked up the receiver.

'Yes, this is the Anderson household, I'm his daughter . . .'

Mother snatched the phone from me. 'I'm Mrs Anderson, what's wrong? When? Why wasn't I called? Why didn't you call me?' Her voice rose hysterically. Michael took the phone, spoke into it quietly as I led her away, held her close to me as she wept, and let her drum her fists against my breast — my pain less than hers.

It was so sudden, so impersonal somehow as if, in the ringing of the telephone bell, Father was gone, extinguished. And I'd lost my chance to grow in understanding of this strange and angry man. I couldn't grieve for him, but felt aggrieved as if he'd gone on purpose, shutting the door against me. Closing me away, as he had always done. There had been a moment in the hospital when we might have reached out to each other, made contact. Now the chance was gone.

The funeral was organised by the army, orchestrated by Michael. I steered Mother through it; forgave her the bolstering brandy; kept her sober enough to stand by the graveside.

I watched the Union-Jack-draped coffin being lowered. I felt detached from it, as though it were someone else's father being planted there in the rich, red murram earth of Kenya. Mother's hand on my arm tightened, her nails biting sharp into my flesh. I winced and put my other hand over hers, loosening the grip, holding her fingers tightly with my own.

Michael, standing to attention on her other side, turned as she swayed and put his arm around her so that, perforce, the back of his wrist pressed against me. I shifted slightly, away from the contact, even while realising he was unaware.

A small stone dislodged and rattled onto the coffin as the flag came upwards, the noise loud and irreverent in the silence. A breeze started up, rustling the long thin leaves of the gum trees along the edge of the cemetery. I felt as remote as if I were witnessing the burial of some stranger.

But how well did I know Habib Amir, anyway? I thought I'd known him well, and yet — why was my mother so bitter, so isolated in the confines of the women's quarters, stifled by purdah? There was surely some reason for her coldness towards me. But then, perhaps theirs was a marriage of convenience, as mine would have been with Shamlu Gadir. Who knows what secret unhappiness she hid beneath the chadri . . .

Mother's startled jump was echoed by my own, bringing me back to the present as the rifles fired a salute. As we left the grave to go, Michael's eyes met mine above Mother's head, and he smiled a brief, correct smile of condolence and compassion.

Yes, you are a nice man, I thought.

I sent a letter to Melika, then wrote to the store owner at Mikendeni who I knew could read, asking him to let Leah know what had happened, and to tell her not to expect me back for at least a fortnight. Leah and Mirriamu would care for Kerri, I had no worries on that score. She was, after all, part of their family.

My days were busy, occupied with sorting out Father's accounts, seeing his solicitors and liaising with Captain Blake about the army house that was Mother's home.

'There's no hurry to move,' he told me. 'Mrs Anderson can continue to live there for at least six months until she sorts things out.'

239

'And afterwards?' I sighed. 'She's been here so long now, it's bound to be an upheaval.'

'Yes, but after a few months the shock of his death will lessen. Then maybe she can look for somewhere else, something to buy. There'll be a good pension, and his life insurance.'

'That's one less worry!' I wanted to see her settled, happy. My mind flicked to Kerri, wondering how soon I could introduce her into Mother's life. Not yet! No, certainly not yet!

Against her protestations, I cleared out Father's clothes, giving them away to the Langata Mission; burnt his accumulation of papers, and changed the rooms around, trying to lessen his presence in the house without erasing it altogether. Mother wouldn't talk about his death, shutting it from her mind, speaking as though he'd return. She was drinking heavily yet denied it shrilly when I tried gently to dissuade her. I found half-filled glasses hidden in the drawers of her dressing-table, empty bottles stashed behind the wardrobe, and I knew then that something must be done to help her. Desperate, I went into Nairobi to see the doctor, taking my chance of an interview without an appointment.

As I crossed Delamere Avenue to go to the surgery, I collided with a bearded man.

'Sorry,' I said, automatically.

'Nina?' His amber eyes sparkled above the beard.

'Paul! I wouldn't have recognised you!'

Funny how beards are a different texture of hair; the thought came irrelevantly into my head. In a moment of stillness and clarity I saw specific things about him I'd not seen before — the line of his brow, wide and clear above his dark brown eyes; a small scar on one cheekbone, white against his tan; his slender surgeon's fingers; his eyelashes, long as any girl's but without lessening in any way his masculinity.

240

'This is Merryl,' he said.

For the first time I noticed the woman at his side. Blonde, smart in khaki trousers and a white short-sleeved shirt.

'I met Nina in Mombasa,' he said, and she smiled.

'I can see you've been at the coast — that super tan!' Her hand on the strap of her shoulder bag had long red nails, a small diamond ring. I swallowed.

'Yes. Well, I had to come home. My father's just died.' It sounded bald, unfeeling.

Paul's smile went. 'Sorry to hear that! Are you okay? And the baby — Kerri? She must be nearly a year old now!'

'I left her . . . down in Mombasa. It wasn't the right time to bring her here.'

A frown flickered across his face. 'You mean, you still haven't told your mother?'

'No — not yet. And she's . . . she's not well enough right now.'

He looked at his watch. 'We're going to have to rush off. Give me a ring and we'll meet for a coffee or lunch — okay?' He handed me a card with his telephone number printed upon it. Blue upon white.

'Yes.' I put the card in my pocket, feeling put down. 'Yes, I'll do that.' I turned and watched as he took Merryl's arm and guided her across the road towards the New Stanley Hotel.

Who the hell is she? Wife, girlfriend — what?

My cheeks flamed with a mixture of anger, shame and disappointment. How stupid I'd been, building so much into the few encounters we'd had in Mombasa. I felt unsophisticated in my well-washed cotton dress against Merryl's obviously expensive clothes, her high heels; and stared blindly into a shop window full of bathroom accessories, fighting the tears that burned at the back of my eyes.

Oh, damn you, Paul! Damn you!

I realised angrily that once more I felt betrayed, when there was nothing for him to betray but my own imagined hopes.

I must deal with Mother — she's the important one right now. And, following that thought, the word 'syphilis' edged its way into my consciousness again. No, not yet, I can't cope with that yet! I knew I'd have to ask the questions sooner or later, wondered how I'd set about finding the answers. Asking the family doctor could prove embarrassing, and yet he would, surely, know the full history?

I needed to open up the subject with Mother, too, but knew I'd have to choose my moment, word the questions with great care, so as not to either shock her by revealing unknown truths, or frighten her into tight-lipped silence.

Perhaps I will ring Paul, meet him and ask the questions, hypothetically! But I knew I couldn't. Couldn't bear the thought that he'd guessed how I felt; that he regarded me as some moonstruck teenager with a crush on him.

Doctor Gordon listened silently as I fumbled for the right words. 'It's Mother. I'm really worried about her!'

'In what way? She's bound to be suffering from shock over your father's death, you know.'

'Yes, I realise that, but she's drinking — she does it all the time!'

He frowned. 'Surely it's nothing to worry about? I could give her tranquillisers if you think that'd help. Otherwise a drink or two will have the same effect. Numbing her pain, so to speak.'

'No,' I told him, 'it's more than that. She's becoming secretive, hiding the bottles, keeping drinks all over the house. And I can't get her to eat.'

'Hmm! I see. Yes, well that *is* a bit worrying. Is she losing weight?'

I sighed, thinking of her sharp shoulder blades, her stick-like legs. 'Drastically! Haven't you seen her recently?'

'No.' He got up and went to the door. 'Bring in Mrs Anderson's notes, will you?' he said to his receptionist.

'Perhaps I'd better come out and see her. I presume it'd be difficult to persuade her to come to the surgery?'

'Yes, she's very touchy — flies at me if I even suggest that she's drinking too much.' My tension relaxed as I realised he was taking the problem seriously.

'All right, Nina, leave it with me. I'll make a routine visit tomorrow. I'll tell her it's normal after there's been a death in the family.'

I hesitated. 'There was something else, Doctor.'

'Yes?'

I wondered how to ask. 'It's just a hypothetical question really. Um — if a man's had venereal disease in the past could it . . . could it cause difficulties in later life?'

His look was keen upon my face.

'Why? Why do you ask that?'

I flushed. 'I just heard it somewhere, I guess. That it could affect someone's recovery if they were ill or hurt, years later.'

'Yes,' he said, and his hand touched mine across the desk briefly, knowing. 'Yes, Nina, it could — and did.'

Anxiety made my voice hoarse. 'What about heredity?'

He smiled. 'In this case it doesn't apply!'

'You mean, I was already born?'

'Yes, you were already three years old.'

'So there's no chance of me passing it on to my . . . to any children I might have?'

'None whatsoever!'

I sighed my relief. 'But what about Mother?'

'That's another story! Part of the reason why I'm concerned now.'

243

There were still so many questions unanswered, burning my gullet with their repression, but there was no more to be learnt from him, he'd already given me more than I'd expected, shocked me into the present.

Next morning I paced the sitting-room, stopping to look out of the window each time I passed it.

Outside in the garden canna-lilies blazed, bright flames of colour against the deep purple of their leaves. The garden boy, Kimau, stooped over the flower-beds, weeding. Through the open window I could hear his high-pitched singing, the Kikuyu words strange and unknown, the sound merging with the cooing of ring-neck doves on the roof above me.

'What are you looking at?' Mother had come into the room silently behind me.

'Just watching Kimau.'

'He's a lazy so-and-so,' she said. 'William keeps saying he'll have to go.'

'Are you going to get dressed, Mum?'

Her head turned towards me, eyes wary. 'Why? Why should I? What's there to get dressed for — what's the point?'

I wondered if she'd already had a drink.

The doctor's car turned into the gateway, and I found my hands shaking, wondering how she'd take his visit.

His voice preceded him into the room: 'I was just passing, Mrs Anderson! Thought I'd pop in to see how you all are.'

She looked flustered, clutching at the neck of her dressing-gown, her hand flying to her hair in an attempt to tidy it.

'Oh dear, Doctor Gordon, I do wish you'd phoned. We're . . . we're fine! Aren't we, Nina?' Her movements were nervous, bird-like. 'I'll just go and get dressed.'

'There's no need for that — I'm only staying a moment or two.'

He took her arm, guided her to the sofa. 'Sit down, please, and let's just have a short chat.'

Her hands were still fluttering, plucking at her dressing-gown. I wanted to hold her, to tell him to leave — forget it.

'Would you like coffee?' I asked.

'Thank you, that'd be lovely!' He smiled at Mother. 'Are you managing to sleep all right?'

She nodded.

'I can let you have some mild sleeping tablets if you want them.' He paused. 'Or perhaps you'd rather just have a small nightcap of brandy?'

'Sometimes I have a small one,' she answered, her eyes evasive. I could see her shrinking away from him on the sofa.

His eyes met mine.

What value the twelve pieces of silver for betraying her? I thought bitterly, and looked away. Why the hell shouldn't she have a drink when she wants it? It's the only thing she's got left, for heaven's sake!

The sun shone outside the window, caring nothing for her pain, for my Judas action. A small golden weaverbird landed on the striped yellow and green leaves of a croton bush, looking exotic somehow, as if it were posing upon the complimentary colours of the plant.

Melika's words of two years before came into my mind:

'I remember when I first came to Memsahib. She was happy then — and pretty, too . . . singing at her work and with many friends.'

I wondered again what had happened to change her so, and by what accident of birth I had been born to them. Would Kerri some day, some place, stand with arms folded, old for her age, and ask the same questions?

I prayed that our relationship would be stronger,

closer than my own had been with my mother, that she wouldn't tread the steps of her life alone.

The garden blurred, became harsher, rock and scrub replacing the flower-beds, as I escaped from the present . . .

* * * *

. . . Through the flickering light from the fire I saw the man move about the hut. My eyelids were heavy and I had difficulty in staying awake. I tried to speak but my lips were dry and no sound came. I didn't know where I was, or how I came to be there. The blackness came upon me again, and several times, I believe, I came to awareness and then sank back. The effort required to concentrate upon who I was and why, was great, so great that the periods of oblivion came as a relief.

'Come,' the man said, his hand beneath my head, lifting it, 'try to drink.'

I felt the roughness of a bowl against my lips and, parting them, let the coolness of water slip through into my parched mouth. I tried to focus my eyes, but the images blurred, doubled and grew grey.

Something whimpered at my side. My eyes all of a sudden flew wide open at this sound, and my drifting senses halted, and alerted.

'Alexi?' I said, the sound hoarse to my ears.

'Aha! young one, you come back to this world!' The man lifted my head once more. 'A little more water, for I don't know how long you have lain so, without sustenance. Judging by your state, it must be some few days!'

I drank obediently. 'Alexi?' I questioned.

'Yes, the animal is alive, but only just. Here, give me your hand, I will place it upon him that you may feel for yourself.' Alexi's small body felt limp beneath my fingers, but he was breathing and his tongue came out to lick my hand.

246

'The horse?'

'Alas, he has, I'm afraid, succumbed to the cold and lack of food. My men and I took him outside, for the smell was strong.'

Tears welled into my eyes at this news, for the stallion and I had travelled far together. The man wiped my eyes, his hand gentle.

'Stay! As fast as I pour water into your mouth, you let it flow outward once more through those large eyes!'

His skin was fair, as was the hair which showed below his hat, and his eyes were strangely light, a blue-green shade which I had never seen before.

'Who are you?' I asked, trying to raise myself, the better to see him.

'I am Malek,' he replied, 'Malek Mirza, and I am from Kalash in the valley called Rumur, high in the mountains of the Hindu Kush.'

'I have not seen one of your colouring before now.'

'There are many fair-skinned amongst the Kafir tribe — Alexander and his men rested along the Brumboret River valley, where lies Kalash, for many years and left behind a heritage of light eyes and hair.'

I lost count of the hours we spent in the hut while Malek nursed me gently back to strength. It was not until several days later that I was awake enough to realise that I was covered with clean furs and that beneath the furs I no longer wore my breeches and jacket, but a long shirt of some finely woven woollen material.

Embarrassed, I looked at Malek, in realisation that it was he who had stripped and cleansed me thus.

'How long were you here before I awoke?' I asked.

'About three days only,' he replied, 'but I think you had been asleep for a good few days before that.'

'Were you alone?'

He looked at me. 'No, I travelled with a hunting

247

party of men. They have gone ahead now to Karainau to get help, for we feared you might die.'

'So there was no woman?'

'No.' His answer was short, and he glanced at me briefly. 'Do not fear, no one took advantage of your weakness!' I thought I saw the glimmer of humour in those strange eyes. 'And it was I who changed and cleaned you, for you were in a desperate state when I arrived. I have sisters of my own, girl, so don't feel ashamed. It was a task which had to be performed for, by Allah, between you and the droppings of your animals, the stench in here was worse than a winter goat-pen!'

'I thank you for taking so much care of me,' I said. 'What have you done with my clothes?'

'All but the boots and hat, I buried with your horse. They were not fit for wearing, and I had no means of cleansing them. Don't worry, I have spare clothes with which to cover your modesty, and my companions will bring more suitable woman's clothing when they return.'

'Oh, no!'

'Why "Oh no!"? What reason for you to travel in man's clothing? And what do you here alone, so far from others at this dire time of year?'

'Oh, please, I cannot tell you now,' I pleaded, 'but I give my word that I will explain when I am well enough to travel onward.'

'Where are you going?'

'I do not care, so long as it is away from Kabul or Merve.'

'Then, please, allow me to take you to Kalash with my hunting party. There you may rest safely from whatever it is that pursues you, and regain your strength. Certainly, you are not fit enough to travel alone at this time.'

I smiled at him. 'Thank you, Malek, I will take up

248

your offer. It will be good to have company and help, for I am sorely tired in heart and body.'

'Your name?'

'Call me, for now, Nadir — that will suffice!'

He asked no more, and my admiration grew for this great gentle man as he cooked and coaxed me into eating until at last I was strong enough to walk.

Alexi, too, grew well again and it was with joy that I watched his spirit grow a little more each day. He seemed bigger, in spite of his long days of deprivation, and his legs had lengthened so that while he was still weak, he wobbled on them. But soon he was bounding in and out of the door and sliding on the now-melting snow. I stood, watching, holding onto the doorway, and decided to try to go by myself to the back of the hut to relieve myself. Great had been my awkwardness at having to void into the large earthenware pot that Malek discreetly provided for me. As I slowly came back, one hand against the wall of the hut to steady myself, Malek stood there to greet me.

'You have done well — but do not rush too fast, lest you fall!'

'Would I could wash my hair,' I said, conscious of my unkempt appearance, dishevelled and wrapped in the fur bedcover.

He heated water and then, wrapping me even more securely, took me outside and carefully washed my head, until I felt clean again.

'Come, do not get cold,' he said, and placing me near the fire, rubbed my hair dry with a clean cloth from his bedroll.

I sat hypnotised by the gentle massaging of my head and the warmth of the fire, content to let myself live in that moment, and determinedly shut the doors of my mind against the memories that knocked.

I handed him a bone comb from my small pile of possessions, and once my hair was dry he sat behind

249

me and combed it free of knots until it sizzled and crackled in competition with the fire. I had never known a man so gentle, nor one who would be prepared to care for a woman in the way he had looked after me. I leaned back against him, sleepy and warm.

'Thank you, Malek — no one has done that for me for a long, long while!'

'Shh, Nadir, it gives me pleasure to see you smile and grow well again,' he said, and I reached back to his head behind me and stroked his face.

'Such a soft skin — most Afghans have hard, harsh bristles!'

'How would you know that? You are no more than a child!' he laughed.

'Not so much a child!' I replied, and drew his hand to rest upon my breast. 'See, I have good breasts, not the small berries that very young girls have!'

'I know, I know!' he said, and his fingers trembled upon my nipple. He drew his hand away, and I felt naked.

'Why do you move away? Am I so unattractive?' I asked, for I needed to be told.

'It is because you are so attractive to me that I do so,' he replied, 'for I do not want to take you in your vulnerability.'

And I, overcome with desire to be held close, to be loved and comforted, knelt up and turned towards him, drawing off the garments that I wore.

'Just touch me — hold me, for I need you so!' I whispered, husky-voiced.

My breasts upthrust thus, so close to his face, he could not resist them, but gently kissed first one, then the other, caressing my naked back and buttocks until I almost swooned for him, and then with a cry he laid me down upon the furs and entered my eager citadel. And, as I wept, he wept, with joy and pain and gladness and remorse, and I covered our bodies over with the

250

sensuous furs of mountain fox and bear until we were warmed and his desire rekindled again and again.

Later I sat up in the soft light of the fire and traced my fingers down his backbone. His skin was honey-brown, golden in the light of the fire, against my darker hue, and his hair curled slightly at the nape of his neck. I leaned over and kissed the place where it formed a small whorl, and then lay back and shut my eyes. Against the darkness of my lids I saw Rsul's face, and I was filled with silent weeping.

Beside me Malek stirred and turned over, and Alexi, the other side, stretched and grunted. I lay wide-eyed, puzzling, then sat up and, shivering, put more wood on the fire. My illness has left me weak-headed, I thought. And here I was with Malek, gentle Malek, surrendering to him willingly the virginity which I had guarded so jealously from Ibrahim. Did it matter? I wondered. It mattered more now to be loved, for I had grown lonely. Dear Malek, with the gentle, caring hands and selfless generosity of spirit! I curled close against him and fell asleep in the comfort of that embrace . . .

* * * *

. . . The banging of a door brought me jolting back into the present.

Who on earth is this new man who has rescued Noeda? I wondered, feeling strangely ill at ease. Had she so soon forgotten Ibrahim? Guiltily, I realised that I had all too quickly responded to Paul, easing Rashidi from my mind.

But Malek?

'No, Noeda,' I said inwardly, 'I'm not sure about this new development.' Michael came into my thoughts then, but I dismissed him quickly. 'Perhaps I'm reading too much into all this, trying to make similarities where they don't exist!' I shook my head, puzzled and somewhat fearful that I should feel such deep concern for someone who, surely, was just a figment of my imagination.

FOURTEEN

The telephone line to Mikendeni crackled and hissed and I could hardly hear what the store-keeper was saying.

'Where is she then?' I asked when he told me Leah wasn't in Mikendeni. 'Has she gone into Mombasa so late? It's nearly curfew time!'

His answer was lost in a burst of static.

'I can't hear you!' I shouted, frustration making my voice shrill.

'She's gone, and Mirriamu, too. There was a letter . . . some sort of trouble . . .'

'What trouble? And where has she gone? And the children? Have they gone, too?'

Kerri!

'They went a few days ago . . . in a great hurry . . . There was some big shauri — trouble . . .' The line went dead.

'Oh, hell!' I dialled repeatedly without success.

Now what?

Trouble could surely only mean Rashidi, but why on earth hadn't they contacted me somehow? I stood by the telephone indecisively, panic escalating as I thought of Kerri and the permutations of the word 'trouble'. The Ruark family, farming in a remote part of the country, had just been slaughtered horrifically. The Mau Mau had not spared any of them — mother, father and small child, slashing them to death with an unbelievable viciousness.

Oh, Kerri! Pray God, oh, pray God she's safe!

I moved away from the phone, then back again. I could think of no one to ask for help, and unless I eventually spoke to the store-keeper again, no one who would give me even basic information.

After futile attempts to reach the Mikendeni number, the telephone exchange informed me that the lines were down, and that they had no idea of how long it would take for repairs to be made.

I roamed the house, packed my belongings, unpacked them again — indecisive and sleepless, hearing Mother cry out in her sleep — painfully aware of her need for me to be there, worried, too, about leaving her alone and in danger.

The rooms felt hot, trapping me, and I went out into the cool darkness of the verandah. The air there was heavy scented with the perfume of moonflowers and, in the star-shimmer, the bush, with its huge, white, trumpet-shaped blooms, seemed alive — quivering and dancing; the motion caused by many large silver-winged moths which hovered and probed for nectar.

How could a night so calm, so silvered and beautiful be full of such fear, such danger? Even now, beyond the hedge, there might be eyes watching, waiting. I shivered and went back into the house, locking the door behind me.

Perhaps it was the very act of turning the key that made me think of law and order and, following that thought, came one possible solution:

'I'll write to the District Commissioner in Mombasa — ask him how I can find Leah and Mirriamu!' I didn't recognise, in my anxiety, that this might put them into danger.

Mother was still asleep when I got back from the post box next day. Her breathing was rough, and her lips had a bluish tinge around them that worried me.

I shook her gently trying to wake her. Her eyelids fluttered then closed again. I called Doctor Gordon who came to the house at once, took one look and phoned the hospital.

*

'Nina?' Her voice was low. I crossed from the chair where I'd been sitting at the window of the side ward. 'Tell them to go away!' Her thin hands beat against the air.

'There's no one here but me!' I caught hold of the flailing hands, held them both in mine.

'Oh, yes there is! They're all here . . . and those . . . creatures!' Her eyes were wide and frightened and she began to shake uncontrollably. I let go of her hands and rang the bell.

'Fetch the doctor, please!' I asked the nurse who came in response.

'There's no need, you know.' Her starched apron crackled as she took Mother's wrist, feeling the pulse. 'This is quite normal — withdrawal symptoms. She's craving alchohol.'

Was this what they called DT's? This trembling fear, the jumble of meaningless words that now tumbled from her lips?

'I'd still like to see the doctor, please.'

The nurse shot me a look of disapproval and went, silent on rubber-soled shoes, returning a short while later to fetch me.

'Mrs Anderson's doctor will see you,' she said, leading me to an office.

My heart, for one painful moment, halted in its rhythm as the nurse opened the door and I saw who was behind the desk. My legs were leaden, refusing to propel me across the floor. I looked down, blinking, afraid that he might see the tears that had started to my eyes.

'Nina!' He stood up, came round the desk towards me and I, like an idiot, stood there trembling.

'I didn't make the connection, hadn't any idea she was your mother!'

I could not answer, still standing with my eyes averted.

'Come on!' He put his arms around me, and my shoulders rounded into their protection, my head coming down against his chest. He smelled of open air, of trees and grass — not of soap and water and surgical spirit as I would have expected if I had been capable of coherent thought.

He was stroking my hair, his other arm holding me close.

'Come on,' he said again, 'cry if you want to — God knows, you've had enough to make you weep!'

I relaxed against him, my tears soaking his shirt, and when they stopped, I didn't want to leave the safety of his arms. He gently disentangled himself, led me to a chair and passed me a box of tissues.

Rsul had taken off my boots and gently massaged my aching feet and legs on the track to Merve . . .

'Better?'

He sat on the edge of the desk, one leg swinging. I saw he'd shaved off the beard again, and his jawline was strong and firm.

'I like you better without the beard!' I said.

'Yes — it was too hot, too uncomfortable!' He rasped his fingers over his chin reflectively. 'What happened? I thought you were going to ring me?'

'So much has been happening, and Mother . . .'

His face straightened and, as if playing for time, he got off the desk and walked round it to sit in his chair.

'She's quite ill. You know that, don't you?'

'Yes, obviously I do. But how ill? What sort of period are we talking about?' Worry over Kerri pushed its way treacherously to the front of my mind.

'I can't give you any sort of prognosis yet.' Paul leaned back. 'She's got to have a lot of tests before we can begin to diagnose and start treatment.'

'I can tell you exactly what's wrong!' I jumped up and walked to the window.

Outside in the hospital grounds the garden boys

tood, swinging their ki-pangas, the long straight pieces
of metal that they used to cut the grass, backwards and
forwards, backwards and forwards. The sound of their
lazy laughter came in with the warm air.

'Mother's an alcoholic, that's what's wrong with
her!'

'Yes, Doctor Gordon told me that. But the alcohol-
ism is a result, not a cause. I want to go a bit deeper
than that, find out why, how long, and so on. It's not
something that we can just switch off!'

I sat down again, tired now. 'The reasons were
here — always have been — despair, loneliness, guilt.
Father wasn't easy to live with.'

She felt unloved, *was* unloved, I thought.

There was silence for a moment then, with an abrupt
movement, he sat upright, picked up a pen and played
with it, turning it end-over-end, making a sharp clicking noise on the desk top.

'Has Doctor Gordon told you anything else?' he
asked.

'You mean the . . . um, the venereal disease?'

'Yes. It affected her, Nina, both mentally and
physically.'

The paper handkerchief between my fingers shredded and scattered small pieces of white over my skirt
and onto the floor. I bent down to pick them up.

'I only found out about it recently — since Father
died.' My voice came muffled from below the desk. 'I
was afraid for Kerri.' Guilt filled me again. Guilt at
the knowledge that my main reaction had been fear for
Kerri, not concern for Mother.

'Understandable.' Paul's look was steady on my
reddened face, 'but unnecessary, or so I gather from
the medical notes.' He studied the file, his long fingers
turning the papers. 'Did you know that she lost a baby?'

'No!' Poor Mother! How many more secret griefs
were going to be uncovered?

257

'When was that? I mean, was it because of . . . ?'

'Yes,' he answered, 'it was a baby boy. She miscarried when she was six and a half months pregnant. Just as well, in the circumstances.'

I didn't understand, but couldn't bring myself to ask. Father's words came back to me, ringing loudly in my head: 'You — who couldn't even mother a son for me!'

Was that what made her hate me — now, and then, — her inability to bear a son?

'Anyway,' Paul's voice brought me back to the present, 'you can see that there's a lot more to look into than just the drink problem!' He sat back in the chair and studied me. 'And you, Nina? Have you been looking after yourself?'

'Yes, I'm fine,' I lied, 'and Kerri's just beautiful. I miss her so much!' The worry flooded forward.

'I bet you do — but I can see your problem this end.'

'Paul,' I blurted, the words rushing out before I could stop them, 'why did you go from Mombasa so suddenly, with no word?'

He looked puzzled. 'I didn't have your address, even if I'd realised you needed to know!'

'Oh! How stupid of me. Of course you didn't have it. It was just that I held on to the thought that you were at Nyali . . . You told me to get in touch if I needed help!'

'You were so independent!' He stopped and, looking at me, must have seen the bleakness of my face. 'What's up now?'

'I'm worried sick . . . I was living in the village of Mikendeni with my old ayah's sister, and when Mother called for me to come I left Kerri there. Now I can't contact them, and the store-keeper says they're gone. I just . . .' the words tumbled over each other in my anxiety.

258

'Hold on a second! Hold on!' His hand on my arm pressed lightly, calming me. 'Let's get this straight. You were living native fashion in Mikendeni?'

I nodded.

'Is this woman trustworthy? I mean, is she Kikuyu and therefore likely to be affiliated to the Mau Mau?'

'No, she's from Uganda, and I'd trust her with my life. Otherwise I wouldn't have left Kerri with her.'

Leah was a part of my past – a link that could never be severed.

'What have you done about trying to locate them?'

'The telephone lines are down, so I've written to the District Commissioner, though what good that'll do, I'm not sure!'

He nodded. 'Well, it could be the best bet. After all, at the moment every movement has to be reported to the authorities — passes obtained, permission granted. There should be records, surely?'

'I hope so. I can't see any other way except by searching for them myself. And how can I do that right now, with Mother so ill?'

He frowned in concentration. 'Give it a couple of days until we've run the tests. By that time you might have heard from the District Commissioner. In any case, we'll take it from there, okay?'

Impulsively, at the door, I reached up and kissed his cheek.

'Thank you, Paul,' I said, and turned to go, quickly. 'Take care! I'll see you within the next few days!' I walked down the corridor and out into the bright sunshine, filled with his presence, my mind fleeting back to Rsul as he sat proud on his horse, his falcons patterning the sky above him. But in Afghanistan — not Africa.

Melika was there at the house when I got back, running to greet me as I stopped the car.

'Melika! What are you doing here?' I hugged her,

unable to believe that she wasn't just another figment of my imagination.

'Oh, Nina! What joy to see you!' Her greeting was warm, although beneath her words I sensed she was ill at ease. 'But such bad news about Bwana dying . . . and now Memsahib! Samwelli tells me she is in the hospital?'

'I've just come from there. She's very ill.'

She shook her head in condolence. 'Where's Kerri?'

'I left her in Mikendeni with Leah . . . Leah, Mirri-amu and my Kerri – they've gone from there! The duka man told me there was trouble, so I thought they might have come to you!'

Her face clouded. 'No, they haven't come to me in Kampala. But I know what trouble they speak of — Rashidi's been caught by the police!' Tears started to roll down her cheeks. 'That's one reason why I've come to Nairobi, to see if this news is indeed true.'

We stared at each other.

'What can we do?' I asked.

'I thought that Bwana Anderson could find out the truth for me — but now I have the bad news about him, and the Memsahib . . . !'

'We'll see what we can do, tomorrow,' I promised, uncertain quite how to set about this task.

I prayed that her information would prove incorrect, but inwardly I knew it to be true, and in my mind many questions chased each other, unanswered.

Oh, Rashidi! I warned you!

Next day the police confirmed Rashidi's internment, telling me that he was at MacKinnon camp, near Voi. There was no way that we could visit him at this time, no information given as to the reasons for his arrest. The voice on the telephone was cold, dismissive, and I turned to Melika with a sigh.

'Nothing, Melika! We can't do anything at this stage.'

260

She sat down heavily upon one of the sitting-room chairs, an unprecedented action on her part. Despite my invitation to her the previous night when we had been talking, she had insisted on sitting upon the floor, and later had curled up on a mat in the hallway to sleep.

Now she sat with head bowed and, looking down at her, I could see the small white coils of hair showing in sharp contrast to the black ones, close against her skull.

You're growing old! I thought, and I was filled with affection for her, appreciating that she had given most of her life to me, without stint, without complaint. And I had brought her nothing in return but trouble.

I put my hands on her hunched shoulders and kissed the top of her head. 'We'll keep trying, Melika, I promise you that!'

The look she gave me was hollow, her dark eyes speaking loud the history of grief and oppression that was the lot of black women.

'Daughter,' she said, 'I know you'll do what you can. But you, too, have many burdens to bow your back!'

'With two of us to carry them, the load will be lighter!' I spoke cheerfully, trying to lift the gloom, but I was heavy with fear for Rashidi, terrified that he might be executed for his involvement with the Mau Mau.

A smile flickered briefly across her face. 'That's true!' She stood up. 'Now, there's much to be done. You should eat, and then it will be time to visit the hospital. We'll let our worries sit in our heads like chickens for now, and see if they hatch some answers during the day!'

I marvelled at her bravery.

The week was full of frustrations and without Melika I would have succumbed to the dark fears and depression which threatened to drown me. I spent fruitless hours on the telephone, getting nowhere, feeling the desperation grow:

'No, the lines to Mikendeni are still down.'

'No, there's no information regarding one Rashidi Mbiti.'

'No, the tests on Mrs Anderson aren't complete yet, I'm afraid.'

The official voices were impersonal.

Outside the sun shone, uncaringly. Bougainvillaea and cannas blazed; blue plumbago contrasted with bright barbiton daisies, and the smell of frangipani filled the cloudless days. I almost hated the beauty of the garden, feeling that it had no right to burgeon thus. It should be bleak, dry and arid as my own soul.

And Noeda, too, seemed to have gone, leaving my sleep filled with incomprehensible and irrelevant dreaming. I felt she and Rsul had abandoned me, betraying my trust . . .

When I went to see Mother at the end of the week, the Sister intercepted me, and led me to Paul's office.

His smile was guarded, and I knew the news couldn't be good.

'Sit down, Nina. We've got the laboratory reports now,' he said, leaning back in his chair, 'and things are pretty grim, I'm afraid. Your mother's liver is in a poor condition. There's not a lot we can do here.' He paused and gave me a long look. 'However, there's a hospital in London which specialises, and really the only hope is to get her there.'

My heart sank. 'How? How can I go — take her all that way?'

'We'll get her well enough to undertake the journey by sea.'

My mind raced through all the reasons why I couldn't leave: the expense — Kerri — the expense — Melika — the expense.

Oh, Paul, help me! Please, please help me! I cried silently. Couldn't he understand?

'I've got no money,' I said.

No money, and I don't want to go — to leave you — Kerri!

'The army must be able to help financially?' His voice rose in question. 'Is there anyone you can ask to help?'

Captain Michael Blake!

'Yes, of course. I'll . . . I'll get onto it, start trying to sort it out.'

Why was I being so stupid? Obviously, Mother had to go to London.

His eyes met mine across the desk and I felt the moment stretch, suspended. I'd been there and back before . . .

FIFTEEN

Samwelli, the driver, handed me a buff envelope next morning. I took it into the sitting-room and tore the flap open. It was from the District Commissioner in Mombasa, telling me that he had no possible way of confirming where Leah and Kerri were. The words on the paper were cold, formal:

'You will appreciate that with the additional work-load that has fallen upon Government offices due to the State of Emergency, it is impossible to spare staff to carry out an investigation into your query. Whilst every effort is made to monitor movement of Africans from village to village, the amount of paperwork involved precludes the keeping of detailed records of this sort.'

Thanks a lot! I thought, crumpling the letter up and throwing it into the wastepaper basket beside the unused fireplace. I telephoned the hospital.

'Paul . . .'

His answer was abrupt, his voice tired. He listened for a while then interrupted.

'Look — I'm up to my eyes at the moment, and I've got a patient waiting. Give me Captain Blake's phone number will you, please, and I'll liaise with him, see what we can come up with.'

I gave him the number and put the receiver down, feeling rebuffed. Sudden anger and scorn for myself swept over me. Why did I behave like a child as far as Paul was concerned?

Thinking about our telephone conversation I realised that he hadn't taken in the fact that it was Kerri I was most anxious about. But then he was, after all, a doctor — and Mother his patient.

Mother! Her emaciated body hardly made a bump in the hospital bed now, but at least her mind seemed clearer. I reminded myself that I'd promised to collect some books from the library for her. Against my shut eyelids the image of her bone-thin hands, trembling on the stiff, white hospital sheets, made me frown with pain.

'Oh, God!' I cried to the empty room. 'Why now? Why does she have to do this now?' Guilt fuelled my anger until I was shaking, and wanted to scream in primordial rage at the inconsideration of her illness.

I got up quickly from the shabby red settee and left the house, walking fast up the hill towards the chapel. The steep climb diluted my anger and, by the time I reached the top, I was hot and out of breath.

The chapel seemed much smaller than I had remembered, the thatch ragged and uncared for. But the aroma was still there — the dusty, rich smell of well-trodden cow dung.

I felt myself sag with an inexplicable relief as I lowered my body onto one of the wooden pews.

Yes! It was there still! Even if the structure itself had diminished in the intervening year, the magic and the nostalgia, overlaid with the ghosts of Rashidi and Jamira and the sound of our shared laughter, were imprinted forever upon the whitewashed walls.

My folded arms rested on the back of the pew in front of me and I laid my head down upon them and waited for the racing of my pulse to quieten after the too-fast walk. The interior of the chapel was womb-like, peaceful and disembodied from the noises outside. As my breathing shallowed, my thoughts calmed. Then, from deep within me, suffusing my whole body, came a flooding of joy, an exaltation, and my head was filled with soft light.

I tried to hold onto the ephemeral moment, but it passed, and I opened my eyes, expecting to find the building filled with angels.

Perhaps, I mused, that was praying? If that was the case, then all the rote-repeated prayers at school were hollow; shallow, unthinking mumbles in the darkness.

I closed my eyes again, hoping to recapture the experience. Instead my thoughts wandered, disjointed and apparently meaningless, as though I had slipped into sleep. I was old and yet ageless; of the past and yet part of the future; many people but only one; multi-tongued. The images whirled in my brain, spinning and distorting, spiralling upwards as though they were about to gush, geyser-like, from the crown of my head.

Frightened, I sat up and blinked. They were gone.

The sun shone like the reflection of a hundred butter-cups through the windows. A small plum-red finch flew in and upwards to the beams below the thatch.

As quickly as joy had filled me, I slumped into depression — emptied, drained, betrayed somehow.

Kerri — oh, Kerri! Her name was a plea — a prayer, too.

I knew that I had to get away, go down to Mombasa to try and find her. Mother was in good care, so far as she could be, and it would take time for Paul and Captain Blake to arrange our passage to England.

I stood up and looked around. I'd never stand inside the chapel again, I knew that with sad certainty. It could never be the same, in any event. Its magic had acted upon my life, and now it was time for separation. I walked up to the altar slowly, my hands running over surfaces, drawing the ambiance inwards through my fingertips; photographing the beauty of its simplicity for storage in my memory.

Then I left fast, turning only once to look back before I started down the hill. How long would it stand? I wondered. What hope had the simple structure against encroaching violence, either from Mau Mau or the burgeoning anti-white, anti-missionary feelings that blew fierce across the continent? I couldn't bear the thought of that small sanctuary's destruction, so I forcibly kept my thoughts turned upon Kerri and how I should start to search for her.

I knew I would have to tell Mother I was going, and was afraid of her reaction to the news. When I got to the hospital that afternoon, I saw her eager gaze, seeking me out amongst the other visitors to the ward.

'Oh! I'm so glad you're here!' she said, reaching out to touch my hands. 'The day seems to have dragged on forever!'

Oh dear! My heart sank.

'I've got you the books you asked for,' I told her, feeling somewhat ashamed at the hurried and arbitrary way in which I had selected them at the Club library on my way into town. 'I hope you'll like them.'

She glanced at the titles, then pushed them to one side.

'Never mind the books now. Doctor Phillips came to see me this morning.'

'And?'

'He says I'm much better, Nina! And I may be able to leave hospital soon!'

What on earth had he told her, I wondered. Surely she must have misunderstood.

'Oh? Well, I'll obviously have to go and see him, find out the details!' I smiled at her excited face, patted her hand. 'I must admit you do look much better.' Indeed, her eyes were bright against the jaundiced skin of her face. 'Are you managing to eat a bit more?'

'Yes — I had nearly all my lunch.' She was less assured and I knew that she lied. 'Do you think I'll really get well?' she asked, her voice betraying the fact that she knew the odds.

'Of course, if you do what you're told!' I poured out

a glass of fruit juice and gave it to her. 'Drink that, for a start!'

She pulled a face but sipped at the juice. 'There's so much to talk about, Nina, so many things I've got to tell you!'

And I had to let her know that I was going to be away, before she built up too much hope.

'There'll be plenty of time for talk later,' I told her, then paused and studied her face. 'Mother . . .' All my carefully rehearsed speeches vanished. 'Mum, look — I've got to go down to Mombasa. To — to collect all my belongings and sort things out there. I came away in such a rush . . .' My voice tailed off as I saw her turn her head away from me on the pillow.

'I won't be gone long — honestly!' How honest was I being? I'd no idea how long it would take.

'You'll go and not come back, like you did before. You'll just desert me!' Her voice was a petulant whine, her eyes and mouth down-turned, her freckles dark against the yellowed skin.

'Come on, Mum! For God's sake!' I kept my voice down, against the impetus of anger. 'I'm only going for a quick trip! You'll be all right here for a few days, surely?'

'Suppose Doctor Phillips lets me out of hospital? What then?' Her head turned back and her eyes stared their challenge into mine. I looked away, determined not to submit to the emotional blackmail.

'If he does, which I doubt, then I've got a surprise for you! Melika's back at the house! She'll look after you!'

'Melika? You never told me!'

'It was to be a surprise!'

'Melika!' Mother's eyes moved from me, her thoughts elsewhere. 'She's been with us so long — seen so much.' She gave a short laugh. 'Good times, and then all the bad ones, too!' A look of distress settled over her face as if the memories had crowded, hurting her once more.

'So there you are!' I said hastily, to deflect her thoughts.

She lay against the pillows again, the jaundiced skin highlighted by the white bedlinen, her lips mumbling at her teeth, back in her half-fantasy world once more.

I sighed and kissed her hot forehead. 'I'll see you tomorrow!'

She didn't wave as I turned in the doorway, and the library books slid with a thud onto the floor beside her bed.

Paul was in the corridor as I came from her side ward.

'Can I speak to you for a moment?' I asked.

His hand under my elbow guided me out on to the verandah that shaded the hospital. 'Of course.'

'What've you told Mother? She believes she's coming home.'

He laughed, 'No, she's got it muddled. I told her we might be moving her. Thought I'd better sow the seeds of the trip to England.'

'Oh, I see.'

His face looked tired, his chin showing dark with a slight stubble, as though he'd not had time to shave that day.

'What I'm hoping for is to transfer her for a few days to Mombasa before you catch the ship.'

'Mombasa?'

'Yes, but it'll be a while yet. Captain Blake's finding out about sailing dates and so on. He'll be in touch with you in the next few days.' He rubbed his eyes, rolled his head on his neck as if to ease its tension.

I bit my lip. 'Paul, I'm not sure I can go to England with her!'

'What do you mean?'

'Well, the money hasn't been sorted out yet, and

269

then there's Kerri. I've got to find her, I can't just abandon her, not knowing where she is or anything!'

He swivelled round to look at me, his back against the verandah rails, his face dark and shaded against the brightness beyond.

'Oh, Nina, I'm sorry, I'd not thought about Kerri!' His eyes narrowed thoughtfully. 'You said you trusted this Leah woman?'

'Yes, I do!' How could he have forgotten Kerri? 'But she's *my* baby, and she must miss me!'

He crossed his arms over his chest. 'Yes, we've got a real problem here, especially since your mother doesn't know about her. But she's only a baby — she'll miss you, sure, but not badly! As long as she's got love and comfort from this Leah, maybe she'll be all right. We've got to weigh up what's the best thing for yourself and for Kerri, too! But your mother needs a lot of attention, and certainly no more shocks!'

I stared out over the gardens, seething. Mother, Mother, always Mother! What's she ever done for me? What did either of them ever do, apart from bring me into the world?

'Yes, I know,' he seemed to be reading my thoughts, 'it appears unfair but she's alone and frightened, Nina. She really desperately needs you!'

'She never needed me before! *She* wasn't there when *I* wanted help!'

'Don't be so bloody childish! She didn't even know about your troubles — now did she?'

Angry tears burned at the back of my eyes.

'You know nothing about it! Nothing!'

I left him on the verandah and ran down the steps into the gardens and around to the car, hot and flushed in the knowledge that I had behaved like a spoilt and petulant child.

In the car I beat my hands against the steering wheel. 'Oh, hell! Bloody, bloody hell!'

I slammed the old Citroën into gear, feeling its long, low-lying body juddering as I let my foot impatiently fast off the clutch.

'Damn the lot of you — I've got to go and look for Kerri!'

My temper had cooled by the time I reached home, and I rang Paul to apologise for my tantrum, for my selfishness.

'But I've got to make some effort to find Kerri,' I said. 'Surely you understand that? Can you delay moving Mother for a week or so, until I come back?'

'Of course. There's no question of her leaving hospital yet, anyway. Go on down to Mombasa and either see that Kerri's all right, or bring her back. We'll arrange something here, I'm sure, but get back as soon as you can!'

Somewhat mollified, I hung up. But I kicked myself, nonetheless, for my immaturity, believing I'd lost my chance to make Paul see me as anything other than a stupid teenager, balanced precariously on the plateau between child and adulthood.

Catching myself in the pomposity of the thought, I laughed out loud and went, still laughing, into my bedroom. He's right, I suppose — after all, I'm not yet eighteen and that behaviour was totally unforgivable!

Melika looked round the door as I stood there smiling at the mirror.

'Have you good news then, Nina?' she asked, black eyes sparkling hopefully.

'No, not really, Melika. Only that I'm going to Mombasa to look for Leah and Kerri.'

'Shall I come, too?'

'Oh, yes! Yes!' I answered, then paused and thought for a moment. 'But no — it may be better for you to stay here so that you can go to see Mother in hospital. She won't feel so alone if you do that.'

Her face fell. 'I would rather help you in the search.'

'I know, and I'd rather you came with me too, but it makes more sense for you to stay in Nairobi. Not only for Mother's sake, but because you may have news here about Rashidi.'

She shook her head resignedly. 'If you say so, Nina, if you say so! But there is no good news to come from Rashidi while he is in MacKinnon Road Camp and it is dangerous, too, for you to travel alone!'

'Mombasa's all right, Melika, it's far from the Mau Mau there!' I replied with an assurance I was far from feeling.

'I'll have to get Mother to give me a cheque,' I went on, wondering if she'd agree, and realising that this was yet one more thing that needed to be sorted out . . . I'd have to get power of attorney so that I could draw the money we would need for the journey to England.

I rang Captain Blake and asked him to dinner that night. 'Sorry it's such short notice, but I've got to get finances sorted out.'

'I understand. I'll get our legal department to arrange for you to be made acting executor, if you like.' His voice was calm and reassuring. 'In the meantime, do you need any cash?'

I hesitated. 'Well, yes, I do. I've got to go to Mombasa in the next couple of days, and I'm not sure if Mother'll sign a cheque.'

'I'll bring some with me. Will £20 be enough?'

'More than enough. Thanks, Captain Blake!'

He arrived promptly at 7.30 pm, his uniform spotless, creases pressed to razor sharpness. His face, round and fresh-shaved, echoed his neatness, like a well-polished apple.

Melika and I had rushed to tidy up the sitting-room, to polish the cutlery and press a tablecloth. The houseboy's diligence had deteriorated badly since Father died, and Mother had been too apathetic to notice or reprimand him. With all our efforts, however,

272

the house still seemed depressingly shabby, the house-boy's long white gown patched and mended and slightly yellowed.

I was acutely aware of the seediness against Michael Blake's meticulous cleanliness, but he was too much a gentleman to show that he had noticed.

'A drink?' I asked, my voice over-bright.

'Yes please — brandy and ginger ale, if you've got it!'

'Of course we have!' I bit my tongue on the sharpness of my retort.

After dinner he smiled across the table. 'I've got your money,' he said, 'And some good news besides.'

'I hope you haven't given me your own cash.' I was suddenly anxious.

'It's all in order. Don't worry about it, Nina. And I've already rung the legal department about Mrs Anderson's funds. But the other bit of news is that I've got you both booked on the "Kenya Castle", sailing in six weeks' time! Sheer luck — they had a cancellation, and it's a good two-berth cabin to yourselves!'

'Six weeks?' My voice betrayed my horror, and the smile faded from his face.

He ran his hand over his neatly cropped fair hair, as if to reassure himself that it remained tidy. 'Oh! Aren't you pleased? I thought Mrs Anderson needed to get to England as soon as possible!'

'But . . . six weeks! There's so much to do — passports, documents, inoculations and so on . . .'

And Kerri — my Kerri! I added to myself.

'Your doctor friend seemed to think it urgent,' he hesitated, turned the glass on its mat, lining it up against his side-plate, 'but if that's inconvenient, I'm sure I can rearrange things.'

His pale blue eyes watched me, waiting for my answer, his lips slightly tight. 'Don't make a snap decision; give yourself a day or two and then let me know.

273

But don't leave it too long or we might have difficulty with refunds etc.'

I felt churlish and ungrateful. 'Sorry — I really am most grateful for your help, Captain Blake.' I rubbed my hand over my eyes. 'I'm just so confused and there's no time to sort things out. I'm sure six weeks will be okay, really!'

His smile returned and he patted my hand. 'Fine, but give me a definite answer in a few days — all right? And please,' his hand stayed on mine for a moment, 'please stop calling me Captain Blake, my name's Michael.'

'Thanks — Michael!' I moved my hand away, picking up my drink, surprised that his friendly gesture had given me a small shiver of distaste, almost of fear. And yet . . .

After he'd gone, I sat in the empty house, my mind whirling, thinking of Kerri and wondering what I should do; how I would cope with the immediate problem of looking for her and the long-term problem of what to do when I found her. It took me a long while to sleep, and when I dreamed it was of Malek, not Michael . . .

* * * *

. . . All too soon, it seemed, Malek's companions returned, for we were heavy with sensuality, and the small rough hut had become a place of great delight to us, seen through the open pores of our desiring. The bed of straw, fur-covered, was a couch fit for my king. And I, the willing concubine, could not find ways enough to pleasure him.

So it was with something akin to resentment at the intrusion, that we sat up one morning, awakened by Alexi's bark, to hear their voices in the distance.

Malek dressed quickly, and I wrapped the fur coverlet around my nakedness.

'How is the girl?' I heard one of the men call, still a little way off.

'Well, by the grace of Allah! Well enough to travel with us.'

There was a murmur of approval from the men, and some of my nervousness evaporated as I heard their voices mingling in glad tones. Malek left the doorway of the hut and went out to meet them, Alexi at his heels. I shivered, my warm cocoon of security suddenly breached, so that all the ghosts of the past rushed in upon me. In my nakedness I felt doubly vulnerable, so I hastily dressed in some of Malek's clothing, needing the protection, needing to stand behind him so that his shadow covered me.

I went to the door and, as the men turned, I heard the gasp:

'But she is beautiful. Malek, you knew what you were about sending us for help!'

Malek's sharp order cut this talk short, and he turned to me, his voice gruff with embarrassment.

'This is Nadir, and she, who prefers to be "he", will travel with us to Kalash. I haven't got the full story of how she comes to be here alone, for her strength is only now returning to her body, and her mind does not want reminding. Let it be so for now. Did you bring clothing?'

'Yes, Malek, though but little for so fair a girl!'

'No matter, for she is happier and more comfortable in breeches to ride astride a horse. Here, Nadir, make your choice whilst we unsaddle and prepare a meal.'

I smarted slightly at the curtness of his tone but, realising that this was for the benefit of the men, made no reply.

How Bibicol would have gaped at my meekness, I thought. Oh, Bibi! I had not allowed myself to think of her since Malek came, and a rush of longing and memory flooded me, so that I had to sit down. Alexi, sensing, as always, that I was troubled, came into the hut and placed a paw upon my knee.

'Ho, Alexi, how long since we saw our beloved Bibi? And does she sorrow too much at our desertion?'

Alexi licked my face and looked towards the doorway, torn between excitement at the activity without, and concern for me within.

'Go!' I said, and patted him towards the door. He gave me a last look over his shoulder and ran off to take his place amongst the menfolk.

I dressed in the girl's clothing for now. What need to hide, since they knew in any case that I was not a man? When the time to leave came the following day, I would once more become a boy.

It was strange to be wearing a skirt. My legs felt exposed and a little awkward. When I came out into the weak winter sunlight, I saw Malek's eyes spark with admiration, and a stab of desire for him burnt my loins.

Among the hunting party there were a few with paler skin than mine, and with lighter hair. But none so fair as Malek. They were all of the Kafir tribe, and told me that they travelled far each year to hunt for the beautiful furs of fox and sable, and sometimes even of the great yellow and black striped tigers, beyond the Hindu Kush. They traded these furs for food and horses, for cloth and for the beautiful lapis lazuli gems from Badakhstan on the eastern borders of Afghanistan.

I sat listening, open-mouthed at their stories around the fire. They were unlike any Afghanis that I had met before, and I found them a delight to be with. They were not bound to Islam, and thus did not pray five times a day, as did the Qashgai. I did not ask their beliefs for I was too interested in the tales they told of Alexander and the tumult of his passage through the land, which had stirred together separate segments of peoples and civilisations.

'Some say he was a devastator, others that he brought new order — but for us of the Kafir tribe, he left a heritage of a different sort, in the colour of our skins.'

'He died too young, before he was thirty-and-three years old!'

'The same as the Jewish leader they called Jesus.'

'Perhaps it is the way of it, that great men so quickly burn their energies that — pouf! — they are extinguished faster than we who are more slow?'

'If it is "good" men who die young, friend, then you will live forever!'

The good-humoured talk went on until well after the sun had disappeared from our sight.

Malek and I slept apart that night, and I hungered for him.

SIXTEEN

The villagers in Mikendeni threw a hedge of silence over Leah and Kerri's disappearance, when at last I got there. Mirriamu, too, had gone, with her husband. The elders, though rigidly polite, were evasive. It was as though I'd never lived amongst them, shared their lives for a year. The women looked at me sideways, and I sensed their fear, their silent sympathy, and knew they dared not speak. I no longer felt myself their companion, but one of the enemy, the Mzungu girl, and although I slept in my old hut, it no longer had my bed in it, and smelled strongly of goat.

In vain I tried to woo their confidence, taking presents for them and sweets for the children, who stared at me, mouths full, eyes large.

'Can't you just tell me if they are safe?' I pleaded in desperation, holding back the desire to scream: 'Come on, come on! Where's my Kerri?'

The men shuffled on their haunches uncomfortably, darting looks at each other. Then the chief cleared his throat, spat into the dust and said:

'We believe them to be safe. More than that we have been sworn not to say. The police came looking; after the letter . . .' He glanced at the others who were sitting, close-circled, around me.

'The letter brought news. News so bad that they went quickly in the night!'

What letter? My heart began to pound painfully.

'Was it from Rashidi?' I asked, but he would say no more, although I promised my silence.

'Times are bad in this country, Nina, and there are

278

informers everywhere! Who can trust even his own brother now?'

I knew then that I'd get no further, and also that if I pursued the enquiries I could endanger not only the villagers of Mikendeni but, ultimately, Leah, Mirriamu and Kerri.

Defeated and miserable, I went down to the beach to walk upon sand so white and fine that it squeaked beneath my bare feet. The warm wind soughed through the fine-needled casuarinas, and set the feathery palm trees a-rustle; the ebbing tide hissed and slapped over coral pools on its outward journey to the edge of the reef, as it had done twice daily since the beginning of time.

As I paced alone on the shore, trying to decide what to do, Noeda came into my mind for no reason, and I frowned, puzzled by the fact that she seemed so fickle. She'd started her journey from Kabul filled with thoughts of Ibrahim, then at Chesht it seemed that Rsul had woken her interest more than a little . . .

Rsul who reminded me of Paul! Or should it be the other way around?

Then Malek had come onto the scene and she was heavily enmeshed with him! Was I as quick to change affections as she was? I wondered. I'd loved Rashidi, until Paul came along . . .

I wondered, too, why our lives, in my dreams, were so closely interwoven, some of the things that happened to her closely following incidents in my present life. And yet, strangely, the dreams sometimes seemed precognizant, almost shaping my actions and reactions in the days that followed.

I wished that I had talked to Leah in more depth. She was the only one who could explain. Anyone else would think I was crazy, placing so much importance on my dreams.

Perhaps, indeed, I was! But then, if they were only

dreams — Noeda, Bibicol, Ibrahim, Rsul — how could it be that I knew them so well? That they reoccurred. That the sequences of events were logical, not distorted and jumbled as most dreams were? I sighed, unable to reach any solution, sure that they were not merely figments of my over-active imagination.

But the questions persisted well into the night and it was late when I finally slept.

Sometime after midnight I was gently shaken awake. My hand went automatically to the revolver hidden beneath the rolled-up jumper that served as my pillow.

'Shh! Nina! Don't shout out, for no one knows I am here.'

'Who is it?'

'Mwange.'

I sat up quickly, rubbing the sleep from my eyes. Mwange was one of the few Kikuyus who had come to Mombasa to work as an ayah for a European family and had ended up married to a Giriama man, making herself an outcast from her own tribe in the process.

I struck a match and lit the hurricane lantern beside my sleeping mat. 'What is it, Mwange? What are you doing in my hut in the dead hours of the night, when only the fisi, the dreaded hyena, is around to eat the dead and the rubbish?'

She squatted on her heels and drew her blanket more closely around her shoulders.

'I should not be here, Nina, but Leah is my good friend, and you, too, are like a sister to us, so I have come silently from my sleeping place to speak with you.'

'Have you news of Leah?' I asked eagerly.

'I have and I have not.' She looked nervously over her shoulder towards the palm-mat that formed my door.

'Life is hard here now, Nina, and it is dangerous to be seen as friendly to the Mzungu! I am still a Kikuyu

280

by birth, and my marriage to someone outside my own tribe has already brought a bad Thahu upon my family at Fort Hall.' She sighed and pensively rubbed one of her long ear lobes, extended by the heavy copper rings and beads she'd worn since early childhood.

'Already I fear the knives which, by being thrust into my heart, would cleanse that Thahu — but to be discovered as an informer would put me in even more danger.' She clicked her tongue. 'I am not a true Kikuyu, for my spirit is small and I do not want to die. The true Kikuyu warrior believes that he who is dead feels no pain, but I am afraid, afraid of the torture, the reprisals which prolong death, making of it a fearful and gruesome ritual.' She shuddered.

'Why do you risk your life coming in here, Mwange?' I asked, putting my hand on her knee. 'I would understand if you couldn't speak! But I must admit I am desperate for any news of Kerri and Leah!'

She nodded. 'This I know! I understand! For that reason, and also because, in truth, I no longer respect my man here, as he is lazy and drinks too much beer, I am prepared to risk helping you.'

I sighed with relief. For a moment I thought she might have changed her mind.

'It will mean journeying to Nairobi.' She cupped her hand under her chin and looked at me intently. 'I have heard of a man there, in the bazaar area, who knows much. He will be able to tell us how to find them, if anyone can. All we know here is that they went. Suddenly, in the night, after the letter came.' She rubbed the fingers of her hands together in front of her mouth, making the sound of the wind. 'Puua! Next morning they were gone — Leah, Mirriamu, Mirriamu's child and Kerri, Like shadows in the darkness — gone!'

I got up, pulled my jumper on over my head. 'When is it best to go, Mwange? I have money enough for the train fare.'

281

She scrutinised me for a long moment. 'Tsk, Nina, how can we travel together? A white girl cannot go in the third-class carriages, and a black woman cannot go in the white carriage, or where the fat Wahindis sit with their pots of curry and ghee!' She spat into the corner of the hut. 'No, we'll have to think about this . . .'

'But I've got so little time, Mwange . . . My mother is very ill and has to go to England, to the doctors there.'

She waved an impatient finger at me.

'It is easy — you travel one way and I the other, as it has always been! Have you money for both?'

I nodded.

'Then, tomorrow, we say we go into Mombasa to buy food, and we'll catch the afternoon train.'

I sighed, wondering if this, too, would turn out to be a wild-goose chase. 'What reason have we got to believe that they've gone to Nairobi? Couldn't they be in hiding here, or at Malindi?'

Mwange shrugged. 'Who knows? But,' and she tapped her forehead, 'in here the spirits tell me that they are far from the coast. For Leah would have taken the child away from any threatened danger. We do not know what the letter said, or who it was from, to frighten them so . . . !'

We escaped in the morning, carrying a kikapu into which I'd stuffed my few belongings, and a small bundle into which Mwange had tied what was most precious to her. I persuaded her to let me travel third-class, feeling ashamed to climb into the comparative comfort of a second-class compartment, and we sat, nodding with tiredness, through the long night, upon wooden benches, amidst bundles and trussed chickens and an assortment of odours.

'When we get to Nairobi,' Mwange said, 'I will leave you and make enquiries about this man. Though

282

whether or not he will see you remains to be found out!' She put her hand into the front of her bodice and brought out her kipande. 'Let us hope I will not be stopped, for there will be questions as to why I've left Mombasa if the Askari look at this!'

'Where shall I go?' I asked. 'Shall I go to my house?'

'No — oh, no! We mustn't let anyone know we are here, or that we search for Leah! No, no!' she shook her head vigorously to emphasise what she said, the large loops on her ears swinging wildly about her face.

I couldn't see what possible harm could come of it. Logically, it seemed the most sensible thing to do, the most natural. However, Mwange was risking her life, not me, so I had to do what she thought best.

Nairobi was overcast, the clouds heavy with unshed rain, but the greyness did nothing to abate the swift up-rise of excitement I felt as we walked out of the station. I looked eagerly at people's faces as we passed, searching for familiar ones. As if I would, by chance, by unbelievable coincidence, see Leah there, or Mirriamu.

We skirted the main streets of Nairobi — Delamere Avenue and Government Road — going instead, circuitously, through to the native quarters where the shops were still, for the main part, owned by Indians, but smaller and dirtier than those in the centre. The smells sent my senses spinning, a malodorous, acrid concoction of urine, decaying vegetables and fruit, rotting meat, curry and spices, overlaid with the musky throat-catching odour of filthy clothes and stale human sweat; coarse cigarettes and cow-dung; alcohol and sickly-sweet perfume. A smell so strong, so pervasive that it seemed to cling, clothing me in the way that dew clothes and permeates a line of dry washing left out after the sun goes down.

I followed Mwange through the packed streets, past the shabby tin shacks that housed the African shops, past the hovels made of broken packing-cases and flat-

283

tened debbis — the ubiquitous rectangular tins that originally contained kerosine.

And everywhere, from each dim interior, from each dark-shaded face, I felt the animosity emanating towards me, like a dark miasmic force. They looked at me with a dull-eyed stare, an almost incurious curiosity that a Mzungu girl should be there, intruding upon the squalor.

'Where are we going, Mwange?' I asked as she pushed her way through the crowds.

'We go to find a woman who can help us,' she replied vaguely. 'She is of my tribe and is therefore as a sister to me. We go to seek her first.'

'But surely the fact that I come with you will make difficulties?' The antipathy, like spear points against my skin, followed me down the streets. 'Perhaps it would be better, Mwange, for me to go and wait for you somewhere?'

She stopped and looked at me for a moment.

'You may be right, Nina, for Nairobi is not as I used to know it, there is a bad feeling here now, which I don't like. You go to the tall trees near the Norfolk Hotel where it is cool, and sit there until I come to you.'

The Norfolk's verandahs were full of Europeans drinking beers or gin and tonics, hand-guns strapped to their waists, and I was tempted to go and sit on one of the slightly battered wickerwork chairs and join them. Instead I pulled my headscarf over my forehead and kept my head down, hoping no one would recognise me. It had been a long time since I'd caroused with the young Nairobi set. In fact I hadn't really been in with the hard-drinkers, the fast set. I'd been kept strictly in line by Father's immovable rules, sneaking only the odd lunchtime session with friends from the secretarial college.

I sat on the grass under the trees and listened to the

284

laughter which roared loud from the Norfolk's bar, and thought how little I had missed.

Drowsing, with my back against a tree-trunk, I didn't at first hear the voice and, startled by the not-so-gentle prod of a booted foot against my leg, looked up to see an African Askari standing over me.

'We-we! Samama!' he ordered.

I stood up obediently.

'Wapi Kipande?' His hand was outstretched for my identity card.

'I don't have one,' I told him. 'I'm a Mzungu.'

He looked at me disbelievingly and paused. It was only then that I realised how sun-browned I was, how ragged my clothes.

'It's true!' I insisted.

'No, you're not Mzungu — you are not a white girl. A half-caste maybe! Where do you live?'

I hastily gave him my address at Karen, cheeks burning under his contemptuous look as he turned and walked away.

Moira's words came flooding back to burn the back of my throat with gall — and yet . . . and yet . . . wasn't that what Kerri was? A chi-chi — half-caste. Despised by both black and white. And I, who loved her so much, was overwhelmed by guilt at my own immediate and instinctive repudiation of the policeman's accusation.

I sat with head down on my arms, letting my hot, shamed tears run over them and splash onto the dust and the red-brown eucalyptus leaves on the ground between my feet.

Christ! What an awful mess I've made of things! I realised. What hope have I now of getting married to any of that lot in the Norfolk's bar — or anyone else for that matter? I thought of Paul, and his apparent inaccessibility made me sob even louder.

'Here! What's the matter with you, Miss?' The voice was cheerful, the accent north-country English.

I looked up and rubbed at my eyes. Two young soldiers stood over me, knees white and knobbly, some-how vulnerable, in their khaki shorts.

I managed a smile. 'I'm okay, really. Just got a fit of the Mau Mau blues, I guess!'

The younger of the two, blond-haired, pink-cheeked, put out a hand and pulled me up.

'Can't have that, can we, Sam?' he asked his com-panion. 'Pretty girl like you, sitting in the park, crying! Come on, we'll buy you a drink, cheer you up!'

'That'd be great!' I cried, then remembered Mwange. 'But I'm afraid I can't, I'm waiting for someone!'

'Lucky bloke!' said the one called Sam. They fidgeted from foot to foot.

'Go on!' I said, turning them in the direction of the Norfolk Hotel, 'I'll be all right now — promise!'

They touched their hands to their army caps and went then, turning to smile and wave at me before going up the steps into the bar.

I wondered how long they'd been out from England, what they made of this war that wasn't their war at all, that was unlike any other war really.

Mwange looked tired when she finally got to me.

'Whee, Nina! That was no easy task! Twice I got stopped by Askaris, and only just managed to convince them that I was not a fugitive!'

'Did you find the man you were looking for?'

'No — but I have contacted my friend who will get someone to take us to him tonight.'

I wondered who he was, this mysterious man who might lead me to Leah.

'Where will we sleep, Mwange? We have to find somewhere, because of the curfew!'

'This, too, I have arranged,' she replied, 'and we go now to rest for a while and eat.'

She led me back through the malodorous streets, down the rubbish-littered alleyways, to the outskirts of the shanty town.

There, in contrast to the rest of the hovels that surrounded it, stood a small and comparatively well-constructed hut. We ducked our heads and entered, at the request of the owner, and my eyes adjusted to the gloom to find that the hut was divided into several sections by thin partitions made of wattle, one section for sleeping in, another for eating in, and a third for some goats, strangely out of place there on the edge of the city, their sharp odour pungent to my nose, their soft bleating and the sound of their feeding, a background to our conversation.

'The man you need is called Muchige,' the woman told us, 'and I will arrange for my brother to take you to him late tonight.' She looked at me for a long moment. 'But I can't see how this girl can go. She is white and, because of this, she will not be allowed into the beer-house that Muchige runs.'

Mwange clicked her tongue, and the two women sat in silence, studying me.

'If it's dark, no one will see me!' I said, impatient now to get moving, having come this far. 'Can't I put mud on my face and cover my hair with a cloth?'

'Ah!' they exclaimed together.

'It may be possible to do something. Certainly, we cannot change the shape of your face, and you are too light to be a half-caste girl.' The woman scratched her head in thought.

I smiled, briefly, at that.

'But,' she continued, 'it's not just the Askari we have to convince and to avoid with absolute care because of the curfew. No, it's those whose hatred is so inflamed that they trust no one — let alone a Mzungu. Those

287

are the ones we have to fear the most. I myself have seen how their brains are turned with too many oaths, too much smoking of "bhangi"!'

I'd only once before heard of the hashish-like drug, and didn't realise then that it was used extensively by the terrorists. I began to appreciate how sheltered I'd been, how totally unaware of the depth of danger that stalked the land, for black and white alike.

Mwange stood up. 'I'll go to the duka and buy some dark shoe polish and some cotton wool,' she announced.

'Whatever for?' I was bewildered, dense with apprehension.

'Tsk! Foolish child! The polish to cover your white skin, and the cotton wool to put inside your mouth, round the gums, here.' She poked a none-too-clean finger into my mouth. 'That will make your lips look larger, more like mine!' She pursed her lips and crossed her eyes, laughing at me until I, too, had to smile. 'Stay here while I'm gone, and rest. Have you the money?' Her hand was held out for the coins.

The woman who owned the hut poured me a mugful of sweet hot tea and we sat and drank it with loud sipping sounds, as was the custom, chatting in broken Swahili, for it was not, of course, her native tongue.

'Where is your man?' I asked her.

She shot me a quick look. 'One does not ask such things in these days. Sometimes he is here, sometimes he is not. I do not question, for the less I know the less I could tell, if the Askaris should take me for questioning. It is not good to be a Kikuyu for you can be taken at any time, sometimes for no reason! And too many who go for "interrogation" do not return!'

'Women, too?' I couldn't believe that the security forces could be interning Kikuyu women for no good reason, or even killing them.

'Oh yes, women as well! For some work, too, for

the freedom-fighters, taking food and supplies up the hidden paths into the forests. And the Askaris, when they find such women, or those who live hidden in caves, high amidst the bamboos, cooking and keeping warm the beds of the men there, those the Askari kill without questioning — shooting them like baboons found in a crop of maize.'

How little I really know! I was silent, taking it all in, my hands cupped for comfort around my warm mug of tea.

My eyes would not stay open in the warm interior of the hut and I curled up on the floor and let myself drift into sleep, dreaming again of Noeda, who was, it seemed, constantly on the move, journeying, searching . . .

* * * *

. . . The track through the mountain passes was still thick with snow, but the weather held fine, and there was enough thaw for us to proceed. In all there were fifteen of us, on sturdy horses whose nimbleness of foot was a necessity for travel along the mountain tracks. I missed the horse I had ridden all this long while, for he and I had grown accustomed to each other, and I had always only to move my hands slightly on his reins for his quick response.

How angry Father will be, I thought, when he learns the animal is dead. This was the first time I had thought of Habib Amir since Malek had found me and, even whilst I thought of him, there was a detachment to it, almost as though he were a stranger. No longer did I feel the pain of guilt and sorrow at having run away. It was as if my spell of deep unconsciousness had severed me from Kabul, but not so with Bibicol, though even she I missed with less intensity. Ibrahim and Rsul came in her footsteps to my mind, but I was not willing to look at my feelings for them. I had dropped into a sort of mindless, dreaming lethargy with high spots of extreme sensuality, and did not want the wounds of the past to open up and fester.

Malek, throughout the long, cold weeks of this journey, was all consideration. Gentle and thoughtful always for my comfort, he cut the distance ridden each day to suit my strength, and his men, with the loyalty born of deep affection, never grumbled or questioned his decisions. Fatigue was my constant companion, for we climbed steeply through the mountainous land, the thin air so cold that it seemed to sear my lungs. Malek watched me constantly, ever ready to wrap me in more and more furs, until I resembled a fat mountain bear.

We reached Bactria as the year began to turn, the nights shortening imperceptibly so that there were more hours in which to ride. We stopped only to barter for provisions, and then rode hard towards the east, until we came to the high plateau they call 'The Roof of the World', a long finger of fertile land that thrust up and out to the east, with the Hindu Kush on one side and Mongolia to the north. Here the people were farmers and landowners, growing crops and tending large herds of Astrakhan sheep and goats. Their wicker and felt houses, the yurts, studded the undulating plain.

Malek knew well the Khan of this area, and we were welcomed as honoured guests to his yurt. We had discussed long the question of my dress and, since I had not yet told Malek who I was, it was difficult for me to insist on my disguise, the more so because the rest of the hunting party also knew I was a woman. I could not, therefore, fittingly sleep in the men's quarters. Because of this, I changed once more into my few items of clothing as a woman, before we reached the Khan's home.

We entered the doorway of the yurt to find it luxurious beyond my imagining. Glowing with the deep warm reds and strong blues of rugs which lined the walls, covered the floors, and with huge cushions for comfort, made seating. The Khan greeted Malek warmly and, enquiring who I was, took us both by the hand.

'Good friend, Malek, many years have passed since you and your father passed this way! Come, you and your friend — "Nadir", is it? — meet here my wife, Maja, and all these chattering daughters!'

They crowded around us, all smiles, but I felt their eyes flicker over my bedraggled clothes. All except Maja, who stood a little apart, and as I looked at her, she smiled, and I felt I knew her well, though I couldn't see how this could be.

Malek saw them looking at me, and spoke quickly. 'Nadir had been very ill,' he said, 'and all her clothes were stolen. I am hoping that you will be kind enough to find suitable garments to make her feel more comfortable?'

'But of course!' said Maja. 'Come, girl, we will soon bring out the beauty that is obviously hidden there!' She put her arm around me and drew me close. My eyes prickled at this unexpected gesture, and I felt a rush of affection for this woman whom I did not know, and yet knew.

'Thank you, I would indeed be grateful to wash myself,' I managed, and I was taken by the laughing, friendly girls and their mother to the sleeping quarters of the women. There they bathed me, washed my hair till it shone, rubbed my thin body with fragrant oils, and finally dressed me in bright petticoats, layer after layer of colour, topped with a darker skirt, a glowing blouse of apricot-coloured cloth, and veils sewn with glass beads.

Maja looked at my ears. 'Why! You have no stud holes, Nadir! Well, we will have to leave the rings for your ears for now. But we'll make up for it with necklets and a headband of lapis lazuli stones to show blue against the glow of your brown skin.'

291

I gasped at all the jewellery. 'I will return these when we go!' I said.

'But no! Of course you will not,' Maja laughed, 'for, truthfully, we all have too much, more than we could wear if we changed every day!' She hugged me, and then stood back to admire her handiwork.

'There, daughters! Have we not brought this beauty to light? Like crystal beginning to shine after the dull stone it was has been polished and polished!'

The girls laughed with her, and each put out a hand to touch me there, or put a bead straight here, a strand of hair into place. Such loving concern warmed me, and I was reminded suddenly of the women's quarters at my father's estate in Kabul. What difference of feeling there to here! I wondered why it was that my mother and sisters had been so cold, so cruel and selfish. Oh! If they had been like this happy group, how different then my life would have been.

The girls brought me a silver disc to see myself, and my eyes grew large as I stared at the stranger looking back at me. My face had taken on a fineness of bone, a delicacy that was not there before I left Kabul, my eyes seemed larger and more luminous, and my hair made a soft and shining frame for the whole. I smiled with pleasure at the sight. I had grown so used to having my hair plaited and knotted on the top of my head, of taking no pains with my looks for so long a while, that the soft prettiness of my reflection took me by surprise.

Maja took me by the hand. 'Let's surprise Malek with this new girl we have found!'

Malek and Timur Khan were deep in conversation, but when they turned at our entrance, Malek's face gave no lie to his surprise and pleasure. I flushed hot at this frank appraisal.

'There!' said Maja. 'Is she not beautiful beyond belief?'

'Yes, oh yes!' Malek replied, and held out his hand to me. 'Come and sit near, Nadir, that I may drink in the intoxication of this new person!'

I sat down, awkward and embarrassed by all the attention, and Maja, seeing my eyes fill with tears, quickly understood and adroitly turned the conversation away.

I slept that night, for the first time in months, upon large cushions, warm and soft and deep.

And once again the voice came — disturbing, strange, and yet familiar.

'Be careful! Be careful!' The woman who spoke had skin as velvety as the night skies, and I knew her. Knew her to be Maja.

'Of what must I be wary?' I asked.

'Take care to search where your real destiny lies, girl. You turn for solace to the nearest shoulder — and your eyes are blinded!'

'But I am happy — I believe, at least, that I am so. Ibrahim is lost to me, and so, too, Rsul, it seems! Am I to grieve for them forever?'

She shook her head. 'Missed opportunities happen to us all,' she said. 'You cannot waste the rest of your life looking over your shoulder, regretting. But neither should you block the memories with hypocrisy.'

'I do not understand,' I said, but she was gone. . .

* * * *

. . . Mwange's voice woke me. 'Nina, get up now! I have brought the polish, look!'

SEVENTEEN

My skin stung underneath the greasy boot polish, and the cotton wool wadged round my gums made me want to throw up.

Mwange was convulsed with laughter at my attempts to talk and, wiping the tears from her eyes, put her hand on my arm. 'You'd better keep the cotton there, Nina, until you get used to it — or else do not speak!' She paused and then hit the side of her forehead with open palm. 'Tsk! What fools we are! You'll have to keep silence, Nina, for you do not speak Kikuyu! We had not thought of that!'

Indeed we hadn't! So it was decided that Mwange should be my spokeswoman, explaining to anyone who asked that my voice had been lost when I was half-throttled during an interrogation. 'That will give you a good alibi, and explain, too, why you need to see Muchige, for I understand he does not open his doors to all who knock!'

'Who does, these days!' exclaimed the other woman, 'for it is difficult to tell who is friend, who enemy now!'

'Have you witnessed the oath-taking?' I asked her. She looked at me from under hooded lids, sucked her lips inward then, obviously deciding I was trustworthy, began:

'I have done so. It was before I came here, while my home was on the shamba of Bwana Watson, near Nyeri. It was truly terrible, Nina, and something that ensured that all the men who took the oath were tied to the Mau Mau by fear, if not by loyalty.' She shook her head. 'The oath-giver came at night and we were all called into a clearing at the edge of the farm. He was armed with a large gun, as were the two men with him.

'Only one man on the shamba had a gun and the oath-giver walked straight up to him and, with his panga, slashed off the arm that held the gun. Then,' her eyes were bleak, hollow in her face as she spoke, 'the oath-giver told one of us to shake the man whose arm had been severed, to bring him back to this world. He screamed — horribly — like a wild pig which has been speared but has not died!'

'Was that the oath?' I asked, puzzled.

'No! No, of course not! There was worse to come. The oath-giver called for the wounded man's wife to step forward, and she approached, trembling. I will never forget her face, with eyes so huge that they looked as though they would pop out from her skull, her skin grey with fear and her belly large with child.

' "Is this your wife?" asked the oath-giver, kicking the wounded man with his booted foot. The man groaned and nodded, "Yes! Yes! She is my wife!"

' "Aha!" said the oath-giver, "so she is the one carrying your seed! And that seed, if it be a son, will take your place as the leader of the family when you are gone?"

'At another nod from the man lying on the ground, the oath-giver pulled the woman's head backwards by her hair and, taking his panga, with one slash cut open her stomach and, taking the body of the unborn boy child from her, threw it onto the man's face.'

The cotton wool in my mouth gagged me, and I spat it out, swallowing hard to keep down the vomit that almost followed it, in horror at her story.

'But why?' I asked, 'why?'

'He told us that the new oath required the dead body of a man and a male child from now on — and he killed the father then. The brains and blood of both father and infant were mixed with mud from the ground. Every man in that group approached the oath-giver and he made a cut in each of their wrists, so that a little of their blood mixed with that of the man and the baby. Then the oath-giver made all come forward again, kneel at his feet and take seven sips of the mixed blood. As each sipped, he made them repeat the words of the oath:

' "If I am ordered to cut off the head of my brother or sister and I do not do so, then the power of this oath will kill me;

' "If I am ordered to kill a European man or woman, or his children and I do not do so, then the power of this oath will kill me;

' "If I submit to interrogation by the Askari, and betray the whereabouts of my brothers in Mau Mau, then the power of this oath will kill me;

' "If I am ordered to slaughter my mother or father, and I do not do so, then the power of this oath will kill me;

' "If I join the Home Guard, then the power of this oath will kill me;

' "If I know of any Kikuyu man or woman who is not a supporter of Mau Mau and I do not either kill them, or warn my brothers of their presence, then the power of this oath will kill me;

' "If I do not take every chance to steal from the Europeans; to kill or maim their animals; to make them leave this country to its rightful owners, then the power of this oath will kill me".'

Her voice had become an intonation, almost as though she were reciting a lesson learned at the blackboard and, when she stopped, the room was still for a few moments, with only the faint rustlings of the goats to break the shocked silence. Then her eyes returned into focus.

Mwange exhaled loudly. 'That is a truly binding

296

oath!' she wiped her hands over her face as if to cleanse it.

I looked at the owner of the hut anxiously. 'What about you? Aren't you putting yourself into great danger having me here in your home?'

She shrugged. 'It was my sister who was killed — her unborn child who was slaughtered. I have no great love for the Mau Mau or their methods!' She spoke quietly, her eyes looking often towards the door.

'But the oaths you heard – aren't you afraid they will kill you?'

'I did not take them, remember, I only saw what they did to the men, how fear and terror is used to force peaceful people into violence.'

'And your husband — what will he do if he finds me here?'

She put her finger to her lips. 'Do not speak of this! I have already told you it is foolish to ask too many questions.'

It was well after dark when the woman's brother led us out of the hut and through the streets, deserted now because of the curfew laws. But though there were no people about, noise came unexpectedly loud, unrestricted by the flimsy walls and doors — radios and gramophones blaring; the sound of an off-key guitar; someone singing; dogs barking — a blast of mixed sounds that assaulted my ears as we went, stepping carefully, keeping to the shadows.

Our guide went stealthily, motioning us with gestures of his hand, reconnoitring each corner as we came to it, shoo-ing us fast backwards behind a pile of cardboard boxes as two armed Askari came by. Occasionally, we were passed by other shadowy figures, who came and went on silent, bare feet, and did not speak.

Eventually, tucked away amongst a jumble of shops and huts, reached by a narrow, unlit alleyway, we arrived at our destination. A small spy-hole opened in

297

the door in response to our knock, and I could hear the whispered Kikuyu conversation that ensued, though I couldn't understand a word of it.

Finally, and so swiftly that it hardly seemed the door had opened and closed again, we were inside, and a light was brought from behind a curtain.

'He tells us to follow him,' translated Mwange. I noticed only then that we had left our guide outside. I nodded, my mouth full of the cotton wool, my heart pounding hard; afraid my disguise would fool no one; that I'd be killed on the spot and buried somewhere — never found! What then of Kerri, of poor Mother? Melika? And Paul — would he grieve at my disappearance? I'd no time for further speculation as we were led down a narrow corridor, flanked on each side by doors from behind which came talk and occasional laughter.

'This is a brothel, Nina!' Mwange turned and whispered, her eye-whites catching the flickering light from the hurricane lantern. 'This is where the men come to spend their money whilst women work on the shambas!'

I gulped. I'd no idea what to expect of a brothel, but it somehow seemed awfully 'ordinary', not at all what I might have envisaged, if I'd envisaged anything. No music; no tartily dressed prostitutes in suspender-belts; no Madame. I furtively glanced into an open door as we passed, and saw only a filthy mattress on a wooden bed, an enamel chamber-pot and an empty bottle of Tusker beer. The occupants had gone. I shuddered at the sordidness.

We were led into a large room at the end of the corridor, well lit and hazy with cigarette smoke. There was a rough wooden bar along one side, and several men stood at it, drinking beer straight from bottles.

The man behind the bar was tall for a Kikuyu, well built, with broad shoulders. He wore a khaki, long-sleeved shirt-jacket similar to those worn by White Hunters, which hung over his grey trousers, and on his head a large and very dented felt bush hat shadowing his eyes.

I could feel his scrutiny upon my face, and moved back slightly so that Mwange stood between us.

'So you are the ones who seek to speak with me,' he said to Mwange.

'Come over to this table here, where we will be far from these stinking jackals,' he indicated the men at the bar who seemed unoffended by his words.

Mwange carefully chose to sit so that the light from the bar lit her face and not mine, but Muchige's eyes still turned in my direction.

'Why does she not speak for herself?' he asked. Mwange gave him our explanation, and I nodded in affirmation.

'And what is it you want?'

'It is her sister who has disappeared, and it is her child, too — from Mombasa. We have been told that as you are the person who knows all movements, you might help us to find them.'

His hands, I noticed, were unusually slim and well formed for an African.

'Mombasa!' he said, and there was something in the way he said it that made my heart skip a beat. Something . . . but I couldn't put my finger on it.

He leaned over and picked up my hand, casually turning it over in his own.

'Hm!' He let my hand go again, and I put it quickly onto my lap under the table.

'Why do you think I would bother with something so trivial as a missing woman and child?' he asked. 'There are so many that disappear now, why so much fuss over two more?'

I drew my purse out of my pocket, putting it onto the table in front of me.

'She has money!' said Mwange, taking the cue.

He pushed the purse towards me with an angry gesture. 'If I help you, it will not be for money, woman,' he said, standing up. 'Do you want to drink?'

He didn't wait for an answer, but strode off to the bar, returning with three opened bottle of Tusker beer.

'Here,' he placed one in front of each of us. 'And what is your name, n'dito?' he asked in Swahili and, as his eyes probed mine, I felt again that unease, an internal dissolution, turning my guts to water. I opened my mouth to speak, and Mwange kicked me hard under the table.

'Her name is Nina,' she said.

For one brief moment I detected a glint of amusement in his bloodshot eyes. 'Well, tell Nina to come to me tomorrow afternoon, alone, and I will try to have some news or some plan for her.' He stood up.

'But she cannot speak . . .' began Mwange.

'She understands — that is all that matters!' he said abruptly. 'I am promising nothing, remember, for a man of my standing has things of more importance to attend to than to search for missing women and children!' He spat contemptuously into the dust.

Our guide was waiting outside the door to lead us back through the dark streets.

Later in the night I lay restless upon my mat, covered, I was convinced, by a thousand fleas which had gravitated to me from the goats, and shivering more from apprehension than from cold. The man, Muchige, wouldn't leave my thoughts. How could I be sure of him, I wondered. Could I trust him to help me, or would I find myself the next victim for an oath-taking ritual? Catching that thought, I realised with relief that a woman wouldn't be considered worthy of sacrifice — the death of one n'dito, a girl, would hardly bind anyone to a cause in Kikuyu eyes. For women were of no value. And yet, there was definitely something that bothered me about Muchige.

I wished to God I could go to Paul, that he'd find time to listen, to help — as Malek had, in that other life. And then there was Maja, too. Yes, Maja, who was so like Leah.

The following afternoon I knocked tentatively at the shabby black door of Muchige's brothel. My progress through the watching streets had been a nightmare, since I was convinced that my flimsy disguise would very quickly be penetrated in the harsh light of day.

Mwange had given me an old and tattered coat, and I had tied my headcloth under my chin, to cover as much of my face as possible, but still I felt my difference shouted loud to all who looked at me.

The spy-hole opened and shut, and I was admitted by Muchige in person.

'Come,' he spoke in Swahili not Kikuyu, 'follow me quickly.' His long legs carried him fast down the corridor ahead of me, a strange loping walk with arms swinging wide of his body. He opened a door and waited for me to enter before bolting it behind me. I found that I was shaking so much that I could hardly stand, and leant against the wall to steady myself.

Muchige sat on the one wooden chair, facing me.

'I know you are not a Kikuyu and, if I could see that so quickly, then so will others. First we must work on your appearance in order that you raise no question in people's minds, though why you can't go back to your home and wait there, I don't understand. Surely that would be the best way?'

'No,' I replied firmly, 'I've tried going through the European channels, and I've drawn a blank there. And the villagers where I left Kerri — my child — and Leah, for some reason know nothing or, if they do, then they are afraid to tell me. The only way I can find them, find any information, is by going to the grass

301

roots.' I looked at him hopefully. 'And you, I was told, are the person who hears more than most, and who knows what is happening in the town and in the forests.'

'Yes,' he said after a moment's long pause, 'yes, a brothel is a place where men talk, their tongues being loosened by beer and by women.' He pulled at his lower lip pensively as he studied me. 'But I don't like it — it could bring great danger to you, and also to me and to what I am doing here . . .' His voice trailed away. Then he stood up and abruptly pulled off my headscarf, letting my hair tumble.

His hands paused in mid air. 'Oh, God! I don't know about this!'

At first I didn't register the fact that he spoke in English. He turned away quickly and stood with his back to me for what seemed an interminable length of time.

I scratched my head, sure that I had fleas, longing to have a bath and wash my hair, my fear suddenly and inexplicably leaving me. I wondered what this strange African had in mind. I was filled with bewilderment, and an odd feeling of *déjà vu*.

He turned back to me suddenly, making me jump.

'Won't you trust me to find them for you?' he asked.

I shook my head. 'I need to find them quickly. And I have to search for them myself. There's so little time. I can't just sit back and do nothing. No, I have to do it!'

He shrugged. 'Right,' he was speaking Swahili again, 'first we must stain your skin properly and deal with your hair and eyes.' I wondered what he meant but he left me no time to ask.

'Take your clothes off.' He gestured towards a grimy curtain hanging across one corner of the small room. 'Go in there if you like!'

I stripped to my underwear, scarlet under Muchige's

302

watching eyes, and stood waiting, while he drew a large wooden box from under his bed, and took out a bottle and some cotton wool.

'We'll have to rub this all over you — or almost all over! We can't risk any white patches! Now just stand still and I'll start on your back.'

The stain had a sharp smell and felt cool as he lifted my hair from my neck and with firm strokes began to massage it into my burning skin. For one brief moment I felt conscious of the fact that I had not bathed, and then realising how ludicrous this was, I relaxed under his gentle hands.

To my shame I found that the massage was filling me with a languid desire, and I remembered Paul's fingers accidentally on my breast, that day so long ago it seemed, in Mombasa. My mind, stilled, slipped backwards . . .

*   *   *   *

. . . It was daybreak, and we were due to follow the rest of the hunting party who had gone ahead to Kalash. My bags were filled with finery, and our provisioning baskets overflowed, for the generosity of the Khan's family was unlimited. They were reluctant to let us leave, and we had to make many vows to return, before they let go of our reins and stood waving us on our journey.

'How generous your friends are, Malek!'

'They are so, and always it is a pleasure to visit them, though I could grow fat and soft through over-indulgence there!' He slowed his horse as we came to the edge of a steep escarpment.

'Stop and look, Nadir — to the south you can see almost to the Hindu Kush and, in the distance, that streak of silver is the Brumboret River which flows into my village!'

The view was breathtaking, and we sat our horses looking out over the valleys and plateaux below us, with the warm breath from our mouths forming wisps of white vapour in the crisp, cold air.

'Let's stop for a short while and enjoy this place.' Malek put up a hand to help me from my horse. 'Also I want to savour your new beauty, Nadir, for I have known you only in the darkness of that small hut.'

I felt a reluctance, a constraint, almost as though I knew him not. But I dismissed this feeling as best I could, and stood beside him looking at the beauty that spread before us.

He turned to me, his hands at the fastenings of my blouse, and I could see the signs of his desire in the swelling of his trousers.

'No,' I said, 'not here!'

'Why not? Oh, please, Nadir, it is many days since I loved you!'

He knelt before me and, lifting my skirt, kissed me soft and gentle on that part of me, until I felt myself respond and my legs part, eager for him to rest between them.

'Wait!' he cried, and drew away to reach for his cloak to lay upon the ground for me, but I didn't now want to wait.

'No, Malek, leave it, I want you within me. Oh, please, please!' He did my bidding then, and all too soon was spent, as indeed was I.

Ashamed after, I sat up and straightened my new clothes, hoping that I had not stained their brightness with the marks of grass or mud. We remounted our horses without speaking, both embarrassed by the sexuality.

He rode ahead of me and I studied his back, wondering. He sat straight, broad-shouldered and slim-hipped, his fair curls catching the sunshine. His light skin had been turned by the summer's sun to a shade of golden bronze, and the fine blond hair on his arms where his sleeves were rolled back from his wrists, gave a shimmer to his bronzeness so that as I looked through half-shut eyes, he seemed clothed in light.

The beauty of this man caught at my throat. I had seen paintings in the cities of men like this, the gods and goddesses of ancient Greece, painted on walls by Alexander's men, golden-haired and shining with light.

Tears came quietly and ran with a certain slow dignity of their own, down my face and I was filled with a deep soul loneliness, though I knew not why this should be . . .

*   *   *   *

. . . 'Why are you crying?' The man in front of me was black, not golden. My tears dried instantly as I realised where I was.

'I cry for my child,' I replied.

His hand on my face was gentle as he rubbed away my tears.

'You must learn to stop the tears,' he said, 'for Kikuyu women do not weep! And also we do not want white marks down your face through the stain, as now.' He laughed and turned me towards a small mirror hanging on the wall. Indeed, the tears had left streaks through the boot polish on my cheeks so that I had a bizarre and clown-like appearance. He gestured to an enamel bowl in the corner.

'There is soap and water. Now wash off the polish and replace it with this stain!' he said.

I was glad to turn my back on him, glad of the greasy polish which had masked my shameful and totally inexplicable rush of desire. As I scrubbed at my skin, I wondered guiltily if there was something wrong with me that I should have these feelings. Surely other white girls didn't feel that wantonness, that dissolving, longing ache?

Once my skin had been darkened, Muchige put drops into my eyes, turning the whites slightly yellow,

305

then showed me how to line my mouth with pads of gum, so that it was less uncomfortable, more secure.

'This way, at least you can eat without such difficulty,' he explained.

My hair was plastered with black dye and scraped back from my face into a knot at the back of my head.

'Keep your kerchief on at all times,' he said, then stood back and looked at me. 'Yes, you might just get away with it on a dark night! Now I'll turn away and you take off your underwear and stain your breasts and that other place — for you are supposed to be a Kikuyu and Kikuyu women don't wear such clothes!'

I blushed again and did as I was told.

'There! Now you are a true n'dito!' Muchige clapped his hands. 'And a good-looking one, too, though too thin for most tastes! To protect you from the men I am going to say that you are my woman, understand? So you will sleep always at my side.'

Oh, God! I thought, all desire gone now. Oh, God! Will I be expected to do all that? What if he's diseased? The word 'syphilis' flashed into my mind again.

'Don't worry, I won't harm you, if that is why your face has fallen! I have no liking for white girls, especially ones as skinny as you!'

Could he read my thoughts as well? I wondered.

'Now go back to your friends — see their reaction to your appearance — and walk through the streets with confidence, Nina, not as if you have something to hide. Come back tonight, before curfew. I want you to be seen with me in the bar, so that questions are not asked later when I appear with a strange woman in the forests.'

My breathing stilled — so we were going into the actual forests. I hadn't expected that, vaguely assuming the search for Leah and Kerri would be in the city. I swallowed hard.

'Ring your home, make some excuse for your delay.

If there has, by chance, been any news of the child, you'll hear it, and we need not go!'

I nodded, still unable to speak.

'Don't worry so! It will make you conspicuous!' His voice was brusque, and he unbolted the door and showed me out into the daylight, which seemed unbelievably bright, revealing, after the darkness inside.

EIGHTEEN

Melika answered the phone when I rang on the way back from Muchige's brothel.

'Melika! It's me — Nina!'

'Nina! Where are you? Are you here in Nairobi?' she asked, her excitement obvious in her voice.

'I can't see you,' I prevaricated, 'but is there any news of Leah and Kerri?'

'No, I've heard nothing. And Memsahib keeps asking for you. What shall I tell her?'

'Just give her my love and tell her I'll be back as soon as I can.' I paused, wondering how much I could say. 'I'm trying to find them, Melika. I'm hopeful that we'll soon have news.'

'Where are you, Nina? Are you still in Mombasa?' she asked.

'No, but I can't tell you anything more. Have you heard any more about Rashidi?'

'Only that he is under interrogation, but that could mean anything or nothing! He is a Bugandan, so how can they keep him in prison camp?' Her voice was weary with worry.

'If he was caught with the gangs then, no matter what tribe he comes from, he'll be in trouble.' There was no way I could soften the blow.

'Oh! Bwana Blake has been ringing! He, too, wants to see you urgently.'

What could Michael want, I wondered. Oh well, he'd have to wait, there were still four weeks before I was due to sail with Mother. Only four weeks! I suddenly realised how short the time was.

'I'll have to go, Melika!' I told her. 'I'll ring you

again soon and let you know what's happening.' I put the phone down and went quickly through the streets back to where Mwange was waiting.

'It's Nina,' I answered her called enquiry from inside the hut. Mwange and the woman came to the door and put their hands over their mouths in astonishment as they looked at me.

'If you weren't wearing Mwange's coat . . .' began the woman, and Mwange interrupted: 'It is only Nina's voice coming from your mouth that makes me know you! And even that is not really your voice!' She turned me round, studied me. 'That is good; very good, Nina! It would be difficult to recognise you. And you could well be of mixed Kikuyu/Somali blood.'

'Not really Kikuyu?' I was disappointed.

'Your nose is too fine, but no matter, for many are of that mixture in these days!'

I explained what Muchige had done, and told them the plans, briefly.

She eyed me solemnly. 'There is much danger in what you do,' she said, 'and I am not sure that Melika or Leah would be pleased to know of this! Do I come with you?'

'No, Mwange, you have done enough — both of you have! I don't want to implicate you in any greater danger. You should go back to Mombasa, Mwange, where at least you'll be safe!' I didn't like the thought of anything happening to these two women who had already risked reprisals by helping me.

'Oh, no! I will stay here, with my circumcision-sister. I have no desire to return to Mombasa, even if it is safer! Besides, if the Mau Mau have already put their mark upon me, it makes no difference where I hide, they will find me!'

I reluctantly conceded she was probably correct in that assumption and, thanking them again, left the hut.

Muchige's bar was full. Most of the men there sat

309

drinking chai, hot sweet tea, out of enamelled mugs; a few had Tuskers in front of them. I wondered how Muchige got away with running this bar/brothel in the heart of shanty-town Nairobi. The police must surely know about it — they weren't stupid. However, it wasn't the sort of question I cared to ask.

Muchige put me to work making cups of tea on a filthy, smoke-belching wood stove at the back of the building. Whenever I came to the bar with a tray of mugs, he smacked me familiarly on the rump, making coarse comments in Kikuyu which I couldn't understand, but which brought appreciative guffaws from the men at the rickety tables. Their eyes followed me speculatively and I was terrified they'd see I wasn't a black girl.

I kept my head down, glad that the stain on my skin hid my burning cheeks, hating Muchige for drawing attention to me.

From time to time Kikuyu girls would come through the door that led into the corridor and hand Muchige coins. They stared at me questioningly, resentfully. I avoided them, busying myself with cups and bottles, my hands shaking.

Late that night, when the last roisterer, the last client, had left, Muchige dragged a mattress through from one of the rooms and placed it on the floor next to his bed. I looked at it with distaste. It was stained and filthy.

'You sleep on my bed!' he said, seeing my look. 'I'll lie on this one — but if anyone should come, then you must move quickly to lie with me!'

This consideration seemed out of character somehow, but I didn't comment, glad only to have the comparatively cleaner bed of the two.

He handed me a saucer.

'Spit your gum pads into this,' he said.

I realised then that I had grown so accustomed to having them that I'd forgotten they were there.

I lay in the darkness, afraid that he might change his mind and take me, like any Kikuyu man would take a woman, as a right. But his breathing grew deep, even, and I knew he slept.

It took me some time to sleep myself, as I imagined what lay ahead, not sure exactly what we were going to do, where we were going to search for Leah and Kerri. I was puzzled, too, that this man should be prepared to take the trouble to help me. That, like Malek, he was prepared to travel with me . . .

* * * *

. . . Malek and I continued towards Kalash, which was a good day's ride. The weather held fair, until — like a jagged wound — the Brumboret valley appeared before us, slashing into the sides of the Hindu Kush. The track grew narrower until it was but a pathway, threading along the boulder-strewn river bank. We traversed the icy ledges along the valley and crossed the great river countless times, walking our horses with difficulty over trembling bridges of slatted wood and rope. Then the valley suddenly broadened and the hillsides grew softer, covered with mulberry trees and tall cedar. The houses were constructed of timber here, cut from the cedar-wood which grew in great swathes to each side of the clearings.

'There!' pointed Malek. 'There is Kalash, do you see, Nadir? The smoke from the fires at the head of the valley ahead — that is my home.' He sat taller in his saddle, eager to be there.

I was inexplicably afraid to go on. Somehow I did not want to meet his family, or the members of his tribe, fearing their questions and scrutiny.

'Malek, I am well now! Maybe I should leave you to greet your family, and make my own way home, too!'

311

'Nadir, what foolishness is this? Haven't you learned yet that you cannot travel alone? You would have died had we not found you, in the snow!'

'I know, and I thank you for that. And also for your patience and discretion in not questioning me.'

'I did not want to break upon your privacy, Nadir, but perhaps the time has come now for you to tell me your story. For I have cared for you well, have I not?'

I felt a momentary flicker of annoyance at his constant reminders of what he had done for me, for these reminders filled me with guilt and remorse.

'You may not wish me to continue in your company if I tell you!' I thought deep for a moment, and wondered how Malek would react to the knowledge of my flight from Kabul. 'I don't wish you to become involved, for if you knew my reasons you would be doubly threatened. Whatever your reaction, the result would not be a happy one for you.'

'You are no criminal, my love, of that I am sure.' He looked long at me. 'But leave it be, for I would not have you distressed. As to your leaving, that I'm afraid I cannot allow, for though you are better than you were when I found you, I still believe there is a long way for you to go before you regain full strength. Come! My family will make you welcome, and you need have no fear that it might be otherwise.'

I was not convinced of that but, because of the guilt I felt over my treatment of this gentle man, I acquiesced, and we rode on towards the village, reaching it in the warmth of the afternoon.

The Kalash women wore heavy black robes, with strange tufted headdresses, threaded and decorated with cowrie shells. Their hands and feet were tattooed with a brown dye, and as they walked there was a musical tinkling sound, which came from small bells which hung from their waist-girdles. Malek called

312

greetings as we approached them, and the whole tribe, it seemed, came out to meet us.

I was taken with dizziness and fear, and could not understand the reluctance I felt at meeting these people who were friendly and polite, and obviously held Malek in high affection. He took my hand and led me to his family, but each step I took was heavy, and my trembling increased.

Where now the brave Nadir who faced capture by Rsul's men; who stood, prepared to fight in the darkness when surprised by Ibrahim and Rsul?

I shook my head to rid myself of the nausea that threatened to overcome me, and forced myself to smile at Malek's people.

'Nadir?' his father asked. 'That is a boy's name, surely?'

'Father, she was all but dead when I found her, and remembers nothing of her past — even her name is gone. But I'm sure, with time and rest, her health and memory will return.'

I forced myself to keep smiling, through jaws that ached with the strain.

Malek's mother stood back after greeting her son. Her eyes were cold as she looked at me, and that cold look travelled over me, from head to feet. She did not speak and I sensed her hostility.

'The girl's clothes come from that region in the north called Bala Hisar.' She spoke directly to Malek, ignoring me. 'Is she of the nomad tribes, then?'

I started to explain about Maja's generosity, but she turned away.

'It is good to have you home, Malek,' she interrupted me, speaking to him. 'These hunting trips are always dangerous, and I fear for you, when you are gone. Jala missed your presence, too!' She put out her hand and a light-haired girl took hold of it, her eyes demurely turned downwards, her cheeks reddened with shyness.

I bit my lip, understanding that Malek's mother was telling me that Jala was the one she had chosen for her son.

Malek smiled, not seeing the animosity which burned the air between his mother and me.

'Jala grows tall, I see. She is no longer the small girl who played so many tricks upon me!'

He put his arm around my shoulders. 'Come, Nadir, you need to rest, for the ride was long, and you are not completely recovered.'

Malek's father made me welcome, asking many questions and showing me into their home. But his mother merely watched our progress, and I could almost feel her disapproval pierce my back like a sharp-pointed spear.

The days grew longer, and I adapted to the quiet ways of the Kalash Kafirs. I grew accustomed to the different traditions, as I had to the variety of skin and eye colouring. So meek and docile had I grown that I blended unnoticeably into the tribe and it was generally accepted that I was Malek's woman, except that is, by his mother, who still chose to act as though I were not there, as if, by doing so, I would disappear.

When talk started about marriage, I steered the conversation away, for it was not something that I wanted. I lived in a form of void, doing my allotted chores and responding to questions, but my mind had formed a shell, shielding me from painful thought, painful reality. I preferred it that way, for I was afraid each time the past pushed forward, and uneasy always in the presence of Malek's mother and Jala.

She approached me one day while Malek and his father were in the forest cutting timber.

'You! Girl! How long do you intend to stay here?' Her finger poked, stiffly and painfully, into my chest as she spoke. 'Don't you realise you are not welcome here? It is Jala who is to be my son's wife. She was

314

spoken for many years ago, and is a suitable and virtuous girl. While you — ' she spat venomously into the grass beside us, '— you are nothing but a peasant, a tramp with no breeding, no chastity.'

I gulped back my quick answer.

'You must leave here, leave my son alone!'

Little did she realise that I shared her thoughts, that I, too, knew that Malek and I were not suited, not destined.

'How can I leave?' I asked weakly, 'when Malek wants me here?'

'You will go — I don't care how! If not, and I am warning you — I will get rid of you myself, without compunction, without regrets!' She turned on her heel and went, her back rigid with disapproval.

I had never felt such hatred, even from my sisters in Kabul. I knew she meant what she said. It was not safe for me to stay in Kalash, and I began to plan my escape.

But then, in the warmth of late spring, I realised that I was carrying Malek's child. The knowledge threw me into a state of acute consternation. Stupidly, the probability of this happening had never occurred to me. Now I felt trapped, caught in a web of my own making. Of my making and of Malek's.

And Malek still hungered after me, at every opportunity, reminding me of how he had saved my life, so that I felt the strands of obligation like cords around my neck, strangling me.

'Alexi,' I spoke in despair to my constant companion, one day out on the hillside where I walked often, 'Alexi, what am I to do? Will we have one more person to share our special bond?'

Alexi, not understanding, lifted his ears enquiringly, and the child within me moved. I put my hand over the movement and, for the first time since my illness, felt the stir of real emotion within me.

315

The unborn child, like an echo of my pulse-beat, an answering flicker, caused a gentle stirring which felt like bubbles sent to the surface by small frogs in a pool. Then Malek came strongly into my mind and the infant in my womb moved violently, causing me to call out. Alexi rushed to comfort me, and I stroked his rough fur as I mused upon the predicament I found myself in.

Now my future and Malek's were linked by the child and my feelings were conditioned by this link, my escape made more difficult.

It was that night that Malek, running his hands over my belly, said: 'You grow plump, Nadir! Is it that we feed you too well?'

'It may well be so,' I replied, and stopped his questioning with the ardour of my mouth, for I still loved his body — the sinew and muscle, the smoothness of his chest and stomach. My hunger could not be assuaged but, as always, I kept my 'self', my thoughts, aside from him, so that though he stormed and took me physically, there remained within the depths of my stronghold, a secret place, locked and hidden, to which he had no key.

As the days passed I grew larger and talk in the village grew proportionately louder.

Malek's mother eyed me up and down. 'You are with child, I'm sure. Does Malek know?' Her voice was harsh, threatening. 'We will have to get rid of the child. I will gather the plants that will make it leave your body.'

'No!' My cry came, involuntarily, from my throat.

I knew now I would have to tell him. That night, therefore, I took him away from the houses, to the privacy of a small thicket where often we met to love, and there I told him.

He was, in his quiet way, overjoyed at the news. 'We must arrange our marriage now, Nadir!' he said.

My breath faltered. I had not, foolishly, thought of marriage. 'There is no need, just yet,' I answered quickly. 'I have business unfinished, Malek, which I will need to attend to before I can make marriage vows!'

'And what of the child?'

'The infant will have you as its father, whether this is sealed by ritual or no. There will be time enough later.' I knew I spoke falsely — there would be no time for us . . .

He was not happy about this, for Malek was a very correct man, and I knew our liaison had bothered his sense of propriety, even while he could not hold himself away from me. There had always been a warring within him over our relationship. I knew he loved me, and yet this love had always had a feeling of guilt about it.

In the same way now I could see the duality of response to my news, for while he was delighted at my pregnancy, he immediately felt the necessity of legalising our union.

I was irritated by this. 'Oh, Malek! What does it matter? Has our loving thus affected anyone else? And if it has done so, will marriage now undo the harm?' Surely, I thought, he can see how his mother hates me. Or has he deliberately shut his mind to this?

'Nadir, it is proper that we should marry, for the sake of the child at least!'

'So be it, Malek. But not now. The baby will know no difference!'

Malek turned away from me, angry at my obstinacy. 'What things have you to do that are more important than our child?' he asked.

'I have to go to seek my father's forgiveness, Malek. I will tell you now that which I have kept to myself. I am the daughter of Habib Amir, Khan of Kabul.'

His indrawn breath told me he had heard of my disappearance.

317

'I left his estate over twelve months ago. It was, perhaps, a stupid thing to do, but I was betrothed to Shamlu Gadir, and could not face the prospect of such a match!' Oh, yes, it was indeed a stupid thing to do, I realised that now; stupid and completely selfish, for how many had I caused to suffer by so doing?

Malek turned to me, his eyes hurt and questioning.

'Why did you not tell me this before? I have heard, as has the whole of Afghanistan, of the Khan of Kabul's lost daughter, of the Khan's grief, and of the reward he offers for your return. But by far the worst, Nadir, is the wrong you have done your father in this way. Had I known this, I would have taken you straight to Kabul, and sought your father's sanction to our betrothal!'

'I knew you would. Perhaps that is why I kept silence. The punishment is for me alone to face, and he may still insist that I wed Shamlu Gadir. But now, I think, because I am with child, he cannot claim the bride price from Gadir, so he will release me from this bond.'

'I will come with you to Kabul, Nadir.'

Oh, no, you will not! I thought, though I didn't know why.

'My name is Noeda,' I said . . .

* * * *

. . . It was three long days before Muchige handed over responsibility for the running of his dubious establishment to one of his friends and, piling me into the back of a lorry, sat up front in the cab with the driver.

'Where are we going?' I had asked him.

'The less you know, the better,' he had replied abruptly. 'Suffice it to say that the driver is a friend and will drop us up in the Thomson's Falls area!'

'Have you heard something, then?' I persisted.

'Maybe!' He would say no more.

The lorry was piled with boxes and tins of kerosine,

sacks full of vegetables, crates of squawking chickens and a miserable-looking mongrel dog with one ear missing. It proved to be the most uncomfortable ride I'd ever had, and I was bruised and unhappy when we ground to a halt in the small township of Thomson's Falls.

'Come on, hurry up!' Muchige lifted a large sack onto my back, and adjusted the head strap that held it in place, so that it pressed hard into my forehead. 'Don't stand there like a Mzungu, expecting me to carry the load! You are a Kikuyu, remember!'

Silently, I cursed at his back as he strode ahead of me, but I had no recourse but to follow him as fast as I could through the town and out the other side. I was grateful for all the months of work in the shambas with Leah, for at least I was fit and could keep up with him.

By nightfall we were well within the forest. We had followed the path of a small river which ran, sun-sparkled, back down the hill to culminate in a beautiful waterfall.

'A sacred place to the Kikuyu,' Muchige told me, 'but desecrated now by the Wazungu who call it "Thomson's Falls", after some white man who was vain enough to think that he was the first man to set eyes on the beauty and magic of the cascading waters.' He turned as he spoke, his teeth bright-white in his dark face as he smiled at me.

'Are you all right, Nina? Is your back breaking from the load? I filled the sack with cabbages rather than potatoes to make it lighter for you!'

'I'm fine!' I said, through clenched teeth, determined that he'd have no reason for scorn.

In the fast-darkening forest, a troop of colabus monkeys leaped from one tall tree to another, on their way to settle for the night, their calls loud and eerie in the cooling air. As if signalled by their noise, all of a sudden the air was filled with the sound of birds of all kinds,

319

a sound so beautiful, so unbelievably rich, that my heart lifted at it, and I slipped the load from my shoulders in order to stand upright, listening.

'Wait one moment, please!' I called to Muchige.

He turned. 'What's the matter?'

'Nothing — just the birds — listen!'

He spat into the grasses. 'Birds! The girl talks about birds, when their noise is alerting every person in the forest to our presence here!' But he came back to me and sat on the ground.

'Here!' He pulled some bread wrapped in newspaper out of his pocket. 'Eat this, we may not have food again tonight!'

We sat eating the dry bread, with only a few birds now to disturb the uncanny stillness. Then, all at once, as happens in Africa, it was dark.

With no moon to light the way, we had to rely upon the feeble glow of a small hand torch which Muchige had brought with him, to find our way up the narrow pathway. We talked very little as we walked, single-file, because talking was too hard on our breathing at that altitude. In the damp forest it was too cold now to stop, so we had to keep moving, our legs and lungs straining to the limit.

Muchige made no sound as he went, unbelievably soft-footed for so large a man and, by comparison, my own progress was loud to my ears.

We travelled, in silence, for another back-breaking half-hour in the fast-chilling air then, suddenly, without warning, we were surrounded by armed and wild-eyed men. I dropped the bundle from my back and stood still, not daring to breathe, wanting to run and, to my chagrin, felt a trickle of urine run, hot, down my legs. I looked upwards, furtively, at the men that stood so close around us that their rancid stench almost choked me. I could see very little in the darkness, but could feel hard hands upon my arms, feel the breath of the man whose fingers bruised my flesh.

Muchige's voice broke into what seemed an eternity of tense silence.

'Stop! I am of the brotherhood!'

The voices then, all talking at once in fast Kikuyu, loud in the night silence of the forest. The hands on my arms let go, and I rubbed at the bruises.

Muchige put out a hand and pulled me nearer. With arms that shook, I lifted the bundle again and followed him, not sure what was happening, whether we were safe or about to meet certain death. Death, I felt sure, would be better than torture, than rape or the usual abuse the Mau Mau terrorists were supposed to inflict on women prisoners.

Dear God, if they've spotted us for what we are, let them get it over with quickly, I prayed, through teeth that chattered. My feet were clumsy and I stumbled often on the path. Muchige looked over his shoulder and said something harsh. Then he stopped and came back to me.

'Keep going,' he whispered, 'they are accepting us, I think. I'm going to hit you now, so be ready for it!' He cuffed my head, and took the bundle from me and, cursing in Kikuyu, dragged me behind him.

We came at last to a small clearing, where a group of people, men and women, huddled round a fire. They were ragged and dirty, faces haggard and thin in the fire-glow. Their eyes were dull and huge in their faces and many of them were coughing, racking, painful coughs.

I followed Muchige into the circle of firelight. All eyes rested on us, coldly speculative, and I sat back, slightly in the shadows behind Muchige, with my pulse racing. I pulled the blanket, which I'd worn tied apron-like around my waist on the journey, close around my shoulders for warmth.

Muchige handed round cigarettes to the men, chewing tobacco to the women, and there was a slight relaxation in the hostility, a shuffling on haunches as they lit up and inhaled, or chewed on the bitter tobacco. My trembling eased a little, and I touched Muchige tentatively with my foot. His hand reached out behind his back and squeezed that foot reassuringly. But I was still mortally afraid, and moved slowly and, I hoped, imperceptibly, closer to him.

I was surprised that the gang had been prepared to take us to this place. Muchige must be well trusted! I wondered how deeply he was implicated in the Mau Mau! Could it be that he was, like Jomo Kenyatta, one of the organisers, those educated Kikuyus who used their membership of the Kenya African Union as a mask for a far more dangerous movement, sponsored by China and other interested parties?

I wished now that I hadn't asked him for help. I felt sure that Leah would never have brought Kerri into such jeopardy. And yet — we'd never found out who had written the letter that put her to flight, or what it said.

The women started to prepare posho for a meal, and obviously must have said something about me, for Muchige turned and put his hand on my head, replying in Kikuyu.

'I've told them you are dumb and also that you're carrying my child,' he whispered quickly. 'Pretend you are unwell, and only eat a very small amount!'

That night I lay with his arms around me, his mouth close to my ear. 'I'm so sorry, Nina, I should have forseen this. I heard of a woman and child in the forest here, and thought it might be the two you are searching for. These men know of me and, because of that, will accept you. But be very, very careful! I have told them that the child-bearing sickness has made you slow and dim-witted and, hopefully, they will leave you alone!'

322

'Have they any news of my baby?' I asked.

'This I have not asked,' he replied. 'We'll have to wait until tomorrow. I don't want to raise too many questions in their minds. I pretend I lie with you now, Nina, to stop the others of my circumcision-group making any demands of their own, because the woman of any man is available to all those who have gone through the circumcision ceremony in the same year as him!'

I thanked him quietly, and was in fact thankful to be within the safety of his arms, though I hardly slept throughout the night, my ears alert for any sound of would-be assassin, and my mind running fearfully over the frightening possibilities the next day held for us.

I couldn't understand why Muchige had brought me here, into the heartland of the Mau Mau gangs; why anyone as intelligent as he seemed to be, with a finger on the pulse of all that was happening, should have made what seemed to be a pretty basic error. He must, surely, have known the danger of bringing a white girl, albeit in heavy disguise, into such a fanatically hostile locale. Even a black woman herself trod carefully here, terrified of saying or doing anything that could cause some doped-up, frustrated and hungry terrorist to raise his panga and finish her. If Muchige was really who he said . . . I frowned at the thought which had come unbidden into my mind. Was he Muchige, the Kikuyu brothel-keeper, or . . . ?

Of course he was! The gang had taken his cigarettes, given us food. There would have been no such niceties if they had had any doubts! No, I'm being stupid — he knows what he's doing! I reassured myself, moving closer within his sleeping embrace, unable to control my shivering on the cold, hard, wet ground.

'Nina, can't you sleep?' he murmured.

'I'm frightened and freezing!' I answered.

He turned me onto my side, curving my back into

323

his front, and wrapped my blanket around us both, so that we lay cupped like two spoons, with his arms tight around me.

'Better?' he asked.

I nodded, silent in the dark, wondering at the strange feeling of comfort I was getting from this close embrace. It was several moments before I realised that once again he had spoken to me in English.

'Paul?' I said quietly. He didn't reply, and I dared not speak again for fear of waking the others, but lay in uneasy wonder through most of that long night, falling into exhausted sleep towards daybreak.

I woke with a start at the sound of voices, of coughing and of twigs being snapped to rekindle the fire.

'Stay where you are!' Muchige's voice, speaking Swahili now, 'at least until I see that your disguise is okay!'

I lay with eyes heavy from lack of sleep, cocooned in the warmth our bodies had created, and was reluctant to move, to face the terrors of the day. Muchige stirred, and I didn't want him to go, to leave me — somehow unprotected. Then I opened my eyes wide, astonished that I should again feel an attraction towards this large, uncouth African. But then — if he was indeed Paul, that would explain it!

For God's sake! I thought, I'm here, in mortal danger from these Kikuyus whom circumstances and superstition have turned into wild and murderous animals; lying, like some loose bitch, with a man I'm not absolutely sure I know, whose motives and loyalties I'm not certain I trust; and once again my traitorous body betrays me!

I suffered Muchige's scrutiny and, after his nod of approval, got up and went into the bushes to urinate.

The trees were ghost-like in the early morning mist and, in the valleys below the clearing, their tops showed like blue, floating islands in a milky-grey sea. One by

324

one, birds took up the morning chorus and, in the distance, I could hear a troop of monkeys whooping. The forest wore its mask of deception well, tranquillity hiding the fermenting frustration which boiled below the swirling mists.

I stood with my arms tight-wrapped around myself against the chill, and puzzled over the enigma that was Muchige. I was almost certain now that he was Paul, and couldn't believe I had not recognised him straight away. And yet, in a way I had, feeling the tug of attraction, of familiarity at the brothel. Surely he knew who I was? He had, after all, applied my disguise!

Of course he does! I thought, of course! How couldn't he know? But if that was true, which it had to be, then why hadn't he said so? Why continue the deception? I rubbed my arms and drew my blanket closer.

He couldn't tell me! I realised, suddenly clear-headed, he's supposed to be Muchige, and doesn't want me, or anyone else, to know that he's not! But, selfishly, I was hurt that he should trust me so little and, following that hurt, came anger that he had exposed me to such danger. But then, I told myself, he didn't do so deliberately — we had run into the Mau Mau gang purely by chance, comparatively low down on the Abadares.

I knew I was too nervous to let him know that I'd seen through his disguise, tongue-tied by my feelings for him. He might be angry, cut me off, as he'd done before. I hugged the secret to myself, holding it, afraid to lose his confidence — however slight that might be. And afraid, too, that in the event that I was wrong, that I'd imagined the likeness out of a wild hope, a desperation, then he would surely abandon me. Abandon the search for Kerri! I shivered, stone cold with fear and uncertainty.

One of the women loomed up out of the mists and spoke in fast Kikuyu.

I nodded, pretending to understand, shrugged and pointed back at the camp site. Then, returning to Muchige's side, I gave him one of the mugs of steaming, un-milked tea which I collected from the fireside. I waited for him to drink it, then had one myself, feeling the warmth of it hit the bottom of my cold and empty stomach.

'What do we do now?' I asked, my face masked by the rim of the mug, my eyes on his face, studying the now-familiar conformation.

Muchige bent forward, as if to examine one of his boots.

'Slowly we will try to make our departure. But this must be open and unhurried or they will become even more suspicious.'

He pulled the heavy bundle I'd carried on my back open, and handed out cabbages to the women. Their hands snatched at the vegetables greedily, for they were hungry, these forest fugitives. Food from the shambas on the reserves was becoming more difficult to steal, and I had already heard how the hard core of the Mau Mau had been thrown back on the resources of the forest. Every edible plant was gathered, animals trapped with wire snares; wild honeycombs complete with the bees; raw monkey flesh — all were eaten without compunction. At times they'd have to go without even this meagre diet and, looking around at the ragged and filthy group that sat close round the small fire to warm themselves, I could see how emaciated they were, how gaunt their faces and hopeless their eyes. They looked so desperate, so famished, that I wondered if the rumours of cannibalism which had reached us in Mikendeni weren't actually based on hard facts. My stomach clenched in revulsion, and I hoped I would not bring up the hot tea I had just drunk.

I stole furtive glances at the men round the fire,

wondering if any one of them was the dreaded Dedan Kimathi, whose reputation for violence and for strangling even his closest supporters if they so much as displeased him in some small way, had made him one of the most hunted men in the forest. Everyone, both inside and outside the forests, knew how dangerous he was. Nothing was more disturbing than the thought of falling into his, or his henchmen's, hands. I shivered, heart racing, thinking about Kimathi, remembering how it was believed he'd been chief instigator of the Lari massacre, when two hundred Kikuyu men, women and children had been cut down, shot or burned to death in their homes in the village of Lari. Killed because it was believed they harboured informers; because, too, they hadn't co-operated one hundred per cent with the Mau Mau.

Indeed, if he is here, I thought, we've no hope — none whatsoever! Even Muchige's silvered tongue wouldn't be able to talk us out of danger and death — or worse! And if they penetrated his disguise . . . !

He was talking to them now — Muchige — and they were shuffling on their heels. Then one answered, and another interrupted, their thin brown hands waving, emphasising, pointing down the mountain.

Muchige's voice was raised slightly, and I wondered why he was becoming angry, what was being said, cursing the fact that I knew no Kikuyu at all.

'We'll have to wait,' was all he could manage to whisper laconically, and with that I had to be content for the moment.

NINETEEN

'They will take us further up the mountain,' Muchige told me later that day. 'There's a large group in some caves up there. It seems it's a centre for food and arms, and therefore there are many women who bring supplies and news from the towns, from the villages. They form the network through which messages and information can be passed.'

I went cold. Further up the mountain? What was he thinking of? I sighed and picked up my blanket. No matter what my fears, there was absolutely no way I could leave, no way I could find my own way down the mountain again, through the razor-sharp bamboo, through the pockets of trigger-happy Mau Mau, through the equally trigger-happy security forces who were combing the forests. No way, either, that I could pursue any other lines of enquiry on my own.

'Come on!' Muchige turned and waved me onwards. 'Well, come on! What's the matter with you? Your face is sad enough to frighten even a buffalo away, and your shoulders are bowed as if burdened by an overload of firewood!'

I didn't answer, but quickened my steps to keep up with him, with a heavy heart and my stomach churning.

The forest hung damply over the path, a dismal panoply of dank, black-green bush, which dripped large drops of cold water onto us as we passed. It was almost impossible for me to keep up with the others, for whom the upward gradient seemed to hold no difficulties. My pulse pounded loud in my head, blurring my vision, and making the steep upward climb even more hazardous, and my breath hurt in my over-taxed lungs, escaping in a loud, rasping sob as I stumbled for the umpteenth time over a tree-root.

Paul came back to me. Muchige, I reminded myself, I *must* think of him as Muchige, always, or I might slip up!

'For heaven's sake, Nina, try to control yourself! Do you have to make yourself so conspicuous?'

'I can't help it!' I was perilously close to tears now. 'I'm cold and frightened and soaking wet! No matter how hard I try, I can't keep up with you! Perhaps you'd better leave me here! Go on — just go and leave me!' Even as I spoke I realised how childish I was being.

Muchige squatted down beside me where I lay on the muddy ground, unable to find the strength or spirit to get up. He spoke softly, so that the men ahead, who stood staring at me, wouldn't hear.

'Nina, you know perfectly well I can't leave you here. Do you want to be raped by perhaps twenty, perhaps fifty men? Do you think you can cope with that? Or with the venereal disease you would undoubtedly contract — if you lived, that is! For the love of God, get hold of yourself and just grit your teeth — it's not far now, I promise you!'

'What's the point, if it doesn't lead me to Kerri and Leah?' I asked sullenly.

'They may not be here — and God knows, I hope they aren't but as I've already told you, this place is a meeting-point, a bowl into which all the news, all the gossip, pours like water into a washing bucket. It's the most likely place to find out if they've been captured, or whatever!'

He pulled me up, shouting and swearing at me in Kikuyu, to give credence to his actions and, holding onto my wrist, slowed his pace and pulled me along the path.

329

The muscles of my stomach had contracted at his words, a fast-falling, down-drop, then an upward rush of my stomach to my throat. I hadn't even imagined that they could have been taken by the Mau Mau. My mind flew desperately from thought to thought. Why? Why should they be of interest to the Mau Mau? Could it be because of Rashidi? But then, he didn't even know of Kerri's existence — no one but Melika and Leah knew who her father was.

'Oh, Holy Mother of God!' I screamed silently within my mind, 'Holy Mother of God — it can't be. Surely to God, it *can't* be!'

The rest of the journey passed almost without my realising it, the physical discomfort being by far less painful than the agonising ache I felt inside.

The possibility that Leah and Kerri might be in Mau Mau hands was more frightening than anything that had happened so far, the whole situation taking on a nightmarish quality that made it almost unreal. Perhaps Noeda was real and I was just a figment of *her* imagination, not the other way around. I wished, as I had so often wished before, that I could change places with her — though even she and Bibicol had faced danger enough, goodness knows. And now, in my dreaming, she was carrying a child! For a moment my mind stilled as I thought about her, and her voice in my head seemed to say:

'There is no escape, girl, no matter which way you turn. Remember that . . .'

Was it her voice? Or Maja's? Or Leah's? I couldn't tell and, pulling away from Muchige's tight grip, I vomited weakly into the wet grass at the side of the path.

'Oh, shit, Nina!' His hand was on my back as I heaved.

The gang members had stopped and their voices were raised.

330

'Better now?' he asked me, then turned and answered the angry queries calmly. Putting an arm around my waist he gently propelled me ahead of him on the path, so that he could steady my progress. In this manner, slowly, we arrived at the well-hidden clearing high on the mountainside for which we had been aiming.

In a way, my fear-induced nausea was a godsend, because it left me so dizzy and with such a headache that I hardly took in what was happening around me. I was only aware of the fact that there was a fairly large crowd of men and women, and that these ones looked minimally better fed than the original gang.

Muchige made me lie down and covered me with my blanket. 'Lie still and try to sleep,' he told me. 'I'll bring you some tea to drink later, and I'll make out that you are suffering from the sickness that comes from the forest, so that they'll leave you alone. In the meantime I'll talk, ask questions, see what I can learn.'

I shut my eyes, trying to block out my desperate, spiralling thoughts about Kerri, and finally fell into a jerky and feverish sleep . . .

* * * *

. . . My mind whirled, confused and uncertain.

Malek loved me, that I knew, and the knowledge filled me with shame and confusion. For though I loved him, too, in a manner, it was Rsul who came to fill my mind, my imaginings. Rsul whose face I thought to see as I opened my eyes to Malek's above me when we loved. Rsul, who had never spoken to me of love, who had merely read my innermost secrets with his brown-gold eyes.

How little he must think of me as Nadir! Young and foolish, hardly cast in his manly mould! He must surely have been puzzled greatly by the interaction between Ibrahim and myself on the way to Merve. Unless, of course, he had guessed! And I wouldn't have put that past him either. If he had indeed suspected that I was

331

daughter to the Khan of Kabul, why hadn't he ridden fast to take the news there? This and many questions chased through my head. And, always, it seemed as though there was someone else with me these early days of my pregnancy. The voice that had come intermittently, puzzling me, on my long journey, came more often now. In this confused state I thought it to be Maja — but why her? I knew her not at all — and yet, when we had met, with Malek, it was as if I'd known her intimately. I was totally bewildered by my strange thoughts, and put them down to the changes my body was going through as the baby grew. And yet — the voices had started way back along the track . . .

I sat watching Malek as he helped his father chop firewood, his brown muscles flexing in the sunshine, and I mourned. I knew that, to the utmost of his capacity, this man loved me. Knew that I should love him, too, as I thought I did at the start. Should love him for his gentleness, for his goodness of heart and loyalty; and I should love him, too, for the child I was carrying. But it was Rsul whose face I yearned to look upon; Rsul's dark, bearded face I wanted beside me. He was not fair-skinned, blue-eyed, as Malek was, not handsome like a Greek God — but his strength was of a different sort and, somehow, somewhere, our destinies were linked — I was sure of that. As sure as I could be of anything.

Malek came to where I sat, and his hand rested for a moment on my head.

'You are deep in thought, Nadir!' he said, 'and your face wears sadness like a veil these days. How I wish we were back in the mountains, in that small, cold stone hut! For then you were happy!'

Indeed, I had been happy with him. Aroused to a sensuality I had only suspected before with Ibrahim, I had been immersed in it, intoxicated by Malek's beauty, and by my own desperate craving for affection.

332

Would I have done the same thing, felt the same passion, for any man who had nursed me back to life then? I wondered.

I smiled at him, remembering his tender care, and loving him still, but in a totally different way. 'Those days were unique, Malek, unreal, for both of us. They will always remain in my memory to warm my heart when it is saddened!'

He sighed. 'You speak in the past, Nadir, as if you could never feel that way again. Already your spirit has left me, and I am desolated!'

I was relieved that he still called me by the name that I had adopted for my disguise, for it forestalled any questioning.

'Oh, Malek!' I answered him, 'don't speak thus, I beg you! My affection for you is still there — and do we not still make love together? That joy is not gone. But, dear heart, I would never be able to settle until I had made my peace with Habib Amir. Nor, if you are honest, would you ever feel entirely comfortable with me until the truth was told. I beg you to let me go to him and return as soon as possible. Then, and only then, will I consider taking the marriage vows. It cannot be right until I have his consent, Malek! Surely you can understand that!' Rsul would have understood, I thought.

He stood up, angry now.

'I still think it better that we go together, after the marriage, and with our child. How could the Khan of Kabul object then?'

'He could, and would,' I replied, 'for he is a man of protocol and we have not sought his permission!' I didn't want his permission, I knew that now.

'And the child?'

'He need not know! The chadri covers a multitude of defects!' I cried, for once seeing the chadri as a useful garment.

333

He turned to go. 'No, Nadir, I cannot let you go, you are not yet well enough. We will go later in the year, as I have already said.'

'But I have to go,' I whispered to Alexi who, as always, was at my side. 'You and I, Alexi, we have to go, just as soon as we can!'

A few days later Malek's mother stood over me, suddenly, when I had thought myself to be alone.

'Drink this!' She held out a beaker of fluid.

'I am not thirsty,' I said, instinctive fear burning my face and tautening the skin on the back of my neck so that the hairs there prickled separately.

Her eyes were like grey stone. 'Do as I say — it is a potion to bring away the child!'

'But I don't want to lose the child!' I protested.

Behind her, through the open doorway, I could see Jala and two village women. Their eyes were furtive, their hands nervously fingering their clothing.

'You will do as I say. There is no reason for us to believe that the child is actually Malek's. Who knows how many men you have seduced, with your big eyes and your look of helplessness!'

I was furious at this and stood up to face her.

'That's not true! Your son is the only one who has known me intimately!'

She laughed, a short harsh laugh. 'You expect me to believe that! You may have Malek fooled into believing your innocence, but why is it that you are running? And from whom? He has not thought to ask those questions, I'll warrant!'

I could not answer her, Malek had obviously not told her who I was. I stood dumb, staring at her. How could a gentle man like Malek have so vindictive a mother? And why, apart from her obvious devotion to Jala, should she hate me so much? It was not normal for any woman to want to destroy her own unborn grandchild. I shook my head and bit back my instinc-

334

tive desire to tell her that I was a Khan's daughter, since she would probably not have believed me anyway.

'Malek loves me, whether you approve or not! I suggested before we arrived in Kalash that I should continue my own journey without him, but he would not hear of it.' I hesitated, wondering if I should tell her that I was prepared to leave now, but anger and humiliation made me keep my silence. That would be my decision, I would go in my own time, and not at her instigation.

'Malek is besotted with you! He is obviously bewitched by some charm you have placed upon him — and he deserves better than some tramp he has picked up and helped on the track!'

If she did but know the truth! 'He is a good and generous man!' I protested, not prepared to allow the implication that he was some easily led weakling. 'He's not like you, Allah be praised, and I would do anything not to cause him pain!' And yet I knew that I was about to do just that.

She advanced towards me, holding the drink, her other hand waving the women outside to come in.

'Your honey'd tongue will not fool me! We have discussed this in the village, and are agreed that the only course is to rid you of the child, then you will have no tie to my son, and you can leave here as quickly as possible!'

'Who has decided this?' I eyed the three other women. 'The whole village, or just you three?'

Jala's eyes were frightened, and the other two women looked anywhere but at me.

'It has been decided! Now, you drink, or we force this down your throat anyway.' She pushed me down to the floor and her hand gripped my hair, pulling my head backwards. 'Come — hold her!' she ordered them.

As the drink came nearer, I could hear her breathing,

335

harsh with her concentration, and saw the perspiration run down her face.

She pushed the beaker against my lips and was tilting it when Malek appeared in the doorway. With a sharp movement, as if by accident, she fast-tipped the drink, so that it splashed onto the earthen floor. From the spilt liquid came a strong smell of something I couldn't at first place. Then, as she made out that she was smoothing my hair, plaiting it, I realised that the scent was that of crushed almonds, and my breathing faltered.

Was that not a poison — known to kill instantly?

She hadn't wanted just to get rid of the child! Oh, no! She was determined that I should present no further problems and, to this end, she was prepared to kill me!

I jumped up and ran into Malek's arms, with heart pounding uncomfortably.

He smiled and held me close. 'I see you are getting to know my mother better, Nadir!'

Oh, yes, I thought, I'm certainly getting to know her better! Out of the corner of my eye, I saw her foot surreptitiously scuffing up the earth on the floor to cover the spilt poison.

You'll not get me that way! I swore to myself. Oh no, I'll not have that! Nor will I allow Malek the pain of having you branded as a murderess. I care enough for him to want to spare him that! My leaving would be less hurtful in the long run, surely?'

I kept close by him over the next few days, but at the same time I was planning my escape. The provisioning and acquisition of items that I needed for such a long journey was made more difficult by the fact that I had to avoid Malek's mother, knowing that I was in mortal danger, whilst not making it obvious to either Malek or his father, needing to keep within calling distance of either of them — just in case!

She had proved that she would employ any means

336

to get rid of me, and obviously knew that Malek's love for me would not cease merely by my leaving. Only my death would give him the freedom to marry Jala. I could not tell her that marriage was the last thing I wanted, for she would not, or could not, believe me. And in a way she was correct. Malek was blind to everyone and everything but me, and while I was there, nothing would change that.

Realising that in my own way I loved Malek, I felt a deep guilt over our relationship, a guilt, too, at the fact that although I loved him, I didn't love him enough.

He was not Rsul.

I knew that the time had come, for I was sore afraid . . .

* * * *

. . . 'Drink this!' The voice in my ear startled me.

'No! No!' I cried, hitting out, spilling the contents of the mug. 'I don't want to lose the child!'

My arms flailed wildly at the man standing over me. 'Shh, Nina! For the love of God, shut up! Do you want everyone to hear you speak — and in English?' His hand clamped over my mouth and I struggled to free myself, still immersed in Afghanistan. In the chill air of the mountain I found myself wringing wet with perspiration.

Muchige's face was anxious.

'You'll give us away completely if you're not careful. I know you're frightened, and there's reason enough for that, but try to understand that because these men have been living in the forests now for a long time, they've developed an uncanny awareness of danger, an extraordinary alertness. They can sense the presence of strangers miles off, and the smell of your fear will all too quickly reach their nostrils. If it does, we're done for!'

'I'm sorry!' I clenched my teeth to stop them chatter-

337

ing with cold and fright. 'I had awful dreams of being murdered, and woke to find danger all around me!' I spoke in a whisper, my face concealed beneath the blanket.

He fetched me another drink and, as I sat sipping it, I saw the eyes of the Kikuyu women upon me.

'I should never have brought you with me!' His voice was still lowered, the tone angry. 'It was a grave mistake, and I really can't understand what possessed me. It's bad enough coming in amongst the real hard-core terrorists myself, never mind bringing you!' His anger was directed more at himself than at me. 'Why the hell didn't I insist that you wait with your family?'

'I pushed to come,' I said. 'I really couldn't have stayed at home twiddling my thumbs, waiting.'

'Yes, but this is madness!' He picked up a twig and broke it in half with a sharp movement. 'But we're here now, and the next step is to get out of this situation without losing credibility. For to do so will undo many months' work . . .'

I wondered just what he was up to, what 'work' he was talking about. And what about the hospital? His work there?

He snapped his fingers in an impatient gesture. 'Damn it! I've got news! That's what I woke you for! There are a woman and child, strangers it seems, down the mountain, about half a day's walk!'

My spirits lifted. 'Can we go to them?'

'Indeed we will, but it'll have to be tomorrow. Don't forget we have to appear cool, uninterested even, for a mere woman and child are of little consequence in Kikuyu eyes, and Muchige, the brothel-keeper, would hardly take precious time to look for them!'

I sank back, disappointed.

After a few moments he put his hand on my arm. 'We'll go first thing in the morning. I'll tell the people here that I have to get back, and that I'm taking you

338

to the Mzee Muganga, the medicine woman, as your sickness is worse.'

The night seemed endless, and I was chilled beyond belief, even with Muchige's arms about me. I lay shivering, staring into the darkness, with his slow breathing close in my ear, and the screaming cry of rock hyraxes rending the night frighteningly, as though murder was being committed all around us.

In my mind's eye was Melika's dear black face; Mother, thin and anxious, so unloved, so bewildered; Father, guilt-ridden and aggressive; Rashidi; Leah; Kerri and, of course, Paul. Paul whom I wanted so much to see me as an adult; as someone of worth.

Silent tears of self-pity rolled down my cheeks, as I grieved for all that could have been — that should have been — if only I hadn't loved Rashidi, if only I'd tried to understand Mother; if only Father hadn't died, hadn't . . .

Muchige snorted in his sleep and his arms jerked, shaking me out of my maudlin introspection.

What was gone was gone. Not much I could do about it, except to try and make amends somehow. Somehow!

Day broke, grey and mist-shrouded, and I got up and rekindled the fire, while the others still slept, unmoving forms wrapped completely in thin grey blankets or rough-cured animal skins, like so many corpses at the scene of a disaster. From the tops of a few of the motionless, unidentifiable bundles, spikes of dreadlocked hair protruded, reminding me of the illustrations from a childhood book about a small girl called Topsy. This twisted and plaited hair was typical of the Mau Mau, who adopted the style to facilitate the cleansing of lice and other parasites from their scalps. My own head itched at the thought and I scratched hard through my kerchief, wondering how much I had picked up from Muchige. His own hair was kept hidden under the battered felt hat which he never removed, not even for sleep.

Our shabby, unkempt house at Karen seemed suddenly like heaven, and I was overcome by a wave of acute homesickness.

One of the women got up and placed a debbi of water on the fire to heat, and spoke to me softly. I nodded and smiled, squatting on my heels in the African manner, and drew my blanket closer around my shoulders and across the lower half of my face as she did.

Muchige took forever to rise, and I waited, trying to control my impatience, as he stretched and spat, scratched an early-morning scratch, and then disappeared into the trees to relieve himself.

I steeled myself to stay absolutely still while he talked and laughed with the men, and to get up slowly, almost reluctantly, when he snapped his fingers at me and spoke angrily, obviously to give the impression that I was an enormous burden to him.

After we had walked for a while through dew-soaked grass, stopping from time to time in Mau Mau fashion to bend back the grasses we had disturbed with our passage, I asked him how he had explained our leaving.

'I did as I said I would do! Told them that you were ill with the forest sickness and, as this passes from person to person as fast as a forest fire in bamboo in the dry season, they were not reluctant to have me remove you from the hide!'

'What excuse did you give them for being there in the first place?' I wanted to know, for it was odd that a city-dweller like Muchige should be accepted so easily by the super-sensitive terrorists. Even more incredible that a white man, no matter how well disguised, should deceive them!

'Ah!' he replied. 'That is another story! Enough to say that I bring them news of what is happening outside the forests, for a man can lose touch with reality up here. Now, stop speaking and walk as quietly as you can — and watch me carefully. If I tell you to stop, then do so immediately and if I gesture so . . .' — he made an up-and-down motion with his hand — '. . . then move as quickly and silently as possible into the trees and lie flat, for there may be soldiers or Askaris patrolling this area.'

'They wouldn't hurt us, surely?' I whispered anxiously.

'Of course they would! We're dressed like Mau Mau, we walk the Mau Mau paths. How could they tell what, or who, we are?'

I hadn't thought of that, and followed in silence, watching him intently.

It was near noon when he gestured me to stop.

'We're near the hideout,' he whispered. 'Conceal yourself in the grasses at the side of the path while I go and see if I can find it.'

The smell of the damp earth and crushed grass was strong in my nostrils as I lay, face downward, waiting. The time stretched, small noises intensified: the buzzing of some insect around my head; the strange gunshot sound of bamboo stems expanding in the sunlight, somewhere in the forest below; and my own heartbeat, echoing in my ears. Then Muchige was back.

'It's okay, I've found the place, made myself known. But this is an even more dangerous gang, Nina, and I will not speak to you. Just keep quiet and stay close to me.'

He led me a short way up a path, so well concealed that I would never had spotted it on my own, leading to a large rock which shielded the entrance to a cave. This had been dug out to make it larger and deeper. In the dim light inside I could see many guns, knives and pangas stacked against the rough-hewn walls.

Boxes of ammunition stood, half-covered by goat skins, to one side of the stinking cave.

The men here were not as emaciated as those I'd seen before, but their faces were hard, their eyes angry, with drug-dilated pupils. There were ten men, all carrying guns, hair in the usual dreadlock style, and dressed in animal skins.

A small group of women sat huddled in one corner. All were silent, and the hostility was a tangible and fearful reality.

Muchige squatted near the men, and I sat behind him. His voice was conciliatory and, once again, he handed out cigarettes. The men took them suspiciously, rolling them between their fingers and sniffing at them, before lighting up.

I stole a furtive look at the women, trying to see their faces in the gloom of the cave. There was a child there and I tried desperately to get close enough to see. The women were so tight-bunched that I couldn't distinguish one from the other. Was Leah there? I blinked, trying to get my eyes to focus. Moving slowly, inch by painful inch, I got nearer to them, keeping my head down until I was close enough, without being obvious.

No Leah. No Mirriamu.

These were all definitely Kikuyu women, with distended ear lobes and broad foreheads bearing the telltale marks of the carrying straps with which they steadied their heavy loads. No rounder, darker Buganda faces amongst them. And there was a child, a small, very dark, very young child — but it wasn't Kerri. Wasn't my baby!

My heart sank, and my whole body felt lead-weighted with disappointment. I wondered if there were any others out of the dug-out, but dared not ask since Muchige had instructed me not to speak.

He shifted his position and took a quick look at me

over his shoulder. I imperceptibly shook my head, and he turned back to the men.

After about an hour, he got up and led me out of the cave, with the hostility unabated, the men's hands still tight upon their weapons.

'Walk quickly,' he said, setting a fast pace down the path. 'That gang were not convinced about us, and I have a feeling they may well follow!'

I was so dispirited that I hardly cared now.

'Are you sure there weren't any more women and children?' I asked.

'No, there were no more. I'm sorry, Nina, it seems my information was wrong this time.' He slowed slightly, seeing that the gap between us was lengthening. 'We'll have to go back to Nairobi now. This is a dead end, and I'm afraid we may have blown our cover.'

Yes, I thought, and even if we have managed to hoodwink the terrorists for now, surely neither of us could get away with it for much longer?

I was torn with indecision, wondering if I should tell him I knew who he was, risking his reaction to that, or whether I should just keep quiet. The knowledge that he was in as much danger as I was — in fact greater danger because of his duplicity — did nothing to help calm my already taut nerves.

TWENTY

Our progress through the wooded upper slopes from the dug-out was fast and we didn't stop to cover our trail as often as we had done before.

The wet grass had soaked us, but I was still sweating from the pace Muchige set. The path was barely visible, and fallen leaves gave the ground a soft, mulchy layer that cushioned any sound.

Then, unexpectedly, we came into a belt of bamboo so thick that only a faint glimmer of light filtered through, even though the sun was high. Old stems had fallen, forming a thick mat of dried poles on the ground, through which new shoots grew, making a tangled, interwoven mass. The thin sharp leaves sliced my skin, and I pulled my blanket round my arms to protect them. There was nothing I could do about my legs, and they stung with a criss-cross of scratches and cuts. As if that wasn't enough, a small breeze rustled through the papery tops, sending a shower of fine, hair-like particles down to fall on my face, making it itch unbearably.

My eyes prickled, and I had difficulty breathing as tears of frustration and self-pity welled up inside me. I swallowed hard and blinked them away, determined Muchige shouldn't see my weakness; wanting just to die, to end this nightmare journey. So engrossed was I in fighting the desire to lie down and give up, that I bumped into him where he'd stopped on the path in front of me.

'Shh!' His finger went to his mouth, bidding my silence. He put his lips against my ear. 'We're being followed — I don't know who by, whether it is those men from the dug-out, or others, or even the security forces! But they are not too far behind — I heard the crack of a stick!'

I wondered how he could have distinguished between that and the intermittent gunshot explosions of the bamboo stems in the midday heat. I had heard nothing, but that was hardly surprising as I had been concentrating solely on fighting my way through the sharp-cutting leaves, and in trying not to trip on the matted poles as we went.

Now I stood, with breath sharp in my throat and lungs, my eyes wildly searching the forest around me, ears alert for any out-of-context sound.

Muchige's hand on my blanket-wrapped arm pulled me forward.

'Come on! There's nothing we can do about it. They know we're here and are following us, so it's pointless to hide! Just keep going, as nonchalantly as you can manage. We'll be out of this bloody bamboo soon!'

Nonchalantly! I thought. How can I act nonchalantly, when I'm so frightened? Panic made me want to run, to career wildly down the path, out of the forest like some wounded buffalo. Above my loud heartbeat, my rasping breath, my own clumsy footfall, I heard it then — the sound of bamboo snapping, under our pursuers' feet.

'Oh God! Oh God! Oh God!' I repeated silently, mindlessly, as I half ran, half walked, hands clenched and shoulders stiff with tension. Tension that made me even clumsier, causing me to stumble constantly. The hairs on the back of my neck tingled, and I expected at any moment to feel the heavy, sharp blade of a panga between my shoulder blades.

By the time we reached the edge of the bamboo belt, with the deciduous forest thick and dark ahead of us, I was almost blind with fear, with the bamboo dust, with perspiration, and I ran with my arms outstretched

345

in front of me, caring nothing now for the cuts that patterned my flesh.

Muchige was bent double, his hands clasping his knees, his chest heaving with exertion. He straightened up as I reached him and held me as I nearly fell once more.

'It'll be easier going from here on,' he said quietly. He looked intently at the thick undergrowth around us, searching for the men who followed, then he turned back to me.

'I'm fairly certain now that it's the security forces on our trail, not the Mau Mau.'

'Why?' I managed to gasp, not really caring who it was, only that we should either escape or be killed, one or the other, but quickly.

'The gangs have learned to move so silently, running on the sides of their feet to leave no footprints, that I'm sure I wouldn't have heard them at all, even though my ears are tuned to each change of sound in the forest!'

'Well, if it's the Askari, can't we call out — tell them who we are?' I was desperate now to get it over with.

'And blow our cover completely to any on-looking Mau Mau, too?'

He pulled me off the path and into the dense undergrowth, listened for a moment, then bent back the grasses and twigs we'd passed through, so there was no mark of where we'd left the path. I wondered about our footprints, but realised how clever he was being. We'd stood for that short moment, still on the matted poles and had left no mark upon the earth of the forest floor.

Moving now very slowly, very carefully, and at each few steps eliminating the traces we'd left, we went deeper into the tangle of new growth in the deciduous forest, until we reached a shallow depression some little way from the path.

Muchige motioned me to lie down and then, almost without sound, covered me with leaves and earth until only my nose, eyes and mouth remained uncovered. Then he left me. Out of the corners of my eyes, I watched him move, snake-like on his belly, on the forest floor, sliding under the lowest branches of the bushes, leaving no trace on the thick layer of fallen leaves.

I lay with every nerve-end screaming in the confinement of wet earth and leaves, claustrophobic and petrified, hyper-ventilating and shivering in my shallow grave.

What if he got caught, leaving me alone here? What on earth should I do? My mind whirled, the trees around me became distorted, went dark, as I sank into blackness . . .

* * * *

. . . 'Quick, Alexi! Quick!' I exhorted as we came through the pass, out of the village of Kalash. My breath was short with fear, and an inexplicable sense of panic filled me. I looked often over my shoulder, half expecting to find myself pursued.

I had forced myself to walk the horse slowly, wondering as I did so if I were destined forever to steal away at the dead of night, like some furtive criminal. This was the third time I had done it, once with my beloved Bibicol, and now twice alone. I thought of her with a pang of longing and felt the tears start to my eyes, knowing that I would never see her dear face again, and realising the extent of my loss. Dearest Bibicol, who had shared so much with me, who had given me unstintingly her love, her trust, all the days of her young life. Oh, Bibicol! The tears rolled, unchecked now, down my face as I thought of her. And following Bibicol — Malek, whose love was undoubted. I comforted myself with the thought that even if I never returned to him, Jala was there. Jala, sweet-faced and docile — his mother's choice! At the thought of his

347

mother my heartbeat quickened and I lifted Alexi onto the horse and mounted behind him, setting the animal at a brisk pace to put as much distance as I could between myself and Kalash.

I hoped that once Malek found I was gone he would be wise enough to let me go, and not set out in pursuit. He would, I was sure, expect me to return once our child was born. But his wounds would heal. If he didn't see the child he couldn't grieve for it, surely? And Jala would give him many fine sons.

I wasn't entirely successful in convincing myself, knowing that I was guilty of too much as far as this man was concerned.

I dug my heels into the horse's flanks and let the cool wind on my face blow away my doubts. In any event I had to concentrate so hard on keeping my seat at the same as holding Alexi from falling, that my introspective thoughts were banished.

I travelled a fair distance before daybreak over an unknown track and, bone-weary at last, I dismounted and found a hiding place where we could rest for a while.

Realising that I had no knowledge of the area, hadn't even asked for directions, I took note of where the sun rose, tinting the sky a grey-pink like the soft breast of a ring-necked dove, so that I would at least continue in a southerly direction later in the day.

Three nights I rode thus, resting during the daylight hours, in the same manner as I had done with Bibicol at the start of this long adventure, and during this time saw not one other person, neither traveller nor peasant. The land was arid and inhospitable and not even goats could have found enough grazing here.

My horse's hooves sounded loud, echoing against the sides of the rocky gorges, the only sound at times in the eerie silence of that dry, empty terrain. I talked constantly to Alexi to retain my sanity, and his eyes

348

rolled, his tongue lolling out of the side of his mouth in joy at having me all to himself.

It was on the third day, as I stretched wearily upon the rug I'd thrown down, that once again I thought I heard hoofbeats in the far distance, but my heart was pounding so loud within my chest, that I could not tell whether it was its echo in my head that I heard.

The baby within me was moving, causing me some discomfort, and I placed my hand over the movement as if by doing so I could still the child. I needed all my senses alert to discern which direction the sounds were coming from, whether they were born of my own apprehension or reality. I held my breath, straining to hear.

Yes! There was more than one horse, if I guessed aright. I got up and mounted quickly, snatching up Alexi, and turning the horse down a shale-scattered slope into a valley below, hoping that the hoof-prints would be lost amongst the stones. Then I doubled back in the direction from which we had come, still keeping the horse slithering on the loose shale, keeping, too, just below the horizon-line, until I thought we were well behind the riders. I tied the horse in a thicket and went, stooping, with Alexi to a small outcrop of grey-green boulders from the top of which I could see a party of some five riders following our original trail.

At that distance I could not tell if it was Malek or not, but it made no difference — whoever it was, I did not want to meet them.

I made my way fast back to the horse and, climbing quickly on its back, proceeded along the same track behind them, my mount's hoof-prints mingling now with those of the five horses. I hoped to confuse the trail completely by circling back to the rocky downcline once again. When I got to the valley bottom I turned southwards, riding along a dry river bed looking for cover and concealment, and finding at last a shallow cave hidden by large rocks and scrubby bushes, I hid the horse there and tied Alexi to a branch while I retraced our steps for quite a distance, brushing away the marks of our passage with a leafy branch, then working my way backwards doing the same thing with my own footprints. This seemed a feeble attempt, but the best I could think of, given the probability that the group could be closing in on us.

I was sweating profusely by now, hampered by my skirts, and cursing the fact that I'd not had time to dress myself in man's clothing once more. When at last I got back to Alexi's enthusiastic welcome, I was dizzy and overcome with nausea, my back aching badly from the long ride and lack of rest.

'Oh, Alexi! Why do I place myself constantly in such difficult situations? Why couldn't I be content to stay in Kabul, or wed to Shamlu Gadir, in comfort and luxury; or to Malek — did his mother but let us?'

Alexi did not answer, and indeed there was no need for him to do so.

I lay down, trying to relax enough so that my heavy, weary body could get some rest, but I was nervous, all senses alert for sounds of my pursuers.

It was some two hours later that I sat up with a start, hearing the distant sound of voices. I bade Alexi to sit quietly, hoping against hope that he would not bark, that the horse would not whinny at the sound of the other animals. Thus, with one hand on Alexi's neck, the other clasping the horse's soft muzzle, I crouched between the two, looking through a small gap in the rocks.

No, it was not Malek, I could see that now as they drew nearer. Nor were they his friends from Kalash. These five looked rough, with large knives strapped to their waists, unkempt hair draggling from beneath their hats, clothes with more than a few days' dust upon them.

350

'The trail stops here!' one called out. 'She must have hidden!'

My heart was thudding, loud and painful in the confines of my chest.

'Or gone upwards, over the stone scree once more!' another answered. They split up, casting about, but the two who came my way, for some reason did not stop to search the rocks, presumably believing that I had ridden onwards.

Alexi fidgeted and I stroked him, calming his excitement, keeping my own panic at bay until they'd passed.

Then there was silence, but I knew instinctively that they'd be back . . .

* * * *

. . . My eyes flew open at the sound of the abrupt voice, the scrunch of boots on the leaves. Above me Muchige stood, arms held tight behind his back by a white soldier in camouflage battledress.

The barrel of a gun prodded me, and another soldier was standing over the slight mound my body made.

'Get up, bloody Mau Mau!' he said and, as I struggled upwards, the gun butt smashed against my head, knocking me down again.

'Come on! Come on, bloody Mickey Mouse!' This was the nickname the security forces gave to the Mau Mau. 'Christ, Joe! It's a bloody mwanamuki, a woman, the bitch!'

I knelt in the leaf-mulch, my head spinning from the blow, fighting off sickness.

Muchige was struggling to free himself.

'Stop it! Don't hit her!' he said.

'This bugger speaks English — uppity, sodding wog!' The rifle butt thwacked against Muchige's mouth, making the blood spurt.

I jumped to my feet. 'Leave him alone, for God's sake!' I said urgently. 'I'm white, and he's helping me!'

They regarded me disbelievingly.

351

'Come off it!' The one called Joe pushed my head back so that the filtered sunlight caught my face, spot-lighting it for his inspection. 'White, my arse — you're as black as the rest of these bastards! What would you be doing up here anyway if you were white, eh? Tell me that!' He let go of my hair so that my head snapped back, ricking my neck painfully.

'You're not going to believe us anyway,' Muchige still spoke in English, 'so why not at least give us the benefit of the doubt and get us the hell out of here! There's a gang not far behind us anyway, and if we stay much longer it'll be all too easy for them to ambush us — if they haven't set it up already!'

The two soldiers looked at each other doubtfully.

'Better take them back to the camp, I guess,' one of them said, 'though it's a bit of a shit really. It'd be easier just to shoot them and leave them here.'

'And alert every terrorist in the area?' Muchige asked. 'Is that what you want? Presumably, there's a lot of you doing a sweep of the forest?'

'How'n the hell do you know?'

Muchige shrugged. 'I'll tell you everything once we get out of here! Hurry up, for God's sake, the light will be going soon, then we'll never find our way.'

The men looked dubious, but let us go and, walking one behind us, one in front, took us down the path.

My breathing eased and I dusted off the remaining loam and leaves as we went.

Muchige, now behind me, cursed under his breath. 'Damn! If any Mau Mau were hidden nearby, they'd have heard all that — my credibility is gone completely now. Damn and blast it!'

'I'm sorry!' I threw the apology over my shoulder as we went. 'I'm truly sorry, especially as it turned out to be a false trail anyway!'

'My own fault, Nina, not yours. I should've checked

352

out the information more thoroughly in the first place . . .'

He lapsed into silence and I bit back the million questions that begged to be asked, knowing that now was not the time.

I puzzled at Paul's role in the struggle between black and white, at the danger he was in, all the way down the mountain, relief at our comparative safety making the journey feel short, easy. In no time at all, it seemed, we reached a clearing at the base of the mountain where several Landrovers were parked among khaki-coloured tents, and armed sentries stood on watch.

Muchige was taken immediately to the officer in charge of the operation, a wiry, ginger-moustached Scotsman, and they disappeared into one of the tents, leaving me still guarded by the two men who had found us. Then, after a while, the officer reappeared.

'Shove her into the Landrover!' he said, winking at me, 'and drive both the silly buggers back to Nyeri for the night.' He turned to me. 'We'll get you back to Nairobi tomorrow, Miss Anderson.' He put his hand on my arm. 'I knew your father well — so sorry to hear of his death, m'dear!'

I smiled my relief. 'Thank you!' I said, somewhat lamely.

At the police guesthouse in Nyeri, where the Land-rover dropped us, we were given a rondavel separated from the rest, two rooms with a bathroom in between.

'Can I bath? What about the disguise?' I asked Muchige, looking longingly at the white porcelain, the silver taps.

'Of course you can now,' he said. 'I'm going to sleep — give me a shout when you're finished so that I can follow you.' He shut the door of his room.

'Paul . . .' My hand moved halfway to the doorknob, then stopped. I frowned and turned into the bathroom, wishing I'd got clean clothes to put on.

Water had never felt so good, soap never soapier as I lathered my hair with it in lieu of shampoo. I lay in the warm suds, letting my tension slowly relax, almost enjoying the stinging of my million bamboo-leaf cuts, my only real discomfort being the bruised side of my face where the rifle butt had smashed.

Afterwards I stared at myself in the bathroom mirror and laughed. The stain was still there — most of it — but faint now, and somewhat blotchy between the cuts. My eyes were still yellowed, but at least my hair was clean. I ran my fingers through it, luxuriating in its softness, rubbing it with the towel that had been left for my use, then tapped at Paul's door.

'Okay, the bathroom's yours!'

The sounds of his splashing only just impinged upon my tired mind. I curled up on the bed with the towel around me, and drifted into deep and, for once, dreamless sleep.

When I woke, it was with a jump.

The man leaning over the bed was indistinct, for it was nearly dark and the lights hadn't been lit.

'Nina, sorry to wake you, but we should eat — I've ordered some food to be brought here. All right?'

I sat up fast, clutching the towel around my nakedness, still sleep-drugged.

'Paul?' I was confused. 'Is that you, Paul?'

He laughed. 'Of course it is, you idiot!'

In the soft light he, too, was blotched and cut, his lip swollen from the blow it had received, but his face was unpadded now, had resumed its normal contours.

'Oh Paul! What a relief . . . !' I started to cry, stupidly, tears of embarrassment and joy flooding my face.

'Why?' I sobbed, holding onto his shirt collar with both hands, modesty forgotten. 'Why the hell didn't you tell me at the start? I needed you so much!' But I still couldn't tell him that I'd recognised him.

He put his arms around me, drew my head against

his chest. 'I couldn't, now, could I? It was difficult enough keeping up *your* disguise, as it was, without you having the additional strain of pretending you didn't know me! Here, I've got you some clothes. They're men's, but that doesn't matter, does it? At least they're clean!'

I couldn't stop staring at him, seeing how different he looked and wondering how he'd disguised himself so well that I'd not spotted it straight away. Yet — I *had* wondered why I felt I knew Muchige . . . And, blushing at the memory, I remembered, too, the rush of desire I'd felt when he'd been staining my back, the wanting when I'd lain close-cupped with him in the cold, wet forest.

'I can't tell you much, Nina,' he said in answer to my questioning over the meal. 'Just that I'm tied up with the intelligence branch of the security forces, helping run the pseudo-terrorist gangs. We infiltrate, get information, that sort of thing!'

'And the brothel?'

'An ideal cover! Good place to gather information, too! Everyone trusts —' his eyes blanked for a moment, '— trusted, the jolly brothel-keeper! Let's hope my cover isn't blown completely, it's taken months and months of work to set up that particular operation.'

'Sorry, Paul . . .' I began.

He put his hand over mine, briefly. 'Enough said, Nina — how could I have let you go, get yourself into danger? I had to do it! But sentiment shouldn't affect my judgment, and it did in this case! Now let's drop the subject, just be ordinary people once again!'

That would explain his strange disappearances from Mombasa, I realised.

We talked all through that night, tired though we were, huddled together on the small narrow bed in my room.

And as we spoke, he pulled the past forward and I

355

felt infinity unfolding around me, saw my part in it; saw how our threads interwove in the tapestry so that we were part of each other and yet apart; separate and yet part of the whole.

The mystery of evolution was there, shining and brilliant within my grasp, our reunion the eternal 'Now'; a breathtaking moment out of time.

This knowledge, coming through words spoken and unspoken, left me breathless and yet gasping for more, and then I was filled with peace and a perfect calmness. We had reached back a millennium, catching stars upon the way, and had broached more subjects in those few short hours than I had even contemplated.

And yet there was no urgency for bodily exploration, we were closer by far than we would have been making love. That could come later. Haste would somehow have lessened the moment. Our closeness was age-old, our trust was being newly forged.

Exhilarated later, we sat on the steps of the verandah and watched the first pale fingers of dawn push up from the east to underscore the night clouds with saffron and rose-pink.

'We'd better get some sleep before we go back to Nairobi,' he said at last. In the half light his face was tired, a new growth of beard blueing his chin, giving him a wild and almost fugitive appearance.

I blinked at the brightening sky, reluctant to move away from the rough wool of his jumper, the comfort of his encircling arm, then struggled up, aware of my returning bodily sensations. My feet were frozen and I had cramp in one leg.

'Yes,' I said reluctantly. 'Yes, we'd better sleep!' I wondered how much time had passed, I'd no idea. An hour? Or several days?

I felt Paul lightly touch my face. 'Cold?' he asked.

'Yes — a little!'

We were whispering, as if we were still in the presence of our past, afraid to leave it, to lose it. Then his hand was under my chin, turning my head towards him, and he was kissing me, gently at first, and then with a wild hunger which matched my own.

And the hunger was a delight, and a fulfilment, and an unbelievable joy.

And afterwards we slept, close-held, in each other's arms.

TWENTY-ONE

The house had a shuttered, desolate look to it, the garden overgrown, unclipped. My calls brought no response from the houseboy or gardener. Of Melika, too, there was no sign.

I leaned against the rough stone wall of the house and turned my face up to the sun, feeling it warm on my closed lids.

My body was still languid with the lassitude that follows a night of love, and my lips tingled. I ran my tongue over them, the taste of Paul's mouth still sweet, still new and exciting — and yet familiar. I could hardly bear to shut my mouth, to swallow, lest I lost its fragrance.

Thinking of him, I stretched, sensuous and feline in the sunshine.

My fingers, with nerve-ends ultra-sensitive, ran over the stone and it felt like silk. Over the blue-flowered plumbago bushes which encircled the house, a bright yellow butterfly hovered, antennae quivering, each tiny filament of its wings clear-detailed to my newly aware eyes.

The languor, the lingering memory of his hands on my anticipatory body; the aching, hurting, wonderful, awesome feeling that coursed through my veins, dissipated slowly into the sun-warming, insect-buzzing, flower-sweet day. And I was empty; drained; hollow; alone. Wanting to weep, with a deep loneliness of soul.

As Noeda had.

From somewhere across the hedges a child cried, the imperious, demanding wail of a very young baby and, with the sound, the worry over Kerri which had been my constant companion for the past long, few weeks returned, earthing me.

Paul and I never spoke about her! I thought. I was immediately beset by an all-pervading guilt that I should have taken so much pleasure with him and forgotten, albeit briefly, about her.

And Paul? I wondered what his thoughts were. Admittedly, he was helping me to search, but I had no idea about how he felt about her presence in my life, about her heritage of mixed blood. He had been abrupt on the journey from Nyeri, withdrawn and silent, and I had let him be, thinking him to be tired. Now, suddenly insecure again, I wondered if he regretted what had passed between us. All that had passed between us. Had I imagined the depth, magnified the importance? I pushed the doubts away.

Where on earth was Melika? I frowned, looking at my watch. It was unusual for the place to be completely deserted. I went to the small block that housed the servants' quarters, tucked discreetly behind a hedge at the back of the house, and pounded impatiently on the doors. They, too, were locked, inhospitable, and I felt panic begin to rise, wondering if some dreadful catastrophe had occurred, causing all the servants to leave unexpectedly.

Had Mother got worse? Died, even, whilst I was away in the forest? Had the Mau Mau raided the house, massacred every one of them, and no one known where to find me?

My mind whirled, imagining the worst, so that by the time Melika walked through the gateway some ten minutes later, I was almost hysterical with worry.

'Nina! Nina!' She held me close. 'Whatever is the matter? What has happened to upset you so?'

I struggled to speak through my weeping, the words staccato. 'Oh, Melika! We searched and searched for

359

Kerri and Leah without success! We nearly got caught by the Mau Mau!'

She looked perplexed. 'What do you mean?'

I'd forgotten she didn't know about Muchige.

'It's a long story, Melika. I'll have to tell you about it another time!' I couldn't tell her anything anyway, Paul had sworn me to secrecy, for his sake and for my own.

She shook her head, forehead puckered. 'I, too, have bad news, and I hate to tell you when you are already so upset. But you have to know. The reason I was not here when you arrived is because the Askari were questioning me. Rashidi has escaped from MacKinnon Road Camp, and they thought I might have heard from him.'

'And have you, Melika? Have you heard from him?' My fear now was not for Rashidi, but for Kerri.

'No! Nothing! Nor have I heard from Jamira in Uganda! Truly, my heart is heavy with fear for both of them, and for Leah and Kerri.'

She sat down heavily on the steps that led up to her room.

'There is so much trouble now! It seems the world has changed too much. Everyone is suffering! Why? Why does God punish so many who have done nothing? And us, Nina, what have we done that our punishment never stops — Bwana Anderson, Memsahib, you and Rashidi, Leah and Kerri! Have we done so much wickedness to deserve trouble?'

I sat down beside her, my own guilt made greater by her words.

'I don't understand either, Melika. If it is me who has sinned — and, yes, I suppose I sinned with Rashidi in the eyes of the church — then it should be me, and only me, who suffers the consequences, if we follow that line of thought. And if we pursue it even further, then we can ask the questions: why should you have

360

so much sorrow? Why should Father be the one to die? Why Mother fall so ill? Leah and Kerri disappear? Who knows the answers? I certainly don't!'

Leah would know, I thought, so would Maja.

I wondered about Rsul — and Paul with whom I'd reached back and thought I'd found the answers. Would Paul know? Paul, the Gemini — one moment all light, all loving, the next closed, dark, untouchable.

Melika put her arm around my waist and hugged me.

'No, Nina, you can't take all the blame on your young shoulders. You haven't been "wicked", merely foolish, allowing your heart to lead where your head should guide. Rashidi is the one who has placed us all in danger, for didn't I raise him to know right from wrong all through his life? And he has broken all the ancient laws, first with you, and then by running with the mad dogs who call themselves "fighters for freedom"! Ach, Nina, what demon has he eaten that he behaves so?'

It wasn't the cause of his present behaviour that concerned me, more the way in which the 'demons' would lead him from now on.

We sat silently for a while, deep in our own private worries. Then Melika got up.

'We must go into the house. You've got to ring Bwana Blake, he asked me to tell you to do so urgently when you got back. Then you should go to see Memsahib at visiting time this afternoon.'

I wondered what Michael wanted so urgently.

'I gather you wanted me to ring!' I said, when I'd finally been put through to his extension.

'Nina! Where on earth have you been? I've tried to contact you for days!'

'Why, what's the matter? Is Mother all right? I haven't had time to see her yet. I've only just got back

361

to Nairobi.' I found myself gabbling, embarrassed for some reason.

'Nothing urgent, really. I was just worried as no one seemed to know where you were, what you were doing!' His voice was calm, soothing me down as if I were some hysterical child.

'I had private things to attend to!' My answer was sharp with annoyance. It was, after all, none of his business.

'Yes, I'm sure you did. Sorry, Nina, I'm not criticising. Your mother'll be glad you're back!'

The criticism was implicit, enraging me even more.

'My ayah has been keeping her informed. She'd have told me if Mother's health had deteriorated!' I lied, knowing full well that Melika couldn't possibly have found me. 'I presume from your remarks that you've seen my mother recently?'

The phone crackled and something clicked against it. I wondered vaguely if it was tapped. Could the security forces have done this, in order to check on Rashidi? I made a mental note not to be tempted to contact Paul on that particular instrument.

'Hello! Nina — are you there? Hello!' Michael's voice brought my mind back.

'Yes, I'm here!'

'Oh good! Thought we'd been cut off! No — what I was saying is that Mrs Anderson's not too good. Doctor Phillips is away, unfortunately, so I'm a bit worried, quite honestly.'

Mother! Oh, God!

'He's back, I think,' I said. 'I'll try and see him this afternoon. Is Mother too ill to travel?'

Guiltily, I recalled the night Paul and I had just spent together. I hadn't had a passing thought for Mother then.

'No — at least I don't believe so! But do get to see

362

her, it'll make a difference if she knows you've returned. She seemed to think you were gone forever!'

'All right, Michael. Thanks for visiting her. I'll go straight away.' I ran my free hand wearily over my hair.

'I'll ring you later,' he said. 'See how you find her!'

I put the phone down and stood looking at it, as if it housed Michael, housed the veiled accusations. Then I turned away, cheeks flushed with indignation.

How dare he tell me off! For that's what he was doing. What right had he to make moral judgments?

At the hospital the ward sister looked at me contemptuously, checked the watch pinned to her starched uniform, and said crisply:

'You're twenty minutes too early for visiting time!'

'Yes, I know that, and I'm sorry! It's just that I've been away, and I understand my mother has been fretting a bit!'

'Mrs Anderson's as well as can be expected. We made an exception in her case, you know, letting in the native woman!'

'Melika? Oh yes, she's our ayah — well more than an ayah really. Part of the family . . .' My voice trailed away. Her eyes didn't change, remained impassively cold.

'It's against the rules, nonetheless. If Doctor Phillips hadn't given orders . . .'

'Is he here?' I hoped my voice wasn't too eager.

She shook her head. 'Not at present. He'll be back tomorrow, I understand!'

So he'd gone back to the brothel after all! I wondered how he managed to get the time away from the hospital.

'Doctor Walters is here, he takes all the cases when Doctor Phillips is away. Do you want to see him?'

I shook my head. 'No. No, it doesn't matter right now. I'd rather see my mother first, if that's all right?'

'Well, I suppose we can bend the rules just this

363

once.' She smiled a small frosty smile, and I thought I saw the glimpse of an echo in her eyes.

'Thanks! Thank you so much!'

The smile was gone. 'Now, don't tire her! Make it a short visit this time!'

Mother's eyes were closed, the lids translucent, patterned with blue veins. Her hands on the neatly tucked bedclothes were thin and bony, the veinous tapestry repeated there. I put my own stain-blotched, work-hardened hand gently over them.

'Mum! I'm here!'

The eyelids flew open, the pale blue eyes, startled, gazed up at me.

'Yes!' she said on a breathless exhalation. 'Yes, who is it? Who is it?'

'Mother — it's me, Nina!'

Her eyes steadied, focused, and her breathing slowed down. 'Oh, Nina! Of course!' She licked her lips as if to say more, but remained silent, staring.

'Yes, I've come back from Mombasa now. Are you feeling any better?' Awkwardness always overcame me when visiting hospital, leaving me devoid of conversation.

'I'm better,' her voice took on an impatient tone now, 'completely recovered! Can't think why they don't let me go home. I keep telling William to pull rank and get me released but he doesn't do anything. As for my daughter — she's off somewhere, without so much as a by-your-leave!'

I wondered how long her mind had been wandering.

'Mother, I'm back now. We'll soon have you out of here and on a wonderful sea voyage!'

She smiled and clapped her hands.

'I love the sea! When can we go?'

'That depends on how you are. I'm seeing the doctor soon, then we can make plans.' I knew it was pointless at this stage to give her departure dates and details. I

sighed to myself. Besides, I still wasn't sure if I'd go.
I couldn't go, leaving Kerri still missing.

The police were at the house on my return.

'We've arrested your garden boy, Kimau. He is the
only Kikuyu, isn't he?' one of them asked me.

'Yes,' I replied, 'but I'm sure he's not up to
anything.'

'Everyone thinks that, Miss Anderson, everyone!'

Yes, I thought, Kimau might want to be loyal, but
would he survive the oath-taking, the pressures — I
doubted it. Poor, bewildered Kimau.

'Why are you here, other than to arrest Kimau?' I
asked. 'Is there any other reason?' I wondered if they'd
say anything about Rashidi to me.

'Just to make sure you're all right, and to check on
your security. We'll be keeping an eye on the place,
too, in case Rashidi Mbiti turns up!'

So there it was. They were looking out for him.

'When did he get out of MacKinnon Road Camp?'

'A week ago, I believe. Now, if there's any sign, a
letter, phone call, anything from this man, you must
let us know immediately. I know his mother works for
you, but you mustn't let this sway you — he could
be — *is* — dangerous, so I'm warning you to be extra
careful, extra vigilant!'

I watched the police car drive away, then went into
the house and bolted the door, pulling the sofa across
to block it as an additional precaution as if, by doing
so, I could possibly stop any really determined terrorist
from breaking in.

'Could you sleep in the house with me, Melika?' I
asked, made nervous by the police interest.

'Of course, what else? We will keep each other company through the dark hours!' She insisted on bringing
in her bedroll, and spread it on the floor of the
bedroom.

Despite her presence, I couldn't sleep, restless on the

soft mattress, with the smallest sounds magnified so
that I lay sweating with fear, puzzled by Rashidi's
change of character, imagining that we were about to
be murdered . . .

* * * *

. . . I'd surely be killed if the ruffians who followed me
found the cave where we hid.

I crouched behind a small bush which shielded the
cave entrance, my eyes drooping with tiredness in the
midday sun. In the heat, the scant bushes quivered
above the track, miraged and ghostlike, to my tired
mind assuming the shape of would-be assassins. I
blinked and rubbed my eyes, and Alexi at my side gave
a great sigh and flopped down with legs outstretched.

Gradually, as the hours stretched, fatigue overtook
me, and I fell into jerky, unrestful sleep in which my
dreams were full of distortions and frightening images.
Then they calmed and there was light and sunshine,
and Rsul was there, tall and dark upon his horse. I
was, in the dream, no longer large with child, no longer
huge of belly and breast, but slim and dressed in Ibrahim's clothes like some brave youth.

Rsul dismounted and, as we looked deep into each
other's eyes, I could see myself reflected in his, slowly
disrobing, dropping the garments around my feet, till
I stood naked like some dryad emerging from a dark
pool. And he, too, was standing proud before me, and
my sight blurred, and the world was there within me,
and around me and there was no end to it.

It was dark when I woke again, stiff and uncomfortable from sleeping in an upright position. I stood up
with difficulty, letting the rock take my weight. My
lower back ached and the child felt heavy in my womb.

'Come, Alexi, it's time we started — it seems the
men have passed by without finding us, thanks be!'

Alexi's tongue curled upwards in his mouth as he
yawned, then he stretched and stood up, shaking him-

366

self. I poured some precious water into my eating bowl and gave it to him, then refilled it and watered my horse.

When the moon rose, we were already on our way, and I dozed again in the saddle, rocked by the horse's movement, jolting into full awareness when dawn was beginning to bring light to the eastern skyline.

Alexi slept, sprawled across the saddle in front of me, head and forepaws hanging down one side of the horse, back legs and tail down the other, for all the world like the corpse of some slain antelope.

I slowed the horse to a halt and Alexi sneezed and woke, struggling to right himself. I laughed at his contortions, and lifted him down to the ground.

The sun rose, pale gold over the hills, and I wondered then how far I had to travel, not sure where I was, or indeed if I was even on the right route. The detours I had taken to avoid being caught had thrown me into confusion and I was muddled over the distance we had covered. I shivered in the cold early morning, almost wishing now that I had taken Malek at his word and travelled to Kabul with him.

Surely, I told myself, Habib Amir will be pleased to see me? He will be so overcome with joy at my return that he will forgive me! At the back of my consciousness, I was afraid that this might not be so, knowing that my actions were almost beyond forgiveness — but then Habib Amir loved me so . . . had always loved me. He would find a way to satisfy protocol — surely!

Drowsing on the ground in the sparse shade of a gnarled tree, I let my thoughts drift.

Once I'd got settled back into the ways of the estate, then I could send for Bibicol, asking her to come to me as a friend, no longer as a servant. My mind conjured up pictures of an idyllic existence on my father's estate, but in my imagination Bibicol and I were young girls

367

again, without the restriction of the chadri, and able to ride free with Harun on my father's horses.

The voice in my head spoke then, breaking the idyll:

'You cannot travel backwards, Noeda . . . the past is done, and your eyes must look to the future. Your freedom comes from within yourself — it cannot come from anywhere else!'

I didn't understand, and suddenly I was filled with loneliness and grief at the unpalatable knowledge that I could be losing all those whom I loved.

The sky blazed white-hot above me, the earth throbbed and pulsed with the heat, hard and inhospitable beneath my tired and bloated body, and I wept . . .

* * * *

. . . My pillow was soaked with tears I hadn't known I'd shed when Melika called me next morning.

'There's a phone call for you. Doctor Phillips, I think!'

I jumped out of bed and ran.

'Can you get away?' Paul asked brusquely and I bit back the disappointment that there were no endearments, no references to what we had been to each other.

'Yes, I suppose so . . .' I wondered how to explain to Melika and Mother that yet again I'd be away.

'Okay, get down to my place this evening!'

'Your place?'

'Where we were before — use your brain!' he said.

I frowned at the telephone. 'You mean at the . . .'

'Be careful!' he interrupted, and I bit my tongue, remembering my earlier fear that the phone might be tapped.

'Oh! Yes — I understand. By why? Have you news?'

There was a minute pause. 'Well, news of a sort. I'll tell you all when I see you — okay?'

I didn't want him to go, wanted to hold on to his voice.

'Paul — I miss you!'

'Look, I can't talk now — see you later, Nina!'

I put the phone down, deflated.

The day dragged. I visited Mother, but decided not to tell her I was leaving again since I'd no idea what Paul wanted, or how long we were going to be away. Then, telling Melika only that I was going to see a friend and might stay for a night or two, I drove my father's ancient Citroën into Nairobi and parked it in the car park of the Norfolk Hotel. The streets were still busy, just before curfew, and I passed unnoticed through the crowds, making my way quickly into shanty-town and Muchige's brothel.

'Have you brought a cloth for your head, and an old dress?' Paul asked after he'd hurried me down the corridor to his room.

I nodded, wordlessly, the pulse at the base of my throat pounding so hard that I felt sure he could see its movement there, longing for him to reach out — to touch me; too shy, suddenly, to say what I wanted to say.

'What's the matter?' He looked at me intently then with one finger under my chin tilted my head upwards and kissed me. I leaned against his chest, hearing the steady pounding of his heartbeat, fighting the onset of inexplicable tears.

'Now, come on!' He pulled away, held me at arm's length. 'This way we'll never get away from this room!'

I sighed, reluctant to move. 'Where are we going? Back to the forest again?'

He shook me, gently. 'No way! I'd never do that again! It was stupid, unbelievably stupid! No, I've got a lead which still necessitates us going in disguise, but it's at Nakuru, not up in the Abadares.'

'Kerri?' My voice came as little more than a whisper.

'Well, maybe! I don't want to raise your hopes too much in case it leads nowhere. Unfortunately, I have

369

to take you, as you're the only one who could identify her beyond doubt.'

I tried to suppress the excitement.

'Did you know that Rashidi has escaped?'

He looked at me, puzzled. 'Rashidi?'

Of course! He had no idea that Rashidi was Kerri's father. I hesitated, not sure whether to tell him or not.

'Let's get you coloured up. I want to be gone in an hour or so.'

The moment had passed.

'How do you manage to get away from the hospital, Paul?' I asked later as we jolted our way to Nakuru in the back of a closed Landrover.

'As I told you before, I'm with the Special Intelligence branch. There's a fellow called Ian Henderson who's setting up a big operation to organise pseudo-gangs — recruiting terrorists who've been caught, men who've got some clout with the top Mau Mau generals. In the end we hope to get enough of them together working with us to find people like General Kimathi!'

'And you?'

'Well, I speak Kikuyu fluently, was brought up with them on our farm, so that I know their ways. Because of this I've been able to pass myself off as one of them. I do go up into the forests, but my role is more the gathering and integration of information. The brothel is, of course, a wonderful cover! It's the heart of an information network — a web of communication lines — going both ways. Because I'm useful as co-ordinator, trusted by the Kikuyus, too, the hospital had little option but to let me go whenever I'm needed.' He smiled wanly, 'and that seems to be more and more frequently now!'

'Why not leave altogether for the duration of the Emergency, then?' I asked.

'No. No, you see that's a good cover, too! If I were to stop being Doctor Phillips, then maybe the Mau

Mau intelligentsia would start asking questions, putting two and two together. They're not complete fools, you know, not the chaps running the job!'

I shivered. 'You mean it really *is* a well-organised revolution, not just a fanatic bunch of hotheads?'

'The whole thing's been well thought out, Nina, planned for years! The Kikuyus kill the Europeans; the Europeans kill the Kikuyus; the Kikuyus kill each other and any other Africans who interfere. Agriculture and commerce come to a complete halt, leaving the land empty — up for grabs. Fear and intimidation take over and the interested outsiders — Chinese, Russians, Asians wait in the cities, laughing, like hyenas waiting for a lion to do the killing so that they can come in and finish the job. Waiting so that they can catch that lion sleeping with a full belly, and bring him to an end, too!'

Paul pushed his battered felt hat back on his head and pinched the bridge of his nose between two fingers. 'The poor old African ends up with even less than he had before!'

I put my head on his shoulder. 'With all the exploitation and hardship that'll bring in its wake!'

His arm slid round my waist and he drew me closer. 'It's a bloody awful mess, Nina! Far worse than anyone realises! The outside world only sees, hears what the media wants to put out! Like all conflicts, it's Joe Doe, his wife and his totos who, unwilling participants, take the brunt of it all! God — I can see *why* they get sucked in, but poor buggers, they'll end up with nothing! Uhuru, freedom, might prove to be a hollow victory!'

I could see why the Africans wanted that freedom, nonetheless.

'Yes!' Paul's voice was weary, 'Yes, it's a sod-awful mess!'

'You can't take it all on board, Paul!'

371

He turned on me angrily. 'I know! I know that! And I'm not leading a crusade! All I'm trying to do is to get at the real bad buggers, the self-styled "Generals" who've been so indoctrinated, so filled with polemic and drugs that they'll kill indiscriminately, spreading terror and confusion amongst black and white alike. God, I've seen some things, Nina . . . !' His arm was no longer around me, he'd gone into some inner tortured world now.

'Paul . . . !' I tentatively reached out, then pulled back, leaving him be, grieving for his torment; for the whole bloody mess.

The Landrover stopped on the outskirts of Nakuru and we climbed down, stiff and dusty.

'It's better to walk from here.' Paul's hand was under my elbow for a moment. 'Not far — I promise!'

I sighed. 'I've heard that before! Last time we ended 12,000 feet up in the Abadares!'

His eyes were creased with laughter, and I was filled suddenly with wanting, my bones dissolving, my mouth drying. I wanted to leave the road, go quickly into the bush, go quickly into the scrub!

His pupils dilated as he looked at me, his answering desire there, an electric charge that sizzled in the hot air.

'Oh, Christ! Oh, Nina, no! We can't.' His finger touched my lips, tracing their outline. I opened my mouth, took the finger between my teeth, saying nothing, trembling and wanton as some twisting, mewling cat in season.

Without more words, we turned into the trees, unable to wait, and in a tangle of grasses, in a tangle of legs and arms and mouths, with the sun warm on our bodies, the electric charge exploded with our simultaneous cries.

Paul's hat had fallen off, and he lay beside me, with the sun dappling his nakedness.

'Bloody hell, Nina! Bloody hell!' The cursing was an endearment, an exclamation of wonder and exaltation.

'I know! I know!' I turned my head to look at him. 'Oh, Paul, I do love you so!' My voice was husky with that love.

He ran his fingers over my cheeks, down my neck, through the shallow cleft between my breasts. 'I've never felt like this!' His voice was low, embarrassed almost. 'Just thinking about you turns my guts to water! It scares me to death! Frightens me more than being up amongst the Mau Mau!' He lay back, one arm across his eyes. 'I can't handle it — not right now! Can't afford the indulgence — it's too dangerous!'

We lay silent, thinking. Far above our heads the high-pitched cry of a fish eagle echoed against the hills, and closer to us in the grasses, came the rasping of a grasshopper.

Paul sat up and looked down at me, and we laughed at the absurdity of it all.

'First time I've made love with my mouth full of gum!' he said.

'Mine went — hope I haven't swallowed them!'

We dressed hurriedly and searched for my gum pads, finding them dusty in the grass.

'Ugh! I can't put those in!'

He wiped them on his shirt. 'You'll have to! Serves you right!'

'Serves *me* right! What about you?' I replied, half indignantly.

We left the bushes stealthily, guilty as two conspirators.

The meet was in a cluster of huts on the outskirts of Nakuru. By the time we got there the sun was low in the sky, taking the warmth of the day with it. I drew my blanket closer around my body. On the slight wind the heavy, nauseating stench of bird guano filled the air, wafting across from the shores of Lake Nakuru, the beauty of the flamingo-painted lake losing its appeal at such close quarters.

The interior of the hut was thick with smoke, stinging my eyes as I entered, close behind Paul. Two hurricane lanterns hung from the rafters above the heads of the men sitting below so that their faces were shadowed, indistinct.

The antenna-like hairs on the back of my neck and on my arms tingled, filling me with premonitions and trepidation. All talk ceased as we came under the scrutiny of a dozen pairs of eyes. I hoped that my shaking was not too obvious, and moved further into Paul's shadow.

'What news do you bring, Muchige?' one of the men asked in Swahili. Paul answered him in Kikuyu, and the conversation was lost to me.

I looked carefully at the men, trying to assess their reaction. It seemed friendly enough on the surface.

Then my stomach turned stone cold, my breathing halted.

Rashidi!

I hunched over, blanket across the lower half of my face, hoping against all hope that he'd not see me. There was no way, at this point, that I could warn Paul without drawing attention to myself.

Rashidi spoke then, and I realised it was he who had spoken in Swahili when we first entered. My heartbeat was so loud, so fast that I could hardly hear what he said.

'Then what is it you want here?' His eyes were hard in his pinched face.

Paul looked at him for a moment, then spoke nonchalantly. 'This bibi here has lost some relatives, a sister and child. It is of little significance, but she has ties to Jomo Kenyatta, so I have to waste my time to keep her silent! She was going to the Askari, so mad-

374

dened is she with her grief. It was safer to promise her help than to expose the network.'

The men nodded and said 'Aaaah!', their eyes shifting towards me scathingly, then away again. Rashidi's look, however, lingered and he frowned.

'Who is this bibi? Is she yours?'

Paul nodded. 'Yes. Yes, the wretched thing is mine.'

'And has she been tested for her loyalty? If she goes running to the Askari over the loss of a sister, could she not be a danger to you — to us all?'

The other men looked at me again, more suspiciously now.

'Is she prepared to honour the oaths? To share the beds of all the freedom fighters, to give her life for the cause? Somehow I doubt it!'

Paul shook his head. 'She is a poor specimen and, truthfully, I would be pleased to be rid of her! Her voice was lost during interrogation, so she cannot speak now, which means she can no longer inform easily if she is tortured. But, as I told you, she has family connections with those in the hierarchy, and for this reason I keep her on as one of my women!'

Shut up, Paul! I begged him silently. Shut up — stop drawing attention to me! He had to answer the questions, I knew, but all I wanted now was to get out of the hut before Rashidi realised, as realise he must — surely!

'This missing woman and a child,' he was speaking again, but his eyes had left me now, 'when did they go? And where from?'

Oh, God! He'd guess if Paul said Mikendeni! I started to cough, feigning a paroxysm to draw attention away.

Paul frowned at me, speaking in Kikuyu and pointing at the door. I lay down, writhing and jerking and he bent over me.

375

'What on earth?' he whispered, so low that even I could hardly hear him.

'Must get out! We must get out!' I answered urgently through closed lips.

He frowned again in bewilderment and then, standing up, angrily shouted. Half-carrying, half-dragging me, he pulled me through the doorway and deposited me outside. Murmurings of suspicion and query followed us out into the darkness.

'For God's sake! What?' He shook me.

'It's Rashidi! The one who spoke — Rashidi!'

His eyes narrowed. 'Has he spotted you?'

I shook my head numbly. 'I don't think so, but he knows Leah!' I still couldn't bring myself to tell him who Rashidi was.

'Okay. Lie quietly here — I'll deal with it somehow.' He drew the blanket over my face and went back inside. Through the open doorway I could hear him laugh and boast about making me submit.

'Bloody Mwanamuki! They're more trouble than they are worth!'

A murmur of agreement, spitting, coughing and laughter came from the others. I covered my ears with my hands, and lay, cold with terror, the flamingo stench foul in my nostrils . . .

* * * *

. . . My sleep must have deepened then, for I woke with a start to the sound of hoofbeats, and the sun blistering my lips.

The rider was coming slowly towards me, following my tracks, and I sat, stupid and confused, watching him approach, the horse seeming to float above the ground on the heatwaves. There was nothing I could do, nowhere I could hide.

I stood up, waiting for him to reach me.

'If you must follow me so, then you might as well be

comfortable!' I spoke with a courage I did not feel, resigned to the inevitability.

The man looked surprised, taken aback, and jumped off his horse some few yards away.

'Did Malek send you?' I asked.

He shook his head. 'No, not Malek!'

'His mother, then?'

His eyes shifted and he made a play of loosening the girths on his horse, but gave no reply, and in his very silence I had the answer. Was I not to be free of her, even here? I sighed, too weary now to question him.

'Come,' I said, 'I will make you food and drink.'

He still eyed me suspiciously, frowning in perplexity that I should offer hospitality thus.

'Where are the others?' I asked, keeping my voice innocent — it could be that with just one I could make my escape.

With mouth full of bread, he spoke. 'They've gone ahead, to lie in wait near Kabul.'

'Why Kabul?'

'That's where you are going, is it not?' he said. 'She told us that!'

'Is she paying you well?'

His eyes shifted again. 'What is it to you?'

'Since you intend either to take me back to Kalash or kill me, and I suspect the latter, then it makes no odds if you tell me,' I replied. 'And if so, why prolong it?'

'I have to take you to the others, they'll know how to deal with you!' He laughed, showing teeth, blackened and broken in his mouth.

The stench of his unwashed body hit my senses . . .

* * * *

. . . 'Nina, quick!' Paul was pulling at my arm, even before I was fully awake. I couldn't believe that I had slept! Perhaps I hadn't — even now I wasn't sure if I was in Africa or Afghanistan. I sat up quickly, head spinning. It was pitch dark now, and no lamps burned.

'What —? What's happening?' I asked. The smell of native beer clung to his clothes.

'They're asleep. I brought some "pombe" and they all got pretty tanked up.'

'I never heard them!'

'No — it wasn't that sort of party! Just a lot of heavy talking and political crap! They talked themselves into the ground! Come on, we've got to get moving!'

He looked back, through the door. 'To tell you the truth, I doctored the pombe! Heavy dose of sedative, I'm afraid!'

'How did you get away with not having any yourself?'

'Spilt it into the ground! Let's go!'

We went, running at a jog-trot out to where the Landrover waited, about half a mile away.

'How,' I gasped, 'how did they know to bring it now?'

Paul leant against the wheel-arch, catching his breath. 'They didn't — I just told the driver to leave it here after we'd gone, so that it would be available if and when we needed to make our getaway!'

It wasn't until we were well out of Nakuru that I asked: 'And how'll you explain our disappearance? Surely they'll wonder?'

'Just have to blame you, if they ask — bloody women! Always a bother! I've had to take you to the doctor, haven't I?'

'Did you learn anything, after all that?'

He looked at me quickly. 'It was difficult, but I did bring the missing woman and child into the conversation again, and I'm afraid that once more it's not them. These two come from Fort Hall, and are Kikuyus, not Bugandas!' His hand rested on my knee.

'Sorry, Nina! Luck doesn't seem to be going our way in this search!'

I swallowed my disappointment, staring out of the Landrover at the dark, mysterious shapes on the plains as we started on the up-gradient of the escarpment towards Nairobi. I wondered bleakly how I could cope with the possibility that I'd never see Kerri or Leah again. Knew I couldn't cope with even contemplating that eventuality.

'What are you going to do about Rashidi?' I asked.

There was a long pause, then I saw the faint blur of his face in the darkness as he turned and looked at me.

'I really don't know what to do about him, Nina,' he said. 'He is Kerri's father, isn't he?'

TWENTY-TWO

Over the next two days I had plenty of time to think about the implications of Paul's question. I'd no idea how he'd worked out the connection between me and Rashidi, and wondered if I was really that transparent, or whether it was just that we were so close that he could read me. Embarrassment and worry had held me back from asking on the way back from Nakuru and, once we were in Nairobi, he'd taken me straight home, bidding me scrub my skin to try and remove the brown stain. Then he left.

I stood on the verandah, watching the Landrover disappearing out of the gate, with my blood running cold in my veins.

'Paul! Wait . . . !' I started down the steps, wanting to stop him, filled with unreasonable apprehension. But he was gone, and I turned back into the house, uneasy.

'Eeh! What on earth are you wearing?' Melika's surprise made an 'O' of her mouth as she looked at my tattered clothes. 'And your skin! You look as you did when you were small and played at making pies in the mud!'

'I can't explain, Melika. It's dangerous for you to know too much!' I told her. But then I was weeping, the tears spurting from my eyes to soak the front of my dress, and I knew I couldn't keep the news of Rashidi to myself.

'What is it?' She mopped my eyes with her apron. 'For goodness' sake, tell me!'

'Rashidi — I saw Rashidi! He was at Nakuru!'

'What did he say? Is he well, Nina?' She was eager for news of him.

I shook my head. 'Don't ask me that, Melika. He didn't recognise me — or at least I hope he didn't. He was with the Mau Mau . . .' I stopped, realising what I'd done. 'You must forget I've told you about him. For his sake!' For Paul's sake, too, or his operation was jeopardised.

Melika looked bewildered. 'But how did you get to see him? What were you doing there?'

'I shouldn't have told you! Now I've put you into danger, too! For safety's sake, I can't explain, Melika. If the terrorists got hold of you, they could kill you for the knowledge! No — try to forget it! All I can say is that I heard a rumour that Leah and Kerri were in Nakuru, but it was untrue. Whilst I was searching for them I saw Rashidi — that's all! If you love Kerri, then try and wipe it from your mind!'

If Rashidi were to find out that Kerri was his daughter! That possibility and its implications had only just hit me. I wondered what he would do if he found out. Didn't want to dwell on that thought.

Melika 'tutted' and muttered to herself, mopping at her streaming eyes with the same apron she'd used on mine. She went, shaking her head, to run a bath for me, and my heart ached for her pain.

'I feel it in my head,' she said when she returned, 'know it in my head, that I will never see my son again!'

'Melika, this fighting won't go on forever! When it's done, then we'll all have to build our lives again.'

'Yes, but I'm sure Rashidi will be gone. Oh, why? Why did he get away from MacKinnon Road Camp? At least there, there was a hope of surviving if he didn't get beaten too hard during interrogation. Now, hunted and running, what are his chances?' Her shoulders were bowed with the weight of her sorrow.

There was little I could do to help lift that weight. I, too, knew that the dice were heavily loaded against

Rashidi. He might flee to the depths of the Abadares, hide like the dreaded Kimathi — but how long for? And, at the end of it all, no matter who the victors — African or European, Asian or Russian — he would not survive, could not survive.

In this battle, ultimately, there would be no winners; all of us would be losers, white and black.

Lying in the hot, sudsy water I couldn't relax, tension still tightening the muscles round my neck and shoulders. So much so that I couldn't bear to linger, and scrubbed fast at my stained body on a rising tide of urgency.

As I towelled myself, it was as though Leah were there beside me, her presence so strong that I could almost smell her musky scent.

I sat down on the edge of the bath, my legs giving way beneath the wave of terror that engulfed me. Oh God! They can't be dead! No, not Leah! And surely not Kerri — not my baby! She can't be! My heart thumped painfully in my chest, and then I felt strangely calm — too calm for that possibility to be true. They *must* be safe! Alive, and hiding somewhere. Oh, please God, let them be safe! Please! Oh Leah, please . . . !

Time was fast running out, and I needed desperately to know, to have reassurance before I went to England.

Leah's presence in my mind disappeared and, replacing her image, came Mother's thin, anxious face. But now, instead of the anger, the resentment, which had filled me, came understanding of her need, her vulnerability and, consequently, an awareness of my responsibility.

Poor darling, I thought, you've never had a daughter in me — we've been so terribly estranged, one way and another!

Kerri will still be here when I get back from England! I tried to comfort myself. Surely it wouldn't take too long to get Mother fit again once we got to the specialist in London.

I sighed, wondering why I was beset by such division of loyalties, always. And Noeda, too, I thought, she's torn — wanting to make peace with the Khan, knowing that she couldn't make a life with Malek, despite all he'd done for her . . . I realised that my feelings about Noeda were changing. I almost resented her intrusion into my life, resented the fact that she no longer offered me sanctuary — her life was as difficult, as tortured, as my own!

And I was so besotted with Paul, so immersed in my feelings for him, that I'd almost resented Kerri and Mother for getting in the way.

Scarlet with shame at my self-absorption, I dressed quickly, wanting to get to the hospital, to make reparation for these unfilial feelings.

As I was halfway through the door the phone rang, a loud, discordant sound which made me jump.

'Hello!' I said, my voice reflecting my deep unease.

'I knew you!' The voice at the other end of the line was muffled, as if the speaker had covered the mouthpiece with a cloth.

I took the receiver from my ear, looked at it, as if by doing so I could see who spoke.

'Who's that?'

'You know who it is, Nina! I don't know how you came to be there, with the brothel-keeper, or why it is you search for Leah and her child!'

So it was Rashidi! And he knew, at least, that I was looking for Leah! My breath faltered, stopped, started again — shallow and fast. He didn't know about Kerri — that was obvious!

'Don't speak,' he commanded. 'Just understand that I did not drink deep of the pombe last night. I saw who you were straight away! Did you think I could forget?' He paused and I was about to answer.

'No — be silent! Don't say my name, for who knows who may be listening? Do you and your friend think I would be so stupid as to get drunk so that the Askari could walk in calmly and collect me? No! I knew you, Nina, and for reasons which you will understand, I let you go. You and your friend!'

'He's not my friend,' I interrupted quickly, concerned for Paul's cover. 'Just a man who I asked to help to find Leah!'

'No matter! If the other men there had suspected, you would be deep in the ground now. Just remember that it was me who saved your life. I will not do it again! And if you tell anyone that you saw me, then you are dead. You and your family!'

The line went silent.

I stood for a long moment with the receiver still held tight against my ear.

Dear God! Rashidi!

Melika looked round the door. 'Who was that, Nina? You'll miss your bus if you don't hurry!'

Her eyes were anxious, and I hadn't the heart, the courage, to tell her. Couldn't raise her hopes again. There might still be a small core of decency left inside Rashidi, but he wasn't coming back; wasn't prepared to leave the Mau Mau. Not yet at any rate.

'Oh! Only Captain Blake, Melika. I'll run for the bus, don't worry.' I wondered if my legs would carry me. I gave her a perfunctory kiss and left, on my way to pick up the Citroën from town before going to the hospital.

Driving fast, to keep my mind off Rashidi's threats, I knew somehow I'd have to get a message to Paul, warning him.

Mother sat in a chair beside her bed, a soft blue bed-jacket round her shoulders, emphasising the colour of her eyes. Her expression was clear, brighter than it had been for a long time. Michael sat with her.

'There you are, Nina!' she exclaimed. 'I was just telling Michael you'd be along to see me this afternoon!'

Michael's eyes narrowed as he looked at me. 'Are you all right, Nina?' he asked. 'You look dog-tired!'

'Fine! I'm fine!' I brushed his concern away.

'We've been talking about my trip to England,' Mother's voice was full of enthusiasm. 'It's only a week or so to go, you know! Have you had all your injections and things? And what about our passports?'

'I've sorted out your passports,' Michael said. 'I hope you'll forgive the presumption, Nina, but I got all the necessary documents from your house — I had to have things like birth certificates and so on, otherwise we wouldn't have got them back in time.'

I shrugged, there was little I could say about it — it was done!

'You'll have to get your inoculations done today though. I tried to ring several times to remind you, but you're always out, it seems.'

'Yes, I've been busy,' I retorted, 'but I'll see Doctor Gordon when I leave here, see what he can do.'

Drat Michael, I fumed, drat him, for being so damn *right* all the time! I knew I was being unreasonable, that he was only doing what he could to help us.

Mother chirped on about the voyage, excitement verging on hysteria giving her cheeks an abnormal rosiness, her eyes a feverishness. I tried to match her mood, not wanting her to realise that I could hardly bear to listen, I was so filled with the sense of unease that Rashidi's phone call had given me.

At the end of visiting time, Michael followed me from the room.

'Nina, are you all right? You look so sallow, and

your eyes are yellow! You haven't got a touch of jaundice, have you?'

I laughed to myself, knowing it would be a few days before the effect of the eye-drops wore off. 'No, Michael! No, I'm fine — really I am! Just to put your mind to rest I'll get Doctor Gordon to give me a check-up when I have the inoculations.'

It would be stupid to go to Muchige's brothel in broad daylight, I knew, so instead I made my way to Mwange, and asked her to get Paul to ring me urgently.

I suffered my injections uncomfortably — TAB, yellow fever, smallpox, after Doctor Gordon had reluctantly given me all of them that afternoon as a matter of expediency, and that night lay hot and restless, with my arm swollen and throbbing, and my temperature high, worrying about all that needed to be done.

I had one week, or just over, to pack up the house and pay off the servants, knowing that I couldn't keep them on, since the army would reclaim the house once we'd left it. Poor devils, I thought, what on earth will they do? There are so few jobs going now, and people are reluctant to take on more staff! I hoped Michael would let me have money enough in advance from Father's estate to give them something, a bit at least, to go on with.

Paul had not phoned during the evening, and I was on edge, waiting for the bell to ring, with my eyes going constantly to the table where the telephone sat, willing it, and yet dreading it in case it should be Rashidi again.

Outside, the crunch of boots on the gravel drive as the Askaris patrolled should have reassured me. Instead it filled me with a deep sense of foreboding.

Then, late into the evening, the sudden ringing made me jump, even though I had been waiting. But it was not Paul, not Rashidi either.

Michael's kind, concerned voice asked, 'Did you see the doctor? Are you sure you're quite all right?'

I sighed with exasperation. 'Stop worrying, for goodness' sake! I'm perfectly fit, and everything will be ready in time.' I put the phone down with a thump, and padded back to bed, then got up again and took the receiver off, not able now to bear the anticipation. Paul could ring me tomorrow — blast him! I'd done my best to get in touch!

In fact he didn't contact me until the following afternoon, by which time I was overwrought and exhausted with trying to pack up the house, and reacting badly to the injections.

'Didn't you get my message?' I asked with some acerbity.

'Mwange came to me, yes.'

'Well, why the hell didn't you get in touch straight away? You might have known it was urgent for me to have taken such a risk with her!'

There was a moment's silence. 'Look, Nina — I've already stretched the safety bounds. . !'

'I know!' I snapped at him, not wanting to be reminded. 'And I'm really grateful. I shouldn't have to tell you that! This is important or I wouldn't have asked — it's just that somebody rang me yesterday, someone we met recently!'

The anger was gone from his voice now. 'All right, I know who you mean! What did he want, or can't you tell me?'

'Oh, Paul!' My own voice broke now. 'I'm so scared, so frightened for us all! He just said he recognised me, and if we reported seeing him he'd kill me, or get me killed! And all my family — meaning Mother and, presumably, Melika and Leah!'

'Did he mention the baby?'

'No — thank God — no! So at least he's not realised that connection!' My despair was spilling down my

387

face now, and I was trying to control the tears, trying not to let him hear them. 'What should I do?'

'Nothing. Do nothing! Certainly don't tell anyone you saw him. There's no doubt whatsoever that he's as dangerous as hell. I've been making enquiries, discreetly, and have learned quite a bit about that young man! He's a bad bugger, Nina, I'm afraid!'

Rashidi! How could it be?

'I'm at the hospital tomorrow. Come and see me when you visit your Mother, okay?' His voice was abrupt once more, and I hung up, feeling no comfort from the conversation.

Next day when I asked the nurse on duty if I could speak to him, she shook her head.

'I'm sorry, Miss Anderson, Doctor Phillips is busy in the maternity ward right now — we've several mothers all giving birth at once! So things are a bit hectic!' She smiled, laid a gentle hand on my arm. 'Your mother's doing quite well, you know!'

She meant to be kind, I realised that, but I felt thwarted yet again, and unreasonably angry with Paul.

Mother, too, was less cheerful than the day before, and I detected a slight note of self-pity in her voice. I was unsympathetic, irritated, and left as soon as I tactfully could, with her blue eyes accusing me as I walked away.

The police were waiting for me at Karen, and my chest constricted painfully at the sight of the black car parked in front of the steps.

Melika, Samwelli and the houseboy stood on the verandah, their faces betraying their anxiety.

A young police officer got out of the car.

'We understand you had a phone call from Rashidi Mbiti, Miss Anderson. Why didn't you report it, as you were instructed to do?'

I glanced at Melika, saw the hurt in her eyes.

388

'He threatened me, threatened all of us!' I stammered. 'I didn't know what to do, quite honestly!'

The police officer's face was stern. 'You were given explicit orders . . .'

'I know that! There's more to it than meets the eye!' I was unsure whether Paul would want me talking about his part in all this; how official his whole set-up was. 'Look, come inside and I'll tell you as much as I can.' I led him up the steps, past the anxious, accusing eyes, and I reached out and gave Melika's arm a quick squeeze as we passed.

Inside I poured a cold beer, offered one to the policeman. He took off his cap, accepted, and I relaxed slightly.

'It's very difficult, this,' I started. 'Someone in the security force is helping me to find my daughter who's gone missing!'

He looked up, startled. 'Why didn't you report this, either?'

I hesitated, twisted my glass in my hands, studying the golden liquid. 'No one knows about her. She's—' I looked at him to assess his reaction. 'She's a half-caste baby!'

He cleared his throat, took a mouthful of beer. 'I see — or I think I do! What you're saying is that your parents didn't know — is that it?'

I nodded. 'She's with my ayah's sister — they've both disappeared!' The anguish rose again, a heavy burning lump in the pit of my stomach.

He sat in thought, then ran a hand over his hair. 'And this "person in the security force" — why has he got to remain nameless? Is he police or Kenya Regiment? Presumably the latter, or I'd know about it?'

'No,' I hesitated, then decided they must surely know of the undercover action, 'one of Ian Henderson's men!'

'Ah!' He leaned back in his chair. 'I see! Sometimes those fellows give us more trouble than the bloody Mau

389

Mau! All the same, he should have told us — the Pseudos are supposed to alert us, so that we don't blunder in and shoot them thinking they're the bad guys!' His eyes regarded me steadily. 'But Rashidi Mbiti — now, that's another question. What's his involvement in all this?'

'We ran into him, while we were looking for my baby,' I replied, relaxed and careless.

' "We"? Who do you mean, "we"? Surely you didn't go into Mau Mau territory?'

I realised my mistake.

'No, not really. We were just making some enquiries.' I thought fast — it could be too dangerous to let them know Rashidi was in the Nakuru area.

'It was at Thika!' I told him. Thika was far enough away, in the opposite direction, almost.

He frowned. 'I still don't understand quite why you're involved. It's against all the regulations, you know!'

He got up, put on his cap, official and stern again. 'Okay! We'll set the wheels in motion in the Thika area. In the meanwhile, be sure you inform us about any more telephone calls, and I'll leave an Askari on permanent duty for the time being.'

After he'd driven away, I paced the room, fuming. How could Paul have done this, put us into such danger by reporting the telephone call! He was the only one who knew about it — I hadn't even told Mwange when I asked her to deliver the message to Paul asking him to get in touch with me. No one else knew. And if the phone was tapped, then there'd be no necessity for me to report a call, they'd know anyway! It didn't add up, was all too uncertain, strange. Paul *must* have told them, anxious for our safety!

But no, surely not. Not after what I'd said about Rashidi's threats!

Melika came into the room and put her arms about my waist.

'You said nothing to me,' she whispered, her voice hoarse.

'No, I couldn't say anything!' I found myself unable to face her, extricated myself from her embrace, and went into my room, with her despair following me. How could I explain what would seem a Judas action?

And Leah was there then, in my head, but I was too feverish, too taut with anxiety to be able to bring her into focus.

I couldn't understand how Paul could detach himself so, that he couldn't feel my worry, understand the increasing fear I had that I wouldn't find Kerri, wouldn't see her before I went to England. Because I knew now I had to go . . . was being forced to go with Mother.

I rang the hospital.

'Stop worrying, for goodness' sake!' Paul said. 'I've got things under control. I'll speak to the police and explain.'

'I told them we saw Rashidi at Thika, not Nakuru . . .'

'What on earth for?' His voice was hard. 'And you didn't, surely, tell them *I'd* taken you?'

'No . . . not exactly.' I recoiled from his anger. He'd not understood that in spite of Rashidi's Mau Mau activities, there was part of me that still belonged to him. Our past, intricately interwoven, couldn't be shredded to order.

'Well, for goodness' sake just get yourself packed and ready, Nina. You've got this trip to England coming up. Your mother really does need urgent attention, you know!'

'But she seems so much better. Can't it be postponed for a while?' I was clutching at straws, I knew that.

'It's symptomatic, I'm afraid. She swings from

391

delirium to seeming really well. But her liver's pretty well shot — and her heart's too dicky for her to fly!'

'You've not told me that before!' I was angry now.

'You seemed to have quite enough on your plate! Now, look, be a good girl and leave it to me from now on. Please! You know I'll do what I can to find Leah and Kerri. Got to go — I'm frantically busy!'

He put the phone down, leaving me empty and puzzled at his apparent duplicity. I wondered where his real loyalties lay.

The post box had only one brown, rather grubby-looking envelope in it next morning. I picked it out, studied it. It was for Melika, postmarked Kampala. My heart raced.

I turned it over in my hands, wondering whether to open it or to wait until I got home.

I knew it was from Jamira. My fingers burned to rip off the envelope, and yet my veins were filled with ice.

We sat, Melika and I, side by side on the sofa, when I got home.

'Open it, Nina!' Her voice was shaking.

I tore at the envelope with fingers that trembled uncontrollably and drew out the small sheet of lined paper.

Jamira had written in English, knowing the letter would have to be read to Melika.

'My dear Mother Melika,

My heart is filled with great sorrowing to have to write this letter to you. Today a man came with news that Leah, Mirriamu and her baby, Kerri, are dead. Killed by the Mau Mau as they slept. He could not tell me where this happened, or why, but only that Rashidi had sent him. My grieving was so great that I did not think to ask him where Rashidi was, or how he knew this dreadful news. I wish I was with you, Mama Melika, to share your sorrow,

and I will come to you within the week, when I can
get leave from my work.

  Your daughter,
  Jamira'

The letter fell from my fingers and the room blurred.
I was cold, ice-cold, and the pounding in my head was
my own heart, and that pounding almost, but not quite,
drowned out the sound of Melika's wailing.

Melika's wailing, and the feel of her body on the
sofa, rocking backwards and forwards.

I turned my head on my stiff neck, slowly, oh, so
very slowly; with the pounding heavy; with my eyes
wide open; unseeing, unmoving; and saw, but didn't
see, Melika with her apron thrown up over her head.
And heard, but couldn't hear, the high-pitched ululations of grief. And no sound came from my throat,
but I knew I was screaming, a silent screaming that
tore from my soul.

And Melika's pain came crashing through, finding
me raw and bleeding and impotent to help, racked with
my own guilt and able to deal with it in the only way
I knew how . . .

                    *   *   *   *

. . . I reached out for the comfort of Alexi's warm
body. He licked my hand and moved closer to me. I
cursed my surly captor, silently, and forced myself to
eat.

'We should sleep now,' I said, 'if we are to travel
tomorrow!' My mind raced, trying to think of some
way in which I could outwit the man.

I lay down, wrapped in my blanket, with the fire
between myself and the ruffian. Alexi growled, low in
his throat, and I could feel his tenseness as he sat near
me.

'Come, Alexi, the fire will keep away the night prowl-
ers!' I whispered, trying to calm the animal. He sat,

quivering, and would not relax, seeming to sense my own tension, my fear.

It was in the dead hours of the night, when I had at last fallen into a sleep born of exhaustion, that Alexi's sharp yelp of pain woke me. I sat up fast and, in the dying light of the fire, saw the man's arm upraised with a heavy stick over Alexi; heard the dreadful cry of pain. I jumped up and grabbed the man's arm, holding him off the dog.

'Stop that! Stop! For the love of Allah! Stop! What harm has he done you?'

The man turned then on me and, struggle though I did; bite and kick and scream as I might, his strength was double mine, and he bore me to the ground. My arms were pinioned in his iron grip, and I fought to free myself, with terror lending me extra strength, but to no avail. His rough beard grazed my cheeks, burning them, his weight heavy upon me so that I could hardly breathe, then his hot, harsh hands were greedy upon my body, tearing at my clothes, and he entered me roughly, whilst I screamed with the pain of it.

Spent, he pushed himself away and got up, spitting on the ground near my face. My body felt bruised, soiled, verminous; my heart pounded loudly in my ears, and vomit rose in my gorge. He kicked at my swollen stomach, standing above me, enormous and ugly.

'You whore!' he said. 'You think your dog can protect you — that stupid animal — I will see to it that he makes no more noise! And you, you bitch! You I take to Kabul, to your rich father. At least you will have served me well that way!'

I spoke through lips that were swollen and bleeding. 'But you and your companions already plan to take me to Kabul . . .'

'Huh! To the devil with them! Now it is I who will take you there. To claim the reward! Who will believe

394

anything you say! You think your word, after all this time, would carry credit in the Khan's eyes?'

'My father will believe me!' My hope was an anguish, and I was sobbing.

'You arrive, heavy with child, with no husband, and expect to be received with honour?'

'When I explain—'

'Explain what? Over a year you have been absent. No doubt he has given you up for dead. His gratitude at my bringing you to him alive will make his generosity the greater, I'm sure. And your punishment will be equally great — of that there is no doubt!'

'You, too, will be punished for this when I tell him!' I tried to get up, but he pushed me hard, so that I fell back against the rough stones of the path.

'Again, who will believe you? You are unmarried, and an adultress. You cannot claim despoilment by me!'

I was too weak to struggle, heart-heavy and racked with pain.

'All right — just take me there — you will get your reward, but leave me be. Have you no thought for Malek, at least?'

He spat again upon the ground.

'Why should I hold loyalty to him? I owe him nothing? He has everything he wants, and I have nothing!'

'You will not be able to return there.' In my whirling, befuddled mind, I wondered if I could perhaps talk this thug into returning under promise of my silence.

'I don't care, for with the reward money I can travel where I will!'

As we spoke I was slowly moving into a sitting position. I looked over to where Alexi lay, unmoving. There was a trickle of blood running from his nose, and I knew he was dead.

Blind rage filled me then and my hand moved fast

to the belt where Ibrahim's knife was strapped at my hip and, with a roar of sorrow, of anger and hatred, I jumped at the man and struck at him again and again with the sharp blade.

He screamed, horribly, his eyes wide with surprise and terror, and as he fell, I struck him yet again, slashing with the knife deep into his body.

Then I stood, with my breath rasping into my lungs, and in the dim light from the fire, saw that my hands, arms and clothes were dark-stained with his blood.

I stepped over his body and went to the small form beyond him.

'Oh! Alexi!' I cried, and cradled his limpness up to my breast. 'Oh, no! Alexi, no!' In vain I listened to his chest, hoping against all possibility that there might be some heartbeat and, when I found none, I knelt, holding him tight against me, unable to control my shivering, and the low, deep moaning that welled up from my centre.

The cold bleakness of morning found me there still, and when I tried to rise I was stiff and weak. I put Alexi down and covered him with my cloak for I could not bear to see him with his brave spirit extinguished.

As I turned then to look at the body of the man, a great searing pain went through my belly, and I knew that my child was leaving me.

'Oh, Allah! It is not time! Not the child, too!' I entreated, then the pains came fast and I felt moisture run down my legs. I know not how long it took, but only that I screamed for Bibicol, for Maja, and then for Bibicol again, over and over. And finally, as the child came from me in a rush of blood, I called for Rsul.

The blessedness of oblivion came over me then, and when I opened my eyes later, Rsul had answered my call it seemed, for he was there with me.

'Beloved girl!' he said as my eyes looked at him

wonderingly, 'I thought for sure that you had flown this earth!' Behind him I could see his horse, foamed with sweat.

'Where have you come from?' I asked, not sure if my imagination was playing me tricks.

'I have searched for many months, Noeda. Malek told me you were on your way to Kabul.'

So — Malek had let me go. Good Malek!

The red mists blurred my eyes, cleared again, and I remembered.

'My baby? Where is my baby?' The question came as a hoarse and anguished cry.

His hand was gentle on my face. 'It was too soon. He had no chance!'

A boy! I glanced down at my body, but I was tidied and the baby was gone. And I was too exhausted to grieve.

'I buried him with Alexi,' said Rsul. 'I am no mid-wife, but I have done the best I could for you.'

It didn't seem important. Nothing seemed import-ant. But my heart lay in my chest like a cold, heavy rock.

I licked my cracked lips. 'The man?'

The man who'd killed my beloved Alexi — and my child, my child whom I'd never seen . . .

'He, too, I have removed.' He asked no questions.

I lifted my hand and saw that it was still sticky with blood. I turned over and vomited weakly into the grass.

Rsul tipped water from his water-skin, gave me some to drink then, wetting a cloth, wiped my face and hands clean. . .

* * * *

. . . My face was soaked with my silent weeping, and my body was numb.

A voice somewhere was repeating, 'No! No! No!' and I realised that it was my own despairing cry.

Samwelli stood in front of me.

'Memsahib Nina! Nina! What causes you this grief?' His hand was stroking my hair. 'What is it? What is it?'

I looked at him uncomprehendingly. Why didn't he know? How could he not know?

I shut my eyes. Tried to concentrate. We'd lost our babies, Noeda and I. Could anyone be unaware of how that tore at the very core of our being? But why, in that silence, in that void, did I seem to hear Leah's voice: 'Nina! Nina — no!' And why, hearing it, did I block my ears, pushing her away, too afraid to confront my grief, come face to face with the truth?

I went through the motions of everyday living. Went to bed, rose in the morning, dressed, made a play of eating, sat empty and bleak-eyed as Samwelli and the houseboy packed around me. Melika was inconsolable, her tears unending. She sat in a corner, keening.

When the telephone rang, Samwelli answered it, then handed it to me. 'It's Doctor Phillips, will you speak to him?'

I took the instrument from him, Paul's voice an intrusion into my numbness.

'Is that you, Nina?'

'Yes.' I forced myself to concentrate, feeling anger beginning to filter through. 'Yes, it's me. Though why it should interest you . . .'

'What on earth do you mean?' His voice sounded genuine enough.

'You know what I mean — if you hadn't reported our meeting with Rashidi to the security forces, then Kerri would still be alive! And Leah!'

There was a long silence on the other end of the line. Then he said, 'Are you trying to tell me you've had news of them? That they're dead?'

'Yes!' I shouted. 'Yes! Yes! Yes! They're dead. Dead because of Rashidi. Because . . .'

'Nina!' he interrupted, 'I promise you I did not tell the police about Rashidi . . .'

'Come off it! How else would they have known?'

'Look, you've got it all wrong! Stay there, I'm coming out to see you!'

'No!' I answered, too vulnerable right now; too wounded. 'No, don't do that — I don't want you here!' But the phone was dead, he'd already left.

By the time he arrived at the house, I'd regained my composure, gathered my reserves, and throughout his visit I stayed coldly aloof, salving my wounds with ice.

'What are you going to do, then?' he asked finally, having realised that I wasn't receptive to his assurances.

I felt I was never going to be receptive to anyone's assurances ever again. There had been too many let-down's, too many hurts.

'Oh,' I said nonchalantly, as if it was obvious, 'I'm going to England with Mother, as arranged. After all, there's nothing left here to hold me back!'

I wouldn't let myself see the pain in his eyes.

'All right, Nina. If you feel that's best — and it probably is!' He tried to put his arms around me, but I pulled quickly away.

At the door he turned back and said, 'You know, I'm not entirely convinced by that letter! Well, the letter's genuine enough, but somehow — and I don't know why — the message from Rashidi doesn't ring true! There's something odd about it which I can't quite figure out.' Then he was gone, and I was left with an embryo of hope, in spite of myself.

'I'll have to find a job as an ayah for someone else, Nina,' Melika said, the day before I left. 'I need to stay in Nairobi, in case I'm able to be of help to Rashidi, and to do that I must have money!'

'I'll give you enough to keep you going until I get back,' I promised.

Worry lined her face and she had lost weight, so that her normally tight uniform hung loose. She sighed and looked up at me from the tea-chest of books she was packing. 'I am afraid that you'll never come back!'

'I will, Melika, just as quickly as I can!'

'You might find England too exciting for you to leave it!' She shook her head dolefully, her hands plucking at her overall. 'Maybe I'll never see you again.' She turned her tear-filled eyes upwards, entreating me to contradict her.

'What! And leave you here alone — never!' I put my arms around her. 'I promise I'll come back — I swear it!' I knelt on the floor beside her, and raised my right hand so that the palm faced forward, fingers straight. Slowly her arm came upwards until our palms were together, fingertips touching fingertips.

When the time came for us to leave, Melika and Samwelli escorted us to the station and stood with unashamed tears to wave us off. Melika's hug was painful in its desperation.

'Remember your promise! And write — please write to let us know how you fare!'

I couldn't answer, the pain of leaving sharp in my chest like a stab wound. I buried my face against her shoulder before climbing onto the train with Mother.

TWENTY-THREE

I caught sight of our reflections in the glass doors of
Mombasa Hospital, next day, and was taken in
memory back to the day, some six months earlier, when
I'd gone, with pulse racing to find Paul and, seeing my
image in that same door, had nearly turned away.

Why was it, I wondered, that our partings always
left me hurt, the misunderstandings leaving bitterness
upon my tongue? That time, unexpectedly I'd found
him gone, the shock of his sudden departure numbing
me so that I'd staggered blindly out into the sunshine.

Our parting at the hospital in Nairobi the day before
had left me equally bewildered and frustrated.

As I walked beside Mother's wheelchair along the
corridors, I felt again the mixture of chagrin and loss
with which I'd walked out of Paul's office.

I had waited outside the wooden door as Mother
was being prepared for the journey, with my heart
pounding, over-loud, my colour high; not knowing
quite what to say, how to break the icy barrier I'd
erected.

'Come in!' he'd said. The gentle pressure of his hand
on my bare arm had made my breath catch, all my
sensors seeming to be concentrated in that small area,
so that when he took his fingers away I'd felt exposed
and looked quickly at my arms as if he'd left an imprint
there, scorched into my flesh.

He was cheerful, polite, as if nothing had happened
between us.

'So! Tomorrow you'll be in Mombasa!'

I'd looked at his smiling mouth as if seeing it properly for the first time, realising his lips were beautiful —

401

sensual without being effeminate, humorous without being sardonic. Then I'd looked away, afraid that the rush of sexuality would show, wanting to feel his mouth on mine; on my neck and breasts. And yet, still eating at the back of my mind was the doubt — I still wasn't sure of him, still wasn't as full of trust as I had been.

'Nina! Are you all right, Nina!' He had been leaning over me, his hand against my cheek. Turning my head quickly I kissed the palm, holding it against my face for a short moment. My tongue felt large and swollen, blocking speech. I cleared my throat, tried to swallow, knowing my anger was unfair.

'Sorry, Paul!' My cheeks flamed. 'I'm sorry!'

He had moved away, and was looking out of the window.

'Don't be sorry,' he said, his voice strange — withdrawn.

We had stared, locked into each other's eyes, then abruptly he'd splintered the moment.

'Are you ready?'

I was trembling and gripped the arms of the chair, fighting for composure, wanting him to take me in his arms, make everything better, as if I were a small girl again. 'Yes,' my voice fought to be heard. I cleared my throat. 'Yes, we're ready!' Numb with grief, it didn't matter any more.

'Good!' He had become Doctor Phillips again. Cool, friendly. And the moment had passed.

'Well, I suppose I'd better go!'

I'd hoped for him to say, 'No! No, don't go! Stay here, Nina!' Instead, he walked to the door, held it open.

'Come on then, I'll see you both off!'

Oh Paul! Paul!

In the doorway I had paused, turning into the semi-circle of his arm as he stood holding the door, and he

402

bent forward then, kissed me lightly, and propelled me towards the car and Mother.

And once again I had felt like a child, and the world was empty. There was no time to mend the tear.

No cure, either, for the pain of Kerri's loss.

After three days in Mombasa Hospital, I moved Mother down to the docks. The ship towered above us, grey and white paint gleaming.

Mother's face was anxious, her hands fluttering again.

'How can I go up that?' she asked. I looked up the steep gangplank and shrugged.

'Don't worry, for heaven's sake — I'll get somebody to carry your chair.'

Thank God the hospital had allowed us that convenience at least.

I explained our predicament to the seaman who stood at the base of the gangplank and, within minutes, two sailors were cheerfully carrying Mother, in her chair, through the large door in the side of the ship normally used for loading luggage and supplies.

'There you are, you see, no bother at all!' I said as we were finally deposited with our suitcases at the door of our cabin.

'First-class?' Mother's voice was querulous. 'We're not going First-Class, surely?'

I hadn't thought about it, Michael had made the arrangements and I'd just accepted them.

'Why not?' I answered with a gaiety I hardly felt. I wondered how long Father's money would last — I'd already spent what I felt to be a small fortune on the trip.

The cabin was small but adequate, two bunks, one above the other, a basin and storage space. I chattered to Mother, more to reassure myself, to deaden my grief, than to comfort her.

'Do you feel like coming up on deck?' I asked when I'd unpacked. 'It would be fun to be there when we sail!'

Fun?

'No,' she replied. 'I'll lie down, I think. I feel so tired!'

'Sorry! I hadn't thought what a busy day it's been! All right, we'll just sit quietly.'

'No! No, you go up. I just want to sleep! Really — I mean it! Go on!' Her thin hands pushed me towards the door and she turned on her side on the lower bunk, facing the bulkhead. I pulled a blanket over her.

'All right, if you're sure! Look, here's the bell if you need to ring for a stewardess.' I put the bell on the table beside her and left the cabin, closing the door quietly behind me.

The deck was bustling with activity, and an all-pervading sense of excitement which, in spite of myself, I found catching. Chains rattled as the derricks loaded supplies from dockside into hold; winches whirred and orders were shouted. The deck was crowded with passengers and relatives seeing them off.

A bell rang, strident above the noise, and a voice came loud over the speakers:

'Will all people not sailing please disembark now!'

More noise and bustle, tears and wavings.

I leaned on the salt-sticky, rounded wood of the railings feeling isolated and alone. The crowd on the dockside seemed smaller now, dwarfed by the huge liner. My eyes searched pointlessly through the faces, looking for anyone I knew, snatching at the hope that perhaps Paul had come down to Mombasa at the last moment.

But of course there was no sign of him, nor of Kerri, Leah or Melika. None of Rashidi or Jamira . . . nor of Rsul or Bibicol or Maja — all the people I loved most . . . I was leaving them all, taking my own path away, and I knew it had to be so . . . Then, in the middle of the sea of faces below me, I thought I saw Leah, so plain, so clear, that I called out — but she was gone and, in vain, I strained to find her there.

An orchestra struck up on deck, traditionally playing us out of the harbour. Ropes were winched in, two tugs pulled the ship around.

I felt my eyes sting, a lump grow in my throat, a hollowness around my heart, and I leaned my head against the metal strut that joined the railing from bulkhead to deck.

Oh God! What am I doing here? I thought, I shouldn't be leaving — I know I shouldn't. Oh, Kerri! Suddenly the careful cocoon of indifference I'd woven around my pain sundered, and I had to grip hard onto the railing to stop myself from falling.

A voice at my shoulder made me jump.

'Are you all right?'

I spun round. 'Michael!'

'Yes, a spot of leave! Last-minute thing really. I thought I'd surprise you!'

'Well, you've certainly done that!' I found myself unreasonably annoyed at his subterfuge. 'Why didn't you tell us?'

'As I said, a last-minute thing! The chance came, so I took it. Thought I might be able to help you, and your mother.'

'That's kind of you, but I think you've done more than enough already!'

He interrupted. 'Nonsense! I'm sure Major Anderson would've done the same!' His smile was friendly, the faint smell of his after-shave pleasant, and yet I wanted to lash out at him, wipe the smile from his round, fresh face.

I couldn't understand why he affected me this way. He had, in all conscience, been extremely helpful, extremely respectful — and yet! And yet . . .

We stood, side by side, but not touching, watching Mombasa's silver-white beaches, palm-fringed and brilliant in the late afternoon sun, disappearing slowly as the Kenya Castle steamed out into the Indian Ocean.

Somewhere, I thought as my eyes strained for every last look, somewhere out there Kerri could still be alive, with Leah and Mirriamu. Oh, God! Please let them be there, let them be alive — oh, let them be alive! And Paul . . .

A large part of me was remaining there, upon those fast-receding shores.

Michael danced attendance upon us, wheeling Mother round the decks, buying me wine, leading me onto the dance floor in the evenings. And I followed, numb and unfeeling. The first-class facilities were opulent, catering for comfort and entertainment, and while sitting in the luxurious dining-room, confronted with mountains of rich food, my mind flickered briefly and guiltily to the simple life lived by the villagers in Mikendeni where they made do with the bare essentials of existence.

The heat was intense as we sailed into the Red Sea, and our cabin airless. A few days out of Mombasa, and unable to sleep, I put on a thin dressing-gown and went on deck to try to get cool. The moon was brilliant that night, diamond-faceted in reflection on the dark waters below, the sky star-filled and — heaven — a slight breeze blew, fresh on my hot face. Longing flooded me, induced by the mysterious romanticism of moonlit water, and I closed my eyes against the deep yearnings, a mixture of joy and sorrow.

I wondered where Paul was at that moment, whether he was Doctor Phillips or Muchige that night — who he was with, puzzled still by his duality, by his apparent indifference to my grief over Kerri.

'Nina!'

I turned quickly, almost expecting to see Paul, my thoughts of him had been so strong. Michael stood there, smiling.

My heart plummeted, and my shoulders sagged with disappointment.

'Oh! Michael — it's you!'

'Of course! Who did you expect?'

Even in his dressing-gown and pyjamas he looked neat, well-turned-out. His hands were on the rails on either side of me, capturing me, the rounded wood pressing into my back.

I shifted uneasily.

'Excuse me, please — I'd better get back to the cabin.'

'No rush! Come on, ease up a bit — it's such a lovely night! Stay and enjoy it for a while!'

'But my mother . . . !'

'Mrs Anderson'll be fine, I'm sure. You'd left her anyway!' His hair was brushed to its usual perfection, and even the breeze failed to ruffle it.

I felt anger threaten. 'I only came up for a moment, to get some air!' I pushed against his chest until he let go the railings.

'You've been here quite a time, Nina,' he said. 'I've been watching you. Standing against the moonlight — beautiful!'

Why wasn't I flattered? Why the irritation?

'Don't be idiotic!'

His eyes in the pale light glittered as he looked at me.

'I wasn't being idiotic! You don't realise how lovely you are!' He lit a cigarette and in the flare of the match I could see his face, gentle and kind — there was no menace there. And yet I was afraid.

He put an arm around my shoulders.

'Michael, please don't! Please don't complicate things!'

407

'Don't be so wary of me — I really think a lot of you . . . and Mrs Anderson, of course. I wouldn't do anything to jeopardise our friendship.'

His arm, however, still lay heavy across my shoulders and I was tense and awkward beneath it.

He eased me round so that we stood, face to face.

'Please let me help you — don't shut yourself away,' he pleaded, holding my face between his hands and looking closely — too closely — into my eyes. 'I only want to see you happy, Nina, there are no strings attached to my help, you know.'

I gulped and stepped backwards from him, fighting tears. It would be too easy to reach out, take what loving help I could from him, let him carry the burdens. Almost, in the magic of the tropical moonlight, I was prepared to let go, to take solace with him, as Noeda had done with Malek.

What hope of Paul? I questioned inwardly, thinking that my childishness had lost him, that he'd gone from me, irretrievably — as Kerri had.

I took another step away.

'Michael — thank you! Believe me, I do value your friendship and help — I really do . . .'

'But?'

'But — I've just got too much on my plate right now. Not just Mother — there's a hell of a lot you know nothing about. Things that only I can do. There's no possible way I can, or could, repay your kindness.'

'Or reciprocate my feelings, seemingly! Is there a man?'

'No!' My answer came too fast, too vehemently.

He leaned, sideways-on to me, one elbow resting on the railings.

'I'll settle for your companionship. No come-backs, no demands, I promise!'

He looked sincere, but I wondered. Selfishly, too, I begrudged the time, still felt the moral obligations

408

would fetter me. He was a nice man, I told myself, and I didn't want to use him. I wasn't prepared either, to let anyone hurt me in the way that Paul had . . . I was too exposed, too raw, my grief making me vulnerable.

Michael went then, and I stared out at the ink-black sea, alone and filled with deep sadness.

'Why do I always seem to be leaving those I love, losing them?' I cried. The cry whipped out of my mouth and was blown by the wind into the sea-spume. And Leah was there, her voice clear and strong . . .

'No, Nina, that is not true . . .' But my confidence was gone, I didn't trust myself any longer, not sure how much was wishful thinking, born of desperate hope. And yet her words enclosed me, cocooned me, leaving me strangely calm.

True to his word, as I would have expected, Michael didn't press me. He was just 'there', always at hand, but I stepped warily.

Once through the Suez Canal and into the Mediterranean, the temperature cooled and Mother became less fretful. Her meals until then had been served in the cabin, but one morning she declared she'd like to eat in the dining-room.

'I'm so much better,' she announced, 'it's time I started to walk on deck, get some sea air into my lungs.'

She was still pathetically thin, but her eyes were brighter, her hands steadier.

'Fine,' I said, 'whenever you're ready!' I helped her dress, choosing grey trousers and a long over-blouse for her. 'These will be smart, and the trousers will keep your legs warm.'

'And hide them, I hope!' she laughed.

I looked away to conceal the sudden up-rush of tears. It was the first time I'd heard her laugh since Father died.

'You'll look great!' I kissed her cheek. 'Let's get your hair done and we'll cause a sensation on deck!'

'Hardly that,' she said ruefully, looking in the mirror. 'Those days have long gone, Nina. I'm old and haggard now.'

Old — at forty-eight?

'Rubbish! Just wait till we get you better, put some flesh back on your bones.'

Her eyes were huge in the thin face.

'I used to be quite pretty once! So long ago. What is it — some seventeen years, I suppose!'

My senses alerted, antenna-like.

'When I was small?' I prompted.

'You were so sweet — fat, round and solemn!' Her voice was wistful, as the memories came.

'What spoilt it?' I hardly dared whisper the question, one of my hands resting on her hair, the other holding the stilled brush.

'I suppose it was my fault.' Hesitantly the words came. 'I was so obsessed with the baby coming, so desperate to give William the son he wanted. He was a very — physical — man, and I wouldn't let him near me. I guess I was frightened I'd lose the child!' Her lips trembled. 'I loved him too much, Nina! Always had done. My mother told me that, long before we married. He never felt the same way, and I knew it, I suppose.'

'But he married you — he must have cared then?'

She shrugged. 'Sometimes I wonder — he came out to Kenya a year before me. I wrote often — passionate letters — and he wrote back, less often. Then I followed him out. Perhaps in a way he felt trapped into marriage!' She gave a short laugh. 'I mean, there I was, on the doorstep, so to speak — what else could he do? Hardly send me back on the next boat, could he?'

Not quite an arranged marriage. But almost . . .

I let her silence hang for a while, slowly resuming the brushstrokes on her hair.

410

'But you were happy then?' I said after a few moments.

'Yes — oh, yes! And I think he was, too, the first few years. It was good in Kenya in those days. We had a full social life, and good servants to take care of us. Then we moved to Uganda — we both loved it there!'

'And then?' I asked.

There was a pause, and I thought I'd lost her. Then her eyes met mine in the mirror and she squared her shoulders.

'Something dreadful happened. I'm not sure I should tell you, but somehow I think you need to know.'

How cruel I am! I thought, letting her strip each layer off, exposing herself. I very nearly stopped her, thought of excuses, but her hand came up, capturing mine, holding the hairbrush still.

'You should know, Nina. Perhaps it'll help you understand why he was so . . . so irascible!'

I nodded, drew up a chair and sat beside her, holding her hand.

'During the early months of my second pregnancy, and with you still very young, I suffered from dreadful morning sickness. It wasn't confined just to mornings, but kept me in a constant dizzy nausea all day, every day. We were in England on leave, and the doctor there insisted that I stay on for a few months, at least until the sickness went. For some reason he was afraid I'd miscarry. I spent a lot of time in bed, I remember,' she pressed my hand. 'You were so good! And I felt so lousy, I'd very little time for you!'

Perhaps that's where the early memories of rejection stemmed from, I thought.

I couldn't remember receiving any love from the other one either — the Mother in Kabul. No, I had never felt any warmth from her . . . I wondered why that was.

'William had to go back to Kenya at the end of his

leave. He was there, oh — about three months, I think, on his own, before I was well enough to travel.' Her lips tightened, then with her head turned downwards, she spoke fast. 'He had a woman. A black girl. A prostitute . . .' Her voice broke. 'A prostitute, for God's sake! I think I might've forgiven him an "affair", but a prostitute — and a native girl at that!'

'She was the one who gave him syphilis?' I asked.

Her eyes widened in astonishment as she looked up at me.

'You knew that?'

'Yes. I'm sorry — it was on his medical notes, one of the reasons he didn't recover.'

'Oh, my God!' She covered her face with her hands. The silence was loud with unspoken questions.

'Did you know he infected me? That I lost his son?'

'Yes, Mum, Doctor Gordon told me.'

'He had no right to!' Anger reddened her face.

I took her in my arms, holding tight against her struggle to push me away, sharing her loss, wanting to share my loss with her, too.

'He had to — I knew enough, guessed at the rest. I was in such a torment — uncertain, feeling unloved, unloving. I forced the answers.'

Her body relaxed against me.

'It was as though it was my fault, Nina! William never forgave himself and, presumably because he couldn't come to terms with what had happened, he turned the blame onto me. It was *my* fault — I'd forced him into a marriage he didn't want; I'd let him down, having a daughter instead of a son; being ill and leaving him to come back alone. He accused me of being no good in . . . you know . . . in bed; he even said that he'd had more fun with that black girl than he'd ever had with me. Then when I got syphilis and lost the baby that was the end of everything!'

412

'Oh, Mum, if only I'd understood — been able to help you!'

'You were too young, how could you have helped?'

I shrugged, stuck for an answer. A mixture of guilt, pity and sorrow washed through me, and I wept, holding her against my chest, the tears falling onto her head, wetting her hair.

'We both had to have treatment, of course. It was dreadful — so worrying, not only because of the disease itself, but also because of the strain of keeping it a secret. We were terrified — William even more than me — that people would hear about it. But Doctor Gordon was marvellous, and the hospital. No one found out or, if they did, it was never mentioned.' Her breath escaped in a long and tremulous sigh. 'But William never fully recovered — mentally, I mean! He just *raged* at me, at you — at everything really!'

'That's why he was so unreasonable about my friendship with Rashidi and Jamira! Of course — I see it now . . . and with justification!' As I spoke I could've kicked myself, but she didn't pick up the words. Now wasn't the time to tell her about Kerri — what point, in any case? Maybe someday in the future I'd be able to confide in her.

Her eyes were ringed dark with fatigue.

'There! Now you've exhausted yourself!'

'No! No, I feel better, strangely enough — just empty, somehow! Like a squeezed-out tube of toothpaste!' She smiled.

'Well, you certainly don't look like one — all folded over and jagged!' I teased. In fact that was exactly how she looked, and yet I sensed her relief at having shucked off the burden of the secret she'd carried for so long.

'If you feel well enough, let's go and wow 'em on the promenade deck!'

'Yes,' she nodded, 'yes, I feel well enough now.'

We walked slowly, her weight featherlight upon my

413

arm, closer than we'd ever been. But the last thing I really wanted to do was to parade, smiling, making conversation. I needed time to digest her words, to come to terms with the history that had shaped my own insecurity, my own inner turmoil.

The ship docked at Marseilles, and Michael took me ashore, leaving Mother in the care of a stewardess for the day.

We explored the old seaport then travelled to the outskirts and found a small restaurant perched high above a vivid green valley.

'It's odd, being on ground again.' I had become so accustomed to the roll of the ship that even now the earth seemed to sway under my feet. It was the first time, too, that I had gone ashore, not liking to leave Mother when we called at Aden, Port Said or Genoa.

Michael poured wine, then looked at me over the edge of his glass.

'It's quite traumatic, coming back to reality at the end of a voyage. Bit of a come-down. I'm not looking forward to it.'

'Yes, but the sea trip's total unreality! It's got a kind of dream-like quality: the thrumming of the ship's engines; the steamy, salty bathwater in those huge, deep baths; all that dressing up and eating and dancing. It's a separate world, on board ship, as though all the horrors of Mau Mau are on a completely different planet!'

He laughed, twisting the glass in his fingers so that the sun reflecting from it made kaleidoscopic patterns on the tablecloth. 'I suppose so — but it's not a bad thing, surely, to relax completely, mentally and physically?'

'It makes me feel guilty — thinking of all the money spent by everyone on board. Unjustified extravagance really!' The wine was going to my head, making me confused.

'Oh, come now — Miss Nina Anderson, setting the world to rights?'

I laughed. 'Yes, I guess I do sound self-righteous . . . but, well, I have *seen* how the Africans live, Michael.'

'Their choice, most of the time! Stop worrying, and enjoy yourself for a change, for goodness' sake!' His hand squeezed mine on the table top.

I sighed, realising I'd never be able to get him to feel the same way as I did.

'Sure!' I said, smiling. 'Let's enjoy it — it won't be long before we arrive in England!'

'And all the relatives to visit!' he replied.

'I've none that I can remember. I'll be staying with some friends of Mother's while she goes through her treatment.' I shivered, feeling a hint of the winter weather that awaited around the corner once we'd sailed out of the Mediterranean.

A faint unease made me restless suddenly, and I looked at my watch.

'We'd better start back soon, Michael — I don't like leaving Mother too long.' Her face was there, sharp, in my mind's eye.

'She'll be fine, I'm sure — but all right, we'll go as soon as we finish the meal.'

The food was good, the wine heady, and Michael a charming and amusing companion. The more I got to know him, the more I realised how unfair I was being. His humour was gentle and slightly wry, his behaviour towards me never changed, always courteous and concerned, ever complimentary and caring. In the pale French sunshine, I relaxed and found my wariness lessening so that when he put his arm around my waist as we went towards the rented car, I didn't pull away.

It was late afternoon when we got back to the ship. As I stepped on board, the purser came towards me.

'Could you come with me for a moment?' he asked and led me down to his office, where the ship's doctor awaited us.

I knew when I saw the doctor's face.

'She's dead — isn't she? She's dead?' Not Mother, too!

The doctor put out a hand. I pushed him away.

'Oh God! God! Why? Why now, when she was doing so well?' I went to the door, hit hard against it with angry, hopeless fists. My forehead, too, hit against the door, as if the physical pain could take away the screaming I felt inside, the tearing pain in my chest. Dry-eyed, I railed at the cabin door, at the doctor, the purser, at Michael. Why, why?

I felt Michael's hands on my taut shoulders, and I shrugged him away.

'No! Don't touch me! Just — don't touch me! If I hadn't gone ashore with you . . . she'd still be here!' I looked at the doctor. 'Wouldn't she?'

He spoke quietly. 'Miss Anderson, try not to blame yourself. It could have happened at any time. Naturally you feel like this, but you've nothing to feel guilty about. We all know how well you looked after your Mother.'

'Well then, what happened?' I gripped my hands together to stop their trembling. 'Did she fall — or what?'

The doctor exchanged a look with the purser, then came over to me and made me sit down.

'Somehow — and this is being investigated — Mrs Anderson got hold of a bottle of brandy.'

'Oh no!' The cry tore from my heart. He held my wrists.

'I have the notes from her own doctor. She was an alcoholic, wasn't she?'

I nodded numbly.

'But she'd been in hospital — dried out?'

416

'Yes.'

'Well, I'm afraid she drank the whole bottle. It was probably too much for her heart. There'll have to be a post-mortem.'

'No — please! Can't you just leave her alone now? It's obvious what happened!' I couldn't take the thought of her being cut open, coldly.

'It has to be done, with any sudden death.' He turned to Michael. 'I'm going to give Miss Anderson a sedative — can you look after her? I'll get the stewardess to put her to bed.'

'No!' I raged. 'No! No! I want to see my mother — now!'

As I stood up, the room spun around me and I vomitted violently across the floor.

All that expensive food! The thought came irreverently into my mind, and I started to shiver. 'Sorry, Michael, all that food wasted — I'm so sorry!'

Michael handed me a handkerchief, and pulled me to him.

'Why aren't I crying? What's wrong with me?' My voice was hoarse and muffled, my eyes dry and gritty, seeing his shirt buttons, magnified by their proximity, the stitches on them making an X through the four holes.

The doctor took me then to the sick bay where Mother lay, an unbelievably slight form, concealed by a white sheet. I gripped Michael's hand as the cloth was slowly pulled away.

The worry lines were smoothed from her face and, eyes closed, she looked like a wax doll. A thin, waxen image; not Mother, not the woman I'd just begun to know.

Startled, I thought: I feel nothing — *nothing!* Why do I feel nothing?

I took my hand from Michael's and touched her cold

417

cheek. The inert flesh was flaccid, discarded, no longer housing Mother.

The three men hovered behind me, ready to help.

'I'll go to my cabin now,' I said, my voice steady.

They looked at each other.

'You can move into another cabin, if you'd prefer it.' The purser's eyes were intense through his spectacles.

'No, I'll be all right. Just take me back there, please, Michael.'

The doctor handed me a small bottle of tablets.

'Take a couple of these if you can't sleep,' he said. 'They'll help a bit.'

In the cabin I sat on the edge of the bunk which had been Mother's. The bedclothes had been removed, the cabin tidied. On the bedside table her hairbrush lay on its side. I picked it up; her hair still meshed the bristles.

'Oh, dear God! If I hadn't gone and left her . . .' I touched the fine hairs with the tip of my finger. Somehow they seemed to be more real than the still, cleansed body in the sick bay.

Slowly the tears started, and my weeping grew in intensity, until it engulfed me in the same way as it had done when I first knew I'd lost Rashidi, as it had done when I lost Kerri. But now my grief was centred on the woman who had been my mother, whose friendship I had only begun to explore.

'It's not fair!' I railed, beating my clenched hands upon the pillow that had supported her head that morning. 'It's just not fair!'

There was no train speeding through an African night to purge my anguish this time; just the gentle rolling of the ship, the throb-throb-throb of the engines, pulsing in rhythm with the loud pounding of my heart, underscoring my sobbing.

And Paul was not there. Nor Kerri. Had I lost them all?

All the while Michael sat, silent in the cabin, allowing me my grief.

The Mediterranean was calm, unperturbed by my anger, uncaring that Mother had died while I wasn't there, that she had cheated me of even that intimacy.

They buried her there, in the bland, sunlit sea.

In the afternoon.

After the post-mortem.

Mother was dead.

Dead . . .

. . . *So, too, is Malek's child, and so, too, my beloved Alexi.*

And Kerri, too?

My head swam as I drifted in and out of awareness, the grief alternating with bouts of anger that she should have gone before we forged the tenuous links. I was bitter and angry with myself for having left her alone, unguarded; for all the wasted years; for having left Kerri in Mikendeni, too much of a coward to admit to her presence in my life . . .

. . . *'Is the loss of my child punishment for betraying Malek's trust?' I ask, and the tears never cease their endless flow down my cheeks, though I am too exhausted to give vent to the harsh sobs that accumulate somewhere behind my breastbone — painfully.*

I felt deserted, riddled with a thousand guilts, and stayed in my cabin, unable to face the stark rock of Gibraltar, the accusing stares of the other passengers. Michael was a constant visitor, solicitous and worried for me. I held him at arm's length, wishing it was Paul who cared for me, longing for Paul.

. . . *Malek was only concerned for my well-being — I realise that, too. And this makes my betrayal worse. For I allowed him, all too eagerly, my body — but never my heart.*

'I'm all right, Michael,' I said testily one evening, shortly after Mother's death. 'You really needn't keep coming down to see me. I'm not going to kill myself or anything!'

I could hear my voice, as though it were thrown like a ventriloquist's stage trick, from somewhere outside myself.

His face reproved me. 'I know that — I just care enough about you to be anxious, that's all.'

There they were again, the thin membranes of the spider's web, enmeshing me. Fine, sticky strands of obligation.

'Look — I really do appreciate all you've done — all you're doing. Nothing's taken for granted, I promise. But — I need to be alone, just for a while.'

His shoulders drooped; he hesitated at the door. 'Yes, very well. Um . . . would you like me to bring you a brandy down later?'

A brandy! The tactlessness was unintentional, I knew, but my answer was waspish.

'No! How can you talk about drinking to me — after what's happened?'

He was immediately contrite. 'Oh, Lord! I didn't mean . . .'

'That's all right.' I flapped an impatient hand at him. 'It's all right — just . . . oh, I'm sorry, I know you're only trying to be kind.'

What a bitch I am, I thought, what a complete bitch!

I put out my hand. 'Come and sit down,' I said, still inwardly sighing. 'I don't mean to be so sharp, really I don't. Please forgive me!'

'Of course I do — there's nothing to forgive, anyway! It's me who should be apologising for my crass remark.'

'Michael! You've been so good to me . . . but, please, I beg you, don't build up too much — expect too much of me, of our relationship!'

He looked down at his hands. 'I'm extremely fond of you . . .'

'I know,' I interrupted. 'That's what worries me! I

can't give you anything in return except friendship. I'm sorry, but that's how it is!'

His hand moved onto the bed, where my thigh mounded the sheet.

Get off! Get off! I shouted silently, for goodness' sake, leave me alone — don't you hear what I'm saying? I clenched my teeth on the words, willing myself not to move my leg away.

With a quick movement forward, he kissed me wetly, upon my lips.

'Sleep well, if you can, Nina! I'll see you tomorrow.'

As he left the cabin my fingers scrubbed against my mouth, erasing the kiss.

What the hell's the matter with him – can't he hear me? I queried, and what the hell's the matter with *me?* He's a nice man, for goodness' sake, a nice man! But I shivered and pulled the bedclothes high around my shoulders, heavy with loss.

So, too, is Malek — a good, kind man . . . a good man . . .

* * * *

. . . My mind is wandering yet again. It must surely be the heat and weakness from the loss of my child. My own child. Malek's child, too . . .

I drift in and out of sleep, vaguely aware of Rsul as he tends me. Each time I return to reality, I long to go back to the painless darkness. When he tries to coax me into eating, I turn my head away, for the effort is too great. I don't know if he has slept during this night, for each time I wake it is to find him sitting beside me, with the fire well fuelled.

Towards dawn I dream again. The man I killed is there once more, his eyes huge and red with lust, and between his legs his manhood stands, an enormous sword with which he tears at my soft flesh.

'Get off me — leave me be! If you must stab me, make it my heart and not my womb!' I sit up and beat at the man with my fists, and sobs of anguish shake me.

'Shh, Noeda, all is well. No one is here to attack you.' Rsul takes hold of my flailing arms and holds me, gently cradling my painful body against his chest.

'Oh, where is my Bibicol?' I ask through my sobbing, lucid for a brief moment and wanting her badly.

'She is well, fear not. I will take you to her later, when you are recovered.'

When I become calmer, I take a drink and look at him. 'How come you to be here?'

'I have never been far away from you, Noeda. I have followed you since you left Bibicol, arriving too late at the hut where you wintered because I could not get through the snow to you. Then, when I saw how it was with you and Malek, I left again. But, somehow, I feel your pain and know when things are not well with you. My regret is that I did not follow my inclination and get here in time to spare you this!'

As I listen to him, it is as though it is not me but someone else he speaks to. I ask no more questions for, indeed, I do not want to have to concentrate upon the answers.

This same day he lifts me onto his horse in front of him, holding me there as I sit, semi-conscious and hot with fever. I do not take much cognizance of the journey, and I do not recall reaching the village where we now stop. I am dimly aware of people about me, of being washed and made to drink, but all I want is to be left alone. I have no will to recover, no wish to face the future.

In the darkness where I am living now I am besieged by strange and ugly creatures, by disjointed words and sounds. Unable to escape, I feel my spirit cower within me, and I lie curled up as small as I can make myself — in hiding.

How long this lasts I do not know, but I awake to

see Rsul, shadowy beside me as ever. I turn my head away, pretending to be asleep.

'Noeda, I have a drink for you. Please try, for me.' He holds my head up and the fluid runs over my dry lips into my throat. I swallow with difficulty, for even that small action seems to require too great an effort.

'There! Was that so hard to do?' he asks.

I make no reply.

He smooths my hair away from my face. I want to move out of his reach, resenting his solicitude.

'Leave me be!' The sound is faint, yet harsh, even to my ears.

'No, I'm not going to let you run away from me yet again, Noeda. You'll feel differently soon, but sleep again now, for that sleep will give your body healing time.'

He does not know that my sleep is a disturbed and unhappy place.

I awake later, wondering why I fight against Rsul, when in the deepest part of my soul I know my destiny is linked somehow with his, and my heart is heavy with loss.

Rsul moves from across the room. 'You are awake. Good!' He takes both my hands in his. 'You dreamed sad dreams, Noeda, for you cried out in your sleep, and your cheeks are wet with tears!'

'I dreamed I lost something I thought was mine,' I tell him, though I cannot recall what it was.

'Maybe it never was yours, but your wishing made it so?'

'No! Oh, no!' I cannot allow that to be.

The room comes into focus, and I wonder what it is we talked about. I lie back and shut my mind.

My body slowly begins to mend, though I fight against it, refusing food and drink until persuaded by Rsul to take a little each time it is proffered. In this way I am eventually able to leave my bed.

I do not know whose house we are in, or the faces of the women who tend me.

When I am able to walk, unsteady though I am, Rsul tells me that he has arranged for me to travel in a litter for the rest of the journey to Kabul.

'It is not more than three days from here,' he tells me, 'even at a walking pace.'

The litter is lined with cushions and has thick dark curtains to shield me from sun or rain. It is strapped securely to a sturdy camel, and I am lifted carefully into it.

'I am not ready to meet my father,' I protest weakly.

'You will not be able to rest easy until you have tried to make your peace with him, Noeda! We can't wait any longer, for it is strange that he has not learned of your closeness already.'

'Who knows I am his daughter?'

'I've told no one, but suspicions must surely have been aroused.'

I do not want to go on to Kabul; a foreboding of great danger leaves me weak and frightened at the thought of seeing my father. But I am too tired to argue, and I know it has to be.

The journey seems endless as I rock uncomfortably in the litter, stifling in the heat. Vaguely I wonder how long it is since I left Malek — it was early summer then.

Rsul is always solicitous, ever ready to halt the animals if my tiredness grows to exhaustion point.

'Why are you doing this, Rsul?' I ask one evening as we rest.

'Do you need to ask? You, Noeda, of all people?'

'What do you mean by that?'

He looks hard at me then, and in his eyes, behind the flickering reflection of the fire, I see once more the uplands of some foreign land and a lone rider at full gallop, but this time the horse stops, and I recognise the rider.

I turn away quickly, and as Rsul starts to speak I break in. 'I'm so tired, Rsul, please let me sleep!'

'Perhaps, indeed, the time is not quite right, but you cannot evade the truth forever, Noeda!'

I do not answer, troubled deeply by far memories, and by some strange view of the years to come. I am not ready to think on these things, and resentment flares in me against Rsul for not allowing my mind to stay quiet and empty. I cannot understand what it is that is pushing at the corners of my consciousness, why Rsul is so much a part of all that was gone and all that is to come. Panic mounts in me as the memories and ghosts will not leave me be.

'Where is Ibrahim?' I ask.

'He returned to Meshed, to Bibicol. They are well suited, Noeda, and a marriage ceremony is being arranged. This also I came to tell you.'

'Ibrahim — and Bibicol?' A stab of jealousy twists in my stomach. Am I to lose them both? I wonder. The mists swirl up into my head.

I rail at Rsul: 'You! You are the one who took away my loved ones, now you've taken this one, too, the child that Malek gave me!' I know I talk rubbish, and I hit at him wildly, screaming with hysteria, fear and guilt.

'No, Noeda!' Rsul holds my wrists, and I struggle to get free. 'No! You are wrong — I would do nothing to harm you, ever.'

I will not be calmed and lie, sobbing bitterly, through the night. Rsul, seeing my wan, exhausted face in the morning light, decides it will be too much for me to travel so, making me as comfortable as possible in the shade of tamarisk trees, he and the rest of the travelling party withdraw a short distance to allow me to sleep.

But my dreams are troubled and it seems a thousand voices call out my name, so that I awake unrefreshed. And yet it is as though, somehow, within that restless sleep I see Rsul for the first time.

I get up and walk to where he sits.

'I am ready! We can travel again.' I cannot bring myself to look at him, and keep my eyes anywhere but on his.

'You are sure?' He puts an arm around my shoulder, and leads me back to the shade.

'But I have questions to ask first,' I tell him.

'Of course!' He sits beside me so that I can speak without the distraction of his face in front of mine.

'Why did you follow me?'

'I returned to Meshed, and Bibicol told me you had gone.'

'Was she much saddened?'

'Indeed she was! You hurt her deeply, Noeda, for she was closer than a sister to you. I tried to explain to her!'

'How could *you* explain?'

'Noeda, I am not so stupid; I guessed who you were the day you left Abdul Pashtoon's estate. Your eyes had told me.'

I remember.

'And yet you didn't speak of it?'

'I was not completely sure until we journeyed together towards Merve. And, for whatever reasons you had, I knew then that you wished to remain undiscovered.'

'That's why you followed?'

'I followed because I had to, it is so written; and also because I was concerned for your safety. I was driven to distraction when I could not reach you in the mountains. When at last I got through, as I have told you, I found you with Malek in close embrace. So deep was your entanglement that you did not see me when

426

I came to the hut. I withdrew then for I knew it was the wrong time.'

'And you followed us, thereafter?'

'Not directly, for I had wounds to heal.'

'Wounds?'

'The same as those that Bibicol was nursing. For I thought I, too, had lost you completely. I returned then to Meshed and let her know you were safe.'

'Yet you did not come to Kalash?'

'No, not then, for the choice of road was yours! I went to Bactria, where I stayed until I felt your danger and need.'

'Malek is a good man!' I say abruptly, guilty about my treatment of that gentle soul.

'Yes, I know, and he, too, is suffering greatly.'

'Should I return to him? He will never forgive me the loss of his son. He did not want me to travel.'

'The decision has to be yours! Give yourself time for full recovery of your body and mind before you do anything.'

'Yes, I think most of my actions have been taken impulsively, without consideration first.'

This time of clarification has tired me, and I sleep there, my head on Rsul's thigh, and then awake refreshed for the first time, some hours later. Rsul stands up, flexing his leg where I have cramped it, sleeping.

'Do you feel well enough to continue?' he asks. 'We will reach Kabul tomorrow.'

My heart sinks and the panic floods back. But it has to be done, we both know that.

'Yes, let's go,' I say, for there is no way around it. I climb stiffly back into the litter, aware of the bruises still painful upon my body. Memory of the man who attacked me comes back in a quick flash, and the taste of vomit fills my mouth as I think of his brutality to my Alexi. I shake the image of his bloodied body from my mind.

427

'Rsul,' I turn to ask, 'what of the man — the man I killed?'

'Leave that, Noeda, I will do all that is necessary.'

As I look down at this tall, dark-skinned man, gratitude for his help and care fills me. I bend down and kiss him quickly on the cheek and he puts his hand up to touch my lips. A great and overwhelming feeling of loss sweeps over me as I look at him — and I know.

Next morning we stand and look down at Kabul, its white domes and minarets gleaming in the sunlight. I can make out the walls of my father's estate beyond the town. Pulse racing, I try to tidy myself, seeing in my mirror how gaunt my face, how hollow my eyes have grown.

By the time we reach the gates I am wringing wet with nervous perspiration, and glad of the protection afforded me by the curtains of my litter. I peer through these as we come to a halt, and see Rsul approach the large studded door. Had I been mounted on a horse, I think I would have turned now and galloped away.

In this moment I know I should have sent Rsul ahead to speak to Habib Amir for me.

My father's headman comes to the door and I see him look in my direction, then Rsul goes into the house with him. I sit, running the edge of my veil through my moist fingers. My mouth, in constrast to my hands, is dry, and my breath shallow.

Rsul comes back and calls me down. The camel kneels and I climb out of my litter, clumsy in my fear, and trip over my trailing veil, so that I sprawl full-length in the dust at my father's feet.

The eyes that look down at me are steely. There is no hint of compassion or love on Habib Amir's face, and his voice is harsh.

'Get off the ground, and cover your face properly with your veil!'

He snaps out an order to the servants who stand

428

behind him, and two come over to me and, roughly pulling me off the ground, take me into the house.

I hear Rsul protest, and call over my shoulder, in a voice so shaking with fear that I can scarce control it: 'Leave it, Rsul, it is my problem, not yours!' Why do I say that, when what I want to cry is:

'Help me, Rsul — Help me?'

The men pull at my arms and walk me fast down the corridors.

Oh, Allah, have mercy! I pray, for I have forgotten my mother and sisters, and it is to their quarters that I am being taken.

I struggle further and pull back, frantic to escape, but with hard hands biting into my already bruised arms, the men propel me through the door. Obviously there has been no time to warn the women for, as I make my undignified entrance, they turn in my direction, and their eyes grow large with incredulity in their well-fed faces.

'It cannot, surely, be the missing daughter of our father?' one of them asks at last and, the silence broken, a crescendo of sound rises until I cover my ears to block it out.

The women circle me, and their acid comments sting out, making me wince as though physically assaulted. In fact not one touches me, but all draw back as if in fear of contamination. I had forgotten their hostility.

My mother speaks: 'So you have returned? We cannot say that we are pleased, for your disappearance caused much trouble here. And you do not seem, by your thin and sickly look, to have profited in the least from this act of disloyalty to the Khan!'

A servant hurries into the room and whispers in her ear. She turns cold eyes in my direction again. 'You are to be bathed to rid you of your odour and then confined until the Khan is ready to deal with you!' She turns her back on me.

I go, at least glad to be away from their venom, and I am wretched at my reception. I pray it was for the benefit of the servants and Rsul that my father has shown no pleasure at my return. Surely, I console myself, once we are alone together he will hear me out and our great bond of love will be restored?

It is not to be that easy.

Once I am scrubbed clean and dressed in a dark chadri, I am put into my old bedchamber with a man-servant on guard outside.

The room seems smaller than I remember and it is desperately lonely. I lie on the cushions, waiting.

This place is nothing without Bibicol, I realise. Oh, Bibi! How I miss you! My heart clenches with the anguish of our separation. Then I think of Ibrahim, and frown. Yet how can I begrudge Bibi the love he can give her? Or he, the loyal and warm affection that I know so well she is capable of giving. I know neither one of them can be mine — but still the strings that hold me to them are not completely severed.

Forgive me, Bibi! Oh, please forgive me! I have no right to withhold anything you ask after what you have been to me, and what I have put you through!

I lie, dry-eyed, in the room that had once been mine. It is empty, and I am utterly alone . . .

*　　*　　*　　*

. . . The cabin is empty and I am utterly alone. I look around, dazed, not sure who I am.

Nina or Noeda? Or perhaps both?

Both places hold terrors. There is no escape from them.

I toss and turn upon the narrow bunk, a girl from both worlds, and my tears fall unheeded upon the pillows at my head. Which is dream, which reality? Who knows! Does Noeda dream of Nina, or Nina imagine Noeda? I cry out loud for the answers, but no one hears.

430

Voices murmur, blurred and just out of sound range inside my head, around me; and faces swim like drowning men, distorted within and without my vision. There is no escape.

I lie for several days on the brink of insanity, but somewhere, from deep within my psyche, my will to fight rises and I am jolted into the *now* with Kerri's name upon my lips . . .

. . . I got up off the bunk and pulled on my clothes, my motions slow and heavy. Within my head Kerri's name still pulsed, drawing me reluctantly forward each time I started to slip back. I knew I must hold on, that I mustn't let go . . . must speak to Habib Amir . . . must find Kerri . . . must . . . But Kerri was dead. Like Mother. Both dead!

The Bay of Biscay was turbulent, the heaving sea emptying the dining-room and lounges. Michael, too, fell victim of seasickness, and kept to his cabin. I walked the decks alone, wrapped tight against the bitter wind, waiting for the days to pass, my spirits as grey and hopeless, as endlessly stormy as the sky that surrounded the rolling vessel; my mind full of distortions, unable to sift reality from imagination. I was sure of one thing only, and that was my longing to be back, transported by the closing of my eyes, to the warmth of Africa, back to the time before my grief, at Kerri's disappearance; at Mother's death; before the burden that *her* grief had placed upon me — the knowledge of how lonely and bitter her years had been.

I spent hours staring out into the uncompromising greyness and knew what it was to be journeying alone.

Leah came into my thoughts, as she often did on those grey days, and it was as if she spoke beside me:

'Each is alone, Nina, each one of us. And yet we are as palm-fronds, woven to make one mat!' But her words did nothing to reassure me.

In the cabin Mother's clothes still hung in the wardrobe, silent and accusing. My hand went forward slowly one day, reluctant to touch them; to touch each garment. I wondered what to do with them, feeling it might be a disloyalty to dispose of them. I buried my face in one of her jumpers, catching the lingering traces of her own distinctive smell, and knew then that she would never have recovered, that she hadn't really wanted to do so.

I pulled the clothes off their hangers and folded them into her suitcase then rang for the stewardess, calm now in the realisation that, as the body had been in the sick bay when I saw it, the clothes were only the discarded trappings of her flown spirit. I knew that I had to let her go, that holding her belongings would not — could not — bring her back.

I just wish we'd been given more time! I thought, then instantly was aware that we had indeed been given just enough for us to reach out and touch each other.

TWENTY-FOUR

Slowly, over the remaining days of the voyage, I confronted my grief, trying to forgive myself for not being with Mother at the end. Trying, too, to untangle the knotted threads of my life.

Still confused and numbed, I was unable to determine truth from untruth, unsure of my identity. I'd been happier emulating Noeda, but she was trapped now, confined within the Khan's estate. She, too, was bedevilled by tortuous circumstances, by guilt and misunderstanding, her relationships, like mine, soured by betrayal; her father — that all-powerful man, the Khan — untouchable, unapproachable, as mine had been.

There were no paradigms for me to follow, no signposts now that could guide my unsteady steps. Only too aware of my inner chaos, my introverted thoughts, I wished with all my heart that Noeda could give me the escape she'd given me in the past. She'd been serene when I was turbulently unhappy; her life exciting, her father loving — now it seemed our lives ran too much in parallel and there was no escape in either.

My thoughts went often to my parents, too, assessing their proportion of blame, wondering how much of what had happened was my own fault. I had carried a great deal of guilt about my part in the relationship between us, feeling myself to be unlovable, a failure in their eyes. Now I could see that I was less culpable than I had believed. *They* had locked the door in my face firmly — how was I to know that I needed to find my own key? There was no blame to apportion — it had happened thus, and no amount of retrospection could alter the karmic records.

And now, when I thought of Noeda, I understood her grief, my heart aching with the echo of her pain . . .

* * * *

. . . The year is fifteen hundred and fifty-seven, and I feel I am near to death now. The prospect is not displeasing to me, for in truth I have been dead in all but body for these many years. Desolate years — since Rsul helped me to return to Kabul.

Still I have not made my peace with Habib Amir, my father. I have not seen him, spoken to him. Indeed, for most of my imprisonment within the widow's quarters, I saw no one but the aged crone who brought my food, who swept my floors and took away the foulsmelling chamber which contained my waste.

My grieving has lessened now, but for the first months I tore and raged and shouted my frustration at these four walls, desperate and near to madness with remorse and self-pity. My hands cracked and bled from beating them against the stone walls, and my voice grew hoarse from weeping, and from calling for mercy, or for company — or even for death to release me.

I forget how long it is that I have been here, for I have no means of differentiating the seasons, or the years, save by the temperature. My time passes in a grey twilight of inactivity. But now, at last, I have Mirri — youngest daughter of my beloved Bibicol and Ibrahim, who came here to bear news of her father's death, and has stayed here working in the kitchens as her mother did before her. Mirri, who in all her generosity of heart gives me her devotion, as Bibicol did before her.

I remember that it was in the third year of my confinement that my solitary life changed. The old crone died and was replaced by one of the women — Katja — who had served in the kitchens when Bibicol was there. She had been told not to speak to me, but took pity on my sorry state, and brings, hidden in her apron, titbits from the kitchens to augment my sparse diet, and always she is gentle with me. Gradually we have gained each other's affection, and I am free to talk to her, knowing she will not speak of it.

It was she who brought Mirri to me — an event which has made my life endurable, and it was Katja, too, who smuggled in the threads, who brought me the small loom, that I might weave to pass my hours. This weaving marks my days, making time more relevant. I weave into the tapestry all the love I feel for those I left — sweet Bibicol, dark Ibrahim, Malek and Rsul. Others are there too, but my mind cannot name them now. Figments of my dreams, images from past and future.

Katja it was who told me what happened during those first years. It seems there was much trouble, much shouting, the day after my return, and my father's booming wrath could be heard even from the kitchens!

The house servants told those in the kitchens that Habib Amir was adamant, there was no way this daughter who had brought so much disgrace upon his house could be reinstated. The law was clear and he had but two alternatives — either to put me to death or to confine me in a place where I could bring no more disgrace or calumny to the other women of the household. I wondered then if it was his intractability, an inherent cruelty I had not seen before, that had made my mother so bitter, so unloving towards me.

'Did Rsul come back?' I asked Katja.

'Indeed he did, but we had been made to swear an oath to the Khan to tell everyone that you were dead. For, as far as he was concerned, you *were* dead — to him as his daughter!'

'Oh, poor Rsul!' I knew how much he must have grieved.

'Yes, he came back, and Harun told him the story. I have heard that Rsul could not believe it and demanded to see the Khan, but he was not admitted, and went fast away, riding as though the very devil himself was upon his heels.'

That night I think my hopelessness was at its deepest, and I prayed to Allah for release into death, for there was no other way I could reach out to Rsul, to let him know the truth. But that release was not granted to me then, and my days continue.

Now, of all the comforts that Katja and Mirri bring me, the most precious is themselves. I wait each day for their visits, counting the moments of their company like precious stones. I stand sometimes listening with my ear against the door for hours to hear their steps. But my mind is often confused, and some days I think they have not been to see me, and I berate them cruelly.

I cannot remember which year it was that Katja told me of Babur's terrible ravaging of the land, and how all the young men were at war against his oppression. Habib Amir, she told me, also was in the north fighting the tyrant. Then one day she came, tear-stained, to give me the news that Mirri brought. News that Ibrahim had been killed in battle, leaving Bibicol — 'Our own dear Bibicol!' — who now had four children, of whom Mirri was the youngest. My dormant emotions had reawakened at this news and Katja and I had clung together in our grief.

My dreams begin to fade, now. It is as if my inner spirit has separated from my body already, and only a small vestige of myself inhabits this old shell. But last night as I lay, wide-eyed, staring as I do into the silence, I dreamed again. It was not strong, and the pictures seemed to pulse and fade. I thought the man I saw to be Ibrahim at first, but then saw it was Rsul, then Ibrahim again — merging with Rsul, who wore different clothes, his hair clipped, his beard gone, too. In the dream he was dark as the night, the moon — pale and yellow — reflected in his eyes as he looked towards me. Then he blurred and Malek took his place — or Ibrahim — or Habib Amir — I could not tell who.

Or was it indeed Rsul, all the time? I knew it mattered not.

The girl, Nina, is here still . . . the one who haunts my destiny . . . she is still here . . .

* * * *

. . . 'Oh, Noeda!' I cry, 'don't leave me!' And her voice comes clearly:

'How, leave you, Nina? For you and I are one, inseparable for all time.'

Then she is gone and I am sitting, desolate and alone.

But why do Noeda and I play so great a role in each other's lives? I ask. The question remains, nagging in my mind like an aching tooth . . . and I am filled with deep sorrow.

The post, brought on board at the mouth of the Thames by the pilot's boat, contained an envelope with an East African stamp on it. I rushed to open it and turned to the last page to see the name.

It was from Melika — and my heart lurched.

'Miss Nina,' the letter started formally, 'I, Melika Mbiti, have a heart full of sadness to hear of the death of Memsahib Anderson. Also my heart is heavy to think of you being alone at such a time. First Bwana Anderson, and now Memsahib, too! I beg of you to take care, for I think I could not bear any more sorrow to come to you.

I have had a letter from Jamira, and she tells me she has heard from Leah!'

437

My mouth dried, and my hands shook so much I could hardly see the dancing words. Leah! Leah?

'How can it be?' the letter continued, 'I pray to God this is the truth, and I am travelling tomorrow to Uganda to see Jamira and find out what she means.

My eyes turn always to the gateway, hoping that your feet will bring you speedily there, and I long for your return. I beg for you to write to me with news of your coming.

Yours truly,

Melika Mbiti'

I put the letter down on my lap and stared blindly at the sea. I wanted so badly to believe that Leah — and presumably Kerri, too — were still alive, and yet I was afraid to do so. Afraid.

Kerri — alive? Kerri! Did I dare believe it? The sound of my heartbeat was loud in my ears, each pulse the echo of her name: Kerri! Kerri!

Michael stood close by, watching me.

'What is it, Nina?' he asked. 'Good news?'

I looked up, vaguely, my mind still with Melika.

'Oh, yes! Yes! At least, I think so!' I thought for a moment. 'I'll have to get a plane back as soon as possible!' My excitement was mounting, hope growing.

His face fell. 'Oh! I'd hoped we could spend some time together in London!'

I felt immediately guilty, as no doubt he'd intended. 'Well, it's imperative I get back, I'm afraid!' I couldn't even contemplate any delay.

'It'll take a while to get a booking, Nina. In the meantime, you're more than welcome to stay at my flat.' He put up his hand. 'No strings attached!'

I knew I'd have to accept, hadn't any choice really. I'd nowhere else to go, no one else that I knew, and I was reluctant to stay with Mother's friends whom I'd never met.

438

'I suppose . . .' I stopped. I'd no money anyway, either for air fare or rent.

He smiled, put his hand reassuringly on my shoulder.

'One of the problems is cash, I presume?'

'Yes — I've no idea how long it'll take for probate on Mother and Father's estates — have you?'

'I'll sort it all out as fast as I can.' He pulled me to my feet from the deckchair and held me by the upper arms so that I faced him.'It could be a little while, I'm afraid. I tried to get an advance for your fare on the ship but got turned down!'

How long? Oh, pray God, not too long!

'Well then — how? You didn't pay it yourself, Michael, did you?' Not yet another reason for my gratitude!

Will he always be there, to rescue me from snowdrift and storm, as Malek had, I wondered, and turned myself away, out of his grasping hands.

His colour heightened. 'Damn, I didn't want you to know that. The army paid for Mrs Anderson, but we couldn't let her travel on her own, could we?' His tone was light, making nothing of it.

'No,' I replied. 'No, of course we couldn't.'

How full of surprises he was, this very ordinary, orderly man. How full of contradictions, yet seeming ingenuous. I wondered what was wrong with me, why I couldn't accept him for what he was. Perhaps I was looking for faults — to stop myself from liking him; to stifle the first stirrings of affection. I studied him as he leant against the ship's railings, looking oddly unfamiliar in civilian clothes, and realised that it wasn't *him* I'd been fighting, not him, but myself. Fighting the urge to use him as I had before, knowing that I must not repeat *that* mistake.

At the same time I knew that his need was still there — and must be confronted.

There was a long silence in which he studied me, then he spoke: 'Nina, I'm . . .'

I sensed the tension in him, guessed what he was about to say.

'Please Michael, let it go . . .'

He shrugged, lit a cigarette, looking uncomfortable, embarrassed, his urbanity gone. And in that moment I felt so guilty, so filled with pity, that I almost turned to him. Then Paul's face came strongly into my mind, and with it a rush of longing that made me shake. I knew that Michael could offer me love, security, devotion and that with Paul there'd always be danger, doubt — and yet . . .

My excitement was mounting; so, too, my impatience to be gone.

When Michael turned to go, keeping his distance still, it was I who put my arms around his neck and kissed his cheek — more for my comfort than for his.

'As you will, Nina!' he said, then straigthened his shoulders. 'You can still use my flat, you know! And I'll try and get the money side of things sorted out — okay?'

'Thanks, Michael!' I hoped he understood, but somehow I doubted it.

I returned to my cabin and sat on the bunk, thinking. Men seemed almost a different species somehow, too difficult to understand! I wondered if it was possible to find one who was prepared to come halfway towards intuition and understanding. I had thought I'd found that one in Paul — we'd reached out in depth, gone back in time and walked amongst the stars. But in the harshness of daylight he'd come down to earth fast, drawing inwards once again, so that I felt I knew no more about him than I had before.

I wondered, too, if all my relationships were formed of need, a desperate reaching out; or even for escape!

And who was I anyway?

440

My thoughts were clouded, and I couldn't concentrate them enough to see . . .

Rashidi had been there always, my playmate, my companion — and our joining had seemed a natural progression. But had it been as innocent as I wanted it to be? Even at sixteen I'd been aware, wasn't unawakened, unevolved . . . the tribal rules were written clear for both of us.

'But what did it matter,' I asked aloud in the empty cabin, 'the colour of his skin?'

And Paul? What did I really know of him that hadn't come from my imaginings? I pictured his tall, lean figure; dark hair; brow high and proud; eyes wide-spaced, dark amber. Immediately, across the screen of my mind, like some old black-and-white film, I saw him riding fast against the wind with cloak billowing behind him. I wanted to put out my hand, pluck that image from my memory and hold it until it materialised in the present and I could examine it more closely. But with that conscious wanting it was gone. I knew it was Rsul I saw.

Elusive Paul, I thought, elusive in just the same way as Rsul was! But were they one and the same, or was that link of my own fabrication? Perhaps I needed to know Paul better, to find the soul inside the trappings of his body, before I really knew for certain.

Against my wishes, Michael intruded upon my thoughts then, as if jostling for a mention. I half-smiled. He would!

It would have been too easy, I knew, to relax into an affair with him. To let him shoulder the worries, sort things out. He was so dependable, so solid. Yes, how easy it would have been to go with him, as I had done with Malek! But he knew nothing about Kerri or Rashidi, and I knew that he wouldn't be able to accept them, or forgive.

Over the picture of his fresh, blond face, Paul's lean

dark features imposed themselves again within my mind, and I knew that it had always been so.

I would have to sever Michael — set Malek free, too . . .

'But you have freed Malek,' Leah's voice in my ear is as clear as though she stands beside me. 'By the very act of leaving, you gave him his freedom!'

'Surely he would have grieved?' I query.

'Indeed he grieved, for he truly loved you. But think on it — wasn't it better for you to leave than to live a lie?'

'I'd been living a lie ever since I left Kabul,' I agree, 'and Malek was such an honest man. He would have been mortally hurt had he known that I'd no intention of returning to Kalash after seeing my father. But, still, I wish I could have told him the truth.'

'He believed you dead. Rsul rode back, after he'd been turned away from your father's gate, and told him.'

I am puzzled. 'Why should Rsul have done that?'

'Rsul is a very special man!' she says.

I know that.

'And Ibrahim — Rashidi? What of them?'

'They were boys, Nina, surely you see that now? You were a challenge to their budding manhood, the foil for their newly sharpened spears!'

'But I loved them, didn't I?' I pause and think for a moment. 'No, they were forbidden fruit for me, too — perhaps that's why I found them so attractive!'

'Of course! But you used them, and the course of their lives was changed because of you. Ibrahim no longer the famed BuzKashi rider, and Rashidi — well, his detention will have been marked upon his kipande — he's lost his chance to go to Makerere!' She sighs. 'And did you really love any of them?'

'I thought I did.' I hesitate. 'Malek I know I used,

442

because I realised I didn't love him once my passion abated. His life, too, I changed . . . But Rashidi — what have I done to him? Oh, Leah! What have I done?'

'But you didn't make that mistake with Michael! Passion and love are never the same thing, Nina.'

Malek's face is there in my mind, so, too, is Michael's.

'I think perhaps you loved Rsul . . .' Her voice is pensive.

My feelings about Rsul are — have always been — ambivalent. I feel deeply for him, trust and respect him.

'Is that love?' I ask.

'You must find the answer to that question.'

I refuse to think about Paul . . . even now.

'But I love Bibicol,' I am sure of that, 'as I love you and Melika; and Kerri! Kerri most of all!'

'Yes, but that again is a different love, deep and instinctive. It is born out of understanding, for you share our sorrows, and our dependence . . . It is so written!'

Her voice fades, and I sit in silence with my thoughts chasing each other . . .

Dependence, that was the clue word. Throughout my life I'd been dependent on them all, unable to stand alone, afraid of the emptiness within me; filling that space with fantasies when I couldn't find substance. So desperate in my search for reassurance that I'd no time to find myself.

With an uncomfortable jolt I sat up straight and looked around, bewildered. It was as though I had returned, too fast, from some long and trouble-filled nightmare.

For a few minutes I remained still, heart pounding fast, letting my wild thoughts calm, remembering what I had just heard. Then I was filled with a rush of sheer

443

joy, as I had been once before in the small chapel on the hill in Africa. My shadowed world lost its opacity, became full of light and clarity so that my senses were lucent, acute: smell, sound, touch.

It was all so simple. 'I don't really need any of them!' I exclaimed. 'I'm *myself*, Nina, and I'm free!'

And my heart lifted as the understanding came. It was as though all the people in my life, the ancestral voices mingling with the here and now, were raised to sing the Hallelujah Chorus.

No, I wouldn't be trapped by my mistakes, by my guilt, as Noeda had been! I was free! And it was Leah who'd given me the answer, started me thinking coherently, looking at my relationships, past and present, a little more objectively, so that I no longer felt subordinated, guilt-ridden.

I could let them all go now, set them loose. And, in that letting go, I would free not only them but myself; free us all from the strands that had bound our destinies, strands which had trapped me in the same way that Noeda was trapped. Strands which had meshed us all.

Freeing me to be myself! Free to find my daughter, my Kerri!

Michael, in some manner, managed to get my money released from probate, not bothering me with the details. He had stuck to his promise and hadn't pressed his attentions upon me while I had been staying at his flat.

I sat, some fifteen days after our arrival with my emigration documents before me — passport, airline ticket, inoculation certificates — ready to return to Africa. My feelings were mixed; excitement and joy at the thought of going back, warring with the uncertainty of what I'd find there. I'd had no further word from Melika, despite my written questions, no word from

444

Paul either, and he'd been away from the hospital when I'd put an international telephone call through to him.

I wondered if I was doing the right thing, what the future would bring, and I rubbed my eyes, trying to shake off the panic which threatened to swamp me. I knew that Michael would give me all I needed if I stayed in England, and I was afraid I might be chasing a dream by going back to Kenya. There was no proof that the information Jamira had passed on about Leah was true — it could be yet another false hope.

Then I shook my head, picked up my documents and stood up, resolute.

'No, I've got to go! Got to try and find Kerri!' I repeated the words aloud, reasserting them in the room, the sound bouncing off my packed cases. There was nothing holding me now; Michael was not the one — I was sure of that; Noeda was gone — she, too, was a myth — hadn't she failed, ultimately, dominated by the Khan into incarceration, losing utterly the freedom she had sought so desperately.

'Oh, Noeda!' I cried — and the cry was of acceptance and farewell.

I pulled on my coat, taking one last look around the room, and went out to where Michael waited with his car.

He drove me to the airport, saw me leave. A Michael quite reconciled, it seemed, to a friendship between us and no more. His blond hair, his smiling face, were there as I turned on the way to the transit lounge. I put my hand-baggage down and ran quickly back to the barrier.

'Thanks, Michael — for everything you've done. For your help and friendship. I needed it!'

I realised that this was the truth, knowing, too, that it was part of letting go. I kissed him then for the first and last time without reservation, before running to catch up with the other passengers.

*
445

The steady pulsing of the aircraft engines filled my ears as I politely rebuffed the blandishments of the man sitting in the seat next to mine.

Rome airport had been noisy, the waiting there in the midnight hours almost unbearable. Now we were on the way to Khartoum, the last fuelling stop before Nairobi. The air hostess flicked off the lights, walked on silent feet down the aisle, handing out blankets — solicitous and smiling. Around me came the rustles and night sounds of passengers settling themselves to uncomfortable, restless sleep for a few hours.

I closed my eyes and relaxed.

Against the darkness a small flame of brightness appeared, and my senses at once were alert. I flicked open my eyelids, wondering if the cabin lights had been switched on, but all was still in darkness, the man next to me snoring slightly. I shut my eyes again. The brightness grew and, emerging slowly, a dark shape against the light — Paul. Or was it Rsul? The features were blurred; he was bearded, then unbearded; wore a burnous, then an Astrakhan hat; then was bareheaded.

I shook my head and he disappeared.

In his place I saw Noeda, but she, too, dissolved and changed, becoming someone else: Leah; Melika; Bibicol; together, then changing, too — disappearing, reappearing; themselves, yet other than themselves; Habib Amir and my father, those magus figures, made to seem hard and unbending to hide their weaknesses — afraid beneath their outer skins; and Mother, whose coldness masked a desperation, but whose lack of affection was my salvation as it had set me free . . . both times!

Consciously, I explained these images as a result of the wine I'd drunk in Rome to while away the waiting, but I knew they were not, knew that they'd always be there — that they were a part of my past, a part of my present, too.

Someone in that past had said: 'Missed opportunities happen to us all . . . but you cannot waste the rest of your life looking over your shoulder, regretting!'

She was right! I opened my eyes. Who said it? It didn't matter who she was or when it was said — she'd given me the answer. I could close the karmic chapter if I wanted to do so. And the choice was for me alone to make.

Nairobi airport was small in comparison with Rome, modern and cool in comparison with the unbearable heat of Khartoum. I stood patiently in line at the immigration desk; looked with growing pleasure at the dark faces around me, hearing the familiar sound of Swahili being spoken. Then I picked up my suitcases and went out into the entrance foyer.

There, silhouetted against the glass doors, dark against the sunshine outside, they stood. A group of three amongst the many, yet to me — suddenly — the only people there.

I stopped, breath held, pulse beating fast at the base of my throat, wondering if my mind was playing tricks again.

For one whole interminable moment the clocks stopped, the time-spool of film that recorded my every movement was stilled in mid-turn. Then my voice broke through, waveringly:

'Paul . . ?'

It was indeed Paul. And Melika. And the baby, grown so large in the weeks since I'd seen her . . . Kerri!

Then there were no words, I was held tight between Paul and Melika, my arms around both, my tears running to mix with hers; Paul's mouth against my forehead. And Kerri's eyes, dark, large with wonderment — not understanding.

'Why did you let me go like that,' I asked Paul when at last I could speak, 'without a word?'

'You had to go, Nina, your mother needed you. There was unfinished business there, between you!'

Yes, that was true!

'Well, why didn't you write? I was desperate to hear from you?' Hadn't he realised my desperation?

'I didn't want to raise your hopes — I was trying to find Kerri for you! And you needed time,' he said, his finger tracing my cheek, pushing a strand of hair out of my eyes, 'you had a lot to sort out, inside yourself!'

There had to be the time lapse, I understood that now. I'd needed the time to test my inner strength, to deal with my inner turmoil.

'Where's Leah?' I looked around, aware for the first time that she was absent.

Melika smiled. 'Leah's with Jamira, Nina, all is well with her!'

'And Rashidi?'

Her face fell. 'Rashidi is dead — he's gone from us now! It was he who wrote the letter to Mikendeni, to protect himself, it seems. It was he, too, who said that they were dead. He was afraid the security forces would find Leah and question her about his activities, though why he thought she'd be able to tell them anything I do not know. Leah, Mirriamu and Kerri went into hiding in Malindi, just up the coast from Mikendeni, until they knew it was safe to write.' She paused, her eyes distant, full of sorrow. Then she shrugged. 'Yes, Rashidi is dead! Shot by the security forces, Nina. The danger is gone!'

I held her tightly for a moment, then buried my face against Paul's chest.

'For a while there, I thought I'd lost you, too,' I said. My voice seemed to come from the far past.

'Not this time, Nina!' he replied. 'No — not this time!'